AFTERThought

A Derange Mystery

by

K.A. Krisko

Published by Tulk Tales Publications

Copyright @ 2014 by K.A. Krisko

First Edition
ISBN: 978-0-9895059-5-6

Cover art and cover design by
KAKrisko

Visit my web page at:
www.kakrisko.com

Dedication

This book is dedicated to the field-level employees of the National Park Service, who have remained committed, through thick and (mostly) thin, to the preservation and protection of some of the most important natural and cultural sites in the U.S., in the face of being assaulted, assailed, and berated by those with more money, more power, and considerably less grace.

Authors' Note:

Here's where I add the obligatory note telling you that any similarities between the characters in this narrative and any real persons, living or dead, is entirely coincidental. Also, of course, anyone familiar with southeast Texas will realize that many of these places, including towns, areas, roads, lakes, swamps, and bayous, do exist (under other names), but they've been altered significantly to protect their locations, to avoid any accidental insult, and to fit my narrative needs. They should therefore be regarded as entirely fictitious locations.

Table of Contents

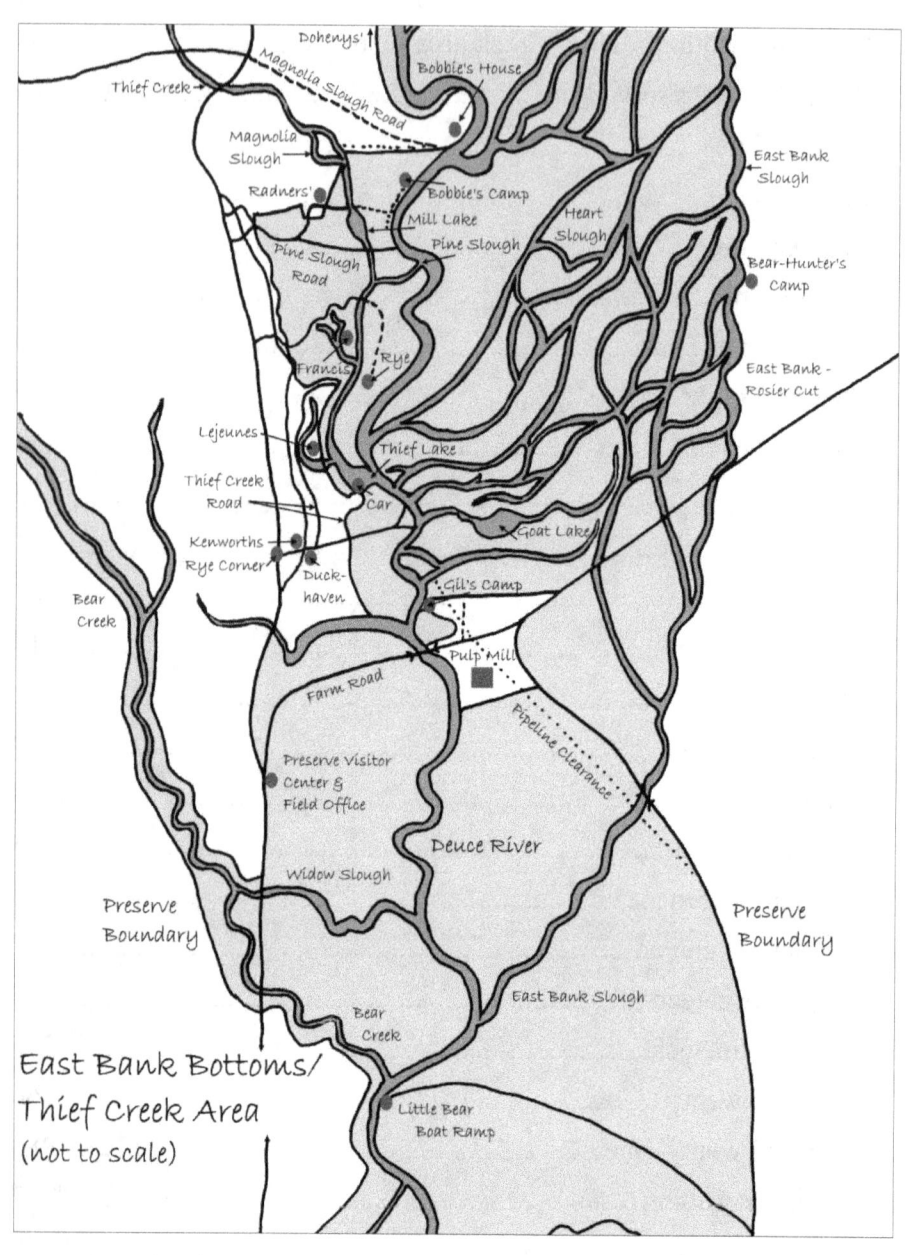

East Bank Bottoms/Thief Creek area map

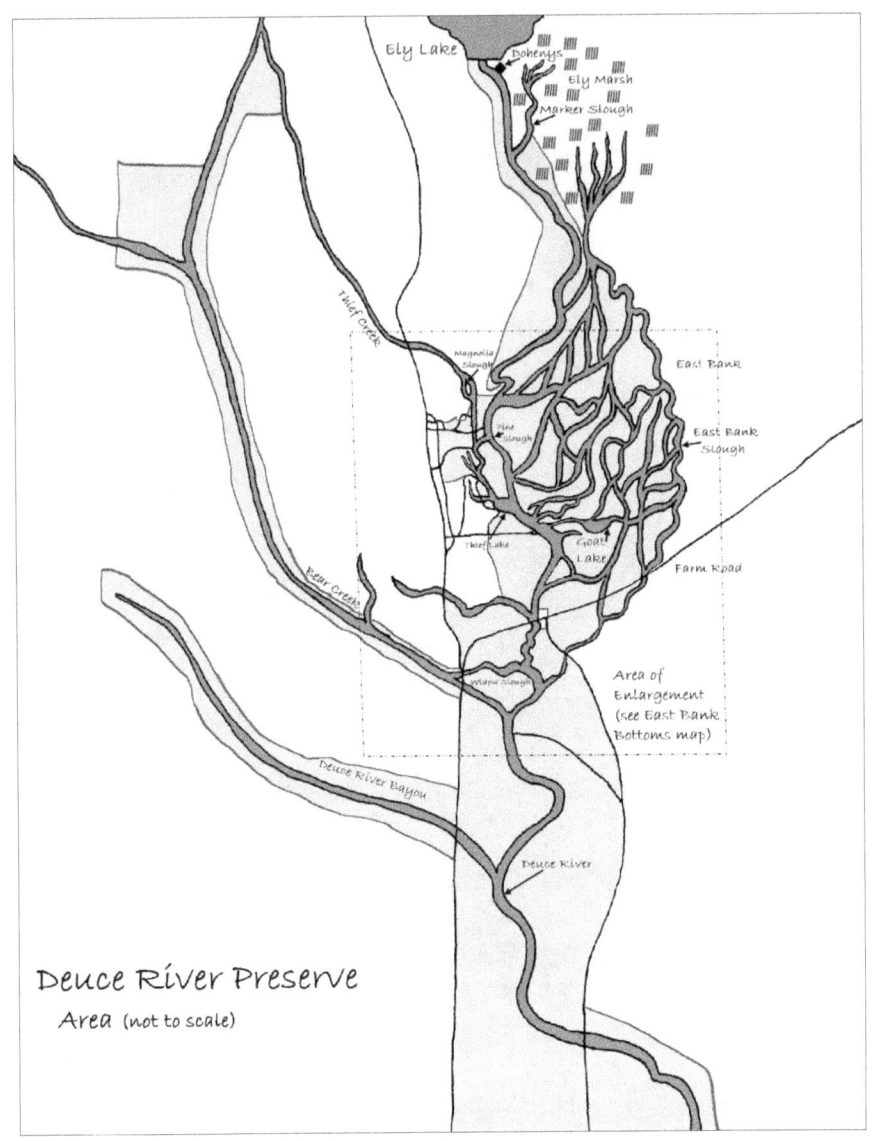

Deuce River Preserve
Area (not to scale)

Ely Lake
Dohenys
Ely Marsh
Marker Slough
Thief Creek
Magnolia Slough
East Bank
Pine Slough
East Bank Slough
Thief Lake
Goat Lake
Bear Creek
Farm Road
Widow Slough
Area of Enlargement (see East Bank Bottoms map)
Deuce River Bayou
Deuce River

Deuce River Preserve Map

Chapter One

Tracey Cole shoved the door of the old Dodge Dart open with his shoulder and fell out into hip-deep water.

The water was about the same temperature as the air, warm as bathwater. Tracey floundered for a few seconds in the eerie, wavering illumination of the car's headlights beneath the surface of the lake. As he found the door-frame and pulled himself upright, the lights flickered and went out.

Brenda Doheny's voice from the pitch-black of the passenger's side of the car rose in volume, resolving from hysteria into fury. "I can't believe you did that! You put us in the lake! You total stupid loser of an idiot moron!"

Tracey made his way around the back of the car, slipping in the sludge on the bottom of the lake. By the time he worked his way over to the passenger door, Brenda was out of the car, fishing for her purse in the flooded floorboards. Tracey grabbed her elbow to help her to shore, but she yanked away.

"Don't you touch me!"

She steadied herself with a hand against the car, then plunged towards the bank. She splashed up the muddy slope, flung her purse over one shoulder, and marched purposefully through the cypress towards Thief Creek Road. The road could be distinguished from the surrounding darkness by a gap in the trees overhead, through which a weak cloud-choked light filtered.

"Leave me alone! Go away! I'm going home," she screamed over her shoulder at Tracey. "And don't even think about following me!"

Tracey hitched up his soaked jeans and staggered after her. "Hey, come on, Brenda! Let me stay at your place 'til morning! I can

1

crash on the porch if you want," he begged. "At least let me use the phone. Or your cell phone?"

Brenda's white blouse faded quickly away through the dark. "Screw you!" she yelled. "My cell phone is soaked! You think Francis is going to let you stay at our house after he finds out you nearly killed the both of us?"

"Yeah, but what am I supposed to do?"

"I don't know. I don't care. Just stay away from me!"

Tracey stopped forlornly. It was no use following Brenda a mile and a half to her house through the rain, in the dark, along a muddy dirt road, if she wasn't going to let him in when he got there. And she was right about Francis. He wasn't any friend of Tracey's to begin with, and he wouldn't be happy to hear that Tracey had dumped his wife in the lake while driving her home from a bar in the middle of the night. Even though it had been a favor, and one Tracey had been conned into doing.

He leaned over and braced his hands on his knees. He'd been driving too fast, too confident in his knowledge of the road and influenced by the alcohol in his system. He'd lost control on the rain-slick red-mud roadway around a sharp curve. The curve lay close to the shore of Thief Lake at a break in the cypress trees, and in seconds they'd been in the water.

The realization of what had happened began to sink in. He felt a little sick. He patted his back pocket to make sure his wallet was there. It was, but that did him little good. He had virtually no cash and no credit card.

If he could get to a phone, he could call Kenworth Tow at Rye Corner. He'd known Ray Kenworth all his life. Ray would pull the car out no-questions-asked, and might not even charge him for it. But on the other hand, it was the middle of the night. The call would be forwarded to the Kenworths' home, where old Willis would be apt to answer it rather than one of his sons. Willis, Tracey was sure, would make a proper report to the police. And Tracey knew that if

2

the police responded that night, he'd likely be charged with drunk driving.

There was another problem as well: the Dodge was registered to Tracey's uncle, Virgil Radner, and if the police ran the plate and called Virg, they'd soon find out he didn't know the car was gone. Tracey had taken it without permission, because he knew Virg would never lend it to him to go out drinking on a rainy night. He needed time to decide what he was going to tell his uncle, and he preferred to be sober when he did the telling. Altogether, perhaps it was for the best that he had an excuse for not reporting the wreck right away.

Tracey turned and squinted through the dark towards the lake. Air escaped from the slowly-sinking car with a burp, nearly drowned out by the rain on the water. Thief Lake was shallow near shore, and the car's back end was likely to remain exposed. But with the lights shorted out, only the sheen of wet glass from the back window would draw attention. Besides, the lake, little more than a wide spot in Thief Creek, was almost entirely uninhabited, surrounded by the Deuce River Preserve. It was unlikely anyone else would be driving along that road until the next morning at the earliest.

Whatever the ultimate solution to dealing with the car, he needed to find a place to shelter for the rest of the night. A quarter-mile up the lakeshore sat the ruin of an old timber mill. Tracey knew it well: it had been a popular party spot when he was a teenager, and it would at least get him out of the rain. Leaving the car to its fate, he fumbled along the lakeshore through cypress and spindly yaupon brush, feeling his way over a fisherman's trail. He clambered up the embankment beneath the mill, tripping over half-buried chunks of broken foundation. Strands of spider webs laced his face as he ducked through the undergrowth, and he tried not to imagine the big yellow-bodied spiders, curved and thick as your little finger, inhabiting them.

He felt his way along the side of the mill, running a hand over the rough, wet concrete. His fingers came across the splintery edge of a piece of plywood attached to the building by a single bolt, and he swung it aside and ducked through the old doorway. It was darker still inside. He groped to the corner at his left and fumbled around on the wall above his head. There was a rim of concrete protruding there, once a brace for some piece of machinery. Sure enough, there were books of matches and the stubs of several candles sitting on the rim, just as there had been ten years ago.

He lit one of the candles after several tries with the damp matches and attached it to the rim with its own wax. The wavering light revealed spray cans and empty beer cans scattered around the room and walls festooned with graffiti. An old ammo box occupied a corner. A campfire circle blackened the concrete floor, and there was a pile of damp newspapers nearby and several broken pallets. He got to work on a fire, pausing once when he heard the whine of a boat motor out on the lake. Whoever that was, he hoped they wouldn't notice the car. But anyone out that late on a wet summer night had probably either been partying at some riverside hunter's camp and would be too drunk to notice the car, or had been out poaching deer or hog and would be concerned with getting his meat home.

The campfire ring was situated beneath a hole in the ceiling where huge beams had once been inserted to brace machinery. The summer rain swept up through the southeast Texas floodplains from the Gulf of Mexico in sheets and spasms. Thunder rolled from one end of the sky to the other above the timbered flatlands and snaky waterways. Raindrops falling through the hole sizzled in the flames, and the shins of Tracey's jeans began to steam. He pulled the ammo box to within a few feet of the fire, sat down, crossed his arms on his knees, and laid his head on his arms to try and sleep.

Chapter Two

A little flat-bottomed boat moved slowly up a narrow slough through the storm. There were no running lights and olive-drab paint made the boat nearly invisible. The sporadic downpours drowned out the sputter of the outboard motor, tilted until the propeller blades nearly cleared the water.

There were two men in the boat, dressed in clothing as drab as the hull. One piloted the little craft. The second crouched in the bow, a hand raised to ward off low-hanging limbs.

The man in the front lurched as the boat gently grounded on a muddy bank. He scrambled out and grabbed the bowline, cradling a rifle in the crook of one arm.

The pilot leaned forward and opened a hatch in the middle bench seat. He unzipped a soft-sided case inside and removed his own rifle, then made his way up the bank to join his companion.

The two followed the bank of the slough west, the pilot leading the way. In a few minutes they turned slightly inland. On higher ground, the forest was suffused with a ghostly light. The moon behind the clouds was nearly full, and it reflected off the steam rising from the river and the flooded bottomlands. Tendrils of mist curled from the sloughs and bayous, twisting like the smokes of cigarettes.

The pilot stopped and crouched in a wooded hollow. It was a good night to hunt: the rain covered up the sounds he made as he moved. He knelt, one knee in the soft wet soil, the other raised, his rifle in his right hand. Heavy drops gathered in cupped magnolia leaves and streamed to the forest floor around him in rivulets. Absently, the fingers of his left hand traced the track of a deer in the mud. He squinted, scanning the thicket ahead of him. Now he spotted the deer: a dark, horizontal shape amongst the vertical tree-trunks, just outside the circle of magnolias.

The deer, a small whitetail doe, quivered in the rain. She was fully aware that something or someone was lurking near her. Her muscles were taut, ready to propel her in whatever direction she needed to go. She hesitated, ears flicking in the mist.

The shot flared in the magnolia grove. The doe leaped straight upward, came down running, staggered for a moment, then dashed away through the underbrush, unharmed. The hunter knelt stock-still. Then, almost imperceptibly at first, he began to move. Slowly he tilted forward. His shoulders collapsed. His arms splayed slightly, and the rifle fell to the mud. A moment later he lay sprawled, legs tangled, elbows jutting, face down in the ooze of last year's decaying magnolia leaves.

A hundred feet away, the second hunter slowly lowered his rifle. He walked cautiously over to the still form. He stood there for a long moment, his breath disturbing the mist. Then he shook his head, flicking the running rainwater out of his eyes. Holding his rifle in one hand, he squatted and quickly ran a finger around his ex-companion's neck, hooking a silver chain. He gave the chain a sharp snap, and it broke. The hunter gathered it into his hand, stared at it for a moment, then tossed it down in the mud with an angry gesture. He patted his companion's pockets, but removed nothing. Then he stood up and for several seconds stood motionless, head bowed against the rain in a posture almost of reverence, or perhaps prayer.

A moment later he removed a cigarette pack from his shirt pocket. He pulled several small objects out of the pack, crouched, and grabbed the dead man by the back of the shirt, lifting him a short distance off the ground. He quickly tucked the objects into the front pocket of the shirt and let the body fall heavily back into the mud.

He stood over the body for a few more moments, fumbling as he replaced the cigarette pack in his own shirt pocket. Then he turned abruptly and hastened away, ducking under low-hanging limbs that shed cold drops down the back of his collar.

6

He was nearly running by the time he came to the steep-sided stream winding through the bottomland, one of thousands that laced the floodplains along the Deuce River. He stepped into the little boat and pushed off.

Several hundred yards downstream the waterway intersected Thief Creek. He fled down it in the shadows, running lights off, guided by the moonlight reflecting on the rain-pocked surface of the water.

He lowered the outboard motor as he passed through the deeper waters of Thief Lake, keeping out of the open areas and close to the cypress, hiding, although there was no one to see. Not far from the ruin of an old mill on the bank, a glint caught his eye. He steered cautiously closer to the shore, where a dirt road followed the lake's edge. As he neared the bank he loosened the tiller and the motor guttered.

There was a car in the water, nose into the lake, trunk in the air, the unlucky result of a Friday night's drive in the rain or the final resting place of a vehicle stolen for a joy ride. The boatman scanned the dark shoreline. He could see no one, but the car had not been there long: large bubbles escaped from it every few seconds.

One of the rear windows was open or broken, a dark triangle just above waterline. He hesitated, then drove the boat slowly up on the downstream side of the car and swung it around. It occurred to him that someone might be in the car, drowned or drowning beneath the warm muddy water, and he shuddered violently, more unnerved by the image of a dying man beneath him than by the reality of the dead man in the hollow. The boat scraped against the side of the car with a dull clang.

Hurriedly, he picked up the rifle and slipped it in through the open rear window. He fumbled in his shirt for the cigarette pack, pulled it out, and tossed it in after the rifle. Then he gunned the motor and took off, leaving the car to settle into the dark water.

Chapter Three

When the sun began to come up, a weak light let itself in from the ceiling hole. Tracey squeezed out past the piece of plywood at the entrance. The plywood had at one time been bolted securely to the building, but the crumbling concrete had given way when determined kids rocked the board back and forth. Now more a formality than a deterrent, the board hung loose, one corner resting in the mud. There was a slightly rusty but official-looking white metal sign nailed to it reading *'Danger - Area Closed - Deuce River Preserve'*.

Tracey scrambled back down the embankment to Thief Creek Road, feeling a hangover coming on. Now he would have to deal with what he'd done, and he hadn't gotten around to figuring out how he was going to explain the whole thing or what he was going to say to his uncle. He peered glumly down towards the waters of the lake.

For a moment he was confused. The car was completely gone. He squinted at the surface of the water. Certainly no one had removed it. But the water level had come up with the rain, and the car must have either sunk into the mud or slowly rolled forward toward the middle of the lake. And the heavy rain had obliterated the tracks made when the car left the roadway. No one would know it was there at all.

Tracey's mood lifted a bit. It would complicate the tow job, but, provided Virg didn't miss the car right off the bat, he now had some time to make a decision about exactly what he was going to do and how he was going to explain things. It could wait until he was rested and recovered and in dry comfortable clothes. He began to walk quickly south along Thief Creek Road, heading for the nearest civilization.

A half-hour later he paused. He could hear a vehicle coming from some distance away, the tires throwing gravel and clumps of mud into the wheel-wells. He hadn't expected anybody out there early on a Saturday morning. The only people who lived up that way were the Lejeune brothers and Brenda. If it was Gil Lejeune he'd hitch a ride, but he didn't particularly want to run into Francis or Brenda at the moment.

The vehicle materialized out of the fog. It was a white Chevy Tahoe with a red-and-blue light-bar, and Tracey recognized it immediately as a Deuce River Preserve patrol vehicle. The driver of the Tahoe would probably be Addie Derange; her partner Ike usually drove a pickup. Tracey avoided Ike, who'd written him several tickets, when he could, but Addie had always been civil enough to him when they'd run into each other before.

As the vehicle came closer, Tracey stuck out a thumb, then gave a hands-up gesture. It was worth a try. After all, he was on Preserve property. Besides, Addie would have no idea what had happened, and he could come up with a story to explain what he was doing there at that hour of the morning.

The Tahoe oozed to a stop and the window came down, squeaking as the wet glass passed the window gasket.

"Hi," Addie said. "What's up?"

Tracey leaned on the open window frame and stuck his right hand into the car. "Tracey Cole."

"Yeah, I remember," Addie said with a slight smile, shaking his hand briefly. "And you already know who I am, I bet."

Tracey grinned. Addie was not from around there and had only been in the area for around two years. But everybody knew who the local cops, wardens, rangers, and agents were, even when they weren't in uniform and driving a marked vehicle.

"You heading out to Rye Corner by any chance?" he asked.

"Well, yeah, that's the only place this road goes."

"Don't suppose you could give me a ride, could you?"

"What's the matter?" Addie squinted at him somewhat suspiciously. "You having car trouble or something?"

"No, girlfriend kicked me out last night," Tracey lied.

"There isn't anybody you can call?"

"From where?" he shrugged. "She wouldn't let me use her phone. And I don't have a cell. Too expensive."

"Uh. You just going as far as Rye Corner, then?"

"To my uncle Virg Radner's place, if I can get there. You know where that is? North of Pine Slough Road, near Mill Lake."

"Mill Lake, huh?" Addie looked over at her passenger seat. "Go ahead, get in. I might as well go up that way. I don't have anything else to do right now."

"Thanks!" Tracey ran around to the passenger side, grinning despite his hangover. Riding with Addie would be a lot more interesting than hitting up Ray Kenworth for a ride or hitching with some trucker out on the highway.

"Sorry about the mud," Tracey said as he got in. His shoes were clumped with it, the legs of his jeans coated to his shins. He tried knocking his shoes together as he sat, but most of the mud remained.

"Don't worry about it," Addie replied. "I brought plenty in myself."

She put the vehicle in drive and it fishtailed slightly as she accelerated. Tracey settled himself in to his seat, sitting a little sideways so he could look at her. He figured her to be in her late twenties, several years older than him. She had short, cinnamon-colored hair, which was sticking up as if she had towel-dried it recently. Her gray uniform shirt was dark with rainwater. He could see the butt of a handgun on her hip, partly concealed by the buckle of the seatbelt. A semi-automatic, he thought, probably a nine millimeter. It protruded from a somewhat battered black holster on a woven black nylon gun belt. There were a few bits of leaves and twigs stuck in the gun belt and scattered around the car. Despite the

10

early hour and the rain, she'd obviously been out somewhere on foot, pushing through some heavy undergrowth.

"So your girlfriend kicked you out in the rain and wouldn't even let you call for a ride," Addie said as she got the car up to speed.

Tracey grinned and shrugged, but said nothing. He knew better than to compound the lie. It would trip him up eventually.

"I was just checking that abandoned mill a few minutes ago. There was a campfire in there. Did you build that?" Addie asked. "Because you smell like smoke," she went on when he hesitated.

"Yeah, I spent the night in there," Tracey admitted. "I just needed to get out of the rain. So are you going to write me a ticket?"

Addie glanced at him. "Well, no. I don't think you were in there huffing spray-paint with a bunch of teenagers or anything. I understand you went in there to get out of the rain. But you do realize it's not safe, right? It's unstable.   Pieces of it could fall off at any time. That's one of the reasons it's closed."

"Yeah, I know," Tracey said. "It wasn't my choice for a place to spend the night."

Addie did not speak again for a few minutes as she concentrated on controlling the Chevy on the slick mud road. She visibly relaxed a little as they hit pavement just east of Rye Corner.

"You're going to have to tell me where to turn to get to your uncle's place. I know the main roads around here and the ones that get you to Preserve property, but some of these old trails are confusing."

"It's easy," Tracey said. "It's right along Mill Lake Road. I see you or Ike go by there sometimes. It's got a big red shed out front, used to be for goats or something but we use it for a garage now." Tracey grimaced. Thinking about the garage reminded him of the car.

"Oh, that place," Addie said. "You live there?"

11

"Yeah, with my uncle Virg Radner and my cousin Billy. My mother's side of the family. I've lived there since I was a kid. My Grandpa Joe Cole lives up this way, too, off Pine Slough Road. You probably know him."

"Of course," Addie replied, with her first hint of a smile. Old Joe Cole Senior was the president of a non-profit historical society that had been contracted to run the bookstore at the Preserve's Visitor Center. He spent hours volunteering at the Visitor Center front desk, and Tracey knew that he was well known to the Preserve employees.

"I bet he drives you folks crazy," Tracey said.

"I don't mind him. He knows a lot about the area and he likes to talk to the visitors. He tells some great stories."

"Yeah, he does like to tell stories," Tracey agreed. He smiled a little: he'd been accused of that, himself. Then he sobered as another complication occurred to him. Old Joe Senior organized fishing trips for visitors to the Preserve and paid Tracey to guide the trips. It had become Tracey's main source of income, and in fact, his previous contacts with Addie had been when she'd checked to see if he was in compliance with the terms of his permit. But the Preserve might blackball him from guiding on their property if he violated their regulations, and they wouldn't be happy with a car, maybe leaking oil or gasoline, sitting in one of the waterways.

"So, you been guiding any trips lately?" Addie asked, as if reading his mind.

"A few," Tracey answered. "I'm supposed to do one this afternoon, but they'll probably cancel because of the rain."

"Too bad."

"Yeah, I could use the money right about now," Tracey said ruefully. He watched Addie adjust the volume on the police radio under the dashboard. He wanted to keep her talking, to distract her from probing further into what he'd been doing at the lake. But besides that, he was curious about her.

12

"So, you've been around here for what, two years now?" he asked.

Addie nodded noncommittally. She didn't seem very talkative, maybe even a little suspicious. He tried again.

"There aren't a lot of folks who aren't from around here who even come here to visit, much less live. Seems like most folks don't even know this place exists. How'd you find out about it? Got family here?"

"No. I have two older brothers, but they live back in Colorado," Addie said in a guarded tone, keeping her eyes on the road. "I didn't know anything about this area before I got hired by the Preserve. I came here specifically to take this job."

Tracey nodded. "That's what I figured. The Preserve hires a bunch of people from outside. Where were you before you came here?"

"Southwest Colorado, where I grew up."

"In the mountains?" Tracey asked. "I always wanted to go to the Rockies."

"Well, where I'm from isn't exactly the mountains. It's high desert, sagebrush and juniper, buttes and canyons."

"Were you a warden there too?"

Addie shook her head. "Only seasonally. This is my first permanent job as a ranger. I got hired here because not a lot of people want to come here. It was a special intake program, and I was looking to move to a different area of the country."

"Must be tough for you, moving to a new place without even knowing anyone," Tracey went on. "This place must not be much like Colorado, either."

Addie seemed to be loosening up a little. "You got that right. The hardest thing for me is that everything around here is flat. That, and it's covered with trees, so you can't see any landmarks. Where I grew up, if you got lost, you just looked for some cliff or butte you recognized."

13

"Who did you get to show you around when you first got here? How do you know where everything is?"

"Well, you know Ike, right? The other Preserve patrol officer?"

"Oh, yeah, I know Ike, all right," Tracey confirmed.

"I guess from your tone of voice that you don't think much of him."

Tracey considered his answer. He didn't want to alienate Addie by saying something nasty about Ike. "Oh, he does his job all right, I guess. He gets out there on the river, checks everybody out. Doesn't slack off."

"No, he keeps pretty busy. Anyway, he showed me the major access points and some of the boundaries when I first got here. I've just had to learn the rest on my own." She waved vaguely at the center console, and Tracey saw a number of folded maps stuck down along the side of the seat.

"But Ike isn't from around here either. I mean, he's been here for a few years, but he can't know the backwaters the way someone who grew up here does. Didn't you ever go out with somebody local?" Tracey asked.

Addie smiled. "You mean, like a guide?"

"Sure. There are folks who've lived here all their lives who know the area real well. Even some people who guide for a living." He grinned.

"I don't think the Preserve has enough money to be hiring guides," Addie said. "If we did, we'd hire another officer instead. And I don't think most of the folks who grew up here would be willing to show us around. At least, not show us anywhere worth knowing about."

"Well, I don't have a problem with it," Tracey offered. "I mean, if you ever need to know where something is or how to get somewhere you've heard about."

"Yeah? What would folks think if they saw you showing a law enforcement officer around the Preserve?"

Tracey laughed. "None of their business. Besides, everybody knows my grandpa works with the Preserve. And I guide on a Preserve permit. Probably they'd just think I had to show you where I go on fishing trips or something."

He'd offered to show patrol officers around the Preserve before, mostly because he thought it would be valuable to discover how much they knew about the area, but they'd always turned him down. It was worth offering again, though. Besides the information he'd gain about their routines, it would be a lot more fun showing Addie around than showing someone like Ike around.

"So, you're serious about that?" Addie said after a minute's pause.

"Sure," Tracey said absently, watching as they passed the Pine Slough convenience store. He was starving, but he didn't have a dime on him. He'd have to wait until he got home.

"Well, it's a fact that these topo maps haven't done me a lot of good. They're old and the waterways change all the time. Plus, I usually can't tell one slough from the other. It's been difficult and I haven't learned all that much on my own," Addie said. "So let's do it. Where's someplace useful you could show me?"

Tracey turned towards her in surprise. Now he was going to have to think fast or he'd seem insincere. He hadn't really expected her to accept.

"Well, there's this old cabin out in the East Bank Bottoms," he improvised. "My grandpa says it used to be a Cole family property, calls it the Bear-hunter's Cabin. It's on Preserve property now. Bet nobody even knows it's there."

"Maybe not," Addie said. "How old is it?"

"Late eighteen-hundreds, I think. I could ask Grandpa Joe. I could take you out there, show you how to get around in the Bottoms."

15

"Sounds like a plan," Addie said. "When do we do this?"

"Friday, maybe? I'll have to check with my grandpa, make sure he doesn't have a job for me, and see if I can't borrow a boat."

"We'll use a Preserve boat," Addie said. "I'll take along a camera and GPS and document the cabin. Then on the way in and out of there, we can look for other stuff."

Addie slowed and turned off on Mill Lake Road. The pavement petered out and became red clay dirt. Scrawny slash pine and short-leaf pine, mainly pulp species, dominated the landscape where the land was higher and drier. As the road sloped down towards the river, the pines were replaced by sweetgum, bay, and stands of cypress.

The Radner residence sat north of the road around a curve, with the eastern property line directly up against the Preserve's western boundary. Near the road on the right was the old shed. The yard was scattered with cars, boat trailers, engine parts, and several all-terrain-vehicles. The trailer itself sat back from the road, up on cinder blocks. It was white, with steps made of two-by-fours leading up to a door in the center of the side. Addie pulled in to the yard and stopped behind a couple of pickup trucks.

"Thanks for the ride." Tracey opened the door. "Guess I'll see you Friday, then."

He jogged to the front door of the trailer, pleased with himself. Not only had he kept Addie from asking too many questions, he'd gotten himself what pretty much amounted to a date. If she got to know him, maybe she'd recommend him to visitors for tours on the Preserve and he could increase his business and pull in some more cash. And he figured she'd be less likely to write him tickets if they were on friendly terms. Besides, she was kind of interesting. He already knew she could drive a boat, and she apparently didn't mind getting out in the rain in the woods. She might be fun, more fun than Liz Durgan, who'd been hanging all

16

over him at the bar at Duckhaven last night, but who never wanted to do anything but watch TV.

He hoped things would go as well with his uncle. The Dodge was kept in the shed out front, and Virg didn't use it a lot. He probably hadn't missed it, and there was a chance he wouldn't notice it gone for several days. If Tracey could get it towed and into the shop before he told Virg what had happened, he could show Virg he had everything under control. He'd have to bargain with the Kenworths for the repair, but if his luck held, nobody would ever have to know the whole story.

Chapter Four

As she pulled away from the Radners' trailer, Addie ran her fingers through her hair several times, trying to fluff it and help it dry. After two years, she still wasn't used to how long it took her hair to dry in the humidity of the south. At home in Colorado, it would be dry in minutes.

She wasn't in the habit of transporting people around the area in her patrol vehicle, but when she'd seen it was one of the Coles she'd decided to help out. She liked old Joe Cole Senior quite a lot, and his relatives had always been friendly and talkative when she'd run into them. That was more than could be said for many of the people she contacted. A lot of them resented outsiders, the government, and Deuce River Preserve employees in particular.

The Deuce River was a long, muddy, silt-bottomed waterway running through the southeast Texas lowlands towards the Gulf of Mexico. The area hadn't been permanently settled until the early 1800s, when a few bear hunters and some criminals fleeing justice in the north had learned to navigate the river's tortuous tributaries and backwaters. She was well aware that some of the residents, including the Coles, were descendants of those early settlers. Some of the families had been in the area for nearly 200 years, and had spent the first hundred of those years living off the land, fishing, hunting, and cutting timber.

In the early 1900s, oil companies and timber companies had bought up huge tracts of land stretching all the way down to the Deuce River and miles out either shore, east and west. The companies provided jobs for the locals, but they also clear-cut the native long-leaf pines, spilled oil and salt water into the swamps, and polluted the river with runoff from the pulp mills.

In the 1970s a coalition of local residents with an interest in preserving the last remnants of the bottomland river corridor managed to convince the federal government to consider creating a preserve or park. The coalition had been organized and motivated by Joe Cole Senior: with the oil and timber businesses slumping and the local economy following suit, Joe had had the foresight to focus on the possibility of creating a tourism industry. Congress had commissioned a study and the Deuce River Preserve had been established. It was designed to encompass loblolly and long-leaf pine forest on either side of the river, as well as the corridor ecosystems of Thief Creek, Bear Creek, and the Deuce River Bayou. On the east side, it also incorporated a large area of flooded forest called the East Bank Bottoms.

But after it was created on paper, the land destined to be the Preserve had to be obtained. Over the next few years, it was carved out of private property belonging to timber companies, oil companies, and individuals, sometimes against their will. There were still local families who hated the Preserve, who believed the federal government had cheated them out of property that might otherwise have been used for oil or timber production. The Preserve also tended to bring in staff from elsewhere, as Tracey had noted, and the locals saw them as outsiders with no understanding of their way of life. And although the Preserve still allowed hunting, fishing, and trapping under permit, federal administration added another level of regulation and bureaucracy many residents resented.

Addie had accepted the assignment to the Deuce as part of an intake program, without knowing much about the area or what it would be like working and living there. After two years, she had made no friends in the community aside from her partner Ike and some of the other staff who worked for the Preserve. People avoided her when they found out where she worked and especially when they discovered she was a law enforcement officer.

There were advantages and disadvantages to that. She spent a lot of her time, both on and off duty, alone, but then, she'd spent vast amounts of time alone as a child, and she was well able to

19

handle solitude. She told herself her lack of connection to the community allowed her to carry out her law enforcement duties impartially. Besides, she hadn't come to the area to make friends with the locals. She was there to do her job, to build a background as a law enforcement officer so she could write her own ticket when she wanted to move somewhere else in the country. Nevertheless, she enjoyed the few good contacts she had with resident users of the Preserve, like the Coles. And Tracey's offer to show her around interested her: it was a chance to see the river system through the eyes of one who was intimately familiar with it.

She backtracked out Pine Slough and turned south on a frontage road east of the highway, running along the Preserve's boundary. As she neared a small dirt track that ran out to the Ryes' in-holding, a piece of property completely surrounded by Preserve lands between Thief Creek and the river, she caught a flash of red and white moving through the trees. Addie quickly wheeled over to the left and cut down along the Ryes' access road.

She caught them just outside the boundary: two people on all-terrain quad-runners, one man and one woman. She recognized the man as Gil Lejeune. The Lejeunes were notoriously anti-Preserve and anti-government, and Addie had argued about Preserve regulations on several occasions with Gil. The woman she had seen before, but didn't know by name. She was small of stature and red-haired, with big, vacant, bright blue eyes, crooked teeth and freckles. The two of them stopped and looked over their shoulders at her marked vehicle as she approached.

Addie pulled up next to them and rolled down her window. She had long ago ceased to be anything but blunt with Gil, since being friendly hadn't gotten her anywhere.

"I hope you two weren't planning on riding into the Preserve on those things," she said. The Preserve was closed to off-road vehicle use, and since Gil pulled a hunting permit every year, and the regulation was printed on the permit, she knew Gil knew that.

"It's a fucking road!" Gil sat back on his seat and crossed his arms. "Cars drive down there, why can't we?"

"Because, number one, people don't stay on the road with four-wheelers, and once we allow them in the Preserve at all, we start having problems with them being off-road, and number two, they're not street-legal, and this is a road, and number three, it's a Preserve. This is one of those things you can't do on a Preserve."

"One of those things? We can't do anything anymore. I wish you all would just disappear back to wherever you came from. It was a lot better here before you showed up."

"Really? You must have been, what, minus five years old or so when the Preserve opened? You have some kind of inherited memory about the years before the Preserve?"

Gil said nothing, but turned away momentarily and spat on the ground. He still had his arms crossed. His jeans and the bottom half of the four-wheeler were soaked with mud. Addie took a quick look at the quads: expensive, new-looking Polaris four-by-fours. Gil's had a gun-mount in front of the handlebars. There was no gun in the mount, and she couldn't see anything else indicating they were armed. But they were in the right area to be the alleged poachers.

"Listen, I'm not going to argue with you about the Preserve. It's here, it's been here for forty-odd years, and it's not going anywhere," Addie said.

"I don't give a shit how long it's been here, it still sucks. You came in here and took away all this land, now you're taking away all our rights."

"Oh, come on. The people who sold property to the Preserve would've sold their property to the timber industry just as fast," Addie retorted, forgetting her own vow not to argue. "If the Preserve hadn't come in, this whole area would be owned by the timber companies and the oil companies. You know how much those companies charge for a lease to hunt their property? The Preserve is open to everybody, even if you're dirt poor and living in some camp

21

back off the river somewhere. You can come in and walk around, free, you can fish or hunt, free, you can run a boat or sit on a sandbar and get drunk, for that matter. There are just a few things you can't do, and riding a quad-runner is one of them."

"I still don't like it," Gil grouched.

"That's fine," Addie said. "You don't have to like it. Just don't try to argue you'd have more freedom to do what you want if this had been bought out by the timber companies instead of the Preserve."

"It would just be better if it was back the way it used to be."

"Yeah, I would agree with you there. It might be better in some ways if it was how it used to be a hundred years ago. But if you wanted to put things back that way, you'd not only have to get rid of the Preserve, you'd have to get rid of the pulp mill and the petroleum industry and all that as well."

"Yeah," Gil said, "you would."

"And then nobody would have a job," Addie pointed out. She paused, but Gil didn't say anything. "What are you doing back here anyway?"

"Looking for my brother. He didn't come home last night. Though I don't suppose you'd give a rat's ass."

"What makes you think he'd be out here?"

Gil said nothing, but glanced at the woman with him.

"Well, was he on a quad? Or did he have a car, or what? Because if I see it I'll check and make sure he's okay," Addie prodded.

"He's probably not back here. Come on, Brenda. I'm not going to sit around jawing with a cop all day."

Addie watched as the two of them retreated back down the access road to the west. When they were out of sight, she drove carefully along the slick mud track until it crossed Thief Creek below Pine Slough on a narrow, one-lane bridge. She turned around

22

there and headed back out. There was no sign anyone else had been that way, although the rain could have obliterated the tracks.

It was a forty-minute drive from there to the Field Office behind the Preserve's main Visitor Center. Addie pulled through a service gate in the tall fence surrounding the property and parked next to Ike's big white pickup.

Ike was the closest thing to a partner she had, although they rarely rode together except when they were on boat patrol. Ike was also the closest thing to a friend she had. But Addie had quickly discovered that she and Ike disagreed on some fundamental issues. Ike was a perfectionist and couldn't stand to have anything out of order, and he held strong opinions about what he believed to be correct and incorrect behavior. Things were black and white to Ike, with no shades of gray. There were some things Addie knew she could never reveal to him, and having to censor what she said at all times strained their communications. Despite that, she trusted him absolutely as a law enforcement officer, and in many ways viewed him as a mentor.

Ike was sitting, or rather sprawling, at a desk in the back corner of the open main room of the little office. His long legs were propped on the desk, the well-worn soles of a pair of rubberized Maine hunting boots exposed. The chair was canted backwards at a dangerous angle, and Ike had his hands clasped behind his head. He contemplated Addie down the length of his nose as she walked in. Addie noted that the nose was slightly sunburned. Despite his dark hair, Ike burned within minutes even on overcast days.

"Any luck?" Ike asked, not changing his position.

"Well, I found the old roadbed Mr. Rye described. It's at the north end of Thief Creek Road, where the west part of the loop and the east part come together. You have to drive over an old concrete slab to get to it, which is why I've never noticed it before. I parked on the slab and walked in. I didn't want to mess up any tracks or anything."

23

"Did you see any tracks?"

"No. The roadbed's overgrown, there's no bare soil."

"What about any hunting stands or feeders?"

"There's an old oil-rig platform back in there. I figured that was the most likely place for anyone who was poaching to set up. You could sit up there and get a good view of the clearing to the west and the creek to the east and north. I walked around there a little bit, but I didn't see anything in particular. When it started to rain again, I left."

"So, what you're saying is, you didn't find anything suggesting anybody's been poaching back there."

Addie shrugged. "No."

"Well, Mr. Rye called again a little while ago. Said he heard shots out there again last night. Actually, he said there was just one shot, around one a.m."

"No kidding? How could he tell, with all that lightning and thunder?"

It was Ike's turn to shrug. "You know the old coot just wants attention. He swears he can tell a gunshot from thunder even in the middle of a total downpour, but I'd like to know what he was doing sitting up at one a.m. listening to the swamp. I'll bet you ten-to-one he's dreaming or imagining things."

"Maybe," Addie said. "Maybe I should have just ignored the rain and kept looking around."

"No sense in that. First of all, there's probably nobody there. Second of all, if there is someone and they've been poaching out there that regularly, they'll be back. We can go out there when the weather's better. I wouldn't waste any more time on it if I were you."

Ike readjusted himself and removed his feet from the desk. "So, while you were out being useful looking for poachers, I spent my morning being useless at the staff meeting."

"Gosh, sorry I missed it," Addie said. She knew Ike hated the meetings as much as she did, but it was his month to deal with their

24

administrative duties and thus his responsibility to attend. "Did I miss anything important?"

"A representative from Roslyn Pulp and Paper was here. They're going to start cutting timber on a piece of property they own that backs up to the Preserve boundary on the east."

"The one out across from the pulp mill?"

"That one. We'll have to start patrolling the boundary out there more to make sure they're not encroaching or felling trees across the line."

"Well, I guess that'll be an excuse to get out and explore an area I'm not too familiar with," Addie said optimistically. "Anything else going on?"

"Not really. A lot of bullshit, you know how meetings go. Old Joe Cole Senior from the Historical Society was there, he stretched things out good and long."

"Yeah?" Addie said. "I picked up one of his grandsons on the way back this morning. He was out near the old mill on Thief Lake."

"Which one, James?"

"No, Tracey. He's younger than James, I think."

"Yeah, mid-twenties, right? Rides a big camouflage-painted quad-runner, lives over there at Mill Lake with the Radner clan, not with the rest of the Coles at Rye Corner. I've caught him riding that quad on the Preserve a couple of times. He'd be a likely candidate for a poacher, especially coming out of there early in the morning."

"Oh? He was on foot today. If he was poaching, he was doing it without a gun. Anyway, I've never heard the Coles are big poachers. I'd think it's more likely it's one of the Lejeunes, given the area. Besides, I ran into Gil and some girl out on quads near the Ryes' road a little later on."

"Any guns?"

"No, and they weren't on the Preserve at the time. Brand new ATVs, though. They said they were looking for Francis. Said he's missing, didn't come home last night."

25

Ike looked up sharply. "Well, that's not unusual, is it?" he said after a moment. "I mean, he's been known to just disappear for a while, from what I've heard. He's kind of an odd duck. What did Tracey Cole say he was doing out in that area?"

"Said his girlfriend kicked him out last night. He offered to show me around the Preserve some time, too."

Ike snorted. "Yeah, he's made that offer before. So has James. They probably just want to find out what areas we're familiar with so they can make sure and set up their illegal hunting stands elsewhere."

"Maybe. I know you don't like the idea," Addie said.

"I don't. Old Joe Senior may have been a major player in getting the Preserve established, but that doesn't mean his relatives are any different from anybody else around here. You run a criminal history on any of his grandkids, I'll bet you'll find a string of citations as long as your arm. I don't think it's right for law enforcement officers to have any involvement with people of questionable background."

"I figured you'd feel that way," Addie said, crossing her arms. "Anyway, I accepted."

"What?" Ike sat up suddenly, almost upsetting the chair.

"I told him okay. We're going out to the East Bank Bottoms to find some historical cabin, probably next Friday."

"What the hell are you thinking? Are you nuts?"

"Look, it'll be a good opportunity for me to look for illegal blinds and trot lines in an area we don't get into much, and besides, you were just talking about the Roslyn cut. I'll figure out how to get back to our boundary through the Bottoms, and we can patrol the cut that way."

Ike said nothing, but from the look on his face Addie could tell he still disapproved. She had fewer qualms about the Coles than he did. They had always seemed friendly enough to her, and Tracey had a disarming grin and easy manner that was hard to resist.

"Look, I'll run a background check on him before I go and leave the printout for you if that'll make you feel better," she said.

"You let me know exactly where you're going, too," Ike demanded. "Take your cell phone and call me so I'm not thinking this dude has bonked you over the head and dumped you in the swamp."

"For God's sake, Ike." Addie rolled her eyes.

"Don't forget you're a law enforcement officer, a Fed, and what that represents to some of these folks," Ike said.

"As if I could forget," Addie replied. "Is there anything else going on, anything you need from me? 'Cause if not, I'm going to go talk to Old Joe about his grandson and get some information on this old cabin. Otherwise I won't be able to tell you exactly where we're going."

"I've got to take the Boston Whaler in to the shop," Ike said. "They want it there by noon."

Addie helped Ike hitch the boat trailer to his truck, then walked over to the Visitor Center. Joe Senior was sitting behind the front desk on a high stool. He looked as though he'd been as slender as Tracey in his youth, but with age he'd developed a round belly that strained slightly at the buttons of his Volunteer shirt. He still had plenty of white hair and the typical gray-green eyes and characteristic perpetual grin of all the Coles.

"So, Joe, tell me about this old cabin Tracey says you call the Bear-hunter's cabin, out there in the Bottoms."

"Huh." Joe crossed his arms over the top of his belly. "I didn't think anybody from the Preserve knew about that old place, or cared. It's not in the Preserve's historical documentation files. I've checked."

"Well, if it hasn't been documented, it should be. Tracey says he's going to show me where it is so I can take some photographs and record whether it's on Preserve property or not."

27

"That right?" Joe raised his eyebrows. "You bring me back some of those photos for the files here. Maybe I'll use some in the book."

"Of course," Addie said. 'The book', an historical treatise about southeast Texas proposed and composed by Joe Senior, so far existed in concept only.

"Well, then," Joe rubbed the side of his nose and looked up at her from under his eyebrows, "I'll get with Tracey and if he does a good job for you, I'll give him a few bucks for going out there. Same as I'd pay him for guiding a fishing trip. You're going to have to go out there by boat, you know."

"I figured that," Addie said.

"Old road washed out years ago, and besides, what's left of it runs through private property now, through the Roslyn property they're going to be cutting over there on the East Bank. They'll probably destroy the rest of the road, so it's just as well you document it now or nobody will ever be able to find the place. Where you going to pick Tracey up?"

"At his uncle's place, I guess."

"Be more convenient for you to just pick him up along the river since you're going by boat, wouldn't it? I'll give him a call tonight and have him meet you out at his sister Bobbie's hunting camp, out there on the west shore. You know where that's at?"

"Sure," Addie said.

"And you be sure and get back to me afterward and tell me how Tracey does, too," Joe went on. "He's a good enough boy, but he's not real responsible, if you know what I mean. Some folks say it's because he got knocked in the head when he was a kid, but I think it's just because all his kin let him get away with it. I hold him to a higher standard, myself."

"I'm sure everything'll be fine," Addie said.

"Better be," Joe said, "if I'm payin' him for it."

Back at her office, Addie dropped the inter-office mail she'd picked up for Ike on his desk. She paused there for a moment. On the wall above his desk hung two picture frames, each with a badge, patch and photo in it. One was the badge of his father and one was the badge of his grandfather. His desk was piled with papers, pamphlets, and bits of junk, as well as commemorative cups, mugs, calendars, and other minutiae.

Addie's family did not include any other law enforcement officers. Her desk was tidy and bare, except for necessary accessories. She had only one frame, leaning against the wall at the back of her desk. It was a picture of herself at about eight years old, squinting seriously into the sun. She was wearing faded overalls that were too big for her, hand-me-downs from her brother Blake. Her hair, nearly collar-length at that age, was blowing slightly in a wind she knew had been hot and dusty.

To her right was a woman, visible only from the shoulders down, ignored by the photographer. She wore a knee-length blue dress and white apron. Her hands were clasped across her abdomen. Her legs were bare, her feet shod in laceless leather shoes.

It was the only picture Addie had of her mother.

Chapter Five

Tracey paused in the kitchen of his uncle's trailer, silently counting the seconds between the lightning flash throu'gh the open kitchen door and the rumble of thunder to the east. The storm, which had continued all weekend, was finally moving off.

He yanked the refrigerator door open and extracted two beer cans. Then he navigated around the peeling red linoleum-topped counter separating the kitchen from the living room, flopped onto the battered couch, popped the top of one can, and drained half of it in a single draft. The refrigerator was old, and the beer was tepid.

Billy came through the side door, wiping sweat off his brow with the back of his arm. Tracey caught Billy's eye and tossed the second beer in his direction. Droplets of condensation flicked off the rotating can, and Billy caught it deftly with one hand. He splayed out next to Tracey, grabbed the TV remote, and flicked on a sports channel with a stock-car racing program on it.

"Glad that's done," Tracey said, swishing the remainder of the beer in his can. They'd just finished laying a new floor in the kitchen and moving the appliances back in. They'd spent Saturday ripping out the old floor, sub-floor, and rotting joists, and Sunday rebuilding what they'd torn away.

"Don't worry, Virg'll have something else for us to do in short order," Billy said, upending his beer. "We've probably got the time it takes him to unload the rest of the lumber to relax."

"Where's he putting the lumber?" Tracey felt a jolt of adrenalin. It would be logical for Virg to put the lumber in the shed, where the car should have been.

Billy gave him a puzzled glance. "Leaning it up against the back of the trailer. We'll be using it up pretty soon, anyway."

Relieved, Tracey settled back into the couch. He'd had to lie about where he'd been all Friday night and why he'd been delivered home soaking wet and muddy in a patrol car. He'd told Virg he'd spent the night with Liz Durgan and that she'd gotten mad at him and kicked him out of her car up the road Saturday morning, a story not unlikely enough that Virg had questioned him. But he'd almost been caught when his sister Bobbie, her on-again off-again boyfriend Gil Lejeune, and Brenda Doheny showed up Sunday morning.

"Did you see Francis Friday night at Duckhaven?" Bobbie asked him. "He never came home and we're trying to figure out where he is."

"I didn't see him," Tracey told her shortly. So he'd spent the night at the mill for no good reason! Francis had been out, and Brenda likely had known he was gone. He could have slept on her porch out of the rain, or even inside on the couch. He shot Brenda a dirty look, but she returned a blank, worried stare.

"So you were at Duckhaven Friday night," Virg remarked casually after the group left.

"With Liz," Tracey said. "She picked me up before you were home from work." Actually, he'd driven out to the old ranch, now converted into a tavern and grill, and met Liz there. She'd been bugging him for most of the night, hanging all over him, and he'd done his best to ignore her. But by the end of the evening he'd changed his mind and offered to drive her home. She'd agreed, provided he gave her friends Sonja and Brenda a ride too. And then she'd ditched him, comeuppance for ignoring her earlier. She'd gotten out at Sonja's house and left him to drive Brenda home.

Virg hadn't questioned him further, but Tracey, now deep into his lies, began to feel a little more urgency to deal with the car. He'd tried to get hold of Ray Kenworth, but Ray was either out when he called, or Virg was too close for him to feel comfortable talking about the car.

Tracey took another sip from his beer and glanced over at Billy. Billy was about six-three, as tall as his father but not yet as

31

broad in the shoulders or as powerfully built. He and Tracey were the same age, and they'd been best friends since childhood. Tracey knew Billy would help him out with the car if he asked. But that would also mean asking Billy to conceal something from Virg, and Billy was both a rotten liar and not prone to deceiving his father.

As Tracey began to think about having another shot at calling Ray Kenworth, Virg walked in through the kitchen door. He slammed it behind him, grabbed a beer from the refrigerator, and flicked the thermostat to trigger the window-mounted air-conditioner. Then he flipped a kitchen chair around to sit on it backwards in the living room, leaning on the top of the backrest.

At forty-nine, Virg was barrel-chested, with powerful arms developed over years of tossing lumber around the Roslyn mill. His dark hair was peppered with gray, but he showed no signs of losing his restless energy. Even on weekends he rarely relaxed, and he expected his boys to keep busy as well, particularly Tracey, since Tracey didn't earn his own living.

Virg Radner was Tracey's mother's youngest brother, and Tracey couldn't remember a time when Virg hadn't been part of his life. Billy and Dennis Radner had spent their afternoons after school at the Cole residence after their mother's death, and with Tracey and his brothers Jackie and James, they'd formed a tight-knit little gang. But as Tracey's dad, Junior, began to drink more and more heavily, the boys had gravitated first to Grandpa Joe's house, then, as they got older, to the Radner property. With Virg at work at the lumber mill, the boys had free run of the place much of the time, as long as they stayed out of trouble. If they did get into trouble, punishment was swift and decisive. But Virg was predictable and rational, which was more than could be said of Junior.

Tracey had moved in permanently when he was eleven, after the head injury he'd suffered at Junior's hands. Virg still provided Tracey with housing, food, and pocket money when Tracey wasn't working, which was most of the time. And their relationship was much the same as it had always been: Virg treated Tracey like an errant child, and Tracey responded by behaving like a petulant teenager.

At twenty-five, Tracey had begun to recognize the pattern, but he had little idea of how to break out of it. He had, after all, failed to ever hold down a decent job and continued to get himself into minor trouble. He was aware his relatives generally thought his behavior was because of his head injury, but Tracey himself wasn't so sure. He'd long ago ceased suffering from anything he could directly attribute to the injury.

"Well, Trace, you got any jobs lined up this week? Or can I get you to finish up in here and do a couple things out back?" Virg asked.

"Nothing coming up. I can do whatever you want," Tracey said.

"Good. Make a run to the dump with all the crap we just pulled out of here. I'll leave you my truck and catch a ride to the mill with Billy tomorrow. We're working the same shift." Virg extracted his wallet from his back pocket and pulled out a couple twenties, which he handed over to Tracey. "It'll take a couple trips. Pay your way into the dump and keep the change. You need a haircut, too. You might think about using some of that change to get one, so you'll look decent for your customers next time you get any."

Tracey pocketed the money, mentally adding it to the few bucks he already had stowed in his bedroom.

The telephone interrupted Virg's description of what he wanted accomplished in the back yard. Virg picked it up, then handed it off to Tracey.

Tracey recognized his grandpa's gravelly voice with the first word. "Got a job lined up for you," Joe said. "On Friday. This is a little different, no fishing involved."

"You talking about going out to the Bear-hunter's cabin?"

33

"Yep, that's it. I talked to Addie Derange yesterday about it. Told her you'd meet her out at Bobbie's camp Friday morning. If you do a good job, come back with some usable pictures and such, I'll pay you for it just like I'd pay for a guiding trip."

"Sounds good to me."

"You remember how I showed you to get there a couple years ago?"

"It was more like ten years ago," Tracey said.

"You couldn't find it?" Joe challenged.

"Yeah, I can."

"All right, then, you make sure you're up and ready to go Friday morning early, and you be nice to that woman. I told her to get back to me, so you'd best do a good job if you want to see any cash."

"I got it," Tracey replied. "Can I borrow your boat tomorrow afternoon? I want to take a look at what the rain did to the river level and check out where I can take clients."

"You got transportation?"

"Yeah, I've got Virg's truck tomorrow."

"Stop by the Visitor Center. I'll be working. I'll drive Rose's car in and leave the trailer hooked up to my truck."

Tracey hung up the phone and grabbed another beer before he rejoined Virg and Billy in the living room. Just as he sat down, the phone rang again. Virg grabbed it, frowned, then extended the receiver towards Tracey a second time.

"Popular tonight."

"Hello?" Tracey tucked the phone under his chin while he popped the top on his beer can.

"Hey. Is this Tracey Cole?"

"Yeah." Tracey didn't recognize the voice. It wasn't someone local, for sure.

"My name's Van. You don't know me, but I heard you run fishing trips out here on the river. That so?"

"Yeah," Tracey said again. "Who told you?"

"A friend of yours. He told me you usually set these trips up through your grandpa, but I figured if we work things out between you and me, we'd cut out the middleman and you'd make more cash on the deal. And maybe I could save a buck or two myself."

Tracey glanced over at Virg. Virg would undoubtedly not approve of him circumventing his grandpa. He got up. "I think we could work something out," he said, dropping his voice as he stepped into the kitchen. "How many people, what do you want to do, and what day were you thinking about?"

"Just two of us," Van said. "I was thinking next weekend. We just want to cruise around, drink some beer, catch a few fish, you know."

Tracey considered for a moment. Friday he'd be out with Addie, and Friday night Bobbie was having a get-together at the hunting camp. He would rather not get up early Saturday morning, given the party.

"How about Sunday?"

"Sunday's good. Can you pick us up at the boat ramp upriver, the one just south of Ely Dam?"

"The one on the west side?"

"No, not that one. Further down, on the other side."

Tracey frowned. "You mean the Dohenys' boat ramp? On the east shore?"

"Yeah, that's the one."

"You want to go out early?"

"No, not really. I'd rather sleep in, and I've got to drive down from Aynesworth, anyway. Mid-morning is fine by me."

"I'll be there." Tracey hung up the phone, but stood looking at it for a minute. The Dohenys' boat ramp was an odd place to pick up clients. Usually he picked them up at a motel in town or at the Preserve's Visitor Center. But then, this was an odd deal. Nobody'd ever set up a trip directly with him before. That wasn't a bad thing,

35

though. Maybe he was getting a reputation. That could only mean more money in the future, and this time he wouldn't be sharing it with Grandpa Joe.

He went back into the living room. Billy was lying on the couch, so he settled into the old recliner. Getting two jobs had put him in a better mood. With the money he made, he might actually be able to pay the Kenworths up-front to haul out the car and start fixing it, instead of cajoling Ray into some deal involving future favors.

The next morning Tracey swung by the Visitor Center on his last trip back from the dump. He was hot and dirty from tossing rotting lumber around, and an afternoon on the water sounded even better than it had the day before. He felt the blast of air-conditioning as he pulled open the double doors and walked in between the racks of books, magnets, postcards, and stuffed alligators.

Joe Senior was ensconced behind the counter at the far end, deep in conversation with a couple of men who, Tracey guessed by the age difference and physical resemblance, were likely father and son. He walked up quietly and stood a little off to the side where his grandpa could see him, but not close enough to intrude.

But Joe motioned him over. "This is my grandson Tracey," Joe told the two visitors. "He runs a guide boat up the river for me once in a while. Trace, this here's Adrian from New York and Andrew from up at Aynesworth. They're the new owners of the glue factory."

Tracey nodded and shook hands. Adrian looked to be about sixty, with white hair and pale blue eyes. He wore a canvas fisherman's hat covered with fishing flies. Andrew was twenty or so years younger but the resemblance was obvious.

"Adrian says he's going to take a look at my book idea. He's got some publisher friends in New York, might be interested in it," Joe said.

"That's great," Tracey said. He figured Adrian was humoring Joe to get a free tour, but that was Joe's business. As long as his grandpa paid him, he didn't care.

Joe slid his truck keys across the counter and Tracey pocketed them. He left Joe discussing Texas history with his new buddies from the adhesives plant.

At Joe's house Tracey parked Virg's truck and cranked up Joe's Ford F250. He took a minute to check the trailer hitch, wiring, and chains on the boat trailer. Then he pulled out of the semi-circular brick driveway and headed east on Pine Slough Road. There was a dirt launch next to the bridge across Thief Creek, and he shoved the boat off the trailer there.

Once he got going the moving air felt good, though it was too humid for comfort. The top part of Thief Creek was narrow and he had to keep it at a medium speed, but at least there was shade from the overhanging trees. He headed south, past the intersection with Pine Slough and underneath the little bridge that led to the Ryes' inholding.

Below the bridge, just across the river from the Ryes' place, was a little slough along the side of a defunct oil-drilling platform. The oil workers had painted a depth-gauge on the concrete so they could tell when to shut the rig down due to rising water. The numbers were still visible in faded yellow paint. Tracey was in the habit of using the gauge to give him an idea of which sloughs and backwaters would be flooded enough to navigate. He motored up the slough to the platform, turned the boat around in a semi-circle, and let off the tiller, allowing the motor to idle while the wake settled so he could get an accurate reading.

As the hot, humid air settled around him, he grimaced. It stank back in there, not so much the sulfur fumes of an oil rig as the putrescence of something dead. Probably a feral pig; there were a lot of them running around in that area, and the rain could have washed out an old carcass.

He heard another boat coming upstream out on the creek, puttering slowly, the motor high and spluttering. The boat went by, then came back a few minutes later. Curious, Tracey mentally cataloged the water level and motored out of the slough to see who it was.

The operator of the boat was Skeeter Doheny, from up at the Doheny's boat ramp. The kid looked about ten, but Tracey knew he was at least fourteen. Skeeter was Brenda's cousin. He had probably been staying at Brenda and Francis' house off Thief Lake. Maybe he was out looking for Francis. Tracey raised a hand, and Skeeter shut down his motor.

Tracey pulled alongside and grabbed the gunwale. Skeeter observed Tracey from below too-long bangs, displaying prominent front teeth that would have had braces on them had he been from a more affluent family. He had a spray of freckles across his nose, and bright-blue eyes.

"Hey, Tracey Cole!" Skeeter said. "What're you doing sneaking around this neck of the woods?"

"Fishing. You got a problem with that?"

"Funny fishing you're doing, up there in the woods. You setting jug-lines? I know you ain't got a permit."

"I was checking the water level, jerk," Tracey replied, dropping the idea of asking about Francis. "Anything else you want, or are you just here to harass me?"

"You scouting our hunting zone? You know we pull the permits for this area," Skeeter asked suspiciously.

"I told you, I'm checking out the fishing. I'm not scouting your area."

"Yeah? I heard you were out with my cousin Brenda the other night. Maybe you're up here because you know Francis isn't around. You better make sure he don't come back and find you out."

Tracey glared at him, thinking up a suitable response to send the little brat packing. He suddenly became aware of the gunwale he

38

was holding onto as they drifted. The gunwale was part of a brand-new jon-boat, without the usual peeling paint and abrasions a few seasons of navigating the sloughs would invariably bring. It was a small, dark green Sea Ark, with no registration numbers on the prow. The boat had a center console rather than a tiller and an over-sized Mercury outboard, which Skeeter had tilted way clear of the water to avoid hitting any cypress knees with the prop. Tracey knew instantly it was way too expensive for Skeeter or any of his family to afford.

"Hey, Skeet, whose boat is this anyway?"

"It's mine!" Skeeter flipped his hair out of his eyes and glared back at Tracey.

"What're you doing with a brand-new boat?"

Skeeter suddenly appeared nervous, fiddling with the wheel.

"You tell anyone else I'm after your cousin, which isn't true anyway, and get me in bad with Francis or Gil, and I'll sure as hell get someone to check out this boat, and check it out good," Tracey said. "So if you don't want somebody poking around your boat ramp, you'll shut your little mouth."

Tracey pushed the boat away. As Skeeter drifted downstream, Tracey noticed that he'd already scratched the new boat, up front just above the water line and along the side of the gunwale.

Tracey lowered his motor and cranked the tiller. He zipped by Skeeter and went on down Thief Creek. Finally he passed the old mill and entered the lake. He swung the boat over to the shoreline near the gap in the trees and let it settle. The water was murky and tea-stained brown. He craned over the gunwale, but he couldn't see the car at all. That was part good and part bad, he supposed. Ray Kenworth would have to dive to hook it up, but it was less likely someone would find it before he was ready.

He went back upstream via the river and Pine Slough to the ramp where he'd parked. He'd left the trailer backed in to the water, since very few people used the make-shift launch, so he was able to load quickly. He stopped to gas the boat up on the way back to Joe's so it would be ready to go. He'd use it to get to Bobbie's camp Thursday night and spend the weekend there. That way he could meet Addie at the camp Friday morning, go to Bobbie's party that night, hang out Saturday, and be ready to go upstream to pick up his clients Sunday morning.

Friday would be an interesting day, he thought: exploring back in the Bottoms, trying to remember where that old bear-hunter's cabin was, and hanging around with a warden. Or rather, a ranger. He wasn't sure about the difference, but he knew the Preserve officers were very particular that they were rangers. It could be a very productive day. He could find out what they did and where they went and what they knew. But there was more to it than that: Addie Derange piqued his curiosity. He knew all about the lives of most of the women he hung around with, because he'd grown up with them and lived around their families all his life. But he didn't know anything about her. He didn't care what anybody else out on the river thought about him going out with an officer, either. Most of them would do it if they had a chance. If he was lucky and planned things right, he might even be able to get her to come back to Bobbie's camp for the evening. That would be a kick, he thought: bringing a warden to a party at a hunter's camp.

Chapter Six

It was still dark Friday morning when Addie left her house. She stepped out onto the front porch and held the screen with her hip as she pulled the door shut. As she turned, she noticed a business card tucked just under the edge of her doormat. She picked it up and read it by the yellow bug light over the door. The rough-textured off-white card had the words '*AFTERThought*' printed in the center of the front. Puzzled, Addie flipped it over and looked at the back, but there was nothing there. She shrugged, trotted down the front steps to her car, threw her daypack, her cellphone, and the card on the passenger seat, and cranked the engine. The car sounded like it was missing on one of its four cylinders. She was going to have to get a tune-up soon.

She had dressed in jeans, sport shoes, and an oversize T-shirt covered with a pale blue sweatshirt. Under the T-shirt she carried her pistol in a low-profile holster, her handcuffs, a clip-on can of pepper spray, and her badge. She'd chosen the low-profile garb to accomplish a couple of things: she would be less visible and more apt to witness any unusual activity on the Preserve, and she would be less apt to attract notice to her guide, who might not want to be associated with law enforcement.

It took her about a half-hour to get to the field office, where she picked up the Chevy Tahoe and a lightweight flat-bottomed aluminum jon-boat, left unmarked for undercover and plain-clothes operations. She ducked into the office to grab the Tahoe keys and checked quickly to make sure the paperwork she'd promised Ike was in order on his desk.

The day before, Addie had accessed the computer database containing the previous year's hunting permit information. She had found about twenty Coles, including Tracey. Tracey's birth-date put him at twenty-five years old, three years younger than her. She had asked the dispatcher for a 'run' complete with criminal history.

Tracey had one D.U.I. conviction on record, but his license was valid and current. His criminal history included a number of misdemeanor tickets and two arrests other than the D.U.I., one for D.U.I. Accident, reduced to Leaving the Scene of an Accident, and one for Evading Police. The dispatcher had run Tracey through local files with the surrounding counties and Parks and Wildlife authorities as well. Two hits had come up: one for running a hunting dog on timber company land and one for driving an ATV along a pipeline clearance near the bayou. He also had two citations in the Preserve's local files, both from Ike, both for riding his quad-runner on Preserve property. Despite these, it was hardly the extensive history Ike had hinted at. There was nothing to indicate Tracey Cole was an officer safety risk or tended towards violence.

By the time Addie was on her way upstream, the sun was completely above the horizon, the rays shooting between the cypress trees, visible in the morning mist. It promised to be a beautiful day.

Bobbie Cole's hunting camp sat on the edge of the river where a piece of property still belonging to the Coles sliced through Preserve land. Bobbie was tall and lean, with stringy yellow hair and the identifiable Cole grin and gray-green eyes, but her height and the broadness of her features belied the Radner blood she'd gotten from her mother's side. She tended to wear a T-shirt with the sleeves cut off, maybe to show off her brawny arms. She was a floor foreman at the Roslyn particle-board factory, and she was making enough money to have built a nice gray brick house along Magnolia Slough Road. She also kept her camp set up by the river, and the Cole clan gathered there on weekends or during hunting season. Addie knew that it was Bobbie's money that had allowed the Coles to hold onto that piece of land at all.

When Addie arrived at the camp, she tied the boat off beneath a steep bank by several others and clambered up to an overshadowed clearing. There was a canvas-roofed cabin to her left, situated in deep shade. A thin spiral of smoke curled from a campfire pit, but she heard no voices and saw no one around.

As she stepped hesitantly towards the cabin, she heard a low, rising whistle. She squinted into the deep woods. Tracey was leaning against the trunk of a tree with one knee up and his arms crossed over his chest.

He chuckled and pushed himself off the tree. Caught off-guard, Addie smiled back at him.

"Bet you thought I wouldn't be awake yet," he said. "Well, you're not too far off. I just got up. Bobbie and James are sleepin' yet. You're not in a big hurry, are you?"

Addie shrugged. "No big hurry, but I guess we'll want to get out there before it gets too hot."

"Sure," Tracey agreed, "I just want a cup of coffee. C'mon in."

Addie followed him around the cabin and through the open doorway. In the far left corner of the room, next to a small wood-burning stove, was a bed made of two-by-fours and plywood. It was covered with foam pads and a number of blankets and pillows, heaped in such a manner that Addie guessed there was someone under them. Along the left wall was a collapsible, military-style cot, with James Cole asleep on it. He was several years older and a little heavier than Tracey, although he was about the same height, five-eight or nine. He lay on his stomach with one arm hanging off the bed. His shoes, kicked off still tied, lay nearby.

There was a Coleman-style two-burner camp stove on top of the wood-burner, and Tracey turned up the gas and lit it. The hiss of gas and the blow of ignition brought some movement from the lump of blankets to the left. Bobbie poked her head out and looked at the stove. Her hair stuck out wildly in all directions. She greeted Addie with a grin of recognition. James remained deep in slumber, although he pulled his arm in to his side.

43

Tracey moved a kettle onto the burner. When the water steamed, he created the coffee one cup at a time by pouring the hot water through a paper filter stuck in a plastic holder. Addie wrapped her hands around her plastic mug and felt the heat seep through into her palms. Tracey took a sip of his, then put it down on a table made of a huge wooden cable-spool. He grabbed the towel he'd used as a potholder and spiked it at James' sleeping form. The towel wrapped around James' head. James pulled the towel off and propped himself up on his elbows on the cot.

"You want your ass kicked first thing in the morning, don't you, little brother?" he growled.

Tracey grinned. "Just thought you'd want your coffee 'fore it got cold." He held the coffee out with one hand from a safe distance. James reached for it. He sipped from the mug while still propped on his elbows. After a minute, he rolled up into a sitting position and noticed Addie.

"Good morning," Addie said.

James replied with a questioning look.

"That's Addie, you remember? She's with the Preserve," Bobbie told him.

James turned back to Addie. "Yeah, but I don't remember last night too good...you stay here?" he asked.

Bobbie laughed out loud.

"I think you got the wrong impression." Addie glanced at Tracey, who was grinning over his coffee cup. "I just came up river this morning."

"Oh." James grinned as well. "Going out on the river with Trace, then? Fishing?"

Addie glanced at Tracey. She wasn't sure what, if anything, he had told them about their trip. Maybe he had led them to believe he was taking her out as a fishing client.

"You remember that old bear-hunter's camp back above Goat Lake, J.T.?" Tracey asked.

44

James grunted. "The one grandpa says was a Cole place?"

"That one. That's where we're going. So if we don't show up by tomorrow, come looking for us."

"Won't be able to find you," James said. "I don't remember where that place is. Besides, those waterways change every time it floods around here. But I guess you won't have to worry about running into anyone else back there. Nice and private."

"Shut up, James," Bobbie said.

Tracey slung a day-pack over his shoulder and motioned to Addie. "Let's get out of here."

They walked out under the thick forest canopy to the bright, sunlit bank, where the morning mist was almost gone from the river. It took a minute for the boat motor to crank and get settled in.

Addie drove downriver until they neared the East Bank Bottoms. There she slowed and pulled to the shore. She grabbed a tree limb to hold the boat in position. "I have no idea where we're going from here on out," she told Tracey.

"Well, I hate to tell you this, but I don't have a real good idea either," he laughed. "Last time I was out to that old camp was probably ten years ago. I ought to be able to get us into the right area, but I'm not making any guarantees."

"Fair enough," Addie said. "I'm just as interested in seeing what else is going on back there, anyway."

"Yeah?" Tracey asked. "What kind of things do you look for when you're out here?"

"Well, you know, anything that might indicate people are poaching or dumping hazardous materials. Stuff like that." Addie wasn't sure if he was genuinely curious, or if he was trying to get information that would help him figure out where the patrol officers were most likely to be.

"Ike likes to catch people boating drunk," Tracey said. "That, and catch folks riding four-wheelers."

45

Addie smiled. "Well, everybody kind of develops his own specialty, I guess. I kind of prefer to get back off the river in these smaller waterways and poke around and explore. I always did like to do that, even when I was a kid: get back into places where other people don't usually go."

Tracey pointed to a slough opening onto the river. "This is Goat Lake Slough. I think we need to go in one of these sloughs just to the north."

They chose one that looked wide, but it petered out within a quarter mile and they retreated. Addie bypassed the next one as too narrow and they tried a third, but it soon became clogged with downed trees.

"Go back to that second one," Tracey suggested as they came out again onto the river.

"It looked really narrow," Addie said doubtfully, but she nosed the boat into the drainage. It was barely six feet wide, but as she headed in she could feel that there was a good outflow of water. She continued up the channel slowly. Eventually the slough widened and became easily navigable, despite its narrow throat. She reminded herself not to question Tracey when he suggested a route. After all, he was the guide.

They intersected several other sloughs. Tracey pointed out the one each time that seemed to be heading east in a general manner. Addie felt clumsy piloting the little boat at such a slow speed, occasionally scraping up against a cypress knee near the bank.

Suddenly, Tracey turned and looked back over his shoulder at her, raised his eyebrows and pointed ahead. Addie swung the boat a little and it stuck out in the shadows: bright pink plastic flagging, tied to tree limbs to mark a route. She knew that flag-lines often led to illegally-placed hunting stands, blinds, and feeders.

"Let's just follow that and see where we get," Tracey said. "This flag-line's far enough back in here that someone's trying to hide it, that's for sure."

The pink flags were widely-spaced and followed a complicated route back through the bottomland. Tracey picked out the flags and directed her left or right. Much of the area was flooded, water running across the ground just a few feet deep, but the flags seemed to follow a deeper, flowing slough.

Finally Tracey pointed to the right. "There's a tack line. I don't see any more flags."

Addie saw a line of thumbtacks stuck in the tree bark of the pines. The tacks led overland to the east, and she could see the abrupt rise of the East Bank fifty yards away through the forest.

"And there's the cabin. We're on East Bank Slough, now. Pull 'er up on the bank, there."

Addie steered the boat to the right and Tracey jumped out and pulled the bow up on the bank.

"You can help me figure out where we are on the map," Addie said. "I'll take some photos for Joe and a GPS reading, too." She looked at her watch. "Let's have lunch first, though."

Tracey tied the boat off to a cypress branch and sat down on the front bench seat. Addie sat on the middle seat. She pulled her small ice chest up and flipped it open.

"So, I heard through the grapevine you and Ike made some kind of bust out on the river," Tracey said, opening his pack.

"Word gets around fast," Addie said. "We busted a guy for boating under the influence Wednesday. We took him out at the Bear Creek bridge and gave him to the county because our truck was at the canal siphon."

"Who was it?"

"Some guy from Buenavista. I never met him before. Name's Doug Raney. He had a little crank on him, too."

"What?" Tracey asked.

"Crank. Methamphetamine. Crystal. Speed. Whatever you guys call it around here."

"Yeah, some folks call it crank around here," Tracey said slowly. "But I hadn't heard there was any going around lately. Not that I would have heard," he added hastily. "I stay away from that stuff. Fries your brain."

"Well, that's what the county guys said, too. They said they haven't been running into a whole lot of it lately, at least not up here along the river. Maybe he got it down in Buenavista. He wouldn't say."

Tracey nodded. "I know Doug Raney. His family's got a butcher shop down in Buenavista. It doesn't surprise me he was boating drunk. Surprises me a little that he had crank on him, though. Hey, do you know Francis Lejeune?"

"Sure," Addie said. "I've run into him and Gil quite a few times. I heard that he might be missing. What do you think might've happened to him?"

"Probably nothing," Tracey said. "Francis is kind of weird. He's been known to disappear for a couple of weeks before. My sister told me Brenda told Gil she had a fight with him last Friday, so he might have just split to make her mad."

"After I dropped you off the other day, I ran into Gil and a woman named Brenda out by the Ryes' road," Addie said. "They said they were looking for Francis. Is that the Brenda you're talking about?"

"Yeah, Brenda Doheny. She's been living with Francis for three, four years now."

"Is she related to that kid who goes by the nickname Skeeter?"

"Yeah, they're cousins. Skeeter lives upriver at the boat ramp by Ely Lake, but he stays with Francis and Brenda a lot of the time. Where'd you run into him?"

"Out on the river yesterday. He was driving a brand-new boat with no registration numbers on it."

"I saw him out in that boat, too, up Thief Creek. Did you stop him?" Tracey asked. "Who did that boat belong to?"

"We did stop him, to find out why there weren't any numbers on it. Turns out all the paperwork was in order, he just hadn't put the stickers on yet. It was registered to David Doheny. He told us that was his real name."

"Yeah, that's right," Tracey frowned. "Seems funny to me they could afford a boat like that. There's nobody up at that ramp nowadays except a bunch of old folks and Skeeter. They don't even do business there anymore. Skeeter's Dad's the only one making any money, and all he does is drive truck."

"Maybe Francis or Brenda bought it and let Skeeter register it in his name," Addie suggested.

"Doubt it," Tracey said. "Francis works up at the adhesives plant part-time. Rest of the time he spends at home, making jewelry. I think he learned that in some jail program. He sells it down in Buenavista at the shop where Brenda works, Doug Raney's sister's shop. He wouldn't be able to afford a boat like that, a new Sea Ark. And it wouldn't be Gil's; he doesn't make enough to have bought it either. Otherwise, he wouldn't be mooching off Bobbie so much of the time."

"Your sister Bobbie?" Addie asked.

"Yeah," Tracey said, "Gil goes out with Bobbie, you know."

"No, I didn't realize that," Addie said, frowning as she tried to mentally catalog the latest interrelationships of the local populace. "What if Francis didn't just take off? Do you think somebody might want to do him harm? Somebody who might have a grudge?"

"There was a thing a few years ago, when he got busted," Tracey said hesitantly.

"I heard about that," Addie said. "The county faxed us a bulletin to be on the lookout for him. The fax said he was arrested for dealing methamphetamines five years ago and he testified against the manufacturer in a plea bargain."

"Yeah, that's what reminded me about Francis, when you said Doug Raney had some crank on him. But I'll bet Francis isn't messed up in that again," Tracey said.

"But he could have some enemies from back in those days," Addie pointed out. "Then again, he could've had some sort of accident. I guess he was probably poaching up there by the Ryes' road where Gil and Brenda were looking for him."

Tracey grinned. "Bet you're right. Not that I know for sure, but Gil's been bringing venison out to the camp pretty often lately. So that's what you were doing out on Thief Creek Road so early in the morning last Saturday? Looking for poachers?"

"Good guess," Addie replied, smiling.

"So you look for poachers and Ike looks for drunk boaters," Tracey mused. He glanced quickly at her. "Ike's your partner, huh? You hang out with him?"

"Hang out? We go out for a drink after work sometimes. But I'm not dating him, if that's what you mean." Addie considered for a minute, wondering if he was just trying to make conversation or if he was expressing interest. There was something attractive about him, but it was hard to pinpoint what it was. Except for his wide and frequent grin, he was average looking, but he had an almost innocent charm.

"So how about you?" Addie asked. "Did you ever make up with that girlfriend who kicked you out a week ago in the rain?"

"Uh, no," Tracey grinned and ran a hand through his hair, looking suddenly shy. "It wasn't a real serious thing, anyway. She didn't, you know, like going out on the river or anything. Not my type."

Addie thought he was leaving something out, but it was really none of her business. She drained the last drops of her soda.

50

Tracey packed up the rest of his lunch and stretched. "You want to go follow that tack line and see where it goes?"

"Sure," Addie said. She set her empty soda can and an apple she hadn't eaten on the bow box next to Tracey's empty can, then climbed out with her camera and GPS unit.

It took only a few minutes to document what was left of the cabin. The remaining pine logs were soft and damp to the touch. Inside, what had been a wood-burning stove was nothing but a pile of rusted iron. Still, it was an interesting bit of local history, especially since Joe Cole could probably fill her in on the specific owner.

When she was satisfied with her documentation, Addie put the camera and GPS back in the boat and they started off inland on foot. There was an old roadbed leading to the southeast, but it disappeared quickly along the crumbling rise of the East Bank. The bank was an ancient river shore, created when the Deuce had run in a wide arc further to the east than its current course, and it was made of layers of silt and sand rather than soil or bedrock.

The tacks were harder to see than the flags had been. They were designed for night use, when a flashlight passed over their reflective caps would make them glow like fireflies. Tracey and Addie moved through the forest sporadically, stopping to search for the tacks, then going forward to the next marked tree.

At the end of the tack line there was a hunter's tree stand. It consisted of a metal chair and a series of pulleys threaded with green synthetic rope. The chair was not bolted or cabled to the tree, which was the normal means of attachment, but was supported with an assortment of home-made canvas bands, knotted to transfer the weight of a person climbing up into it in such a way that the chair was pulled in to the tree and would not slip down. The pulley system could be used to raise or lower the stand.

"That's different," Addie said, looking at the set-up. "I should have brought the GPS and camera."

Tracey grunted. He was staring at the stand.

"You've seen this before?" Addie asked.

"No," Tracey said quickly. Addie glanced at him, but he avoided her eyes and continued to study the stand. She was pretty sure he was lying. She decided not to push it. If he knew whose it was, he would probably tell that person it had been found, and it would be removed. Besides, she wasn't at all sure it was on Preserve property. The property line ran close to the East Bank and was poorly marked or not marked at all back in here.

She wandered around the stand area, looking for anything else interesting. There was a set of faint tracks heading east, and the tack line continued on the opposite side of the trees.

"So the guy can either walk in from somewhere off the East Bank, or maybe ride a four-wheeler, or he can come in by water," Tracey said, examining the tacks. "These haven't been here long, either. No rust."

They made their way back to the slough, following their own footprints in the mud. Addie walked down towards the rear of the boat. Tracey untied it and gathered up the bow-line in one hand.

As he stood up, there was the crack of rifle shot and one of the empty cans on the bow crumpled and fell into the boat. The bullet continued into the water, whining as it tumbled.

Tracey flinched and ducked. Addie, after a second's surprise, hit the ground on the bank, partly in the water, and rolled onto her left hip to yank up her T-shirt and draw her pistol. But she could only point it into the woods in the general direction from which she thought the shot had come. There was no one to be seen or heard.

"Tracey!" Addie hissed. "Get down somewhere!"

Tracey was half-kneeling. He moved cautiously in the direction the can had fallen, putting the boat between him and the shooter. As he moved, a second shot cracked in the forest, and the apple disintegrated into pulp.

This time Tracey went to his belly. He made his way around the stern of the boat in the water and came up the bank next to Addie. Addie was still lying on her stomach, her pistol pointed into the trees.

"He's not shooting at us," Tracey said.

"Sure as shit seems like he is to me," Addie snapped, "seeing as how we're the only ones around here, and those shots are coming really, really close to us."

"He hit the can and the apple," Tracey pointed out. "Either that was a really big coincidence, or he's a really good shot. And if he's that good a shot, he could've had us by now."

"Yeah," Addie agreed. "But what's the point, then? A warning? I'm not in uniform, but I bet there are people who still recognize me."

A third shot took out the second can on the bow. Addie scanned the forest frantically, but saw no one.

"Damn! What's he want?"

"I don't know," Tracey said. "Those shots are coming from a long way away, though. He's a damn good shot, whoever it is."

Tracey got cautiously to his knees. "Stop shooting, you fucking idiot! You're gonna kill somebody!" he shouted into the woods. Addie reached up and grabbed at him, trying to pull him back down unsuccessfully.

The shout was greeted by silence. Tracey remained on his knees, looking into the woods. After a minute, he reached over the side of the boat and groped around until he caught the handle of Addie's ice-chest. He yanked it out, opened it up, and pulled out Addie's second can of soda. Then he crawled forward and put it on the bow.

They waited. Five minutes passed, and Addie had to re-adjust her position. She sat up slightly, taking the weight off her elbows. Her heart rate was beginning to decrease.

"I think he's gone," Tracey said. "It was some kind of a joke or some kind of warning or whatever, but I think he's gone now."

"What kind of joke would that be?" Addie asked angrily, getting up to her knees and replacing her pistol in its holster.

"I don't know, someone sees a couple cans set up like that and takes the opportunity to prove what a great shot he is," Tracey shrugged. He took the full soda can off the bow, popped the top and handed it to Addie.

Addie sat down next to him on the bow, took a swig, and offered the can back to him. Her jeans were soaked to the hip with brown swamp water.

"You doing all right?" Tracey asked, studying her. He was also wet and muddy, but he didn't seem to be nearly as alarmed as Addie.

"I guess," Addie said. "I don't care for being shot at."

"Me neither. But I think it was some smart-ass who wanted to shoot those cans off the bow. I bet he didn't even know who we are."

"Maybe the person who put up that stand," Addie said, glancing at him. "But how did he get in here? I didn't see any boat."

"No, but he could have parked it up one of these sloughs. Or he could have come in overland."

"I thought your grandpa told me the overland route was washed out. And part of the old roadbed goes through Roslyn Pulp and Paper property, isn't that right? So whoever it is, they'd have to be able to access Roslyn property and know where the old roadbed was."

Tracey hesitated. "It isn't that hard to get onto Roslyn property if you really want to. But he'd have to know the area pretty damn good to know where the old road was and be able to follow it, and to be able to find this same area by water as well."

Addie nodded. "So it's someone who knows this area like the back of his hand. As well as you."

Tracey smiled. "Better, maybe."

They exchanged the soda can a few more times until it was empty. Addie continued to watch the woods in the direction from which the shots had come, but she saw no movement of any kind.

"There's no running-lights on this boat," Tracey commented, looking down at the bow by his legs. "Isn't that illegal?"

"Not if we don't run it at night," Addie said.

"Then we better get going," Tracey said, "because it took us about three hours to find our way in here, and you have to get down to the ramp, too."

Addie looked at her watch. It was five o'clock. It would be getting dark by 7:45 or 8:00. But going back should be easier and quicker, and they wouldn't stop to check out the things she'd wanted to examine on the way in.

"Want me to drive back?" Tracey offered. "That'll give you a chance to look around."

They made good time at first with Tracey at the helm, but the flags proved harder to see on the return trip. A couple of times they took a wrong turn and had to back up when a slough petered out altogether. Addie sat up on the bow-box, leaning this way and that, trying to spot the next flag in line. The sun was getting much lower in the sky, and their southwesterly direction of travel put it right in their eyes, making it even more difficult to choose a route.

Finally the sun disappeared behind the trunks of the cypress. Addie opened the middle seat box. Inside was a Q-beam, a battery-operated spotlight. She pulled a car battery out from under the bow-box and clipped the light to it with alligator clips. Then she flicked the switch, testing it.

As darkness settled in to the Bottoms and the trilling of the night-insect world rose in volume, Addie lay across the bow-box, trying to keep out of Tracey's line of sight. It was an awkward position, with her knees in the bottom of the boat and her elbows propped on the metal platform. She held the spotlight with both

55

hands and turned it back and forth. Shadows wheeled across the water in the opposite direction from the swing of the Q-beam. With only the spotlight, it was difficult to tell what was slough and what was just flooded forest. The swamp was eerie and primeval in the dark, with the strange shapes of cypress knees poking up and rattan vines and moss hanging down.

Finally the beam passed across what appeared to be a more open space. They came around a corner, through the narrow slough entrance, and were out on the river. Addie sat up. "Shut it down for a minute so I can call Ike," she said, pulling out her cell phone.

Ike answered on one ring. "Where are you?"

"We just got back out on the river. It'll be at least forty-five minutes before I can get down to the ramp."

"I tried to call you a while ago," he replied accusingly.

Addie looked at the screen of her phone. "Oh. I must have been out of range. Sorry. Anyway, we're heading for the camp."

"After you drop Tracey off, you'll be alone," Ike reminded her. "That boat doesn't have any running-lights, nobody else coming up river will be able to see you. Can you operate the Q-beam and drive at the same time?"

"If I have to," Addie said.

"Why don't you just spend the night at the camp and then go back in the morning?" Tracey asked.

Addie looked at him doubtfully through the dark.

"Nobody would mind," Tracey went on. "It's just the Coles and the Radners and the Kenworths that'll be up there. Gil Lejeune'll be there, but if he gives you any trouble just tell one of us. It won't be a problem."

Addie hesitated. Spending the evening at a hunters' camp on the river would be an interesting experience. She tried to think how to explain it to Ike. "Why don't you just go home for tonight?" she said into the phone. "I'll stay up here and come on down tomorrow morning."

"Where are you planning on staying? In the boat?"

"No, I'll stay at Tracey's sister's camp."

There was a moment of silence. "You sure you're okay with that?" Ike asked.

Addie could hear the hesitancy in his voice. She was glad she hadn't mentioned the shots in the woods. "Yeah, yeah, it's fine. Call me about eight tomorrow."

Ike didn't reply. Addie brought the phone away from her ear and hit the "End" button.

Chapter Seven

Finally the light picked out the river bend where Bobbie's camp was located. Tracey turned the boat to the western shore. Addie scrambled out on a narrow strip of sand beneath the tall, crumbly bank and tied the boat off to a root.

Tracey killed the motor and scrambled forward over the center seat. "Ready?" he asked.

Addie debated with herself. She didn't really want to go up to the camp wearing her gear. If she was going to be there for the night, she might as well relax and try to enjoy herself. Besides, she'd have to take her gear off eventually so she could lie down and sleep. She stepped back in the boat, removed her belt and everything on it, and put it all in a plastic garbage bag. Then she stowed it in the middle bench seat, which had a padlock, and slipped the key in her pocket.

Tracey climbed up the bank and extended his hand. Addie grabbed hold and he hauled her up. At the top, he held on more than long enough to be sure she had her footing. Addie could see him grinning in the dark. She figured he was getting a kick out of bringing an off-duty federal officer to a hunting camp on the river.

She could hear music and a number of voices. There were maybe thirty people there. The fire pit crackled and a few sparks wandered into the air. Addie stood off in the dark by the cabin while Tracey went over to Bobbie, who stood near the two-track road in the light of a lantern. She saw Bobbie glance in her direction. Tracey stopped at a plastic tub to retrieve a couple of beers on his way back. A dark-haired, lanky guy Addie didn't recognize accompanied him as he skirted the fire pit.

"Want a beer?" Tracey popped the top for her before she could answer. She took it and gulped at the cold beer gratefully; she was a little dehydrated from spending all day out in the heat. As she tipped the can, she noticed Gil Lejeune sitting on a log at the fire pit. He turned his head quickly as she looked in his direction.

"I told Bobbie you're going to spend the night here," Tracey said. "We'll figure out someplace to sleep later. You hungry? Let's get something."

Tracey led her towards the cabin door. The dark-haired man followed them, sticking out his hand. "Ray Kenworth," he slurred. Addie thought he was probably already drunk. He had a wide-eyed look, almost alarmed, and his hair looked as though someone had run a brush through it the wrong direction.

"Addie Derange," she said, wiping the moisture from the beer can off her hand on her jeans.

Ray stared at her, swaying slightly on his feet. "That's some name, there."

"Derange? Yeah, it used to be 'Deranger', from the French," Addie replied, lengthening the vowels. "My ancestors were clothing makers. They specialized in creating huge ruffles for blouses that were sometimes called derangers."

There was a pause while Ray appeared to take that in. Addie didn't volunteer any more. She had no idea if Ray knew who she was.

The cabin was lit by a couple of Coleman lanterns. The cable-spool table was loaded with bags of chips and plastic tubs of dip and salsa, potluck dishes, and the like. Tracey retrieved some bread and cheese from a shelf near the stove. They made themselves sandwiches, and Addie offered to make one for Ray, who seemed too distracted to accomplish the task himself, but he refused her offer. Instead, he retrieved two more cans of beer from his pockets and offered them to Tracey and Addie. Addie realized she'd already finished her first one, drinking it too quickly. She reminded herself to drink more slowly, but took the can Ray gave her.

Gil Lejeune stepped into the cabin and walked over to the cable spool. He reached into a bag of chips. Addie raised her eyebrows and looked at him.

"So how's the warden business?" Gil said acidly. Ray shot a quick glance at Addie, then at Tracey.

"About like it always is," Addie replied.

"You a warden?" Ray asked in surprise.

Addie took a swig of beer. "I'm a ranger for the Preserve. Some folks call us wardens."

"What do you do?" Ray asked, still staring at her.

"Mostly spend a lot of time trying to convince people that I'm a normal human being and that the Preserve is a good thing," Addie said.

Ray grinned. "Yeah? Bet you know old Joe Cole Senior. My great-aunt Rose is his wife. That makes Tracey and me second cousins. I think."

Gil snorted, grabbed another handful of chips and walked out. Ray shrugged. "Bad mood, maybe."

"Yeah, I think just seeing me puts him in a bad mood," Addie said.

Ray grinned sloppily again and patted her hand. "Don't worry. I won't tell anyone who you are."

When they were done eating they went back outside. Addie sat down on a bench up against the side of the cabin, just out of the ring of light from the fire. Tracey told her he'd be back soon and hauled Ray away by the arm. They disappeared into the dark around the end of the cabin, but a minute later Tracey returned alone. He handed her another icy can of beer and sat down beside her.

"Damn, Ray is wasted already. I was hoping he'd be sober enough to talk to, but he's not."

"Got something you need to discuss?" Addie prodded. It hadn't escaped her that whatever Tracey wanted to talk to Ray about, it had been something he didn't want her to hear.

60

"Mmm," Tracey muttered noncommittally. He took a long drag on his beer, his eyes roving around the camp over the top of the can. He jumped up again. "I'm gonna go say 'hi' to Sam Rye, over there. He sets up guide trips for me sometimes. I'll be back. Don't go anywhere."

"Wasn't planning on it," Addie said. She watched as Tracey worked his way back through the crowd. Obviously he hadn't wanted to talk about his business with Ray. She was curious, but she didn't care a whole lot, either. There was no reason Tracey should trust her with his private business any more than she'd trust him with hers.

As the evening wore on, Tracey came and went, usually bringing her beer or food. He sat next to her on the bench between forays to the ice chests or to the fire pit to talk to one person or another. Addie began to feel more comfortable at the camp and with him. He introduced her to several people, but never told them what she did for a living, and as far as she could tell, neither did Ray. People seemed more relaxed about her presence than Addie had expected. She guessed it was because she was there with Tracey.

The height of the bonfire seemed to rise in direct proportion to the level of intoxication of the people around it. During the intervals when Tracey was gone, Addie amused herself by studying the folks at the party. From her position outside the circle, she could see the expressions on the faces of those seated around the fire and observe their interactions and body language, but they, looking out into the dark, would have a harder time seeing her. It was a familiar position for her: outside, looking in.

She knew Dennis Radner, Tracey's cousin: the Preserve did business with his air-conditioning shop in Buenavista. He was dark-haired, good-looking, and neatly dressed, with a recent haircut. She guessed the woman with Dennis was his wife. The long-legged, broad-shouldered young man sitting next to them was Billy Radner, Dennis' brother and Tracey's cousin. Bobbie Cole was a center of

61

attention, often standing in the midst of a noisy group who appeared to be the hard drinkers at the camp. James, also a center of attention wherever he went, was a full-time flirt and a tease. He seemed to enjoy wrestling and shoving with some of the other guys, including Tracey, but it looked good-natured enough, and Addie didn't see anyone who appeared to be put out by it.

Tracey was less of an obvious flirt than James, but Addie could see people gravitated to him. He liked to talk and he laughed easily. He obviously reveled in the attention he received from the people at the camp, though he had seemed to feel at home out on the river and in the backwaters as well. With the river rolling by in the dark on one side and his friends and relatives on the other, he was in his element.

Gil Lejeune, however, appeared to be almost as much an outsider there as Addie herself. The only people who paid him much mind were Bobbie, a couple of men she didn't know, and Skeeter Doheny. Skeeter showed up from the river, apparently by boat, and skulked around the outskirts of the camp, trying to make off with a beer or two. He sat next to Gil at the fire pit, while everyone who passed by him casually, continuously, and ineffectively removed beer cans from his hand.

Tracey had just removed another beer from the kid and was navigating around the fire ring towards Addie when James reached out from his seat and wrapped an arm around Tracey's leg. Tracey tripped over a rock near the fire ring, dropped the nearly-full can onto James' chest, and staggered backwards into a tree, smacking the back of his head soundly on the trunk.

James jumped up immediately. Addie thought he might be angry about the beer, but instead he grabbed Tracey by both arms with a look almost of fear on his face.

"You okay?" James demanded.

"I'm fine. I don't break that easy," Tracey replied, shrugging off the help and rubbing the back of his head.

"Yeah, whatever," James replied. "Watch your ass. Kick me if I get too stupid. None of us are in any shape to be driving you to the hospital tonight."

"And I ain't going," Tracey said, slapping James on the chest. "Nice shirt you got there, slob. Girls love a man who smells like stale beer."

James stripped off his shirt and sat back down on the log bare-chested, and in a few seconds Tracey was relaxing on Addie's bench.

"What was that all about?" Addie asked. "Are you okay?"

Tracey popped the top of a beer. "No big deal. James was just playing."

"I could tell that, it was his reaction when you fell that surprised me," Addie said.

"Oh, that. He just freaks out sometimes. I had a skull fracture when I was a kid." He glanced at her. "That's why I got laid off from the Roslyn factory. I guess they had some policy about not letting people with a history of a head injury drive their big machinery." He laughed shortly.

Addie remembered that Joe Senior had said something about Tracey having cracked his head as a kid. "How'd you do that?"

Tracey hesitated, and Addie hoped she hadn't asked the wrong question. But after a moment, he answered.

"Well, I didn't do it by myself. I was eleven. It was on my brother Jackie's thirteenth birthday. There were a bunch of kids over at the house. My mom was out somewhere with the littler kids. We all were running in and out. Junior, that's my dad, was off work, he was sitting there drinking beer and trying to watch the T.V. He kept yelling at us to shut up. Finally, I guess, he just lost it and jumped up and grabbed me. I don't remember, I just know what James told me. We had this brick fireplace, he slammed me up against it real hard. James says that when he dropped me, I just fell like a sack of potatoes. Then my dad sat back down, popped another beer and kept

63

watching T.V. Dennis called Virg on the kitchen phone and Virg came over, punched Junior once, and knocked him cold. They had to call a second ambulance for him. When I got out of the hospital, I went to stay with Virg for good. So did James and so did Jackie for a while, before they packed him off to Austin."

"I'm sorry," Addie said. "I didn't mean to pry."

"No," Tracey grinned at her. "Everybody around here knows it. We all grew up knowing everything about each other, you know? After a while, we'll start knowing stuff like that about you, too."

Tracey popped another beer, handed it to her, and scooted close enough to her on the bench for his leg to press up against hers.

"You know, all these people here know me like we're family. Have known me all my life and I've known them," he said, motioning to the group around the fire. "Sometimes that's great. You don't have to tell anyone what you're about, you know? But sometimes it can kind of get old. Sometimes you kind of want to change things. It's hard when everybody thinks they've already got you pegged. They treat you just the same way they did when you were a kid. It's almost like you never get to grow up. Sometimes you just wish there was somebody who doesn't know everything you've ever done in your life and who you don't know all about, either. Somebody who'll give you a chance to be different."

He was sitting with one arm extended behind Addie's shoulders along the top of the bench. Addie thought he might be pretty drunk. But then again, so was she. She relaxed against the bench back, enjoying his attention in the midst of all the people he could have been talking to.

"On the other hand, I always have somewhere I can go," he continued. "It's too bad you don't have any family around here. What would I do without these folks around? Who'd I get to help me out? I don't have to explain what I mean when I say something, they just understand. I don't have to tell them what I need or what I want. But

64

that doesn't mean it's bad to get to know different people, see things in a different way for a change."

Tracey slid his arm off the bench back and around Addie's shoulders. Addie smiled at him, but she was distracted. She was thinking about the connection Tracey felt with his siblings and about her own brothers. Of all the people she knew in the world, her brother Blake was her least favorite. She had hated him as a child and had nothing to do with him as an adult. But there had been a connection with Logan. She even remembered the first time it had happened, the first time he had looked at her and acknowledged her as a human being, someone with her own volition and desires. She had been nine years old. And then it had grown, during their teenage years and after. She would have done anything for Logan. She had left so that she wouldn't have to. And now she hadn't spoken to Logan in two years.

"You doing okay?" Tracey asked gently, bringing her back to the present.

"Yeah, great," Addie replied.

"Well, hang on a minute and don't disappear. I gotta go visit a tree. You want another beer when I come back?"

"I don't need any more beer," Addie said.

"That's not what I asked," Tracey grinned. He jumped up, and Addie subsided against the bench back, staring out through the trees at the moonlight reflecting off the river, lost in her own musings.

The bench rocked slightly as someone sat down upon it, and Addie glanced to her left to discover Gil Lejeune, alarmingly seated quite close to her. She uncrossed her arms and sat up straighter on the bench.

"You don't fool me," Gil said intently, leaning towards her, his dark eyes penetrating.

"What are you talking about?" Addie replied, scowling back at him. Her initial alarm turned quickly to irritation.

65

"You're not off duty. You never were. You were out there all day with Tracey, sneaking around, just not wearing your uniform is all. And you're doing the same thing now, sitting back here trying to catch what folks're doing."

Addie maintained her eye contact. "You're right, I was on duty today. But what I was doing has nothing to do with anyone here, and nothing to do with Tracey. You're wrong about tonight. I'm not on duty now, or I wouldn't be drinking beer, would I?"

"Huh," Gil snorted. "You may get something going with Tracey, but if you think you're ever going to fit in here, you're wrong. Nobody wants you here. You can say you're off duty all you want, but I know better. You're never off duty. You sit back here and just watch, and the next time anything comes up at the Preserve, you use whatever you saw."

Addie didn't answer. In a way, he was right, but his mistrust stung.

"You don't know how things are around here. You'll never know, 'cause you'll never be from here. You can hang out with Tracey all you want, but it won't change things. You don't belong here, and nobody will ever trust you. The quicker you get that through your head, the better. I'll deal with you out on the Preserve because I have to, but I don't want to see none of you when you ain't in that uniform."

"I don't think it's your choice or your business where I hang out, or with whom," Addie said, growing angry. "This isn't your place, far as I know."

"No, it ain't." James stepped over to the bench. "Gil, get the fuck away from her and leave her alone, would you? Mind your own goddamn business."

Gil got up wordlessly and brushed by James, knocking shoulders. James scowled, looked momentarily like he might punch Gil, then controlled himself and let Gil go on by. He shook his head.

"Sorry about that," he said. "He's probably drunk. But don't let him tell you shit like that."

James began to sit down on the bench next to her, but Tracey came up behind him and shoved him out of the way, then sat down himself. He grinned and immediately returned his arm to its place behind her shoulders. James rolled his eyes and skulked off towards the fire pit.

"You doing okay?" Tracey asked again, offering another beer. "You about to give Gil what-for? Too bad James rescued him, I'd of liked to see it."

Addie took the beer. She was relieved to have Tracey sitting next to her again. It wasn't just that he acted as a buffer between her and this camp full of people she didn't know. She wanted to be associated with him, wanted people to know that she was there with him, wanted to be a part of this thing that he was obviously so intimately a part of. Perhaps she was lonelier than she liked to admit to herself. And partly, perhaps, it was that Tracey seemed younger than she knew him to be, and with the atmosphere of the camp, she was reminded of being a teenager. She had always felt that she'd missed out on something during her teen years, when she'd been isolated on the family farm.

Addie noticed Tracey looking past her, and turned to see Bobbie Cole coming their way. "She's plastered," Tracey grinned, nodding at Bobbie as she approached. Bobbie sat down heavily on the bench on Addie's other side, pulled out a pack of cigarettes, stuck one in her mouth, and began making attempts to light it. She was obviously too drunk to aim properly, so Addie took the lighter and lit the cigarette for her.

"Thanks," Bobbie slurred, eyelids heavy. "I saw Gil over here. He's kind of a butthead sometimes. You just don't pay him no mind."

She turned and studied Addie, holding the cigarette out to the side away from them. "You heard his brother's been missing?"

"I heard."

"Francis. That's his brother," Bobbie continued woozily. "And then somebody trashed his house, too."

Tracey leaned forward to see Bobbie better. "Trashed whose house?"

"Francis'. You know Brenda's not staying there no more. Some asshole probably knew that and figured nobody would notice if they went through it, with Francis gone to wherever-the-hell he went. Went through Gil's, too."

"When'd that happen?" Tracey asked.

"Ah, this week. Wednesday, maybe. Ask Gil." Bobbie swayed and sucked on her cigarette.

"Did he report it to the police?" Addie asked.

Bobbie snorted. "No. Gil ain't any too big on the police."

"He should still report it," Addie said. "They could get fingerprints."

"Yeah. I'll tell him he should," Bobbie nodded. "But he better not disappear like he did last weekend. Pissed me off. He told me he was coming over Friday night, you know? And then he didn't."

Tracey leaned around Addie. "He said he was going to your place."

"When?"

"Last Friday. He dropped Brenda off at Duckhaven around seven and hung around for a couple hours. Then he said he was going to your place and left."

Bobbie leaned forward to look at Tracey. Addie leaned back to let them talk in front of her.

"Well, he never came to my place. Whole weekend, the little shit. He better watch what he's up to, he wants to hang around here."

Tracey shrugged. "Your choice," he said, sitting back. Bobbie rubbed her face, then got to her feet and staggered off in the direction Gil had taken before.

"I wonder where he did go, then," Tracey mused, "because I ended up having to drive Brenda Doheny home."

Addie thought about that, and glanced at Tracey quickly. She was pretty sure he had been talking about last Friday night, and Saturday morning was when she'd picked him up near Thief Lake, without a car. How, then, had he driven Brenda home?

Tracey put his empty beer can down on the ground under the bench and turned a little more towards her, tightening his arm around her shoulders and pulling her closer to him. Addie slid one arm around his waist.

"You getting tired?" Tracey asked into her ear. "I think folks're crashed on all the beds in the cabin and the truck beds and stuff, but we could go on out to James' houseboat."

Addie hesitated. Despite her attraction to Tracey, she wasn't at all sure that spending the night with him was a good idea. She needed more time to get to know him, but she was drunk and tired and didn't feel like thinking too deeply about it.

"How would we get there?" she asked. "It's a ways away. I can't drive a government boat after drinking."

"We could take a four-wheeler up along the shore," Tracey said.

"That would be illegal, not to mention pretty unsafe in our state," Addie pointed out. You weren't allowed to access the houseboats, which were more like floating homemade shacks, by riding four-wheelers through the Preserve.

Tracey turned his head, resting his cheek on her forehead, and was silent, as if thinking. Addie, looking over his shoulder, noticed that a big pale blue pickup had arrived, and she saw a man with whom she was not familiar step out. She studied him curiously. He was older than most of the people at the party, with thick dark hair going gray above the ears. He was also taller than most of the Coles, and much larger of build, with broad shoulders and powerful-looking arms. But there was something about him that reminded her

69

of Tracey and James and Bobbie Cole, something around the mouth, the eyes. Even more, she realized, he reminded her of Billy and Dennis Radner.

"Who's that guy?" she asked.

Tracey turned slightly. "My uncle," he said. He tensed and removed his arm. Addie sat up straight on the bench, catching his tension.

"Does he come out here and party with you guys pretty often?" she asked.

"No," Tracey said. "He must be looking for somebody. Just as long as it's not me."

James and Sam Rye were near the truck, and she saw James offer Virg a beer. They stood talking, and, she thought, occasionally looking her way. After a few minutes Virg made his way over towards them. Addie glanced at Tracey, who was watching Virg intently. She could see the tension in his jaw.

But Virg simply nodded at Tracey when he arrived, then squatted down on one knee in front of the bench and offered his hand to Addie. She automatically shook it, and he held onto her hand as he talked.

"Virg Radner. I hear you got stuck out here for the evening," Virg said. "I thought maybe you'd rather me take you into town. I could drive you back to your place, if you want." When Addie hesitated he continued, "I've only had one beer. No problem there."

"Thanks, but it's quite a ways. I live out west of Buenavista, and I have to come out here tomorrow morning and get my boat anyway. I'm sure I'll be okay."

"Well, you could come back to my place and stay there. It's not far. Billy's going to crash out here, anyway, so you could take his bed. It'd be a whole lot more comfortable there."

"Well..." Addie hesitated again.

"You'll be hard pressed to find a decent place to sleep here. No sense staying out here when you could have a real bed," Virg

70

said. "Besides, James said you got dunked out there on the river today. You could throw your clothes in the dryer at my place. You don't want to be wet all night. And I'll drive you back out here tomorrow morning to get your boat. Nobody'll bother it tonight."

Addie glanced at Tracey.

"Might as well," Tracey said resignedly. "We stay here and I guess we'll have to curl up on the ground somewhere, huh?"

"I'll be leaving in about fifteen minutes," Virg said. "That's my truck over there, the blue one. I'll see you over there." He released Addie's hand and stood up. Addie felt either manipulated or charmed, she wasn't sure which.

"Not that it would be a bad thing to curl up on the ground somewhere," Tracey commented, grinning. He seemed to have relaxed now that Virg had moved on.

"You're going to come, too, right?" Addie asked, relieved to have avoided the decision about going to the houseboat.

"Sure. I might as well sleep in my own bed. I can get a ride back out here tomorrow."

"I need to get some things out of the boat and make sure the bench box is locked."

"I'll help," Tracey said. "It's hard to get back up that bank in the dark."

They made their way between the campfire ring and the cabin to the riverbank and slid down to the waterline. Addie crawled into the boat, put the Q-beam away, and checked the bowline.

"Let's go upstream a little," Tracey said. "There's a little inlet where we can get up easier. I'm too damn drunk to crawl back up this bank."

Addie followed Tracey along the waterline to the north. The area between the bank and the water was narrow and sloped and the sand gave beneath her feet. Tracey put one hand out behind him to guide her. Addie held on and tried to keep her balance stumbling along in the dark.

71

As they approached the inlet, they could hear two voices and see the dark outline of a boat. Tracey stopped abruptly and Addie bumped up against him and stopped as well.

After listening for a few seconds, Addie could tell that the two people were Bobbie and Gil. They seemed to be having some sort of argument.

"I don't want you cluttering up my place with more of your crap," Bobbie said. "That spare bedroom was supposed to be a guest room, not a storage closet. James is already bitching about all your stuff that's there."

"Come on," Gil urged. "It's just a couple of boxes. Small boxes. I can't keep 'em out at the old camp up Widow Slough anymore. That little trailer out there is all leaky and there's a ton of mice. They'll get ruined."

"What's in 'em that's gonna get ruined?"

"It's just some boxes of stuff that Francis had. I just need someplace to keep them for a while."

"Well, where are they now? You got 'em in your boat, or what? 'Cause you're not going back up to Widow Slough in the middle of the night to get 'em, so what's the hurry?"

"They're in the boat right now."

"Why can't you keep 'em at your house? Or stick 'em in Francis' house?" Bobbie complained.

"Listen, are you gonna let me put them at your place or not? Just tell me, one way or the other," Gil said.

"Shit. Go ahead. What do I care?" Bobbie said. "Help me up the goddamn bank before you leave, if you're gonna take off."

Tracey and Addie remained standing at the waterline until Gil pushed the boat off and started it. Addie saw the running lights come on as the boat slipped away. Bobbie crashed up the bank through the brush and disappeared.

"Guess he's not staying tonight either," Tracey said.

They made their way back to the top of the bank, following Bobbie's route. Addie thought she caught movement off to her left from the corner of her eye. She glanced that way, but the woods were dark and she could see nobody. Perhaps it had only been an animal, or some drunk from the camp wandering off to find a place to crash.

"Sorry about getting lost like that today," Tracey said.

"No, don't be sorry. We did what we intended to do. We found the cabin and we found that stand, too. And besides, I had fun."

"Even though we got shot at?"

"Well, that part wasn't so fun. But it came out all right in the end. And I really enjoyed being out here at the camp. You do this a lot?"

"Yeah, almost every weekend in the summer. Sometimes we get together at Bobbie and James' house, too." Tracey paused by the door of Virg's truck. "So you think you're gonna need any more guiding any time soon?"

"Sure. I could always use a little guidance."

"Well," Tracey said, "I could take you around on your day off some time. We could go up the bayou, or way up Thief Creek past Magnolia Slough. Bet you've never been back that way."

"I haven't. It sounds interesting," Addie said, "but this week I have to take my car in to the shop. It needs a tune-up really bad, or maybe something more major, I don't know."

"I could take a look at it if you want. I work on Virg's cars all the time."

"Really? That would be great," Addie said. "If you could at least figure out what's wrong, I'd have a head start going in to the shop."

"You think it would make it up to Magnolia Slough one of these evenings?"

"Probably."

"Let me talk to James and Bobbie. You could come up next time we get together there and I can use James' tools."

Virg popped open the driver's side door behind them and Tracey jumped. Addie turned and crawled into the middle of the truck's bench seat, and Tracey got in beside her.

"So I guess you two got a little lost back there," Virg said, starting the engine.

"Not really," Addie shrugged. "We just spent too much time looking at stuff and ran a little late. The boat I brought doesn't have running lights, so I didn't want to go back down river in the dark."

"Did Tracey talk your ear off?" Virg grinned and glanced over at them.

"No. Not at all," Addie said.

"Well, he can be a little bit like old Joe Senior. You get him going and you can't shut him up. Tracey always did talk to anybody. When he was a little kid, you'd take him to the supermarket, he'd disappear. Five minutes later, you'd find him in the cereal aisle, talking to some little old lady about Cheerios."

Addie smiled. "I'd rather be out there with someone who will talk to me than someone who won't."

"True enough," Virg agreed. Then he swung the big pickup around through the trees in the dark, turned on the lights, and started down the rough, rutted mud track.

Chapter Eight

By the time Tracey woke up Saturday morning Addie was gone and Virg was already back from dropping her off at the camp, bringing Billy back with him. Tracey's hangover was complicated by a sense of frustration. Addie was close and guarded, hard to get to, as if she was concealing something, or maybe she wasn't sure she wanted to be seen with him. And it seemed like every time he thought he was getting somewhere, somebody interrupted them.

He'd planned on grabbing Ray Kenworth that morning at the camp when both of them were sober, but before he could take off on his ATV, Virg cornered him and Billy and got them working around the property. While Tracey was under the hood of a gold Chevy Chevette, he noticed Virg heading for the shed. He swore internally and tried to focus on the engine.

A minute later Virg came around the Chevy and stood there waiting until Tracey pulled his head out from under the hood, which was propped open with a board.

"Where the hell is the Dodge?"

Tracey wiped the grease off his hands with an old shirt, trying to gauge Virg's mood from his tone of voice.

"How do you know Billy didn't take it?"

Virg glared at him.

"It's at Bobbie's," Tracey said quickly, internally cursing himself. He had now moved from simply not talking about the car to actively lying about it. The responsible thing would be to tell Virg what he'd done, take whatever he had coming to him, and get it off his mind.

"What's it doing at Bobbie's? And if it's there, why are you running around on your four-wheeler instead of driving it?" Virg persisted.

"It's got a dead battery. I need to jump it or get a new one," Tracey said. He pulled off his T-shirt and used it to wipe the sweat off his face and neck, avoiding eye contact with Virg.

"When did you take it?"

"Last week, Friday. Before you were home from work." That, at least, was the truth.

"How long were you gonna wait before you told me you borrowed it?" Virg was sounding a little more upset.

"I figured if it came back with a new battery, you wouldn't care," Tracey said.

"Yeah, well, I care. Get it back here. And next time, ask me." Virg walked away towards the trailer, then turned. "I want it back by Wednesday. You see if the battery in that Chevy is any good and take that. I'd rather have the Dodge running."

Tracey looked down at the Chevy's battery, wondering if he was going to have to lie about that as well. He glanced up at Billy, who shook his head.

"I was over at Bobbie's house two nights ago," Billy said. "I sure as shit didn't see that Dodge there."

"Yeah, well, it's not there, it's somewhere else. I just didn't want Virg to know where," Tracey said.

"You better be careful. He'll be pissed off if he finds out it's somewhere he doesn't want it to be and you lied about it."

"He's already pissed off," Tracey said.

After lunch Tracey managed to slip away while Virg was chain-sawing up old floor joists in the back. He grabbed Virg' work cell phone off the counter and stuck it in his pocket. He told Billy he'd pick up some more beer and snacks as an excuse in case he didn't get back before Virg noticed him gone. Then he ran his four-wheeler out Pine Slough Road to the intersection with the highway, where there was a mini-mart.

He shut down the ATV and punched in the number to the Kenworths' towing and auto-body shop at Rye Corner. Willis

Kenworth, Ray's father and the shop owner, answered the phone. Tracey asked for Ray.

"He's not here," Willis replied.

"Well, do you know when he'll be back?" Maybe Ray hadn't made it back from the camp yet.

"Some time Thursday evening, I figure."

"Thursday?" Tracey repeated incredulously.

"Yeah, I sent him and Henry over to Houston this morning. They're gonna get that old truck Ray drives overhauled, put a side-load winch on it, get it repainted, and pick up a new slider-bed truck from the manufacturer on Tuesday. Then they gotta get the light bar I want on it installed. Can't get the decals and screening done until Wednesday, and it's gotta sit twenty-four hours to dry after that. Cost me a bundle to put the boys up for that long, but it'll be a good break for 'em."

"Well, can you have Ray call me as soon as he gets back?" Tracey asked. He ended the call and stood for a moment staring at the cars passing on the highway. The money from the two trips would pay for the tow, but that was useless if Ray wasn't available to do it and keep it secret. He couldn't just call another company. First of all, they'd charge him more, and second, they'd ask questions. Most of them knew better than to tow wrecks without verifying that the accident had been reported.

But now Virg wanted the car by Wednesday. He wasn't going to get it even if it was towed out by then, because it certainly wouldn't be running. Tracey could see he was going to have to come up with some other excuse. Maybe it would be better to just not be around for the next few days.

James picked him up that evening and the two of them spent the night out at Bobbie's camp. Sunday morning Tracey got up at sunrise and made his way down to Grandpa Joe's boat at the bottom of the cutbank.

Before he headed up river, he steered the boat down along the east shore. He found the narrow-mouthed slough above Goat Lake and ran up it until he found the pink flag-line. It took a lot less time to get back to the bear-hunter's cabin than it had with Addie, now that he knew the route and didn't have to hunt for the flags.

When he got to the tack line he saw a boat pulled up on the bank. He cut his motor and secured his own boat to a cypress. He took a closer look at the one on the bank. It was a new aluminum jon-boat with clean registration stickers, and at first he thought it was Skeeter Doheny's. It looked a lot like that one, but Skeeter's had a scrape on the front left side, and this one didn't. He looked around to make sure no one was watching, then opened the seat box. There was a Q-beam in there, an extra battery, and a soft-sided rifle case. Tracey squeezed the rifle case. It was empty.

There was a very recent set of footprints leading inland from the boat. Tracey examined them: about his own size, with a court-shoe tread. He looked along the tack line, memorizing the route as far as he could see it. Then he stepped off-line into the woods and paralleled the route east and inland.

Tracey walked quietly in the soft soil, hyper-alert and aware of everything around him. Although he couldn't see it, he felt sure he was getting close to the tree stand. He knew who the stand belonged to: there was only one person he could think of who rigged a stand that particular way, with the canvas straps and the balanced knots and pulley system.

He had just caught sight of the cream-colored bands strapping the metal stand in place when a man stepped out from behind a tree just a few feet in front of him. Tracey stopped short. The man held a rifle across his body, the barrel resting gently in his left hand. He was just slightly taller than Tracey, thinner, with darker hair and several days' worth of beard.

"Well if it ain't Tracey Cole!" the man grinned. He put a foot up on a log, rested the rifle on his thigh and stuck out his right hand.

Tracey leaned forward and shook it. He hadn't seen George Cole in five years. George was a distant cousin, one of the so-called "upriver" Coles whose family had split off from Tracey's in the early 1900s. He was older than Tracey by a couple of years, but Tracey knew him well enough. He had always been one of the best hunters and the best marksmen Tracey knew, even as a child. Then five years ago, George had been arrested on methamphetamine manufacturing charges. At that time, he'd been doing the manufacturing and Francis Lejeune had been doing the dealing. When they'd been arrested, Francis had cut a deal and testified against George. Now George was obviously back in the area, and Francis was gone.

"Long time," George said, grinning. "What brings you back this way?"

"I saw the stand the other day. I knew it was you," Tracey said. "What the hell was that all about, taking a bunch of pot-shots at us?"

"At you? C'mon. If I'd been shooting at you or the boat, I'd of hit it. You just left those cans set up so nice. And I knew you'd figure out whose stand it was. I didn't mean to scare your girlfriend though."

"You're damn lucky she didn't shoot your ass. She had a gun, in case you didn't notice."

"I couldn't see her after she hit the deck," George said. "What did she have a gun for? You back here picking up some deer?"

"She's a warden on the Preserve. You just took a couple shots at a fed."

George ran his fingers through his hair. "Well, hell, I figured her for a Rye or something, with that red hair. I hope you explained I wasn't shooting at her. I didn't figure her for a warden, not hanging around with you."

"I didn't explain anything. I didn't figure it'd make her feel any better to tell her some ex-con dope dealer was shooting at us."

George raised an eyebrow, then stepped over the log and sat down on it, readjusting the rifle across his lap. The rifle was new-looking, with a scope and matte-polished dark wood stock. He pulled a somewhat crushed pack of cigarettes out of his back pocket and lit one. He offered one to Tracey, who shook his head.

Tracey sat down on an old stump a few feet away from George and took a better look at him. "How long you been back around?"

"Six months, give or take."

"You living around this area? Down here on the river?"

George glanced at Tracey. "No, hell no. I'm living up north, outside Aynesworth. Living back off the river where folks don't know me on sight. I came down here to set stands because I know this area like the back of my hand. I didn't figure there'd be a lot of other folks way back in here."

"Did you know Francis Lejeune is missing?" Tracey asked bluntly.

George pulled the cigarette away from his mouth and studied Tracey. "No."

"Well, nobody knows where the hell he is. I heard the cops have put it out that he's missing. I guess they think something might've really happened to him."

"Shit," George said emphatically.

"I'd have thought you'd be happy about that," Tracey said.

"Hell, no. I mean, I wasn't any too happy with Francis when he turned evidence on me, but on the other hand, I don't know I wouldn't have done the same, given a chance. Anyway, having him missing is no good at all."

"Why not?"

"Why? Because they'll be looking for me, is why. They'll suspect me right off the bat."

"So you don't have anything to do with it?"

George shot a look at Tracey. "No, I didn't make him go missing. I didn't come back here to kill Francis Lejeune and go back to prison. I have things I want to do with my life."

Tracey considered that. "What are you doing, anyway?"

"Setting trot-lines and picking up a little game here and there. I'm doing all right." George shrugged. "I got another line of work too, looking after a place when the rest of the folks aren't there. A little guard duty, so to speak." He grinned. "Learned that during the last few years, though I got my own technique. I'm making a little money at that."

"Enough money to buy that boat out there on the slough?"

"No, that's borrowed." George sucked on his cigarette. "I'm trying to avoid registering things in my name. I'd just as soon people not know I'm back around, because they'll just start suspecting me for anything that happens around here. Like Francis being missing. Even you."

Tracey was beginning to feel bad about that. George ran his hand through his hair several times.

"I'd go someplace else altogether if I thought I could. But this is what I know, you know? The river and the bayou, where to hunt, where to set stands, where to set trot-lines. I figured if I couldn't get any kind of job, if nobody'd hire me, I could make it off the land, at least for a while." He looked around him as if evaluating the potential of the area. Then he grinned again.

"You and me, we're a lot alike, Tracey. We don't fit in to the rest of society. Both of us, we'd rather just be out here on the river. We would've done fine a hundred years ago, living off the land. You wouldn't catch us dead working in some stinking rotten pulp mill."

"How do you know I'm not working in the pulp mill? Or the lumber mill?"

"Oh, I know what you're doing. You're working as a fishing guide through old Joe Senior. Just because nobody knows I'm here doesn't mean I don't know what's going on." George studied his

81

cigarette thoughtfully. "I could probably help you find a little cash, if you need it."

"If you think I'm gonna start making crank, you're crazy," Tracey said. "First of all, I don't want to get busted, and second of all, Virg would kill me with his bare hands."

"No. Come on, Tracey, do you think I'd come back here and start in on that right away? I'd get popped for sure. Back to jail I'd go. I'm not stupid. I'm not in that game anymore. I did it because it was outside, you know, not outside in the air but outside of the companies and the industries and the whole damn system. But it was a nasty job. And all the crap - you have to get rid of it. I used to dump it all down this old uncapped oil well. But I figured some of it might leach out into the river. I couldn't deal with that. I've gotta eat what comes out of this river, you know?"

"So what are you talking about, then?" Tracey asked.

George stretched his shoulders. "I could set up some guide trips for you, tap into the market up around Aynesworth. We could skip using your grandpa as the middle-man. All the cash goes straight to you. I won't take a cut, myself, for setting it up."

"And in exchange I don't tell anyone that you're here?"

"That's up to you," George grinned. "But I prefer the cops don't know where to come looking for me, and you could pick up some easy money." He snubbed out his cigarette and stuck the butt in his pocket instead of dropping it on the ground.

"Too late to get anything this morning," he noted. "Guess I'll head back before there's a lot of people out on the river. I've got to come and go by boat now, 'cause Roslyn is starting up with that timber cut right where the old road in to this place used to run. There's too many people running around out there for me to come in that way anymore."

Tracey walked back with George along the tack line to the boats. George placed the rifle carefully in the case in the seat box.

"You want to follow me out or you know where you're going?" he asked.

"I guess I'd better follow you," Tracey admitted.

"You going downstream or up?"

"Upstream."

"Well, I'll work us out of the bottoms further up than the flag-line, then. Save you some time."

George pushed off into the slough, then spun the boat around and headed out. Tracey followed him through the bottoms, thinking. It was an odd coincidence, indeed, Francis missing at the same time George showed up again. But then, George had said he'd been back for six months, and he'd sounded sincere, not like Tracey would have expected if he'd been concealing something.

Out on the river, George ran upstream to the west-side boat ramp below Ely Dam. Tracey raised a hand as he passed the ramp, which was just downstream and on the opposite side of the river from his destination. He pulled up at the Dohenys' a few minutes later.

Two men were sitting in the open-sided porch above the river. When they saw him, they got up and walked down the ramp. One, a tall blond guy wearing military-style cargo pants and a dark-green T-shirt, introduced himself as Van. Tracey shook his hand, thinking that Van was going to get awful hot in that dark shirt. The other man, who called himself Howie, looked younger, closer to Tracey's age, with a smile that turned up sharply at the corners and close-cropped red hair.

They had several coolers, which were quite heavy. Tracey popped the top off one after heaving it into the boat. It was full of beer and ice. He raised his eyebrows, and Howie grinned.

"Hey, we're not driving," he said. "This is our recreation day."

After they were loaded and aboard, Tracey pushed the boat off and let it drift.

"So what do you want to do today?" he asked.

"Get to know the area a little bit, mark some spots for fishing later," Van told him.

"You planning on coming back?"

"Sure," Howie said. "We're living up in Aynesworth. Might as well come on down and do a little fishing since we're here. But I don't know much about river fishing. I grew up on a lake. A big lake."

"You're living in Aynesworth?" Tracey asked, curious. George had said he was living up in Aynesworth as well. "What're you doing up there?"

"We work at the adhesives plant," Howie said. "You know it got bought out a while ago by a new company. They brought in a new team of folks when they re-opened it."

"The glue factory," Tracey nodded. His grandpa's two new friends had been introduced as the new owners.

"I want to get to know the area better," Van said. "You know, get a feel for how the river system works, what flows into it from where, so I can find my way around if I need to."

"Okay," Tracey said, "I'll point out the major waterways. We can go up any of them you want, or back into the bottoms or up the bayou. Just let me know."

"Good. I brought a set of topo maps of the area so I can keep track." Van pulled a set of neatly folded topographic maps out of a day-pack he'd brought. They were marked up with ink notations and yellow highlighter.

"Things have changed since those maps came out," Tracey said. "You always mark your maps up like that?"

"I used to be a surveyor," Van said. "Habit, I guess. I like to get a visual idea of where I am on a map. It's easier for me to figure things out that way. These numbers are from my GPS unit." He brought out a black GPS receiver with a stubby antenna. "I've been

84

doing some exploring on my own. But there's nothing like having a real person show you where things are."

"Do you guys know Francis Lejeune?" Tracey asked casually. Francis worked at the same adhesives plant these guys claimed to work at, and the coincidence that George now lived in Aynesworth and had said he knew people in that area was too much.

Van and Howie glanced at each other. "Yeah, sure. He works part-time in the warehouse," Van said.

"Did you hear he's missing?"

Howie shrugged. "Yeah. Deputy was up there asking people if they'd seen him. We told him we haven't."

Tracey twisted the tiller and brought the bow around downstream. Van adjusted his sunglasses and turned his ball cap around so the brim wouldn't catch the wind. Howie leaned forward with his elbows on his knees, staying out of Tracey's line of view as they cruised down the river.

Above Widow Slough there was a long stretch of river with few tributaries and heavy timber on either side. The timber gave way suddenly on the eastern shore where the Roslyn pulp mill lay. The mill gleamed in the morning sunlight, metallic and over-sized.

Howie turned and shouted back at him from the bow. "Is that the Roslyn pulp mill? It looks like it's from some science-fiction show."

Tracey slowed the boat to drop the motor noise. "Yeah, that's it."

"Is the pulp mill in the Deuce River Preserve?" Van asked.

"Kind of. I mean, the river runs through the Preserve. The pulp mill itself is on private land, though."

"That's pretty incredible. Stinks pretty incredible, too. Bet you wish it wasn't here, huh?" Howie asked.

Tracey shrugged. "A lot of folks around here work for the timber companies, and a lot of 'em work for the pulp mill. My uncle and cousin both work for Roslyn. I used to, too."

"Does it pump waste water directly into the river?" Van asked.

"There are filters and settling ponds back in there by the mill, on their property. But there is a big outflow pipe back in the woods. I've been back there. It bubbles up into the middle of this little lake like a big spring. It doesn't look bad or smell bad, though. But there's a dioxin advisory for some of the fish downstream from the mill."

"So the fact that the outflow doesn't look bad doesn't mean anything," Van pointed out, "because obviously the dioxins are coming in from somewhere."

"A lot of them are leftovers from the past, I guess. Eventually they'll all break down and go away," Tracey sidestepped. He'd learned that it was best to avoid discussing controversial and political issues on his trips.

"You know any of the rangers or wardens around here?" Howie asked.

"Sure, I know 'em all," Tracey said. "I get my guiding permit through the Preserve and they check me from time to time, make sure I'm doing stuff right."

"I'm sure you wouldn't do anything wrong," Howie said with a grin.

"Not me. Not so's I'd admit, anyway."

Tracey twisted the tiller again and got the boat up on plane. Great blue herons and egrets took flight from their night nests in the cypress trees, winging heavily downriver before the noise of their boat. Two swallow-tailed kites performed aerial acrobatics over the treetops. Mist rose in tiny tendrils from the water's surface. Despite the pulp mill, the river in the morning light seemed primeval, unspoiled.

When they reached Widow Slough, Tracey cut back the motor and maneuvered the boat upstream at a few knots per hour.

"Who did this area belong to in the past?" Van asked, waving a hand out at the deep forest on either side. The property was all

86

Preserve land, now, west of the river all the way out to the highway and on either side of Bear Creek.

"Mostly Lejeunes, I think," Tracey said. "There was some Rye property here, too. Cole property was mostly to the north."

"The Lejeunes, huh?" Van asked. He had one of his maps out, and he wrote some notes on it with a ballpoint pen. "As in Francis Lejeune, the missing guy? What do you know about them?"

"I guess their family showed up in this area around the 1820s, right about when mine did," Tracey said, trying to remember what he'd heard from Gil. "They came down from Canada, French Canadian, you know, and Gil says they have some Indian blood, too, like a lot of the trappers from up there did. They're Spanish or Mexican or something on their mother's side. But the only Lejeunes I know of around here anymore are Gil and Francis. They both live on a piece of property off Thief Lake. There's a couple houses up there and a boat ramp."

"Is that the only property they own anymore?"

"I think so, other than their hunting camp by the pulp mill. They sold the property south of the camp to the timber company years ago. That's where the pulp mill sits now. My grandpa says they used to have land running west from the river all the way out here to where Bear Creek meets Widow Slough."

"They got any old camps or anything out there?"

Tracey hesitated. "Well, seems to me I've heard they have a little camp out this way, up Widow Slough somewhere, but I don't know exactly where. Why are you so interested in the Lejeunes, anyway?"

"Because we've been using the Lejeunes' hunting camp, the one by the pulp mill," Van said.

Tracey frowned. "Using it for what?"

Van popped the top of another beer, then glanced up, almost warily, from under his brows. "As a training camp. We were looking for someplace we could fix up and somewhere to set up some stuff

87

in the woods on fairly dry land. That's hard to come by around here, I've found."

"Wait a minute," Tracey said, loosening his hold on the tiller. "Are you trying to tell me the Lejeunes are running some kind of camp? I thought you said you didn't know Francis very well."

"The only thing the Lejeunes are doing is letting us use their property. We're a militia," Van said. "You know what that is?"

"Yeah, I'm not an idiot," Tracey said. "You guys get together and practice for the end of the world and shit."

Van laughed.

"So what do you guys actually do?" Tracey asked.

"Most of the time we're just like anybody else," Howie said. "But in our spare time we get together and do different types of training. Not really for the end of the world; for self-sufficiency."

Tracey considered that. "Okay. So how many people do you have out there at the Lejeunes' anyway? Because I haven't been hearing anybody talking about it, and I'd of thought I would have. Gil goes out with my sister, you know."

"I know that. But we don't live there, we all live up in Aynesworth. And there's only about ten of us right now. These things start out small, you know?" Van said.

"So are you trying to recruit more members?" Tracey asked.

"Yeah, you," Van grinned. "Why'd you think we're telling you about it? We want people who aren't roped into the system, who have some time on their hands when they won't be missed, and who know their way around here. You fit the bill."

"Sounds like George Cole fits the bill, too," Tracey said.

Van laughed. "Oh, yeah. Who do you think recommended you as a guide?"

Tracey shook his head. "George isn't hanging around the Lejeunes' camp, though, is he? I can't see that, after what happened between him and Francis."

"Francis hardly ever comes out there," Howie said. "Besides, that's in the past. People can often put aside their differences when they've got a common goal."

"What's that, survival training?" Tracey asked skeptically. "George I can see getting into that, but not Francis. He makes jewelry, for crap's sake."

Howie grinned. "Maybe that's why he doesn't come around."

"So, you going to come by some time and check it out for yourself?" Van asked.

"I'll think about it," Tracey said, trying to sound sincere. One thing he really wasn't interested in was military-style discipline.

"Besides, you could make some good money. We've got access to a little bit of cash." Van turned, watching for low-hanging limbs in the slough. "We intend to set this place up as a permanent camp. We'll need people to take care of it when we're not around. Gil's getting a good deal from this thing. We're letting him use our boats and we bought him and Francis two quads in exchange for us using the land."

They continued upstream for a while and eventually intersected Bear Creek. Tracey turned southeast and headed down it. Out on the river again, they ran up past the Lejeunes' property on the east bank. Tracey couldn't see up over the bank to check out the camp, but he figured he would ask Gil what the hell he was doing hanging out with a bunch of nuts next time he saw him.

Howie and Van drank steadily. Tracey was tempted, and they repeatedly offered him beer, but he refused. The worst thing he could think of would be getting stopped by Ike or a Texas Parks and Wildlife officer and arrested for boating under the influence. He'd lose his license for sure, and the Preserve wouldn't let his grandpa name him on his incidental business permit. And he didn't need to add anything to the problem he still faced with the car.

Near Goat Lake Slough, Tracey tied off in the shade of a cypress so they could fish for a while. Van lounged in the bottom of the boat, sitting on their life jackets with his feet on one seat and his back propped on another. Tracey thought about what Van had told him. He had picked up Van and Howie at the Dohenys' boat ramp. George had connections with the Dohenys through his family, and it made more sense that he'd be hanging around the Dohenys than around the Lejeunes. Possibly Van's group was using the boat ramp as well. That might explain the boat Skeeter was using.

"So I'm getting a little more curious about this militia thing," he said. "Maybe it would be a good deal for me. Tell me a little bit more about it."

Van turned around to face Tracey more fully. "Okay. Why don't you have a beer?"

"I'm driving," Tracey said.

Van opened an ice chest and pulled out a can. He handed it to Tracey. "Gotta make room for the fish."

Tracey took it reluctantly. One beer couldn't hurt. He popped the top.

"So, look," Van said, "this militia thing is really no big deal. It's not like a paramilitary organization. It's not like we march around in formation or something. None of us would be doing it if it was like that. It's more like a bunch of guys who get together and drink on the weekends, and sometimes we do target shooting or practice using the GPS or something. Usually in the company of a bunch of beer. Like I told you, we've got a little bit of money available, so we've got some good toys to play with. We've got a bunch of quad-runners, boats, computers, guns, whatever."

"You're not making that kind of money working at the adhesives plant," Tracey said.

Van grinned. "No, we have other ways of getting a few bucks now and again. You can learn all about that later, if you want to. Right now I'm just extending an offer for you to come by some time and check things out."

"Maybe I'll do that," Tracey said. It was beginning to sound a little bit more interesting. He drained his beer, threw the can in the boat, and started the engine. They were about an hour downstream from the boat ramp, and it was mid-afternoon. He figured both the guys would be unconscious by evening, at the rate they were drinking. Besides, Howie was a redhead and he looked like he was beginning to bake.

At the ramp, Tracey walked directly behind Van in case he slipped or fell. Although Van seemed less drunk than Tracey would have guessed he'd be at this point, he didn't want to take any chances. Van plopped down in a plastic chair under the awning at the top of the ramp and Howie lay flat on his back on top of a picnic table.

Skeeter Doheny appeared from the big house to the south of the ramp. "Hey, Skeet, get those ice chests out of the boat, would you? Your buddies here need a little hand," Tracey said.

Skeeter took a look at Van, then silently went down the ramp to the boat and heaved out the ice chests, turned them over, and dumped the remains of the ice. A couple beers rolled away into the water. From the top of the ramp, Tracey watched Skeeter stick two beers inside the over-sized military shirt he was wearing like a jacket. He shrugged; not as if he hadn't pirated a beer or two himself as a kid.

"Hey," Van said, readjusting himself in the chair. "I got some money for you." He reached into a side pants pocket and pulled out a battered envelope, which he handed to Tracey.

"You gonna stick around and have a beer with us?" Howie said.

"No, I gotta get back," Tracey glanced at Skeeter. There was no way he was going to drink at the Dohenys' boat ramp.

"Some other time then," Van said. "You know where we live, so to speak. You drop by on a weekend and we'll show you what we're up to. I'm sure we can figure out something you can do to earn a few bucks."

"All right," Tracey said, this time meaning it. Van was getting to him with the offers of money.

"I might even be persuaded to front you the money for your own boat, so you don't have to borrow someone else's to do your river guiding," Van continued. "But I'd have to get to know you a little better."

Tracey looked up sharply. Why would this guy he'd just met offer to front him money for a boat? He must be really drunk, Tracey figured. Still, it was something to keep in mind. Maybe he could ask around, find out if he could trust these guys.

Van raised his beer can. "Later."

"Yeah," Tracey said. "You take care now. Don't fall down the goddamn ramp into the river."

Back at the boat, Tracey pulled out the envelope and counted the cash. There was two hundred dollars in twenties. He wondered if Van had meant to give him all that, but he wasn't going to argue. If these guys were going to pay him like that, he would take them out and let them get drunk on the river any time. He could be a designated driver as well as he could be a fishing guide.

Chapter Nine

Addie was northbound on the highway near Rye Corner Friday afternoon when she got a call from her dispatcher regarding a car off the road at Thief Lake. According to dispatch, the county was already on the scene. Since the Preserve shared jurisdiction with multiple other agencies, whoever got the message first generally responded first. Addie decided she was lucky she had been notified at all. Sometimes the county took care of events on Preserve property without bothering to tell the Preserve what had happened.

She pulled up at the sharp bend in the road along Thief Lake ten minutes later. Two elderly men with a truck and boat trailer were standing off to one side. They had launched their flat-bottomed boat off the side of the road at the bend, and it was moored to a cypress tree downstream. Deputy Buster Brighton was there as well, and Ray Kenworth with his big tow truck, with a new-looking winch that could be rotated to let down off one side of the bed. Since Ray was already there, Addie figured the county must have received the call a while ago.

Buster Brighton irritated Addie a little bit. He talked and looked like some stereotypical southern cop. But she suppressed her irritation because he always eventually called the Preserve when something happened within their borders. She also had come to realize that Buster's manner was mostly an act, concealing an organized mind and a lifetime of information about the backgrounds of local residents.

Buster was tall and not really overweight, although he was tending towards a beer belly, which gave him more room on his shiny black leather belt to hang a variety of equipment. He had an oval face with a double chin, which made him look heavier than he really was.

Addie walked over to Buster and stuck her hand out. Buster grinned and shook it, then hitched up his duty belt and turned to the water. He spoke slowly, and Addie suppressed the urge to finish his sentences for him. She gritted her teeth and listened instead.

"These boys here was launching off the road when they say they ran the prop into something underwater. So they took a good look, and seemed like they could see a license plate. Went down the road to Duckhaven and gave us a call."

"You know when it went in? If anybody's in there?" Addie asked.

"Well, I'll tell you. According to these old boys, there weren't any tracks going off the bank when they pulled up. The only tracks here come from their truck and trailer. I checked that out myself. So I'd say it would've had to go in before, or during, the time when we was having all that heavy rain. Which was right about two weeks ago. Rain would've taken the tracks out pretty quick."

Addie glanced over at Ray, who was studying her from the bank. He gave her an exaggerated shrug and a pained expression, then turned quickly back to the lake as Buster looked in his direction.

"As far as somebody being in the car," Buster continued, "there's only one person around here that I've heard is unaccounted for, and that's Francis Lejeune. But I hadn't heard any of his cars were missing along with him. We'll know in a minute."

Buster watched Ray wade into the water hip-deep. Some teenager who was riding with him fed Ray the winch cable. Ray dunked and fished around under the water for a place to hook the car.

Once it was secured, Ray ran the winch up. As the rear license plate cleared the surface, Buster wrote it down and handed his notepad to Addie. "You wanna run that for registered owner?" he asked. "Not that it's necessary. I'd know that car anywhere. 1968

94

Dodge Dart 270 four-door sedan, V-8." He pointed with his pen at the slowly emerging car. "Belongs to Virg Radner."

Addie grimaced as Buster identified the vehicle. "I'm afraid I know who put this car in the water," she admitted.

Buster looked at her and grinned. "Oh, I'd guess it wasn't Virg. He's not the type. My guess would be he loaned out his car to his nephew Tracey, the one that lives with him. I've picked Tracey up before for DUI and for not reporting an accident."

"Yeah, that's what I was thinking," Addie said. "I picked up Tracey right near here about two weeks ago, hitchhiking. It was right during those rains, a Saturday morning. He said his girlfriend kicked him out the night before."

Buster snorted. "Only people live farther up along here are the Lejeunes and old Mr. Rye. Only girl I can think of would be Brenda Doheny, and she's been living with Francis Lejeune for three, four years." Buster sucked on his teeth and contemplated the lake. "Why don't you call in that plate, just to verify?"

Addie went back to her Tahoe and called in the plate. It showed a current registration to Virgil Radner of Mill Lake. She wrote down the information and tucked it in her shirt pocket. The car was now sitting clear of the water, and Buster snapped photos from different angles. Addie walked around it. It was covered with silt and river vegetation. Underneath the grime, it was an off-brown metallic color. On the right side, near the back window, there was a wide scratch under the silt. There was a little front-end damage, and one of the front tires was flat. There were also shiny new scrapes on the trunk lid, probably where the prop from the two older men's boat had hit.

Addie looked in through the less silty, downstream front window. No corpses, that was good. Looking through the open rear passenger window, she saw a collection of sticks, vegetation and trash collected on the floor, washed in by near-shore eddies in the current. There was something else in there that didn't look like a stick.

"Hey, Buster. There's a rifle in here." Addie stuck an arm in the window, trying not to get muck on her uniform shirt, and grabbed the gun butt. She pulled it out of the junk and slowly-draining water.

Buster walked over and looked at the rifle. "See if you can find a serial number on that," he said.

Addie took it to her vehicle and wiped it down with her towel. She turned the rifle back and forth until she located the engraved numbers along the right side. She ran it, but it didn't come back as stolen or with any registration at all. She cleaned the stock and examined it. It was well used, not new, with no obvious brand name, and there were initials apparently hand-carved in a rough ornate scroll on the end of the stock. Addie called Buster over.

"G.C." Buster read off the stock. "Now there's only one person I can think of with those initials who it makes any sense might have been in a car with Tracey, and that's George Cole."

"I've never heard of him," Addie said. "I just looked through last year's hunting permits the other day, and I'm pretty sure no one by that name pulled a permit."

"No," Buster said. "He's an upriver Cole. The Cole family split up some time in the early 1900s, half of 'em went north, half of 'em stayed in this area. This guy's a small-time meth manufacturer, went to prison about five years ago." He thought for a minute. "Probably due to be out by now. I can check on that."

"Would he be likely to be riding around with Tracey?" Addie asked. "And then leave his rifle in the car when they wrecked? Or borrow a car from Virg Radner?"

Buster shook his head and frowned. "George wasn't no particular friend of Tracey's, I don't think. Virg Radner wouldn't tolerate him around, that's for sure. But blood is thick, and I'll bet Tracey wouldn't turn him down if he needed a ride somewhere.

Funny thing, though, being so close to the Lejeunes. George got busted along with Francis Lejeune. Francis was doing the dealing, George was doing the manufacturing. Francis gave evidence to save his own butt."

"That's quite a coincidence," Addie said.

"Yeah, it sure is." Buster shook his head again. "I don't know what's going on here, but I sure would like to know. This is looking like a little more than a car wreck to me now." He took the rifle from her and studied it. "This is probably about thirty years old," he said. "Looks hand-carved, like a kid decided to put his own stamp on it. Loaded, too."

"You want to inventory the car, see if there's anything else in it?" Addie asked.

"Yeah, I guess we better," Buster grimaced. He walked over to the driver's side door and opened it. He stepped back quickly as water poured out.

Addie opened the other front door and began scooping out handfuls of wet junk, sorting through it before dropping it on the ground. She found a soggy Camels cigarette pack, which she placed on top of the car.

Buster popped the trunk open while Addie finished the back seat area. After a minute, he slammed the trunk shut again. "Well, that'll do it for me," he announced. "You find anything?"

"Just this cigarette pack." Addie handed it over to him.

Buster, who was wearing a pair of latex gloves, took the cigarette pack and carefully opened the flip-top. He pulled out a couple of sodden cigarettes, then raised his eyebrows. Using his fingertips, he pulled out several tiny plastic bags, each with a semi-transparent yellow-white lump inside.

Addie took one of the bags and examined it.

"One, two, three, four, five, six." Buster counted. "Looks like crystal meth to me. All packaged up like maybe for sale."

Addie tried to keep her voice neutral. "You don't think Tracey's been dealing methamphetamines?"

"Well, I've never known any of the downriver Coles to be mixed up in anything other than a little pot here and there," Buster said. "Plus, Tracey don't smoke, so it'd be funny of him to store his stash in a cigarette box. And I wouldn't guess Tracey as a user. He's a little goofy, but it's not from doing drugs. Besides, I doubt he'd risk it, living in Virg Radner's house. Virg ever caught anybody with drugs in his house, or his car, he'd beat him six ways from Sunday."

They both stood for a minute in silence.

"So what do you think?" Addie pressed.

Buster shook his head. "We've got to get the story from Tracey. He's gonna have to talk to us. Let's go take that rifle up and book it into evidence and get this stuff to the lab. We'll wait 'til after shift-change at the Roslyn plants, then go visit Virg Radner and see if Tracey's there. If not, we'll tell Virg what's going on and get him to bring Tracey in. I know Virg. He don't like drugs, he don't like liars, and he really don't like not being in control. And he sure is going to want to know exactly what happened to this little car of his."

Buster turned to Ray. "Ray, come on over here."

Ray left his truck and walked over to them. Buster put an arm around Ray's skinny shoulders and squeezed hard enough to buckle them. Ray looked even more alarmed than usual.

"Now, Ray, I know damn well you've been listening to every word we've been saying here," Buster said. "And you are not going to go back to the shop and give Tracey a call and let him know. Because that would be interfering with an investigation, and I will personally come back and cite you into court for it if I have any idea you might have been talking about this here investigation. You are just gonna sit on this vehicle and not do anything for right now. 'Till I tell you you can. Isn't that right?"

Ray nodded and glanced at Addie. Buster released him, and Ray rubbed his shoulders and hastily returned to his tow truck.

"I'll follow you," Addie said. They waited until Ray pulled out, then headed out to the highway and Buster's substation to book in the rifle.

In the back of the substation, Buster laid out the cigarette pack to dry and labeled the little bags. Addie took a last look at the rusty rifle.

"You sure this belongs to George Cole?"

"No," Buster said, "but it's a damn good guess. Until I get some story that tells me otherwise, I'm going to assume it's George's."

Addie left her Tahoe at the substation and jumped in with Buster for the drive up to Mill Lake and the Radner property. Buster parked his patrol car out near the road and they walked across the front yard to the door of the trailer. They stood down off the steps and Buster reached up and knocked. In a minute Virg opened the screen, looking tired and hot from work. His thick salt-and-pepper hair stood up in front like he'd been running a hand through it, and he squinted a little looking down at Buster.

"Hey, Buster. What's up?" Virg sounded just slightly suspicious.

"Hey Virg. Sorry to get you like this right after shift. Tracey around?"

"No. Why? He in some kind of trouble?"

Buster sucked his teeth. "You happen to know the whereabouts of a rust-colored Dodge Dart, registered in your name?"

Virg said nothing, but his gray eyes became sharply focused.

"Yeah, I was wondering, this look like it?" Buster handed Virg a digital camera with a photo of the car on the screen.

"Yeah, that's it all right." Virg handed the camera back and met Buster's gaze.

"Mind if we come in and discuss this with you a little bit?" Buster asked. Virg stepped back out of the doorway and held the screen open. Buster went in to the living room and sat down on the couch across the room. He sank deep into it and threw an arm across the back. Addie remained standing, leaning on the bar-height counter. She had stood there before recently, drinking a cup of coffee early in the morning.

Virg yanked a kitchen chair out into the living room, turned it around, and sat down straddling it.

"So that car, that one in the photo, that is your car. Is that right?" Buster began.

"Oh, yeah. It's my car all right."

"So, Virg, any idea of how that car might have got there in Thief Lake? 'Cause we were a little perturbed to find it there, you understand. Didn't know if we was going to be pulling out a dead body or two, or what. Plus, it's in the Preserve, so we had to get Addie out there. Federal property, you know? Had to get Ray Kenworth out there to haul the thing up the bank, too."

Virg raised his eyebrows, but said nothing. In his almost impassive calmness, Addie perceived a slow burn, building up under the surface.

"So I can't see you dumping a car in the creek, way up by Lejeunes', then not getting it hauled out. But it didn't come back reported stolen, either."

"No, it wasn't stolen," Virg agreed, "but you know damn well I didn't dump it in the lake."

"Now, I gotta tell you something, Virg. First of all, we found a loaded rifle in the back seat of that car when we pulled it up."

Virg looked puzzled for a moment, then looked at Addie. "It's in the Preserve, that right? Can't have a loaded rifle in the Preserve out of hunting season."

"Well, that's part of it," Buster continued. "Seems like the rifle might belong to George Cole. And that car was in Thief Lake, at the bend in the road just below the Lejeunes'. Now, Francis Lejeune, I don't know if you know this, but he's been missing for about two weeks. Any idea when that car might have ended up in the drink?"

Virg studied the floor for a moment, then looked up. "Probably during those rainstorms about two weeks ago."

"Uh-huh. And, one more thing, I found a bunch of crank, crystal methamphetamine, packaged for sale, up there in the front of that car in a Camels cigarette pack."

Virg met Addie's eyes for a moment. "I hope you don't think I had anything to do with that."

"Well, right now, here's the thing," Buster said. "It's your car. It's registered to you, you're responsible for it. We got failure to maintain control, leaving the scene of an accident, failure to report accident. We got federal charges, loaded rifle in the car, and crank for sale. Plus we got some kind of possible connection to a missing man. No report of it being stolen. So right now, this is all coming back to you. You understand?"

Virg nodded, tight-lipped.

"Now, Virg, I know you. Known you all our lives. I know damn well you're not dealing drugs. I know damn well you wouldn't tolerate anyone dealing drugs around your place. I know you're not running around with George Cole, and I know you didn't wreck your '68 V-8 and then just leave it there. I'm a fair man, Virg, you know that, and I do my best for this community. All's I want is the whole story. What I'm gonna do is, I'm gonna leave things alone for the time being. I'm gonna give you some time to get things under control. A few days from now, if the responsible person gives me a call and tells me the story of how that car got in there, comes up with some good believable information that matches what I know about the facts, well, we'll take it from there. Fair enough?"

"Fair enough," Virg said. "You will get what you need. I promise you that."

Buster nodded. "I knew I could count on you, Virg. So I'm gonna go ahead and release the car. I could hold it, but I trust you, Virg. I know you won't let me down. You can get Ray to haul it over here so you don't have to pay any more impound lot fees. You'll have to pay for the tow, though. You'll see some damage on the trunk where the old boys who found it ran their boat over it and hit it with the prop. The rest of it don't look too bad."

Virg stood up and let them out the door. "I'm sorry to run into you again under these circumstances," he said to Addie as she started down the steps. "I was hoping our next meeting would be a little different."

"Me, too," Addie said, "but I don't really think you had anything to do with the car."

As Addie returned to the patrol car, her mind turned to Tracey. She had been thinking about him a lot during the past week. She had enjoyed the evening at the camp and her time with him on the river and she had been hoping they might be able to get together at Bobbie's house so he could work on her car, as he'd promised. But one way or another, it looked as though he had at least wrecked the Dodge and then failed to report it, and he had probably lied to her when she'd picked him up near the mill. Nevertheless, she was determined to remain as neutral as she could until she had all the facts. It could be there was an explanation for all of this. Although, at the moment, she was at a loss to figure what that might be.

Chapter Ten

Friday afternoon Tracey drove his four-wheeler over to Bobbie's house on Magnolia Slough. He let himself in and helped himself to a beer. Out of curiosity, he pushed open the door to the spare bedroom. It was pretty packed with stuff, including two slightly damp-looking cardboard copy-shop boxes near the front. He'd thought about asking Bobbie if he could move in with her and James, but with Gil there half the time and the room being used for storage, it didn't look like a possibility.

Bobbie showed up with Gil a little later, and Dennis and James a few minutes after that. Dennis called for his wife, Janet, to drive over for the evening and Bobbie called Billy.

"Hey, James, can I use a few of your tools this evening?" Tracey asked.

"Sure. What for?" James asked as he stripped off his work shirt.

"I told Addie Derange I'd work on her car."

James raised his eyebrows. "No kidding?"

Tracey grinned and shrugged. "I thought maybe I'd call her up here, if you guys don't mind."

"Sure, go ahead," Bobbie said. "At least she's got a good job. She can support your sorry ass."

Tracey called Addie at her house, but she didn't answer. He figured she wasn't home from work yet or was in the shower. He didn't leave a message. He'd call back a little later.

Janet came in with a couple of bags of groceries. A minute later Billy opened the screen door. Bobbie handed him a beer as he walked in.

"Hey, Trace, Dad wants you home," Billy said as he popped the top.

"How come?"

"He said you'd know. He sounded kind of pissed."

"Crap." Tracey studied the floor for a minute, feeling his stomach knot. He'd had to lie again to explain why he hadn't gotten the car back by Wednesday: he'd told Virg it was at the Kenworths' getting the wiring re-done. He wondered if somehow Virg had discovered it wasn't at the Kenworths' after all, or, worse, if the car had been found in the lake and the cops had called Virg and told him. He couldn't think of any other reason for Virg to be pissed at him: he'd done everything he was supposed to around the trailer and out in the yard.

"I guess I better go."

Billy put down his beer. "You need a ride?"

"Yeah."

Tracey hopped in Billy's pickup, leaving his four-wheeler in Bobbie's yard.

"So what's going on?" Billy asked as he started down Magnolia Slough. "You in some kind of trouble?"

Tracey drummed his fingers on the door, out the window. "You know the Dodge?"

"The one you said was at Bobbie's, which isn't."

"Well, I dumped it in Thief Lake two weeks ago."

"Two weeks ago? You mean you just left it there?"

"Yeah, well, Ray's going to pull it out for me tomorrow morning. Unless it got found, which is kind of what I'm thinking could have happened."

"Shit, Tracey. Dad is going to kick your ass."

"I know," Tracey said.

"Why didn't you tell someone?"

"I figured I could take care of it myself. Besides, I didn't want you to have to cover for me. You're a crappy liar."

"Well, you could've asked me to lend you money and not told me what for," Billy said. "And you know Bobbie or James would've loaned you the money too. That was just stupid."

104

"You gonna come in with me?" Tracey asked as they pulled into the yard outside the trailer.

"Hell no!" Billy said. "I'm not even getting out of the damn truck. But I'll tell you what, I'll go pick up some beer and I'll stop back by in a half-hour and make sure you're still alive."

"Yeah, thanks." Tracey slammed the truck door and surveyed the trailer. He had that same feeling in his stomach he'd had when he was a kid and he'd gotten in trouble at school. He took a deep breath and headed inside.

He went in the front door and pushed it closed behind him, not quite latching it. Virg was standing directly across from the door by the bar-height counter that separated the kitchen from the living room. Tracey said nothing. He attempted to find something to look at besides Virg.

"You better start talking, Tracey," Virg said. "You got about three seconds to tell me what my car was doing at the bottom of Thief Lake before I start kicking your ass."

Tracey felt around for the doorknob behind his back in case he needed to retreat in a hurry. "I lost control in the rain and it went off the road. That's all there is to it."

Virg slammed his fist down on the counter and Tracey jumped. "Goddamn it, Tracey! You took my car, you didn't even have the decency to ask me or the guts to tell me the truth about where it was. You must've been drunk off your ass to put it in the lake. Then you left it there for two weeks! Two weeks, rotting in the goddamn shit-water of Thief Lake!"

"Ray was going to tow it out tomorrow. I was trying to get it out of there," Tracey protested, knowing at the same time that his best bet would be to keep his mouth shut and let Virg get it out of his system.

"Yeah, trying to get it out without letting the cops know what you did. For a damn good reason, looks like. You wanted to get all that stuff out of there so you wouldn't have to explain it. Well,

105

you're going to have to explain it now. And you better hurry up, because I'm right about at the end of my rope with you."

"What stuff? What're you talking about?" Tracey searched his memory for anything he might have put in the car that evening that shouldn't have been in there, but he drew a blank. He didn't even think he'd thrown any empty beer cans in the back.

"Goddamn it, Tracey, you can't cover this up," Virg growled. "Just when did you decide it was a good idea to go driving around with George Cole, a loaded rifle, and a bunch of drugs in my car? What the hell were you thinking?"

Tracey stared at him in confusion. He'd come in expecting to have to explain about wrecking the car, but suddenly Virg was yelling at him about drugs and a rifle. And he couldn't figure out how Virg knew he'd seen George Cole.

"Did you really think you were somehow going to get away with all this? That you could somehow fix things up so no one would notice? The car is the least of it at this point, Tracey. Buster Brighton was over here this afternoon, and you are in some deep shit. What in the hell were those drugs doing in there? What were you doing at Thief Lake? What in Jesus' H. Christ's fucking name are you doing anything with George Cole for? Did you have something to do with Francis Lejeune? You start telling me what the hell is going on."

"How can I tell you what's going on when I don't even know what the hell you're talking about?" Tracey snapped, his temper rising along with his frustration. He wished Virg would give him a minute to think.

In a few steps, Virg was across the room. He slammed the door all the way shut and leaned on it with one arm, looking down into Tracey's face from a foot away.

"Buster found that crank, or whatever you call it, inside my car. It didn't somehow just float in there. I won't tolerate that, not in my house, and not in my car, and not with my money. You have got

106

me right in the middle of something I sure as shit don't want to be involved in. The cops are going to hold me responsible for this wreck and for everything they found in that car, including those drugs. My ass is on the line here just as well as yours, and I have a right to know what's going on."

"I don't know anything about any crank. All I did was wreck the car. I don't know what Buster told you, but it's a bunch of bullshit!"

"The only bullshit around here is what's coming out of your face," Virg snarled, then lowered his voice and leaned in closer, threatening. "I looked in that box in your room where you keep cash, and there's nearly four hundred dollars in there, Tracey. You've only done two guiding trips lately. You better not even think about telling me Joe is paying you two hundred bucks a trip."

"What the hell were you doing in my stuff?" Tracey snapped, furious. "It's none of your god-damned business how much cash I've got!"

"It is my business!" Virg retorted. "I'm the one Buster's holding responsible for this. Do you understand that? If you hadn't had any cash in there, maybe I'd believe you aren't dealing dope. But that's not what it looks like to me now. George Cole's rifle, crank packaged up for sale in a car you were driving, and a bunch of money you're not explaining to me, it all adds up in one direction. You've been lying to my face for two weeks. You better start telling me the truth."

"I am telling you the truth, damn it! I said they're not my drugs! I don't know whose they are, I don't know how they got in there, and I didn't get that cash from dealing anything. You don't know everything I've been doing!"

Virg grabbed him by the front of the shirt. "That's obvious! Why should I believe you? Nothing you've said for the last two weeks has been the truth and nothing you're saying now sounds anything like it. I swear to God, if I have to knock the truth out of you, I'll knock it out of you!"

"Oh? What're you gonna do? You're being a fucking asshole," Tracey spat back into his face.

A second later, Tracey was flat on his back on the floor, the wind nearly knocked out of him. He lay stunned for a few moments, unsure how Virg had taken him down so quickly. He rolled and tried to scramble up, but Virg swept one of his arms into the small of his back and leaned on it. Tracey went down onto his chest. His legs, not quite far enough under him, slid out with Virg's weight on his back.

Virg paused for a moment, breathing heavily. Then he put one knee in Tracey's back. Tracey made another attempt to get to his hands and knees, but Virg leaned forward, keeping the pressure on.

"Jesus Christ, Virg!" Tracey gasped. "I'll tell you whatever you want! Just give me a chance. I'm sorry! I swear!"

Virg hesitated. Tracey could feel the sweat trickling down his temple and the pressure in his shoulder from the position of his arm. The combination of humiliation, adrenalin, and anger was making him nauseated.

"I'll tell you whatever you want," he said again, trying to bring his voice down to calm Virg. "I promise. Just please let me up. Give me a chance to explain. Please."

Virg didn't move for what seemed like minutes. Tracey didn't dare say anything else. Finally Virg leaned back a little, taking some of the pressure off Tracey's back and arm.

"Start talking," he growled.

"Let loose of my arm. You're gonna pop my shoulder out," Tracey begged.

Virg moved his knee down further into the small of Tracey's back, and Tracey slowly brought his arm around to a more normal position.

"Let me up."

"Start talking," Virg repeated. "I'll let you up when I'm convinced what you're telling me is the truth. You can start by telling me when you decided it was a good idea to sneak off with my car."

Tracey swallowed and tried to keep his voice even and calm, talking over his shoulder. "I took the car Friday two weeks ago. I told you the truth about that. The only thing I lied about is where it was at."

"That's not the only thing. You told me it was at Bobbie's, then you told me it had a dead battery, then when I wanted it back by Wednesday and it didn't show up, you told me it was at Kenworths' garage getting the wiring redone. All of those were lies."

"Okay, you're right, but it was kind of all related," Tracey said. "I mean, the thing was, I didn't want to tell you I put it in the lake until after I got it pulled out and at least cleaned up a little bit."

"Why'd you take it without asking in the first place?" Virg's voice was shaking, but his tone was lower. "I usually lend you things when you ask for them proper."

"I went to Duckhaven for a party," Tracey admitted. "I pretty much figured you wouldn't let me borrow it if you thought I was going out drinking."

"Damn right," Virg said.

"I didn't really plan on driving around in it," Tracey said defensively. "I was just going to drive there and drive back later."

"But at some point you ended up at Thief Lake, which isn't exactly on the way home."

"Yeah, it's a long story. I'm telling you the truth, Virg, can you please let me up now? You're hurting my back."

After a few seconds, Virg pushed himself to his feet. Tracey scrambled up. Virg sat down heavily on the couch and extended his legs. He took a deep breath and released it slowly.

"I don't know what it is with you, Tracey. You're not stupid. You got good enough grades in school, better grades than Billy, for sure. You just make some damn bad decisions, and then you don't take care of things that have got to be taken care of. Well, you're going to have to take care of this now. You're going to tell me exactly what happened and what you have got yourself into. You are going to explain to me about the car, about who was there with you, about what you were doing at Thief Lake, and about the gun and the drugs and George Cole and Francis Lejeune. You are going to explain to me in a way I can believe where that cash came from, too. Don't piss me off any more than you already have, either, because I'll be back on you so fast it'll make your head spin."

Tracey sat down on the arm of the recliner. "I get it."

"So talk. I'm listening," Virg said.

"I was at Thief Lake because I gave some of the girls a ride home from Duckhaven. Like I said, I wasn't planning on driving around, but it was raining, and they needed a ride."

"Which girls? Liz Durgan doesn't live up that way," Virg pointed out.

"No," Tracey shook his head. "I had Liz along, but I gave Sonya Gomez and Brenda Doheny a ride too."

"So you went in the lake with all of them in the car? And nobody talked about it?"

"No, I dropped Sonya off first. She lives out along Rye Road, towards the river. I was going to drop Brenda next and then go up to Liz' house last. But Liz got out at Sonya's place, she was pissed off at me because I blew her off earlier. So I got stuck with Brenda and I had to drive her home."

"Where was Francis?"

"I don't know. He doesn't get along with Sonya's brothers, so I guess he didn't come to the party. Brenda said they had a fight about it. She got a ride there with Gil, but he left early."

"Who else was in the car?"

"Nobody else. Just those three. I swear, they were the only people in that car that whole night."

110

"Buster said the rifle he found in the car belongs to George Cole. So how did that get in there?"

Tracey shook his head. "I don't know. I really don't. George wasn't in that car, I didn't put the rifle in there, and I think I would've noticed if any of the girls had brought a rifle in."

"So you're trying to tell me you haven't seen George Cole, spoken to George Cole, or anything. That somehow his gun got in there without him ever having been around you."

Tracey hesitated long enough for Virg to notice. "Tracey, you are going to have to stop lying to me. You may be in big trouble here. Francis is missing, George is back around, his rifle and a bunch of drugs are in the car you were driving, and the car gets found in Thief Lake, which is on the way to the Lejeunes', and it ended up there the night Francis disappeared. You see where all this is heading?"

Tracey slumped back in the chair. He did, indeed, see where it was heading. "I saw George, but not at Duckhaven and not that night. I didn't even know he was back around until last weekend. I saw him Sunday and I talked to him for a few minutes, that was it. He had a rifle with him when I saw him, and that was a week after I dumped the car in the lake."

"What in the hell are you doing even talking to George?" Virg asked in disgust.

Tracey studied the armrest of the recliner. He was for damned sure not going to tell Virg that he'd done a guiding trip George had set up for him. "I swear to you, I don't know how any rifle got in that car. Not his, not anybody's."

"What about the drugs? Buster said there was a Camels cigarette pack in the car with crank packaged for sale in it. I know you don't smoke, but if George Cole wasn't in there, and you're telling me you aren't dealing it, which I sure as hell hope is the truth, then where did that come from?"

111

"I don't know anything about that either. It must have been Brenda's or one of the other girls'. Buster can ask around all he wants and no one is going to tell him I've been dealing."

"Then where did that four hundred dollars come from, Tracey? That's two hundred more than I figure you should've racked up lately."

"It all came from guiding. I swear to God I haven't been dealing drugs out of your house, Virg, or out of your car, or at all. I did a trip you don't know about that I set up with some guys from up north, and they paid me real good. I knew I should go through Grandpa Joe, but I figured I could make more money if I went direct with these guys. I've been saving it all to get the damn car out and repaired."

"Why didn't you just tell me instead of letting it sit there in the lake and rust, then? What difference would it make if you had the money to pay for it beforehand or if you just paid me back later?"

"I know I should have told you about it, I know that. I almost did, a bunch of times. But I knew you'd be pissed off, and I just wanted to be able to tell you I had everything covered, that I screwed up, but I could take care of it. I wanted to prove to you I could deal with my own goddamned problems that I always seem to create. That's all."

Virg looked up and met Tracey's eyes. Something in what Tracey had said seemed to register then, and his expression softened.

"Yeah, I get it," he said, in a more normal tone of voice. "You wanted me to think you could take care of things yourself."

Tracey looked down at his hands and realized he was shaking. He tucked his hands into his armpits.

"So, what are you trying to say, then?" Virg continued in a minute. "That someone put that gun in the car after you wrecked it? When it was in the middle of the lake?"

112

"I know what it sounds like," Tracey said. "If you don't believe me, there's nothing else I can say. You don't really think I have anything to do with Francis being missing, do you?"

"I don't want to think that, but that's what Buster thinks, I guarantee. And I still don't think you're telling me everything. You better consider naming names, because otherwise, and maybe anyway, you're gonna at least get charged with possession of this stuff."

Tracey said nothing. As far as he knew, there were no names to be named.

Virg let out another deep breath. "You're going to have to tell all this to Buster," he said. "I'm gonna get Ray to tow the car over here tomorrow so I don't have to pay for storage. I want you to clean it up and start doing whatever you can towards getting it fixed. I can't believe you wrecked that little car, Tracey."

"Drop me over there tomorrow and I'll pay for the tow and the lot fees. I'll pay for all the work or I'll do it myself. Maybe I can get Joe to set me up with some more guide trips soon."

"Yeah, you blew that, I guess," Virg said. "You think the Preserve is gonna let Joe recommend you if they think you've been messed up in drugs? You can kiss guiding good-bye if you don't clean up your act. You can probably kiss your warden friend good-bye, too. She was over here with Buster today, so she knows all about this."

Tracey glanced quickly at Virg. He'd been worried about what Addie would think if she found out about the car and his failure to deal with it, but Virg was right, this was even worse. There was no way she'd hang around someone she thought was involved with drugs, or maybe with the disappearance of Francis Lejeune.

Virg sighed. "Tracey, I still don't really understand what's going on here. I'm pretty pissed off, and I still think you're not telling me everything. This is going to be a big hassle. I expect you're going to court for not reporting the accident, with your background, at the very least."

"I know," Tracey said. "I'll just have to deal with it somehow."

"Well, we'll cross that bridge when we come to it," Virg said. "Right now, I'm tired and hot, I want a shower and dinner, and I don't want to talk about it anymore. I don't want to think about my sixty-eight Dodge sitting at the bottom of goddamn Thief Lake. You go back to Bobbie's or wherever you were, but tomorrow I expect you to get in touch with Buster and tell him what you told me, and later you and me are going to talk about what you are going to do to make it up to me. To show me that you can deal with it yourself. You understand?"

Tracey nodded and sat still while Virg got himself a glass of iced tea from the kitchen and then headed towards the back of the trailer to shower. When he heard the water come on, Tracey got up and fetched a beer.

He held the cool can up against the middle of his chest for a minute before popping the top. In one sense, it was a relief to have the car out in the open, to not have to conceal it anymore. But he was confused about the rifle and the drugs, and he still felt guilty. Virg had a temper, but he'd never really hurt Tracey, unlike Junior. Virg had rescued him from his own family and had raised him like his own son. Over the years, Virg had bailed him out of jail, paid his fines, loaned him cars, given him pocket money, given him a place to live, and been there to help him out when he needed it. And over the years, Tracey had lied to him, been unable to support himself, wrecked the cars he'd been loaned, and gotten into trouble.

Tracey leaned his head on one hand and massaged his own temples, trying to think. The best he could do to make it up to Virg would be to work on the car and try to get it back to the shape it had been in before he wrecked it, or preferably better. He tried to think

114

of how he was going to explain things to Buster to make it sound the best that it could.

Billy showed up about a half-hour later, as promised. "You're still walking," he grinned as Tracey hopped in the truck. "Dad couldn't have taken it that bad."

Tracey shook his head. "You don't want to see bad, then." He cranked down the truck's passenger side window to feel the wind. His adrenalin was still pumping, but it was almost exhilarating, as though he'd narrowly escaped danger.

At Bobbie's, Tracey carried in the beer Billy had bought and started pulling it out of the case, inserting cans into slots in the crowded refrigerator.

"So what was that all about?" Bobbie asked suspiciously. "What did Virg want you for? You in some kind of trouble?"

Since there was no longer any secret, Tracey told them about the car in the lake and the odd circumstances with the rifle and the drugs.

"So how pissed-off was Virg?" James asked when he was finished.

"Pretty pissed," Tracey acknowledged.

James laughed. "Wow, I wouldn't want to get Virg mad, myself. You're braver than I am."

"Stupider, you mean," Bobbie said. "Why didn't you just tell him? Or come to one of us? We would've loaned you the money."

"I didn't want to get anyone else involved," Tracey shrugged. "I thought I could deal with it myself. Guess I was wrong, as usual."

"You gonna call your little warden friend up here now, and tell her you got in trouble and need some sympathy?" James teased.

"My little warden friend already knows. She probably thinks I'm a total fuck-up now," Tracey said, throwing himself into an armchair. "I guess I'm going to have to talk to Buster and try and convince him I'm not dealing crank."

"I don't even know anybody who's got it, lately," James said. "I'll keep an ear out. It's pretty weird about George's rifle, though."

"Yeah," Tracey said. "I can't figure that out." He hesitated, studying the floor for a minute. "I did see George, though. I ran into him back by Goat Lake."

Bobbie grimaced. "I didn't even know he was back around."

"I did," Gil said quietly. Everybody looked at him. He shrugged. "They notified Francis when he got out of jail."

"Well, don't you think he could have something to do with Francis disappearing, then?" Bobbie asked, alarmed.

"No," Gil said. "No, I don't think so."

No one said anything for a minute. Then Bobbie turned back to Tracey.

"You haven't been hanging around him, have you? You better stay away from him. He's a big-time loser."

"I just talked to him for a few minutes," Tracey said. "I'm not hanging around him."

Tracey sat back in an armchair, listening to the summer night outside the open window near his head and finishing off his beer. Of all the things the car had led to, his altercation with Virg, trouble with the law, having to face Buster Brighton, and who knows what else, Addie Derange's opinion was the one thing that nagged at him the most.

Chapter Eleven

Billy dropped Tracey off at the Kenworths' garage Saturday morning, and Tracey handed over the cash to Willis while Ray winched the Dart up on their new flatbed truck. Tracey also bought a new battery, oil, coolant, and brake fluid.

He jumped in the passenger seat of the tow-truck with Ray. "So, Ray," he began as they pulled out of the lot, "you don't happen to know anybody around here who's dealing crank these days, do you?"

Ray was silent. Tracey looked over at him and raised his eyebrows.

"Ray! I thought you quit that stuff a couple years ago."

"Yeah, well, I did."

"I thought you were pretty messed up over at Bobbie's the other night. You're not dealing it, though, are you? You're just using it."

"Well, I'm not dealing it."

Tracey shook his head. "You getting it regular?"

"No, no. I just got it once, lately, in fact. Well, twice, but from the same guy."

"Who?"

"Doug Raney. I got a little from him down in Buenavista when I was doing a tow job. Then I guess he got busted, but he showed up at Bobbie's camp the other night with a little more, saying he was looking to get rid of it fast. He practically gave it away."

"He was at the camp? I didn't see him."

"No, he left when he saw your warden friend there. Made him a little paranoid. I guess it was her that busted him."

"Yeah, but she busted him for boating drunk. That's his own fault; he probably wouldn't have got caught otherwise. So Raney's making it? Or is he just passing it on?"

"Just passing it on, I guess. He said he was getting it from somebody else, George or something, I think."

"George? Like in George Cole?"

"What?" Ray looked over at Tracey and swerved slightly on the road. "No. George Cole? Is he even back around?"

"Yeah, he's around."

"I didn't know that."

Tracey thought for a minute. "Is there a lot of stuff around lately? 'Cause I haven't heard much about it."

"Me neither. This is the first time I knew anybody that had it in a while." Ray paused. "This have to do with that stuff they found in your car yesterday?"

"You know about that?"

"Yeah, I was there when they found it. Buster told me he'd charge me with interfering if I told you what was going on before he got to you. I did try to call Bobbie's place, though. But the phone was busy."

"I appreciate that, Ray. Could you let me know if you hear anything else about anybody dealing?"

"Sure. Sure, I'll keep an ear out. Folks won't think it's so weird if I ask around a little. Heck, they know me."

At the trailer, Ray let the car down off the flatbed and swung back into the cab. Virg had gone food shopping early and wasn't back. Tracey thought he probably didn't want to be there to see the Dodge when it arrived. He knew Virg had a soft spot for that car. Tracey decided that he'd scrub it up good first thing, make it look better, so Virg wouldn't feel so bad when he saw it.

He walked around the Dodge, taking a good look. Ray had washed the major gunk off for him with a pressure sprayer. It didn't look too bad, except for the new dings on the trunk and right side.

The one on the side was at an odd angle, from the rear wheel well towards the rear window, diagonal, not horizontal. Tracey couldn't figure out how that one had gotten there. He didn't remember hitting anything.

He examined it carefully, running his fingers along the scratches. Whatever had hit the car had caught on the trim, bending it up. And the trim was bent forward, from the trunk towards the hood. If Tracey had hit something while sliding into the lake, it would have been bent backwards. The pressure sprayer had removed the silt, but there was still what looked like green paint rubbed into some of the scrapes. The color resembled the dark olive green often used to paint jon-boats.

Ray had told him that the car had been discovered by some guys who were launching their boat off the road, and that they had hit it. But the marks of their prop were on the trunk. The trunk had been the highest part of the car, and therefore the body of their boat had passed over the rest of the car without touching it, the low-hanging prop scraping only the trunk lid. So the boat that hit the trunk couldn't have hit the side of the car.

Tracey stepped back and thought. If the car had been a little above water, at an angle, and if a boat had driven up alongside it, the angle of the scratch would match. The right rear window stuck halfway down. It had been covered with plastic sheeting duct-taped to the inside, but the tape had been coming off even before the crash. If someone had come up alongside the car they could have tossed the gun in the open window. Tracey suddenly remembered hearing a boat coming down the lake when he'd been at the mill. Then he remembered something else.

"Damn." Tracey studied the ground for a moment, thinking. Then he went inside and dialed Addie's home number. He waited impatiently, but there was no answer. He realized it was Saturday, and she was probably working. He dialed her work number. There was no answer there, either. Her cell phone number gave him only a recording, stating that she was out of range. He hung up in frustration and paced in the living room for a minute. Then he grabbed Virg's work cell phone, which was lying on the counter, and headed out the door.

Tracey started up his four-wheeler, stuck the phone in the storage box on the back rack, and took off out of the yard. He worked his way down a pipeline clearance through the Preserve, across Pine Slough Road, and then down along the west side of Thief Creek. He crossed the nameless dirt track that ran in to the Rye's in-holding. Then he made his way through the magnolia groves between Thief Creek and the slough above the old oil platform.

At the intersection of the slough and Thief Creek, Tracey shut down his four-wheeler and walked northwest, following the slough inland. He smelled it long before he saw it. In a hollow fifty yards off the slough, he found a camouflage-clad figure. Shafts of sunlight through the magnolias highlighted a gun butt and a pair of black leather boots. Francis Lejeune lay face down in the ooze of last year's decaying magnolia leaves, elbows jutting, ankles tangled, shoulders collapsed.

Tracey leaned forward, his hands on his knees. There was a buzzing in his ears that was only partly the flies. Other than that, the magnolia grove was silent in the humid heat, not even a breeze disturbing the forest canopy.

After a minute he straightened, and, trying not to breathe until he was out of range, hurried back to his four-wheeler. Even there he could smell the odor of decay. He shuddered as a wave of nausea swept over him. He could feel the sweat running down his temples, partly from the humidity and partly from his own reaction to the corpse.

He pulled the cell phone out of the box behind the seat and dialed Addie's cell phone number again. He waited impatiently, transferring his weight from one foot to the other. She answered on the third ring.

"Hi, Addie, this is Tracey Cole."

"Hi, what's up?" Addie asked. She sounded a little hesitant.

"Listen, I know I need to explain to you about the car," Tracey said hurriedly, "but there's something more important right now. I found Francis Lejeune. He's dead."

"What?" Addie said. "Where are you? Where is he?"

"Do you know that old road that leaves off the top of the Thief Creek Road loop? The one that starts from that old concrete foundation?"

"Sure, I was just back there the other day."

"Can you meet me there? I'll show you where he is. He's back that way, up along a slough."

"Okay," Addie said. "I'm south of the Field Office, so it'll take me a little while to get up there. Wait for me. Don't go anywhere."

Tracey started his ATV again and retraced his tracks to the Ryes' road, then followed the road west around the top forks of the slough. He cut down through the woods from there towards Thief Creek Road and the old foundation at the top of the loop.

He was a few hundred yards from the slab when the four-wheeler quit running. He realized he was out of gas; he'd been driving it a lot lately, and he hadn't checked it recently. He put it in neutral, got off, and began pushing it. It was a big quad-runner and it was hard to roll across the damp, spongy ground through the trees. By the time he got to the slab, sweat was dripping from his temples and matting his hair. He wiped his face on his shirt and sat down on a cinder-block foundation wall in the shade of a magnolia.

Pushing the ATV had used up some time, and he didn't have long to wait before he saw Addie's Chevy Tahoe pull up, followed by a county cruiser. So Addie had called Buster to go with her. He had hoped she might come alone, so he could talk to her in private.

121

Tracey met Addie at her vehicle and pulled the door open for her as soon as she began to get out. Buster heaved himself out of his cruiser and joined them.

"I had a hunch I knew where he was this morning," Tracey said. "I went back and checked to see if I was right. I was."

"I'm sorry," Addie said. "This must be unpleasant for you." Buster crossed his arms.

"I can explain where he's at, if you want," Tracey said. "I'd rather not go back there again."

"You shouldn't have gone back there to begin with," said Buster. "You should have waited and let us do it. Who knows what evidence you disturbed?"

"I didn't touch anything," Tracey said. "I didn't even go near him. I backed out as soon as I saw him."

"Yeah, well, you could have stepped on tracks. Besides, it's a convenient excuse now, isn't it, if we find any evidence that belongs to you there."

Tracey crossed his arms defensively. He'd been afraid Buster would try to pin this on him, what with the evidence in the car and all.

"Let's not get ahead of ourselves," Addie cut in. "We still have to go back and establish that this is Francis Lejeune. Do you know if he's on Preserve property?"

"Yeah, I'm pretty sure he is."

"Okay. Describe to me how to get there. I've been back in this area before, I ought to be able to find it. You don't have to come back with us."

"No," Buster said, "but you have to stay here. Don't even think about going anywhere until we get a chance to talk to you."

Tracey described where he had found the body. "You could get there from the Rye's road, too, but it's harder to tell you how. You'd have to be sure you went down the right one of the little

122

sloughs. If you go from here, you just have to cross this big slough and then work your way up it 'till you find him."

Tracey watched as Buster sat in the passenger side of his car, changing out of his spit-shined shoes into a pair of military boots. When Buster had his boots on, he and Addie crossed the concrete pad and disappeared into the woods along the old roadbed towards the derelict oil-drilling platform. Tracey waited impatiently. He had a feeling he wanted them to hurry, though he knew it was unwarranted. After all, Francis had probably been lying out there for more than two weeks.

Ike showed up within a few minutes. Next were a couple more county patrol cars and a cube truck with the county search-and-rescue crew aboard. When the coroner and an ambulance arrived, Tracey pushed his four-wheeler back off the concrete slab and sat on it under the magnolia out of the way. He watched as the search-and-rescue crew put together a litter with a big all-terrain tire attached to the bottom. Ike stayed in his vehicle, talking on the radio, with the door open and one leg out. Tracey thought he was keeping an eye on him. He didn't even try to talk to Ike. He knew what he thought of him.

Buster came back out of the woods about forty-five minutes later. His pants legs were wet where he'd waded through the slough, and sweat soaked his uniform shirt as well. He was breathing hard in the humidity and appeared to be in some distress. A few minutes later Addie followed. She was less wet; perhaps, Tracey thought, she'd used a fallen tree to cross the big slough, one that Buster was too uncoordinated to walk on. She also looked less sweaty and less disturbed by the heat. Her apparent composure when compared to Buster's misery amused Tracey. Just desserts, he thought, after the accusations of earlier.

Buster hitched up his gun belt and walked over to Tracey.

"Sit on down there on the wall."

Tracey stepped back over the wall and sat, and they waited for Addie to join them.

"Well, he was right where you described," Addie said.

"Is it Francis?" Tracey asked, squinting up at her.

Addie pulled an old cinder block over to where she could sit down in front of him. "We don't know yet. But whoever it is, I'd say he matches Francis' description."

"Can you tell why he died?"

"Well, there appears to be a gunshot," Addie said, "according to the coroner. Under the right arm. It'd be a hard place to shoot yourself accidentally, or even on purpose."

Buster sat down on the wall next to Tracey and adjusted his belt so he could lean forward. A few drops of sweat hit the concrete between his legs. "You've got some explaining to do, Trace."

"I know," Tracey said. "But I swear, no matter what it looks like, I didn't have anything to do with Francis."

"Hold it," Buster said, raising his hands. "We're gonna take it from the beginning, all right? First I want you to know that you're not in custody, and you can get up and go any time you want. You understand that?" Buster said.

"I don't want to leave," Tracey said. "I want you to not think that I had anything to do with Francis Lejeune's death."

"Okay then," Buster said. "Start all the way back with the day you took that car. I want to know it all, from how you decided you were gonna take it to now."

Tracey told them about the night at Duckhaven tavern and about the car accident, skipping a few incriminating points like how much he'd had to drink.

Buster shook his head and gave Tracey a skeptical look. "So you couldn't report the accident because Brenda was too pissed off to let you use the phone, and it was too wet to walk all the way to Rye Corner in the middle of the night," he said, echoing the excuse

Tracey had given him. "Or did you even try asking Brenda if you could use the phone?"

"I did," Tracey said quickly.

"Why didn't you report it the next day when Addie picked you up hitchhiking?" Buster pressed. It sounded less like a question than an accusation, pointing out what both of them already knew: Tracey had failed to report the accident in a timely manner, as he was required to do.

"All right, look," Buster went on when Tracey did not reply. "We both know you were too drunk to be driving and we both know you didn't want Virg to find out about the car, because you didn't have permission to take it. I can't get you for drunk driving at this point anyway, so why don't we just agree that was the case, and go on from there?"

"Okay," Tracey said resignedly, studying the concrete slab between his shoes. Drunk driving on a dirt road, and even running a car into the lake, was not really considered much of a disgrace by his peers and family, other than Virg, but he had a feeling Addie viewed it as a little more serious.

"So Brenda saw Francis before she left home with Gil, and people should be able to place you at Duckhaven from the time he was last seen until your accident," Buster went on. "That covers the time period from about five 'til about midnight or twelve-thirty. But we'll have to establish the time of death, which might be tough at this point."

"Old Mr. Rye might have heard the shot that night," Addie interjected. "He reported a single gunshot coming from that area at one a.m. He thought it might be poachers."

"We'll see what we can get out of Mr. Rye, then," Buster said. "But there's still the drugs and the rifle."

"I swear they are not mine," Tracey said, looking Buster straight in the face. "I swear it. The only thing I can tell you is who was in my car that night. And George Cole was not one of them."

125

"Well, those three girls ought to be able to verify whether or not George Cole was in your car with a rifle or not. If not, I'd say most people would have a hard time believing that after you dumped the car in the lake, you walked up here, drunk, in the dark, went out with Francis in the woods, and shot him to death. And then took George Cole's gun, if that turns out to be his gun and the murder weapon, and went diving to put it in your own car. It just doesn't make a lot of sense. Of course, maybe we'll come up with some other scenario that I can't think of right now."

Tracey glanced at Addie. She was balancing her chin on her hand, her elbow on her knee, studying him. He couldn't read the expression on her face.

"Okay," Buster said. "Why don't you tell us how you happened to know that Francis would be up this slough?"

"Well, I just took a look at the car this morning," Tracey said. "It has a scratch on the side of it that has to have been put there while it was in the water, but before it sank all the way. There's green paint in it, like boat paint. And I heard a boat come down the lake right after I left the car, probably around one-thirty. So it seems to me that a boat was there and hit the car before it went under."

"Okay. So? Maybe somebody was coming down through the lake and saw the car and went over to check it out."

"Yeah, but I saw Skeeter Doheny out in a boat the other day that had a scrape with the same color paint on it as the color of the car, right where he would have hit the car if he'd driven the boat up to the side," Tracey said. "If he did that, he could have dumped George's gun in my car through the back window. When I saw the scratch on the car and remembered Skeeter's boat, I remembered that last week I ran into Skeeter right at the bottom of the slough where Francis is. Then I remembered smelling something, well, dead, back there. I figured it was a feral hog or something."

Buster nodded. "Well, there sure have been some hogs back in there, unfortunately. So you think Skeeter's boat ran into your car

126

that night, huh? Well, we ought to be able to get a match between the paints, then."

"It's a sixty-eight Dodge Dart four-door sedan," Tracey offered. "The color's called Bronze Metallic."

Buster raised a hand. "We can get that later. But there's one problem with your theory. If Skeeter was up that way that night, he would've gone north up Pine Slough to the river and home to the boat ramp, or south to the Lejeunes'. He would never have come down through Thief Lake."

"Shit," Tracey said. "I didn't think about that."

"That doesn't mean someone else couldn't have been driving that boat. Or that Skeeter might not have had a reason to go through Thief Lake," Addie said.

Buster considered Tracey for a long moment. "I have to assume Francis went out hunting that night. His own rifle was there with him, underneath him, and he's dressed in camouflage. There was a bunch of ammo in his pockets, too. There's deer tracks all over that hollow. I'd say he went out with someone else, because there's no car or boat or four-wheeler around that we've found, and he had to get here somehow. It would have to have been someone he trusted. Not likely to have been George Cole."

Tracey shrugged. "It wouldn't have been me, either. I never did get on with Gil or Francis so well."

"Would George be apt to let Skeeter Doheny use his gun?"

"Sure, I guess. They're related somehow, if you go back far enough."

Buster raised his eyebrows. "It doesn't make sense to me that Skeeter would kill Francis, though. He practically lived with Francis. I don't really think you would've, either. But you being out with Brenda that night looks pretty bad, Tracey. It gives you a motive. And I'm going to tell you something else. We found drugs with Francis' body, and they were packaged just like the ones in your car. They are going to get the exact chemical make-up of that stuff, and they will compare it to the chemical make-up of the stuff I found in your car. And if it came from the same batch, they will be able to tell. And the rifle will be tested to see if we can tell if it's the one that killed Francis."

Tracey was silent.

"Is there anyone else who might have been using that boat, who might have had George's gun, who might have crank on them? Anything you know about anybody dealing lately?" Addie asked.

"Well, you know about that guy you and Ike busted a week or so ago," Tracey said. "Doug Raney. You said he had crank on him."

"I already thought about that," Addie said. "But I was wondering if there was anybody else you might have heard about, anybody using it, anything."

Tracey hesitated. He didn't want to get Ray involved, and he didn't want to have to tell Buster about his recent association with George Cole, so he needed to be careful with his answer.

"Tracey, it'll be in your best interest to give us any information you've got," Buster said.

"Well, I heard a rumor that Raney had a little bit more last week. But from what I heard, it wasn't much, and he got it from someone else and passed it on. Supposedly he said he got it from somebody named George."

Buster blew out his breath and glanced at Addie. "Well, Tracey, this is a big mess," Buster finally said, "and it sure looks to me like you are right smack in the middle of it."

"Are you going to arrest me?" Tracey asked.

"I'm not going to arrest you," Buster said, "because I don't have the probable cause right now. I'm not saying you're not a suspect, you understand. We're going to be talking to all three of those girls who were in your car and a lot of other people if we can find them. But right now, all I have on you is a shaky possession charge, motor vehicle accident stuff, someone else's rifle in your car, and the fact that you knew where a dead body was located. You have anything else you want to say or explain?"

Tracey shook his head.

"You'd help yourself out a bunch if you'd tell me which one of those girls you think might have dumped that crank in your car, if that's what you're claiming happened."

"Believe me, if I knew who had it, Virg would've got it out of me last night," Tracey said.

"Okay. I'm going to write you two citations," Buster said. "One of 'em's for Fail to Maintain Control. One is for Fail to Report Accident. I should get you for DUI, but I'd have a hard time proving that now. Don't think I don't know you were drunk when you put that car in the lake, though. And don't think I'm not going to be keeping an eye on you every time I see you behind the wheel."

Buster paused as if waiting for his statement to sink in. "Addie, you have any citations you want to add from the Preserve?"

"Not right now," Addie said. "We'll see what happens."

"Okay, that's where I'm gonna leave it for right now. You are gonna have to work out how to pay these, and how to pay what you owe to Ray Kenworth for the tow, and God knows what you'll owe Virg. Don't blow it off. If I get a warrant on any of these because you didn't pay or show up in court, I'll come pick you up. You understand?"

"I'll take care of them," Tracey said.

Buster continued to eye Tracey for a moment, then put his hands on his own knees and got up off the low wall. He ambled over to his patrol car, pulled out a clipboard, and brought Tracey back a Witness Statement to fill out. Buster wrote the two citations standing up, balancing his leather basket-weave citation book on his left arm. Tracey was still completing the Witness Statement when Buster handed him the two cites and went to meet the search-and-rescue team, who were wheeling the litter, loaded with an incongruous bright blue body bag, out of the woods.

Tracey signed the paperwork and looked up. Addie had not moved. She was still sitting in front of him on the cinder block. Tracey met her gaze for just a second, then glanced away, self-conscious with the turn of events.

"I thought I could get that car towed out of there without anyone finding out," he said. "Pretty stupid, huh?"

"Yeah, I wondered how you drove Brenda Doheny home Friday night with no car," Addie said. "Remember, you told me that out at Bobbie's camp."

"I never thought about that," Tracey said.

"Is that what you were trying to talk to Ray about?"

"Yeah. He was going to get it out this morning. I sure wish I'd just reported it that night, or told you the next morning when you picked me up." Tracey shook his head. "The longer I put it off, the worse it got. But I don't have anything to do with the drugs or the rifle. I swear I don't."

Ike was standing nearby, watching the search-and-rescue team load the body-bag into the ambulance. He was probably within earshot, Tracey thought.

"Can I call you later? There's a couple of other things, maybe they don't mean anything. I don't want to talk about them here," Tracey said.

"Sure. You can call me even if you don't have anything else to tell me," Addie said. "If you just want to talk. It must be pretty nasty to find somebody you know lying out in the woods dead."

Addie seemed to have dropped some of her formality when Buster walked out of earshot, and Tracey was encouraged that she still seemed to like him enough to suggest he call her just to talk.

"I wish it wasn't me that found him, but when I started to put two-and-two together this morning, it just all seemed to lead this direction," he said. "I know it looks kind of bad, but I hope you don't think I did any of this."

"I think you put that car in Thief Lake and didn't deal with it," Addie said. "But people have done worse things than that before."

Tracey sighed. "You know, I was just driving Brenda home to be nice that night. Buster's making it seem like I was after her or something, but it's not true."

"I believe you," Addie said.

Tracey studied the Witness Statement for a few moments as if he was reading it over, but his eyes weren't focused on the paper. He wanted some further reassurance that he hadn't blown everything with Addie completely, especially now that she seemed to be opening up a little bit, even protecting him in front of Buster.

"You remember when we were leaving Bobbie's the other night, after we went out to the bear-hunter's camp?" he asked hesitantly.

"I remember," Addie said, smiling a little.

"Well, do you still want me to work on your car some time? Because I really meant that I would work on it for you. I was even going to call you to come up last night, but then all this stuff happened."

Addie nodded. "Sure. The problem hasn't gone away."

"Good. I mean, not good that it needs to be worked on." Tracey paused awkwardly. "I already asked James if I could use his tools. We can do it soon, maybe even this weekend."

Addie glanced quickly towards the patrol car where Ike had retaken his seat. "You give me a call, then. We'll talk about it later. Are you done writing out that statement?"

"Yeah, that's all I can think of."

Addie took the form. "You can probably go now, if you want. You don't have to sit around and watch us wrap this up. It's going to take a while."

131

"My four-wheeler ran out of gas. I'll have to call someone to give me a ride," Tracey said. "Unless someone here can haul it for me."

"Better call somebody," Addie said. "You need to borrow my cell phone?"

"No, I've got one."

Tracey called the trailer. Virg was home, and not happy that Tracey wasn't there working on the car. He was less happy to find out that Tracey was calling him on his own cell phone, one signed out to him by Roslyn for work purposes only.

"Why don't I just bring you some gas and you can drive the four-wheeler home?" Virg suggested.

"Why don't you just bring the ramps and let me put it up in the truck?" Tracey answered. He knew it wasn't smart to argue, but he didn't feel like riding the four-wheeler all the way back. "Come on, Virg, I've had a hard day already."

"All right, I'll bring the ramps," Virg said. "You can explain to me what you've been doing instead of fixing the car on the way home."

Virg showed up about a half-hour later in his International pickup. He swung it around and backed onto the slab. Tracey pulled down the tailgate and slid out a metal jerry-can of gasoline.

While Tracey filled his tank so he could run the four-wheeler up into the truck bed, he watched Virg head over to the patrol vehicles and shake hands with Addie. Virg held onto her hand a little longer than necessary, Tracey thought, the way he had at the camp the other night. Tracey closed the can and pulled the ramps out of the truck bed. He ran his four-wheeler up and secured it with a couple of straps. From the truck bed, he watched Virg and Addie. He knew Virg well enough to tell from his body language that he was flirting with her.

Tracey hopped down and slammed the tailgate to get his uncle's attention. Virg returned and jumped in the truck. Tracey got in with his citations and threw them on the bench seat between them. Virg looked at them and raised his eyebrows.

Tracey shrugged. "Buster wrote me a couple tickets."

"Sounds like you're lucky that's all," Virg said as he pulled the truck back onto Thief Creek Road. "Addie told me about Francis. I guess Gil's going to be pretty upset."

"Guess so." Tracey slumped in the seat and stared out the window. He didn't feel like talking about it.

At the trailer, he gathered up his citations and went quickly to the bedroom he shared with Billy. He threw them down on the small desk near the door. As he did, he saw that he'd accidentally picked up a couple of other papers from the seat of Virg's truck. He examined them curiously. One was a scrap of cardboard, with Addie McCain's name and home number on it.

Chapter Twelve

Addie finally pushed open her front door Saturday evening hours late, after wrapping up the crime scene with the county investigators and Buster. Buster had offered to take her to dinner, but she'd declined, telling him she needed a shower more than she needed food. Now that she was home, however, she realized she was starving.

The house was dark, and as she walked in to the living room she saw the blinking red light of her answering machine reflected on the wall of her kitchen. She dropped her day-pack on the floor and went to the machine. Maybe Tracey had called. She didn't have any problem believing Tracey had crashed a car into Thief Lake because he was drinking and driving, but that was a far cry from being involved in a murder, and she just couldn't make the leap from one to the other.

A shock coursed through her when she pushed the button. The voice was not Tracey's, but her brother Logan's.

"Hey, Addie. Give me a call, okay? I need to talk to you. I'm looking for a map, and I need your help..."

Addie hit the 'end' button and Logan's voice cut off in mid-sentence. A map? It had been two years since they'd spoken, and he called to get her help finding some map? Of course, he couldn't just call to see how she was doing.

She stood motionless for a minute, her finger still resting on the answering machine. She had half a mind to just erase the message without listening to the rest of it. The phone call had awakened emotions she usually tried to suppress. She and Logan had disagreed, but there was no way to forget all that had come before, the childhood they had shared. And the truth was, she could have called him, too, and she hadn't. Now he had taken the first step.

She pushed 'play'. The machine mechanically gave her the time and date of the call. She listened through the first sentences again.

Logan continued, "...finding it. It's a specific map, not something I can buy. I know it sounds weird, I'll try and explain if you call me. Hopefully it's not too late already. I'm still at the same number."

Too late? What was that supposed to mean? It sounded like some drama Logan was adding to make the call seem more important. He tended to do that. And there was no ending 'hope you're doing well' or anything of that nature. Just an assumption that she'd call him if he asked her to, if he wanted her help with some project or another.

Exasperated and ambivalent, she shoved some cheese and crackers in her mouth and took a quick shower. Rather than think about whether she should call Logan back or not, she decided to organize the notes and paperwork she'd brought in from her car. She picked up the pile of papers from where she'd dropped them. As she did, she noticed that she'd brought in the odd business card she'd found in her door a week before. She studied it again.

There was certainly nothing else printed on the card except the word '*AFTERThought*'. She grabbed her laptop from her desk near the door, sat down on the couch, brought up a search engine on the Internet, and typed in *AFTERThought*.

She came up with unlikely websites about memorials and a band in Seattle, then finally hit on an environmental website with an archives section. In the archives she found a six-year-old article in a New York environmental magazine. It was about radical environmental-advocacy groups. One of the groups the article mentioned was *AFTERThought*, the Alliance For Tactical Environmental Response.

Addie clicked on the link to the group's website. The link brought up a page with a logo with the words *AFTERThought* in the same type and print style as on the card. The words "A Michael Gerschoff Foundation" were underneath, underscored by a menu bar.

On a page entitled *About Us*, Addie found an opening statement. The organization had been started by Michael Gerschoff as an environmental lobbying and advocacy effort, but was now run by his daughter June. One of the functions of the foundation, according to the statement, was to receive communications from radical environmentalists who committed crimes in the name of environmental protection and wanted publicity for their efforts. The page specifically noted that *AFTERThought* had nothing to do with the actions themselves, only passed on the information.

The communications were listed by date and location. Photographs of burning buildings and wrecked machinery accompanied some of them. After perusing the accounts attached to some of the more recent photographs, Addie scanned quickly down the list of dates and places.

Then she stopped cold, her cursor hovering over one particular link. It was from a little more than three years ago, an arson at an expansion of a ski area in New Mexico. The ski area's new slopes encroached on prime elk calving grounds. She remembered the controversy well. Logan had talked about it incessantly, and had been almost gleeful about the arson.

She clicked on the link and read. The anonymous author who claimed responsibility for the fire stated that his group would stop at nothing to protect the environment from corporate abusers. He claimed the group was untraceable and that they would strike again wherever such abuses occurred.

Addie backtracked out of the link and clicked through the rest of the website. She found a list of corporations and companies identified as particularly objectionable. She scanned the list and focused immediately on the name Roslyn. Roslyn was the parent company of the local pulp mill and particle-board factory, and they had major corporate complexes in both San Antonio and Houston.

She sat back in the couch and stared blankly at the screen. There seemed to be some sort of connection: a card from this website, *AFTERThought,* in her door; the website identifying nearby Roslyn as an objectionable entity and therefore a potential target; and her brother, who had been supportive of one of the website's prior actions, calling her from out of the blue. Was her brother's call really connected, or was she making something out of nothing in her mind?

She pulled the laptop closer and looked through the rest of the website. There was another list that focused on corporations involved in creating environmentally friendly products. There were several wind farms and fuel cell companies listed as well as the manufacturers of solar systems, but nothing else caught her attention or seemed tangentially connected to her life.

She clicked back to the 'About Us' page. Addie studied the picture of June Gerschoff featured there, a woman in perhaps her late thirties, on horseback with a backdrop of western-American pine forest. She had long, dark-brown hair done in an elaborate series of French braids which started near her face and continued back before merging into a single plait. Her features could have shown ancestry from any number of races and ethnicities: Asian, American Indian, Hispanic, Caucasian, most probably a mix of several. She wore jeans and an elaborate but well-used western-style shirt.

There seemed to be something familiar about the picture, but although she studied the backdrop, she couldn't identify the place and she didn't recognize June. Addie's eye was drawn to the pinto horse June sat upon. It had distinctive markings, as unique to each horse as a fingerprint. And Addie suddenly realized she'd seen that horse before. In fact, she knew it quite well: it belonged to her brother.

In the lower right-hand corner of the page Addie saw something else: a spiderweb-shaped logo she recognized. A line of text above it read "We support Circle of Life". Addie clicked on the link, and it took her to a page of the Cortez Indian Rehabilitation Center for Learning and Education site, abbreviated CIRCLE. The center was an hour or so from her childhood home. Logan had been involved with them off and on. He could have met June Gerschoff there, Addie surmised, if *AFTERThought* supported the center.

The page featured a photo of several people framing a large piece of metal wall art. It was eye-catching, a stylized set of interconnected southwestern scenes. The sculpture depicted canyons, mesas, clouds, the sun, and other southwestern landscape features, done in a variety of methods, from arc-welded rusty iron sheet-metal through bundles of thick wires following the topographic outlines of hills and valleys. The sheet metal was etched to add further dimension, creating a topographic effect. There were a number of small holes in the piece, arranged in a circle like a clock face; Addie wondered if perhaps it would eventually be used for such a purpose.

She read the text beneath the photo: "Circle of Life Director (left) with 'Art for Life' Group Final Project. This piece was commissioned by a group of collectors and will be wall-mounted in a private home. Twelve historic silver pieces will be mounted in the holes. The Group is proud of their accomplishment. Payment for the piece will go to support CIRCLE. Congratulations!"

Addie ran her hand through her hair. She was tired, too tired to puzzle any of it out that evening. Maybe some of it would come together in her mind while she slept. Or maybe she'd make some sense of it in the days to come, when she'd had some rest. Reluctantly, she closed the browser.

It was getting dark outside, and she flipped on a few lights around the house and set the laptop back on her desk. She thought about getting in touch with Tracey to find out what he'd wanted to say, but it was a little late, and calling would mean phoning Virg Radner and asking to talk to Tracey instead. Since Virg had just asked her for a date, it would be pretty awkward to call his house and then not want to talk to him.

In her conversation with Virg during her ride back to the camp Saturday morning, she'd learned that he'd been a widower for twenty years, never remarried after his wife and youngest son had been killed in a boating accident. He'd raised his sons and Tracey alone, working shifts at the lumber mill and eventually promoting to a second-level supervisor. Now that his sons were grown and he was working less variable hours, he was finding time to do some things for himself, and one of the things he wanted to do was take her on a date. She wasn't involved enough with Tracey, or with anyone else, to have a good reason to say no. Besides, he was charming in his own way, and she was curious about him and his life.

In the end, Addie procrastinated and didn't call anyone. Instead, she sat in bed and read until she fell asleep.

She went in to the office early the next morning and sat down in front of the computer to begin entering information in the case-incident reporting system. Buster called about eleven o'clock. The county had the lead on the case, since they had the investigators and facilities available and the experience to do a murder investigation, at least until such time as the FBI accepted or declined investigation. Buster, who was a beat cop and not a detective, was not the case agent. However, since he was the lead officer for Tracey Cole's car accident, which seemed to be intertwined, he was working with the detectives on the murder investigation.

Addie paced the office with her phone under her chin as Buster talked. He told her the medical examiner had recovered a single rifle bullet from under the corpse's left armpit. It had traveled through the chest from just under the right armpit, breaking a rib and going through both lungs and part of the heart, and lodged in one of the left ribs. Gil had positively identified the clothing and rifle as belonging to Francis, as well as a broken silver chain found in the mud near the body. Further identification would have to await dental records.

"We did a bunch of interviews yesterday evening and this morning," Buster said. "The bartender on duty at Duckhaven the night Francis disappeared said Tracey came in early, around five, ate dinner and had a couple drinks before the party started. He was sure Tracey was there 'til around midnight."

"How about the girls?" Addie asked.

"We talked to Sonya and Liz last night and they both gave us about the same story. They got dropped off there together around seven. Tracey was already there. Liz remembered seeing the car parked up front by the door, under the lights. Both of 'em said Tracey was there all evening. Liz is pretty sure he didn't leave at all, because she was hanging around him all evening. She's your competition, so to speak."

"Pardon me?" Addie asked.

"You know, I am a local boy," Buster said, "and I do hear things, sometimes when I'm off duty, sometimes when I'm on. Now, Sam Rye was over to a place I eat supper at, down south of Bear Creek, and he just happened to mention you were out at Bobbie's camp, getting friendly with Tracey one night last week."

"Jeez," Addie said, slightly embarrassed.

"No need to explain," Buster said, "I always wondered why the Preserve folk didn't get more involved with some of the local folks. You'll end up getting a lot more information that way. And the Coles aren't a bad lot, the ones down in these parts, anyway."

"I'm sure you're right," Addie said. "What else did you find out?"

"'Course, James is probably closer to your age, and he's got a good job at the air-conditioning place with Dennis Radner."

"Buster! Please!" Addie said.

"All right, all right. I'm just ribbing you. Liz said they all left together around midnight. She thought the doors of the car weren't locked because she didn't remember Tracey unlocking them. Also, she said one of the back windows wouldn't roll up and had plastic over it. Sonya and Brenda sat in the back and Liz sat in the front. She said she would've noticed if there'd been a long gun anywhere in the front. Sonya said she sat in the back until she and Liz both got out at her house. Said Tracey was pissed because he thought he was going to drive Liz home last, but Liz thought he'd been ignoring her and decided to stay at Sonya's to spite him. So he got stuck driving Brenda home, which they both thought was pretty funny. Of course, neither of them claimed the cigarette pack."

"Of course not," Addie said. "But that gives us three people who could've been in possession of it who were in that car, plus we know it was unlocked and someone else could've thrown it in there. It'll be hard to make a possession charge stick with that."

"Yeah, you're right. Which'll be damn good for Tracey if that crank ends up being the same as the stuff found on Francis. Brenda was too upset to talk to us much last night, but we talked to her this morning, just a bit ago, and she basically confirmed what Liz and Sonya said. She sat in back and didn't notice any rifle back there. After Liz and Sonya got out, she got in the front seat. Tracey was driving pretty fast, lost control around that sharp turn, and they went in the drink. She said she was pissed off and scared, so she walked away and wouldn't let Tracey help her. She said he didn't follow her. She walked the rest of the way home, took her about an hour. Said she got in about one-thirty."

"Of course, she didn't claim the cigarette pack either," Addie noted.

"No. She was smoking when we talked to her, Winston Lights, not Camels. And she absolutely denied Francis was involved in crank again. She said we could search his house, which we didn't, but we may later."

141

"That also makes three people who didn't see the rifle in Tracey's car," Addie noted. "Did she tell you that Francis' house got robbed?"

"Yeah, she did. She hasn't been living there for ten days or so. She went down to Buenavista to stay with her sister Pet. Gil's house got gone through, too, I guess. She said nothing was taken as far as she and Gil could tell except for a laptop computer Francis had borrowed. Somebody just jimmied the door and tossed the place and went through both houses real thorough. Francis had metal-working tools and pewter, which they didn't take. Didn't even take the liquor, which is weird if it was kids."

"Somebody was looking for something specific, like the laptop or something smaller," Addie said.

"Yeah, and on the subject of missing stuff, we asked her about the silver chain found near Francis. She said it was his and that he usually wore a silver pendant on it, made to look like a curled-up mouse, I guess. But we didn't find the pendant. A couple guys are going back out there with a metal detector to see if it got buried in the mud."

"That's kind of a strange thing to get stolen, if it's not there."

"Yeah," Buster snorted. "Brenda said it's an Indian symbol of the artisan, or some shit like that. Said it was his pattern, that he made a mold from it and made pewter copies that he sold down in Bug Raney's jewelry store. She thought he made it during his work-release program."

"The one he was sentenced to after giving evidence against George Cole?"

"Yeah, it's some special program he qualified for. You got to be able to prove you're one-eighth American Indian. This program brings 'em out to somewhere in Colorado for three six-month stints, and they're supposed to learn some trade to keep 'em out of jail."

"It wasn't Circle of Life, was it? The Cortez Indian Rehabilitation Center for Learning and Education?" Addie asked.

142

"Yep, that's it. How'd you know that?"

"I grew up not far from there," Addie said. "What did Brenda say Francis was doing that night?"

"She last saw him about seven o'clock. He's been getting deer pretty regular out in the Thief Creek area across from the Ryes. She thought he'd been hunting up north in the swampy areas, going out in his truck along the Ryes' road. She said he was planning on going out that evening. He was just going to wait until the Ryes' lights went out."

"Well, that explains the shots Mr. Rye kept hearing," Addie said. "You know, I was out there Saturday morning two weeks ago, not more than a couple hundred yards from where Francis was found."

"Yeah, and Brenda said she went up there with Gil and looked around, since that's the last place they knew he'd been planning on going. But they went in the road leading out to the Ryes' place and walked down the west fork of the slough. That was the east fork he was actually on. Plus, his truck was at home, so Brenda wasn't positive he'd actually gone out hunting, or poaching, as the case may be."

"He usually took his truck?"

"Unless he went out with someone else. Brenda said he might have taken a couple of friends out recently, guys he knew from the adhesives plant, which is where he worked, but she couldn't remember their names as of this morning. Said they weren't locals."

Addie frowned. "Any idea what time Francis might have gone out that night?"

"Well, Brenda said the Ryes' lights usually went out about 11:30 or twelve, and Francis maybe had a few beers before he left because she found empty bottles out on the porch when she got home. So say he sat around and had a few, watched old Mr. Rye's house for the lights, then went on up there, got involved in hunting, and bam."

"She didn't happen to keep those bottles, did she?"

Buster paused. "Shit, I didn't think about that. I'll call her right up after I talk to you and make sure she doesn't take out the garbage. They don't get any pick-up there so they have to take the stuff and dump it themselves. Since neither of them has been around to do it, I'll wager those bottles are still there. I'll get 'em dusted for prints soon as I lay a hand on 'em."

"Did you hear Tracey say Brenda told him she'd had a fight with Francis that night?" Addie asked. "That was why Gil gave her a ride to the party and Tracey gave her a ride home."

"Yeah, I picked up on that. I asked her about it and she said it wasn't a big deal. It had to do with Sonya's party and how he doesn't get along with her brothers. She said she figured he just took off for a few days because of that, but she was a little worried because his truck was still there. But she thought he might've called one of his buddies from the adhesives plant to come get him."

"That does make her a suspect, though," Addie said.

"Yeah, of course. But if the shot Mr. Rye heard at one a.m. was the one that killed Francis, she wouldn't have had time to get up there any more than Tracey, and it doesn't explain the drugs and the rifle. Unless she and Tracey are in cahoots, somehow. Unless they went in the lake after they killed Francis, later than they both said it happened."

"Still doesn't explain the drugs very well, or George Cole's rifle," Addie said. "Did she say anything else useful?"

"Well, she said when she was walking home that night, she heard a boat go down the creek. She figured that would have been around one-fifteen."

"Same as Tracey. Did you ask her anything about Skeeter?"

"Yeah, I asked her what he'd been up to lately and where he got the boat. She said she thought the boat belonged to Gil. She said Skeeter wasn't there Friday night and she didn't know where he was. I asked her why she thought the boat belonged to Gil, and she said that he's been involved in some group lately that's been buying him expensive stuff. She didn't use the word, exactly, but it sounded from her description like some sort of militia or a neo-nazi group, or something like that."

"That's interesting. I hadn't heard anything about that from anyone else."

"Me neither. She said Francis and Gil both got new four-wheelers through this group. That's who Francis borrowed the laptop from, too. She said Skeeter has maybe been involved with the group, hanging around them, and that she warned him to stay away from them 'cause she thought they were up to no good," Buster said. "Also, she said she had to get a ride home from Tracey because Gil left early. She didn't know where he went."

"What did Gil say? Someone must have talked to him when he came in to identify the clothing."

"Yeah, he was pretty thrashed, though. It was a bad scene. Francis was his only kin around here."

"I understand. Did he say anything at all?"

"He admitted Francis had been poaching. He's still got some venison in the freezer, if you want to go for that. Nothing was taken from his house during the break-in. And he denied that Francis was involved in crank again, which is probably true. I don't know what you know about Francis."

"I don't know much about him other than that he and Gil are pretty anti-Preserve," Addie admitted. "I've run into him a couple times, that's all." She remembered him as shorter and thinner than Gil, with the same black hair and eyes, but somewhat darker complexion. He'd been more ingratiating than Gil, too, covering his criticism with smiles, which made Addie more suspicious than if he'd been angry.

"Well, Francis was always a little bit of a scammer," Buster went on. "You know, he'd do what he had to do to make a buck. Course, there's a lot of folks like that around here, with the way the economy's been. But Francis always had some angle, something that was supposed to make him money but usually wasn't very well thought out and ended up getting him in trouble. But he seemed to be straightening up with this jewelry thing."

"No word on anybody dealing crank or anybody seeing George Cole around?"

"Well, yeah. None of the girls have seen George around at all, although he was apparently released about six months ago. But I did get a little information that Ray Kenworth may have had some crank lately. He's a crank-head from way back."

"Interesting," Addie said. "I'm not that surprised. I guess it would be worth talking to him as well. And I'd like somebody to re-interview Doug Raney, the guy Ike and I busted for boating under the influence. I guess we could test the crank we took off him and see if it's from the same batch as the other two samples."

"Yeah, there are a lot of directions we could go. If you want to lend a hand with any interviews, we could probably use the help."

"I'd be happy to. Can you let me know what else comes up? Anything about the ballistics or the drugs?" Addie asked.

"Sure will," Buster said. "You want to see if you can find out anything else about this boat Skeeter has been driving? His real name's David, but of course it's probably registered to someone else."

"Me and Ike stopped him the other day because there were no registration numbers on the boat. He had the paperwork with him. It's registered to him, all right. I've got the number somewhere in my notes. I'll see what I can do about finding out who bought it and where it came from."

After Addie hung up with Buster, she flipped through her pocket notebook until she found the notes she'd taken the day she and Ike had stopped Skeeter out on the river. Then she called the Texas Parks and Wildlife office.

146

Addie gave the clerk the Texas registration number and began taking notes. The registration was only three months old. The boat had been bought outright, with no liens against it. After she hung up, she slapped a telephone book down on the desk and flipped to the Boat Sales section. There were a number of local dealers who sold Sea Ark boats. Addie dialed the first one on the list, asked for the manager, and identified herself as a law enforcement officer.

"I need to check and see if you sold a particular Sea Ark fourteen-footer with a center console during, say, the last six months. I've got a serial number."

The fourth place Addie called was a boat dealer north of the Preserve, near Ely Lake. He found the serial number quickly.

"Yeah, I sold it about four months ago," the manager told her. "You want who I sold it to?"

"That'd be great," Addie said.

"Guy named Delevan Bates, according to the receipt," he said, stumbling a bit over the name. He spelled it out for her and Addie spelled it back to make sure she had it right. "I've got his address in Aynesworth. He paid cash for it. I sold it to him for five-thousand even, with the motor and trailer."

"Can you fax me any information you have?" Addie asked.

"Sure. You want anything else, like what this guy looked like or anything?"

"Well, yeah. You remember that?"

"Sure. I remember him real well. He bought four boats from me and four motors. Two 14-foot jons and two 19-foot utilities. The little ones were new, the utilities were both used."

"Wow. I guess you would remember him. So what'd he look like?"

"Tall guy, probably six-one or so, blond hair cut real short, almost military, you know? And he was wearing those military pants when he came in. My girl who works the register here and the parts girl were talking about him after he left, said he was good-looking,

147

if that means anything to you. Though that's not exactly the term they used."

"How old? And what was his build like, his weight?"

"Oh, about thirty-five to forty, I guess. Looked like he worked out, but he wasn't real built up, you know? And he said he was from up north somewhere, I don't remember where. Maybe Washington or Oregon. He was friendly enough, pretty talkative. We made the deal and he came back with three other guys and paid with cash, like I said, and picked up all the boats. There was another blond guy, a little shorter and younger, could've been kin. There was one heavier guy with kind of long black hair, a little older, and he was a darker-skinned guy, too, but I couldn't rightly tell you what race he was. Then there was a young guy, maybe in his late twenties, reddish-blond hair cut short, kind of an arrogant S.O.B. I don't remember any of their names, but I do remember that they called the first guy Van."

"This is great," Addie said. "Thanks a lot. Fax me the rest of that stuff, would you?"

When the fax came out of the machine, Ike, who was working in the office on case reports, pulled it out and looked at it. He sorted the papers, then handed her the stack.

"Here's your stuff," he said. Addie took it from him, but Ike remained standing near her. After a minute he leaned back against the wall near her desk and crossed one ankle over the other.

"So, I guess your buddy Tracey Cole is in pretty hot water," Ike said casually.

"I don't know about that," Addie said. "There's no real evidence that the drugs or the rifle were ever in his control."

"Sounds like to me he wrecked a car drinking and driving and then tried to conceal it. And sounds like to me he's involved with this George dude who's a meth manufacturer, at the very least."

Addie put the papers down on her desk. "So, what are you trying to get at?"

Ike shrugged. "I'm just pointing out that it's a bad idea to get too attached to this guy."

"Ike, there's nothing going on between us," Addie said impatiently. "But since you're being a busybody, I'll tell you what I think about him. He's sweet, he's smart, and he's funny. And yes, he's a little bit of a screw-up. But that's not the end of the world. You have to make decisions about what you're willing to accept in another person and what you're not willing to accept. Nobody's perfect. Maybe I can accept some things in other people that you can't accept. And I'll tell you one thing, there's no way I believe he's involved with this murder, or with the drugs in that car."

She stood up, took the fax and the rest of her report from the desk, and slung the day-pack she'd brought in with her over her shoulder.

"I'm going home to work on this case file. If you need anything, you can call me there."

At home, she spread a bunch of her paperwork out on the coffee table in her living room and tried to organize things into piles, creating categories with little sticky-backed papers. She made notes to herself on her laptop as she sorted. But she kept getting distracted by her own thoughts.

She took a break and leaned back on the sofa, gazing around the living room. The house she had rented was small, a compact two-bedroom of gray brick, with a wedge-shaped fenced-in yard. She kept it tidy. Her decor was sparse, mainly prints of southwestern scenes. She'd only been buying her own furniture and accessories for the last two years; prior to that, she'd lived with Logan, and his house was well furnished. She hadn't needed much of her own stuff.

Today, in the heat of the early evening, the house was silent, and she noticed the silence more acutely than usual. Her mind turned to the bustle of Bobbie's hunting camp on Friday night, the tinny sound of the boom box, the snap of sparks from the fire, the murmur of voices punctuated by laughter now and again, and the

149

background drone of the river and the cicadas and frogs out in the dark. She remembered the buzz of excitement she'd felt through the alcohol when Tracey sat next to her on the bench, and her desire to be a part of the close-knit, relaxed circle of relatives and acquaintances around him. She wondered if she would always remain an outsider in that community as Gil Lejeune had asserted.

Finally Addie got up and headed for the shower. It would be a moot point anyway if Tracey turned out to be a drug dealer or even somehow involved in a murder. As little as she liked to admit it, Ike was right in that regard. She was, after all, a law enforcement officer, much as she sometimes wanted to escape the special constraints it placed on her personal life.

And she reminded herself that Tracey might not even be interested in hanging around with an officer, despite his actions out at Bobbie's camp and his ongoing offers to work on her car and show her around the Preserve. Or, he might have ulterior motives. And anyway, he had competition now, in the form of his own uncle.

Chapter Thirteen

The phone rang shortly after Addie stepped out of the shower. She snatched it up quickly, feeling the mix of adrenalin and anticipation the bell usually caused: it might be an emergency call, or it might be someone she didn't want to talk to. Or, then again, it could be someone she did want to talk to.

"Hi, it's Tracey."

"Hi. I was just thinking about you."

"I bet."

"Really," Addie said, sitting down on a bar stool in her kitchen. "There's something I wanted to ask you about. I found out who bought that boat Skeeter has been driving. Guy named Delevan or Van Bates, from up north of Ely Lake, a town called Aynesworth. That ring a bell?"

"One of the guys I took out last week on a fishing trip was named Van."

"That's interesting. It's not that common a name. Any way he could be associated with Skeeter Doheny?"

"Yeah," Tracey said hesitantly. "I think so. There's a couple things I want to talk to you about. I was wondering, can we meet somewhere? I'm talking on Virg's phone and he's gonna be home pretty soon, and I'd just as soon he doesn't hear me talking about this stuff. He's not too happy with me lately."

"Okay. Where would you like to meet?"

"Well, can you come up to Bobbie and James' house on Magnolia Slough? I can work on your car tonight, too."

"Sure," Addie said. "Tell me how to get there."

Magnolia Slough Road was a rough dirt track leading towards the river north of Pine Slough. Addie took the highway out of Buenavista and turned off at a fading wooden Missionary Baptist church sign leaning up against a fence post. Past the church the main road turned south towards Pine Slough Road, but Addie continued east, her car tracking in the ruts. She crossed Thief Creek just below Magnolia Slough on a one-lane bridge. From there the land rose to a prominent bluff on the river, the magnolias and sweetgum and tangled undergrowth giving way to pines.

Addie pulled up at Bobbie's gray-brick house around five-thirty. There was grass growing around it and a V-hulled boat on a trailer parked against the side of the house. On the other side was a large metal shed, with a narrow pathway between it and the house. An arc of trees intruded into the clearing, butting up against the shed and shading the back patio. Bobbie's big pickup was parked haphazardly in the yard.

Tracey met her out front. He seemed a little shy or awkward. Addie thought it was probably because he was still embarrassed about the car.

"Bobbie's in the shower," he said. "James'll be here pretty soon. He has to drive up from Buenavista. Him and Dennis work weekends a lot because that's when people want their air-conditioners working. Pull it up over there and pop your hood and let me see how it runs before you shut it off."

Addie popped the hood and watched while Tracey peered into the engine compartment. She knew a nominal amount about car engines. She'd watched her brothers tinker with their own cars enough times to be familiar with most of the parts, at least. But she'd never been allowed to help them with any actual work. Tracey seemed to know what he was doing, and Addie kept her mouth shut and stayed out of his way, except to turn the engine off or on at his request. She figured doing something for her that she couldn't do herself was a good way for him to regain his confidence with her. She did want to go over the investigation with him and hear whatever it was he wanted to tell her, but she thought maybe it would be better to wait until he wasn't distracted. Maybe they could go out for dinner and talk about things there.

While Tracey was working under the hood, James drove up in a big white pickup. He backed in next to the house near the boat and jumped out, grinning as usual. He was wearing a white polo shirt with the logo of his air conditioning business on the pocket.

"How's it going? Tracey get that thing running right for you?" he asked, joining Tracey and leaning over the engine.

"Running a lot better, anyway," Addie said.

"You gonna stick around for dinner? We're gonna throw a few things on the barbecue on the back porch."

Addie glanced at Tracey. "I thought I'd take Tracey out to dinner to thank him for fixing my car." Tracey looked up and grinned.

"Aw, give him a rain check on that!" James urged. "Come on, I want to hear all about what's going on in the Preserve these days. You know, where you all are patrolling this year, so's I can figure out where to set my illegal stands."

Addie raised her eyebrows. "And you were thinking you were going to pull a hunting permit this year?"

"I was just joking," James said. "You'll get used to me. Seriously, you can hang out for a little while, can't you? Have a beer?"

"Sure, I guess. I'm in no hurry," Addie said. James grinned and walked away towards the house, stripping his shirt off.

"I guess I'll owe you dinner another time," Addie told Tracey.

"You don't owe me anything," Tracey said. "Did you know you're missing a lug-nut from two wheels, the front right here and the back left?"

"I didn't notice that," Addie said, checking the wheels herself. "I wonder how long they've been gone."

Tracey shrugged.

"Well, I think I've got a couple of locking nuts," Addie said. "I don't like to use them, they're a pain to get off and on."

"Do you have them here?" Tracey asked. "I'll put 'em on for you."

"They might be in a box in the trunk," Addie said. "I think I tossed them in there when I moved."

She yanked the trunk-release handle and Tracey pulled out a couple of cardboard boxes, still sealed with packing tape.

"Which one?" he asked.

"Don't remember," Addie said. "I have no idea what's in which one. Open them up and let's see."

Tracey took a jackknife out of his pocket and slit the tape on each box and pulled the flaps loose. Addie knelt down and dragged one of the boxes towards her. Obviously whatever she'd packed in them had been nothing she'd needed in the last two years. She began pulling things out, letting Tracey go through the other one. Her box contained mostly spare car parts and a few tools. Down underneath everything else, she found a plastic bag with the locking nuts in them. After a search through the loose items in the box bottom, she also found the tool with the correct shape to fit the lug nut pattern. She turned to Tracey.

He had pulled a pile of stuff out of the other box and was kneeling with a handful of photographs in one hand.

"These pictures were just loose in here. I didn't want to smash 'em," Tracey said.

"Thanks," Addie said. "I forgot they were in there." The memory of what she'd packed in the box came flooding back. These were the photographs she hadn't wanted to frame or put in her albums, but hadn't been able to throw away. They were the ones that were poorly exposed or blurry, but in particular, they were the ones she preferred no one else see.

"Who's this?" Tracey held up the pile with a washed-out photo of a chunky blonde kid on top.

"My brother Blake." Addie fought down a sudden unreasonable urge to snatch the photos away from him.

Tracey flipped through a few more, putting each one underneath the pile. "There's Blake again, huh? Who are the other kids?"

"The skinny dark-haired one is Logan. Logan's four years older than me, Blake's two years older."

"This where you grew up?" Tracey tapped a photo of several buildings in the distance, taken looking down the dirt farm road from where the school bus stopped along the highway. Addie moved closer to him and looked over his shoulder.

"That's the farm. There's a ravine behind it where I used to walk when I had nothing else to do. The coyotes used it as a trail, and there were crows and other birds and sometimes deer down along the creek. You can just see the tops of the trees that grow down in there to the left of the house. Every once in a while I would find a worked piece of stone, left there by the Pueblo people, the ancient Indians who used to pass through on their way to their hunting grounds."

"Is that where you got the idea you wanted to be a ranger? From that area?"

"I guess so." Addie sat back on her heels. "I spent a lot of time alone, so I knew I could deal with working in isolated places. And a lot of the time I felt like I had more in common with the animals down in the ravine than with anybody else."

Tracey flipped through a few more pictures. "Here's your brother Logan again. I bet this is his first car."

"Yep." Addie took the photo from him and studied it. Logan, at sixteen, was leaning against the hood of a big pale-blue two-door sedan. She felt an unexpected surge of emotion at seeing her brother's windblown dark hair, the way he leaned with one shoulder up, and the familiar old sweatshirt he was wearing. She had spent many hours in that sedan while Logan maneuvered it, bouncing and banging, up dirt roads in red-rock canyons.

Tracey went slowly through the other photos, handing them off to Addie as he went. Addie took them from him almost automatically, the memories following one after the other.

"Any pictures of your mom in here?" Tracey asked after a few minutes.

"No, I don't think anyone ever bothered to take photos of my mom," Addie said, remembering the picture on her desk. "They ignored her, just like they ignored me when I was a little girl. I was afraid I was going to end up like her, you know. Get out of high school, marry some dry-land bean farmer, and spend the rest of my life picking tomato caterpillars and playing cards with my daughter at the kitchen table."

Tracey glanced up at her. "But you didn't."

Addie laughed shortly. "No."

"So somebody must have helped you. Your mom? Did she want you to get away from that, too?"

"My mom died when I was seventeen. She just laid down on the bed, crossed her arms, and was dead when I came home from school. I lived with Logan after that. I lived with him all through college and during the three years after I graduated when I was working seasonally, before I got into the intake program."

"How often do you go back and see your family?"

"I don't," Addie replied, trying to keep her voice neutral.

Tracey raised his eyebrows. "Not at all? Not even Logan?"

"No," Addie said. "Not since I got here two and a half years ago. I never got along with Blake anyway. He lives on the farm now, with my dad. My dad's in too poor health to manage things by himself, so I guess I owe Blake some respect for that. Logan and I had a kind of parting of the ways a couple years ago, when I got into the intake program. I haven't seen him since."

Tracey studied the next photo on the stack carefully, then handed it to Addie without a word.

156

The photo was of Addie. She was half-kneeling on red soil, squinting up at the camera. She was holding a piece of Indian pottery, with the painted pattern faded by age and a sheen of dry red Colorado dust. She had tipped the bowl with one hand so the hole in the top was towards the camera. Between the fingers of that hand, she held a large wedge-shaped chunk that had broken cleanly out of the pot.

"How old are you in that one?"

"Seventeen," Addie replied softly. "It was right after my mom died."

"Where did you find that? I mean, was it just sitting around, or was it buried somewhere?"

"It was buried. It was in a caved-in place, an old pit house, which is a house that's made partly underground."

"Is it old?"

"Probably about eight hundred years old."

"Worth a lot of money?"

"Not with that chip out of it. It could be glued together, it's a pretty clean chip, but it still wouldn't be worth as much as a whole one."

"Pretty cool anyway. Is there a lot of stuff like that around where you grew up?"

"Quite a bit," Addie admitted.

"And it had been there for eight hundred years, until you found it?"

"Probably."

"Did you keep it?" Tracey asked. "Or did you have to turn it in to a museum?"

"I gave it to my brother." Addie leaned forward and gently took the rest of the photos out of his hand. She sorted through them slowly. Then, after some hesitation, she handed him one. It was another photo of Logan, as an adult this time, standing in the middle of a room lined with shelves. The shelves held Indian pots, vases, bowls, and other artifacts of various sizes and shapes.

"Wow," Tracey said, examining the photo. "Is this stuff all at his house?"

"Not in any kind of public area of his house. In a special room."

"That only special people get to see?"

"You got it."

"So what you're saying is, this isn't legal," Tracey continued, tapping the photo. "You're supposed to turn these in to a museum or somewhere. It's kind of like hunting or trapping on the Preserve, I guess. You have to have the right kind of permit to do it."

"You can't even get a permit to do this, not on public lands, and sometimes not even on private land," Addie said. "Logan is a dealer of Indian pottery and other art, most of it made recently specifically for sale. But he also moves historic and prehistoric pieces, some of it collected legally and some not. He knows how to make the pieces look as though they came from legitimate sources, to launder them."

"So the people he sells it to don't know where it really came from?"

Addie thought for a moment. "Yes and no. Most collectors want to know exactly where the things they collect come from. Logan supplies a cover story, but he also gives his clients information about where the pieces were actually found. Most clients like to maintain a kind of a secret record, sometimes a map with marks on it, or a computer file of GPS coordinates, or even a book with the pages dog-eared."

"And Logan found all this stuff himself?" Tracey asked, examining the photo again.

"Some he got through other people with the intent of selling it. But he does search out some of it himself. He's pretty good at finding places."

"Is that what you and Logan had a falling out about?" Tracey asked.

"Yes," Addie said. "Before I got into the intake program, I wasn't working in law enforcement. When I got accepted, I knew I couldn't be associated with Logan's dealings. Logan couldn't promise me he'd quit and stick to legal brokering. So I had to leave, had to make a break. It wasn't easy, walking away from the only person in my family who believed I could do something with my life. We argued at the end; it was pretty nasty and hurtful on both our parts."

"Are you ever sorry? I mean, about what you decided to do?"

Addie hesitated, her thoughts returning to the recent phone message and her reaction to it. "I made my choice. There's no use spending time wondering what things would have been like if I'd made some other one. This is the way it is."

Tracey studied her. "I can't really imagine what it would be like to not have any family around, not to be able to go to them if you need to."

Addie shrugged, trying to appear nonchalant. "You get used to it. You find substitutes." She gathered up the photos and put them back in the box, then put the box in the trunk. "I found those lug nuts. Here they are."

Tracey took the lug nuts and the insert for the end of the tire iron that fit in the locking nuts' pattern. As he tightened the second one, he glanced up at Addie again.

"Does Ike or any of the other folks over there at the Preserve know about Logan?"

"No," Addie said, shaking her head. "That's one reason I moved away from that area, so there wouldn't be any concerns about my having to deal with my own relatives, any kind of conflict of interest."

"All the cops around here have to deal with that," Tracey said. "I mean, any of them that grew up around here, like Buster

159

Brighton. Everybody knows about their past and sometimes they have to bust their own relatives. It shouldn't make any difference as long as you aren't doing that kind of stuff yourself anymore."

"I'd still prefer they didn't know. It's just easier that way," Addie said.

"Except that you have to keep a secret. You can't talk to anyone about your own family."

Addie smiled, and a little bit of relief crept in with the realization. "I guess I can talk to someone about my family now."

Tracey grinned and dumped the tire iron back in her trunk. "And I promise I won't tell. Come on, let's go see how James and Bobbie are doing with dinner. You can look at all Bobbie's photos up on the walls. She's got a bunch of me. There comes Gil, right now."

Addie followed Tracey inside. Gil didn't say a word to her during dinner or over the next couple of hours when they sat outside on the paved back porch in the warm evening air. She hoped he was accepting that she was going to be around. Then again, perhaps he was too upset to even want to argue with her. He spent most of the evening slumped in an old armchair on the patio, nursing a beer, which was replaced when empty by whoever was going into the kitchen at the time.

Around nine o'clock, she went in the house to use the bathroom. As she came out of the hallway into the living room, she noticed the photographs Tracey had been talking about. They were mounted on the walls, all in matching whitewashed wooden frames. She paused at a large one and studied it.

The photo was of the entire set of Cole kids, seated left-to-right, oldest-to-youngest. They were sitting sideways on some kind of carpet-covered bench in the photographer's studio, like a sled. The older, bigger kids had dropped their legs off the sides. The smaller kids had their legs tucked up around the kid in front of them.

On the far left was the oldest boy, looking nearly adult. On his right thigh he balanced an infant, the only child out of age order. In front of him were the two girls and three other boys of the Cole family. Addie squinted at the photo, looking back into Tracey's life as he had looked back into hers, trying to imagine what it must have been like.

She felt a presence and glanced over her shoulder to find Gil standing directly behind her. She crossed her arms automatically and turned towards him, her heart thumping.

Gil avoided eye contact, but pointed a finger around his beer can at the photo. "You know who all of them are?"

Addie shook her head. "I recognize James, Tracey, and Bobbie, but I don't know the others."

Gil took a step closer. "That's Joe Trey, the oldest one," he said. "Next is Bobbie and James, you know them. Then Jackie, you don't know him, he's been gone for years. Then Tracey, then Eleanor. The baby's Thomas."

"Thanks," Addie said.

Gil stared at the photo. "Francis was my only brother."

Addie ducked her head. "I'm sorry."

"Yeah." Gil took a swig of beer, turned abruptly, and stalked off towards the bathroom. Addie let her breath out slowly.

Tracey was waiting for her near the corner of the porch in the dark as she came out.

"You want to take a walk down along the bluff?"

Addie nodded and slipped after him around the corner of the house. They walked through the dark past Bobbie's property and followed the bluff away from the scatter of houses. The river cut close to the bank here, and there was a good thirty-foot drop to the water. Upriver of the bluff the Deuce made a sharp turn. Eventually it would cut through and take on a new course, isolating its old stream-bed into an oxbow lake.

161

At the top of the bank, Tracey sat down on a log positioned so they could look over the river. Addie sat down close beside him and waited.

"You remember when we went back to the cabin and we found that stand back in the woods on the tack line?" Tracey began.

"How could I forget? We got shot at, remember?"

"Yeah, I guess you wouldn't forget that. Well, the only person I ever knew who set stands like that was George Cole. I didn't know he was back around until I saw that stand. Then when he shot those cans off the boat, I knew for sure. He was the best shot I ever knew. That's why I wasn't as worried as you were. I figured he wouldn't shoot me."

Tracey told her about his meeting with George Cole and George's apparent surprise at finding out Francis was missing.

"It doesn't sound like you think he killed Francis, then. I have to admit it's almost too good. A known meth manufacturer shows up back in town, the guy that testified against him is murdered, then his rifle and some crank is found near the crime scene and there are the same drugs on the body as well. But your theory about Skeeter Doheny bothers me. He's just a kid, fourteen if I remember right. And from what I know, Francis was always nice to him, let him stay at his house and all."

"Yeah, but what was he doing in a brand-new boat that I think hit my car, then? And what was he doing at the bottom of the slough where I found Francis, giving me strange stories about why he was checking me out?"

"I don't know," Addie said, "Maybe it was an accident and Skeeter's too scared to admit to it. Maybe somebody else uses that boat, too, like the guy who actually bought it. And it wouldn't be strange for Skeeter to be in that area, would it?"

"No. He could have been setting jug lines for catfish or just cruising around in the boat, I guess. That area's on a direct route

162

between the Lejeunes' and the Dohenys' boat ramp, through Pine Slough."

"So you got any more theories?" Addie asked.

"You remember when we were sitting on that bench at Bobbie's camp? And Bobbie said that Gil hadn't been at her place Friday night?"

"Well, I don't actually remember too well," Addie laughed.

"Come on. You remembered that I said I gave Brenda a ride home in a car I didn't have the next day."

"Guess I wasn't paying attention, then." Addie did remember, but she wanted Tracey to tell her what he thought about what they had heard.

"Well, Gil dropped Brenda off at Duckhaven around seven. He left a couple hours later and told me he was going to see my sister. But Bobbie said he never showed up that night."

"So where do you think he was?"

"Well, I didn't know he'd done it, but George set me up with a river trip with a couple guys who work up at the adhesives plant last Sunday."

"And one of them was the guy named Van you told me about on the phone. And they have something to do with Gil?" Addie guessed.

"Sort of. They were drinking, you know, and with the heat and all, they started talking, like people do when they're wasted. They told me that they're part of some militia group. And they said they had a training camp at the Lejeunes' hunting camp. Lejeunes have a little place on the east bank. It's on the bend just above the pulp mill, below Goat Lake Slough. It's a little ratty place, but good enough to spend a night. So I was figuring, Gil might have run down river through Thief Lake and gone out to his camp Friday night. Might have been meeting these guys out there."

"That's one thing I was going to ask you about," Addie said. "Brenda told Buster that Gil was involved with some militia. If

163

George set you up with these guys, and they're also in the militia, and one of them is Van Bates, who bought Skeeter his boat, then all of them would be connected."

"Yeah, and I think they're using the Dohenys' boat ramp too. That's where I picked Van and this guy Howie up."

Addie frowned. "Isn't there some connection between George Cole and the Dohenys?"

"The upriver Coles are related to the Dohenys," Tracey confirmed. "George used to hang out at the boat ramp before he got busted, when there were a few more people living there. I bet he's known Skeeter since he was born."

"Hmm." Addie thought for a moment. "So do you think Ray is involved with these guys too?"

Tracey looked over at her quickly, but didn't answer.

"I got a little information that Ray might have had some crank lately, Tracey, so you don't have to worry about ratting on him," Addie said.

"Heck," Tracey said, "I didn't even know that until a couple days ago."

"Me neither, but when stuff like this happens people start making connections. Is there any way he's involved with this?"

"Oh, no. No way. But he did tell me he got some from Doug Raney a couple times, just a little bit, and Raney told him he got it from somebody named George. But George Cole told me he wasn't making it, he didn't want to risk being busted and he was being watched too closely."

Addie considered. "Maybe someone is trying to make it seem like George is making meth again, trying to set him up for this murder. I wonder what this militia is about?"

"I don't know. I think they work at the glue factory, the adhesives plant. You know Francis worked there, too, right?"

"Yeah, I remember you told me that before, when we were talking about who could have bought Skeeter's boat for him. What did he do?"

"Stocking and inventory, I think, part-time. I remember Van and Howie said he worked in the warehouse."

"What does the glue factory make? I mean, it makes glue, obviously, but what kind?"

"It's not glue exactly," Tracey grinned. "They make adhesives that stick particle board and plywood together. The plant used to belong to Roslyn, but they sold it off last year. The new owners brought in a bunch of new people. That's what Van said."

"Did Van or George tell you what the militia does or what their ideology is?"

"Nope," Tracey said. "Van said they're pretty laid back, that it's not real strict, it's mostly fun. I didn't really think anything about it at the time, you know, so I didn't mention it before."

Addie readjusted herself on the log. "It would've been good to know, because these groups are usually anti-government. But I know about them now. So, let's think about the people we know would've had an opportunity to kill Francis that night. George Cole, but you think that's unlikely. I have to admit, it would be stupid to kill someone with a gun with your initials on it and then purposely leave it where it's sure to be found. Brenda, if she went out with Francis after he went home. She did admit that she had a fight with him that night. That's why she had to get a ride with Gil. You and Brenda together, maybe." She put a hand up as Tracey began to protest.

"I'm just coming up with all the possible scenarios. Let's say you did want to get something going with Brenda. That would give you a motive to get rid of Francis, right? That's what some people are going to think. And you could have lied about when the car went in the lake if you and Brenda were in it together. You could have killed Francis and then been driving out of there with the gun and the rest of the drugs and wrecked the car then."

"I swear to God," Tracey said, "I was not after Brenda. I don't even like her. I sure as shit wouldn't have killed somebody over her. Besides, we would have stopped at Francis' house in that case, right? Where else would we have gone? So we wouldn't be leaving that area together."

"Okay," Addie said. "Let's say those aren't very reasonable theories. So, next on the list is Skeeter, and there's some evidence his boat was out and about that night. And he could have known about your car from Brenda, and he could have had George's gun, conceivably. But he is also only fourteen and on the small side, and that moves him down on the suspect list at least a little. Besides, he doesn't seem to have any motive. So, what about Gil?"

"Gil wouldn't have killed Francis. They're half-brothers, but they were always really close. They stayed here together when the rest of their kin moved away ten years ago or so."

Addie didn't think Gil had killed Francis either, given his reaction, but she persisted in order to work through every possibility in her mind. "Yeah, but you don't know where he was that night, and nobody else does either. Is there any way Gil could have been driving Skeeter's boat?"

"Sure," Tracey said. "Skeeter lives with Brenda and Francis about half the time. I don't know if you've ever been back there, but Gil's house and Francis' house are on the same lot right on Thief Creek, with a boat ramp in between them. If Skeeter's boat was there and Gil wanted to use it, he'd of just used it. But he has his own boat, and he doesn't have any reason to kill his own brother."

"Then let's look at the drugs angle. If Francis actually was into meth again, he might have had a connection with this guy Raney, who is apparently dealing it."

"No," Tracey said. "First of all, there hasn't been any going around, according to Ray. And Doug Raney's a friend of Francis, all

166

right, but I can't see him getting into a meth deal with him after what happened last time. The Raneys run a butcher shop in Buenavista, and I bet Francis was fencing his venison through there. But I don't think he'd be fencing meth out of there, too. That would be pretty stupid."

"He wasn't too worried about the law if he was poaching on a regular basis," Addie said, thinking about Buster's description of Francis as a scammer and opportunist.

"That's different," Tracey said. "You're probably not going to go to jail for it, and it doesn't do anybody any harm. It's just food. Not that I agree he should've been doing it. It screws the rest of us when folks hunt out of season. We don't get a chance at the biggest deer and you take the does before they have a chance to have babies. And most of us don't want the Preserve cracking down on hunting permits either. But still, poaching a deer every once in a while is a lot different than making crank."

"Yeah, I have to agree with you there." Addie rubbed her neck. "You remember overhearing Bobbie and Gil arguing that night when we were out at the camp, down by the water? Just before Gil left?"

"Yeah, Bobbie didn't want him storing stuff up here anymore."

"What did he say he wanted to store? It was something of Francis', wasn't it?"

"Yeah. He said it came from their other hunting camp, which I guess is out Widow Slough somewhere."

"I wish I knew what it was," Addie said. "It probably doesn't mean anything, but it was something of Francis'."

"I guess we could ask Gil. Or better yet, I don't ask Gil, I just go in Bobbie's spare room and look at it."

"Be careful. Gil wouldn't be happy with you pawing through his stuff, I'll bet. But I admit, I am curious. Maybe you can do it later tonight." She subsided into silence, listening to the insect-heavy night and the muffled sounds from the houses behind them.

After a minute, Tracey glanced over at her. "So I guess you think I'm a total jerk for not telling anybody about that car for two weeks."

"I don't think you're a jerk. Sometimes you make one bad decision and these things just take on a life of their own."

"Yeah, I'm not known for making good decisions."

"I'm insulted," Addie said. "You agreed to take me out to that bear-hunter's camp and you fixed my car for me. And you promised to keep quiet about my brother. Were those bad decisions?"

"No, I guess not."

Tracey fell silent. The moon filtered into the clearing through the pines, tall and heavily-branched trees not logged for many years. Addie looked over at him. He was breaking a small stick into multiple pieces and tossing the pieces on the ground between his feet. She could hear the snap as the twig fractured.

"Are you doing okay?" she asked, using the phrase he frequently used himself.

Tracey nodded and looked out at the river.

"Anything else on your mind?"

"Yeah," he said hesitantly. "Did you go out with Virg?"

Addie crossed her arms defensively. "No. Not yet."

"But he asked you."

"Well...he asked."

"Are you going to go?"

"I said I would. How'd you figure that out?"

"Saw your home phone number on that piece of cardboard in Virg's truck."

"Oh."

"You like him?"

"I barely know him. I don't know that we have a lot in common."

"He's a lot older than you."

"I know."

They were silent again for a minute. Tracey moved a little closer on the log and slid his arm around her. She leaned up against him and wrapped her arms around his waist. Tracey put his hand gently on the side of her face and kissed her.

The night was warm and the moonlight flickered and reflected off the river through the tree trunks. Tracey slid down off the log onto the sand and pulled her down next to him. For the moment, Addie forgot about the feeling of isolation the old photographs had provoked earlier that evening. She allowed herself to imagine that she could be a part of Tracey's world: the casual, unhurried, intermingling of families and friends with generations of history behind them.

She squirmed a little. Tracey was lying partially on top of her, supporting her neck with one forearm.

"I'm not squishing you, am I?" he asked, raising himself a bit on his elbows.

"No," Addie said, "but I'm getting eaten alive by mosquitoes. I need to go inside somewhere."

"Okay," Tracey said. "Do you want to go back to Bobbie's house?"

"Are you staying there tonight?"

"Wasn't planning on it," Tracey replied.

"Where else could we go?"

Tracey considered. "We could go out to the camp. There's no one there tonight, I don't think. But we'll have to ditch your car and take my four-wheeler, 'cause that car won't make it down that road."

"I don't really want to leave my car parked outside Bobbie's."

Tracey considered. "We could go to your place."

Addie nodded in the dark. They headed back towards her newly-tuned car and its trunk full of photographs, tripping now and again over stray sticks and rocks in the dark.

Chapter Fourteen

Addie slept fitfully that night, unused to the presence of another person in her bed. Finally she got up, wrapped a bathrobe around her, and wandered out to the living room. She quietly opened the sliding glass door a crack and slipped out onto the back porch, feeling the cool of the flagstone under her bare feet.

She felt, as she'd felt before when she was with Tracey, younger than she was: as if she could abdicate her adult life and return to her teenage years, if only temporarily. She knew she felt that way because Tracey still lived as though he was a teenager, and she realized that on some level she resented the constraints being a law enforcement officer placed upon her. She craved his freedom, not working shifts or schedules, unhampered by any concern about what his family or friends would think about him, secure that they'd be there and his life would continue substantially the same, no matter what.

But on the other hand, she wasn't willing to jeopardize what she'd sacrificed to get. Her relationship with Tracey was questionable at best, when viewed from the standpoint that she, as an officer, was subject to more scrutiny of her personal life than the average person. And there was more at stake than simply her career. She couldn't afford to have people examining her past in too much detail. She knew she needed to choose her friends carefully. Ike was right about that, and despite her growing feelings for Tracey, if he was involved in any of the crimes he appeared to be involved in, she wouldn't be able to maintain a relationship with him.

And again, she was unsure of Tracey's own motives. It almost seemed as though he'd rushed to make his move because of competition with his uncle, although at the camp she'd felt his desire before she had ever met Virg Radner. Or maybe he wanted to regain some measure of control over their relationship after the embarrassment of the situation with the car.

She gazed up through the limbs of the pines at bright scattered clouds moving quickly across the face of the moon. Tracey seemed sincere, and she wished she could allow herself to take him at face value. She wanted to keep her thoughts in the moment and to ignore the constant second-guessing of her own actions, both in relation to Tracey and in relation to her own choices.

Her thoughts turned to her brother and her memory to the times she had spent as a child roaming in the silence and sunlight of the red-rock canyons near their home. She remembered the first time as clearly as if it had just happened. She had been nine, Logan thirteen, and she had begged to be allowed to go with her father and brothers on one of the rare occasions when her father had the time to take them anywhere. On those occasions they would drive into the canyons to the northwest and hunt for arrowheads. Her brothers had not wanted her along, but she was no help in the kitchen, only underfoot, so her mother had requested that her father take her and he had acquiesced.

In the heat of the afternoon they wandered along a sandy bench above a creek, scanning the gravelly outflow from a side canyon. She was silent, isolated from the boys and her father. She roamed idly, not as interested in the hunt as in being away from the farm. But then she saw it, peeking out of the gravel. The shape, the texture, was all wrong for a cobblestone. She bent and picked it up: a beautiful, complete arrowhead, gray-black and an inch long.

Suddenly Blake was there. He snatched it from her hand and ran to his father. "Dad, Dad, see what I found!"

Addie stood silent and still. She had learned not to contradict Blake. The retribution would be severe. But her eyes met Logan's, and she knew he had seen what happened. And she knew, from the look in his eyes, that he was thinking, not just accepting. He was looking at her as a person, as one who could suffer a wrong.

Logan didn't contradict Blake or say a thing to Addie. But that was the beginning.

Addie had a knack for finding not only arrowheads, but also other artifacts. She abandoned searching for arrowheads soon and preferred to pick up pottery shards, in which her brothers were not interested. Later, Logan became interested in them, or at least in the idea that the existence of shards pointed to the possibility of the existence of entire pots in the area.

By the time Logan was sixteen, when the photograph of him with his first car had been taken, he had discovered that the old pottery could be sold for a great deal more money than any arrowhead. There were those in the area who laundered illegally-collected Indian artifacts, created provenance for them so that they appeared to have been collected legally, and jacked up the price when they passed them on to collectors. It wasn't hard for Logan to get in touch with them, and he began to build a reputation as a supplier, someone who could get what people wanted, and began to learn the skills needed to pass the pottery off without being caught.

He was driven by a combination of the thrill of the hunt, a genuine, if misplaced, appreciation for the art of the pieces he collected, and a desire to make money in a way that was as disconnected from the normal and average as it was connected to the land in which he lived. Addie had shared some of that, but the desire to get away from the place where she'd spent a childhood with very little joy overwhelmed any connection to the area and the farm.

Addie turned and stepped back through the glass doors. She was not going to resolve a lifetime of conflict in one night. She was instead going to return to bed and enjoy the time she was spending with Tracey, wherever it might lead. In the morning she'd take the new information she'd learned from him the evening before and try to put it towards exonerating him. If accomplished, that would, at least, solve one of her problems.

173

The next morning Addie got up and made a pot of coffee. While she waited for Tracey to get out of the shower, she called Buster Brighton.

Buster told her the dental records from Francis Lejeune confirmed his identity. In addition, ballistics reported that the rifling inside the gun barrel and the bullet that killed Francis were consistent, although two weeks of rust made the comparison less than positive. And tests showed a close match between the chemical composition of the drugs they got out of the car, the drugs found on Doug Raney, and the ones found at the crime scene.

"Well, this isn't anything we didn't expect," Addie said.

"No," Buster said. "Brenda called this morning. She said she remembered that one of the guys that's been hanging around recently with Francis is named Jesse. Another guy she remembered as either Silas Casey or Casey Silas, and one she thinks is named Van. We sent someone over to get those beer bottles last night, and the latent print tech picked up some partial fingerprints and some whole ones. We submitted them to AFIS, that's the Automated Fingerprint Identification System..."

"I know what AFIS is," Addie interrupted impatiently.

"Yeah, sorry, well, some of them came back to Francis, some of them came back no match so far."

"Okay," Addie said. "Let me know if anything else develops, would you?"

She was sitting on the couch with her notes spread out on the coffee table when Tracey came out, with his hair wet and tousled, wearing only his jeans. Addie observed him as he walked through into the kitchen. He was slender, and his jeans sat well down on his hips. He was not tall, perhaps five-eight, and his hair needed a cut. But there was something appealing about him. His smile was frequent and un-self-conscious, and he was easy to talk to. He functioned, she realized, almost entirely on charisma; that was what

174

made him so popular out at the camp, and probably why his relatives continued to happily support him.

He poured himself a cup of coffee, then sat down on the couch next to her and looked at the piles of paper.

"Trying to figure things out?"

Addie nodded and sipped from her own mug. "Buster says the drugs in your car and the ones with Francis are a close match."

"Which means that whoever dumped the drugs in the Dodge got them from the same place as the ones that were found with Francis," Tracey said carefully.

"Right," Addie said. "We can't come to much more of a conclusion than that. We need to figure out where the meth is coming from."

"Maybe Doug Raney will tell you," Tracey said.

"Maybe, but I doubt it," Addie said. "And anyway, we know someone named George has been implicated by at least one person."

"Well, Doug Raney would know if he bought the stuff from George Cole. He's lived here all his life and so has George. I know they know each other. It must have been someone else. Besides, George told me he wasn't making crank anymore. He said he didn't want to do anything to draw attention to himself. He even complained about how he used to dump the chemicals in the water, and now he has to eat what comes out of the river. It just sounded like he was telling the truth to me."

"Do you think it's possible George might have shown these guys in the militia how to manufacture it? Even if he's not directly involved in it himself?"

"Maybe, but if they're making it, they're selling it somewhere else," Tracey said, "because there hasn't been enough around here to get rich off. Not enough to account for buying four boats and motors, anyway."

"True enough," Addie said. She considered. "Well, what we do know is that Brenda told Buster that several guys have been hanging around with Francis recently. If these guys know each other through the adhesives plant, they could all be part of this militia group, which means they have an association with George, which might give them access to a rifle belonging to him. They'd have access to the boat Skeeter Doheny has been using as well, either through George or through Gil and Francis. And they'd be familiar enough with the area to be able to get out without a guide, probably by boat."

"But there has to be some reason for them to have killed Francis," Tracey said.

"How afraid of George do you think Francis was? Given that he testified against him, I'd think Francis might be pretty worried about George being around again."

"Yeah, I'd think so too, but so what?"

"Well, if Francis found out George was involved with people who were making crank again, would he threaten to tell the cops in order to get rid of George? That would give someone a motive to kill him."

"That makes about the most sense of anything I've heard yet," Tracey said, nodding. "And then they set up George so he'd take the fall for the murder, to save themselves. They planted the crank on Francis and put some of the same stuff in my car, which they would've found by accident on the way back down to the Lejeunes' camp, and then made sure somebody heard George was dealing again. And they threw the rifle in there for good measure."

"But both George and Gil are still hanging around with this militia, right? It doesn't seem like either of them could know what's going on if that's what really happened. Otherwise, both of them would be pretty upset, I'd imagine, George because he's being set up, and Gil because they killed his brother. I wonder how much Gil really does know about this group?" Addie mused.

Tracey grinned. "I suppose you can always go ask him, now that you two are getting on so well. I mean, he didn't bug you at all at Bobbie's last night." He drained his coffee mug and stretched. "What do you want to do today? You don't have to work, do you? You want to go down to the beach at High Island or something like that?"

"Maybe," Addie agreed, "but what I want to do first is see what I can find out about this adhesives plant that these guys all seem to work for. Would you pour me another cup of coffee, please?" She handed him her mug and seated herself in front of her computer, which she had snapped into its docking station in order to use the full-size keyboard and screen she preferred.

Once on-line, she did an Internet search for the Broadbase Adhesives Plant and found a write-up on an industry website. Roslyn, the company that owned the pulp mill, particleboard factory, and lumber mill, had sold it off just eight months earlier. After a brief shutdown and an upgrade to some of its machinery, it had been re-opened by the new owners.

The factory employed fifty people and was separated into two divisions. One division manufactured anhydrous ammonia; an innovation by the new owners was a cost-sharing agreement to operate that division in cooperation with a nearby fertilizer plant. The manufacturing facility was located on Broadbase property, but the fertilizer plant provided both capital and personnel. Much of the anhydrous ammonia was bottled on-site and trucked directly to the fertilizer plant.

The second division of the adhesives plant then combined carbon dioxide, a by-product of the ammonia manufacturing process, with the ammonia to manufacture urea. They also made formaldehyde and phenol on-site. They used those chemicals to formulate formaldehyde-based wood adhesives and resins for lumber laminating. Some of the urea and formaldehyde was also sold to the fertilizer-manufacturing plant.

Addie frowned. Most of that meant nothing to her. She continued searching. The web page had a link to an EPA site that

177

showed formaldehyde and ammonia off-gassing records and listed on-site chemicals. Addie had little idea of what most of the chemicals were, but she did recognize toluene as a solvent that could be used in certain methamphetamine manufacturing processes, and she remembered that anhydrous ammonia could be used for the same purpose.

The purchaser of the plant was Sora Industries, a corporation based in New York with a picture of a wading bird as its logo. Addie located a page describing the corporation. Interestingly, other than the adhesives plant, its holdings were wind-farms and fuel-cell manufacturing companies.

Addie scanned the names of the holdings. Several of them rang a bell. A quick check showed that they were listed on the *AFTERThought* website as environmentally friendly businesses.

The major shareholder of Sora Industries was a man named Adrian Sora. There was a photo of him on the page, a middle-aged, respectable-looking man with watery, pale-blue eyes.

Tracey brought her the fresh cup of coffee and put the mug on the computer desk next to the keyboard. Addie was sitting on a wooden dining-room chair, and Tracey swung one leg over the back and slid down between her and the chair back. Addie slid forward a little to accommodate him, and Tracey put his arms around her waist and rested his chin on her shoulder, looking at the computer screen. Addie could feel his wet hair on her neck.

"Huh," he said, pointing to the picture of Adrian Sora on the screen. "That guy looks like Adrian."

"That is Adrian, Adrian Sora, the owner of the adhesives plant," Addie said. "Do you know him?"

"Yeah, he's a new friend of my grandpa," Tracey said. "I met him and another guy at the Visitor Center one day. My grandpa said Adrian was going to look into his book idea. He knows publishers in New York."

Addie turned her head to look at him over her shoulder. "Well, that's kind of interesting. This does say he lives in New York. I guess he could have been visiting his new adhesives plant. But I'm kind of interested in how this whole crew of guys, who all happen to be part of the same militia, all got hired at his plant at once. It almost sounds like someone in management at the plant has some involvement with this militia and got them all hired as a group."

Tracey grinned. "Adrian isn't exactly the militia type, if you ask me. He was wearing one of those canvas hats with a bunch of fishing flies stuck in it. He looked like somebody's grandpa."

"Who was the other guy with Adrian?"

"Andrew. I think he's Adrian's son."

Addie clicked back to the Broadbase Adhesives Plant page. The General Manager was listed as Andrew Sora.

"Sora Industries owns wind farms and fuel cell companies," she told Tracey. "That doesn't really fit with a militia group. The only connection I'm seeing is the possibility that the militia is using the adhesives plant to supply them with anhydrous ammonia for methamphetamine production. But I can't imagine why Sora Industries would want to be messed up with a meth manufacturing ring."

"And it still doesn't answer what happened to Francis."

"Well," Addie said, "I guess there are a couple possibilities. One, a member of the militia killed him because he threatened to expose their drug business, which may or may not be connected with the adhesives plant. Two, maybe Francis found out something else about this group, and they tried to make his death look drug-involved to cover up the real reason they had to get rid of him."

"But what would he have found out about this group? I mean, other than that it was a militia, which I guess isn't illegal, or making meth, which is your first theory."

"No, simply organizing as a militia wouldn't be illegal." Addie crossed her arms, leaned back against Tracey, and contemplated for a minute. Her eye fell on the *AFTERThought* card on the computer desk.

"What if Francis figured out that they aren't really a militia," she said slowly. "They may be organized like a militia, and even behave somewhat like a militia, but what if they aren't one, at least not the way we usually think of one? We think of militias as being extreme anti-government or extreme anti-establishment, but not as being extreme environmentalists."

Tracey raised his eyebrows.

"Look, I know that somebody associated with this group *AFTERThought* must be around this area," Addie said, showing him the card. "This business card was left on my porch. I looked this group up, and it's connected to cells of people around the country who commit crimes in the name of environmental protection."

When Tracey still looked puzzled, Addie brought up the *AFTERThought* website and showed him some of the articles and pictures.

"The founder of this group, Michael Gerschoff, was based out of New York. It's a big city, I know. It might not mean anything. But Adrian and Andrew Sora are also from New York, right? And look at Sora's other holdings, besides the adhesives plant: wind farms and fuel cell companies. Several of those companies are listed here on the *AFTERThought* website. But then Sora buys an adhesives plant in southeast Texas, of all places, and hires a bunch of people who call themselves a militia to work at the plant. So, what if they're not a militia, but a cell of extreme environmental activists? What if the militia thing is just a front?"

"But what has any of this got to do with Francis at all? Other than the fact that he worked there?" Tracey asked.

"I'm not sure," Addie sighed. "Maybe I'm completely wrong and I'm reading something into this whole series of coincidences that isn't there. But let's say I'm right: let's say these folks are here to commit some kind of crime that'll focus attention on an environmental problem. What might their target be?"

"Easy," said Tracey, "or maybe not so easy because there are so many of them. Could be the adhesives plant itself, I guess, or the fertilizer plant, or Ely Dam."

"Could be Roslyn Industries," Addie put in. "They seem to be a focus of attention on the website."

"Then the most logical target would be the pulp mill," Tracey continued. "It's run by Roslyn, so that would fit in, and it's also right near the Lejeunes' camp where these guys are supposedly set up."

Addie nodded. "That makes the most sense, I think."

"So what do we do now?" Tracey asked.

"Well, the problem is, all this is just conjecture right now. We don't have any proof."

"You want to go out and look at that militia camp, or whatever it is? I can show you where it is."

"Well, yeah, I do. But it would probably be a good idea to do it while I'm on duty and have a couple of other people with me. Especially if it turns out that there is a meth lab out there. It seems likely that if they are making it, they'd be making it in a nice isolated spot like that camp."

"Yeah, but remember they're hanging around the Dohenys' boat ramp, too. There are a bunch of abandoned houses up there on Marker Slough they could be using. They could just run an extension cord from the big house and get electricity. It would be a lot harder to cook anything at the Lejeunes' camp if they needed electricity. And, if George is doing it, or showing them how to do it, he'd probably be using the Dohenys', not the Lejeunes'."

Addie considered. "What do you think about the possibility of people hanging around out at the Lejeunes' camp today?"

Tracey shook his head. "Van said there were only about ten people involved in this. And he said they all have regular jobs and

181

most of them live in Aynesworth, they just get together on weekends and evenings."

"So there's probably no one out there at this time? On a Monday?"

"I wouldn't think so."

"Is there any way we could see what's going on at this camp without going onto the property itself?"

"There's a pipeline clearance that runs through the Preserve right near it. We could walk along that and then cut down to the river. The Preserve boundary runs right along the side of the Lejeunes' property out there."

Addie hesitated. "Well, let me call Ike and tell him where we're going to be. Just in case."

She picked up the phone and called the office. She told Ike she was going to be checking out the Lejeunes' camp, but she didn't tell him her suspicions regarding *AFTERThought*. She knew it sounded far-fetched, and it would take too much time to explain how she'd reached all her conclusions. She asked Ike to try and run the names Delevan Bates and Silas Casey or Casey Silas through dispatch, and if he couldn't get a match in Texas to try northwestern states like Oregon, Idaho and Washington, based on the memory of the boat-seller in Aynesworth.

Ike called her back forty-five minutes later.

"No luck on anybody named Delevan Bates in any state I've tried," he told her. "No luck on Silas Casey, either, unless you're looking for dead guys."

"How dead? Could it be an assumed identity?" Addie asked, perking up.

Ike laughed. "Real dead. Before social security numbers, even. You know I'm a Civil War buff. Silas Casey was a Union general. He died in New York in 1882. I'd say it was just a coincidence that this guy has the same name. Maybe he's even a descendant. Except for one thing."

182

"What's that?"

"Delevan Bates was a Union general, too. I guess he was white from his photo, but he commanded an all-black regiment and was wounded in action twice. Unless these guys know each other from some society for descendants of Civil War generals, those are both pseudonyms. You're not planning on contacting these guys today, are you?" Ike asked. "I don't like this. You shouldn't be going out there on your own."

"I'm not going to contact anybody today," Addie said. "Tracey is just going to show me where this camp is, we're going to walk down there on Preserve property and take a look, see what we can see, and then leave. I don't want to spend my whole day off working."

"Oh, great," Ike said. "I really feel a lot better knowing you're going out there with the main suspect in a murder investigation."

"I wouldn't be going out there with him if I thought he was the main suspect," Addie said, lowering her voice so Tracey wouldn't hear. "There's a lot of things that don't add up in that direction. Going out to this camp may help me come up with some concrete evidence. Don't tell me you don't want to know who the real criminal is. I know you; you're a good cop. You don't want to solve a case by pinning it on the first guy you see. I know you'd rather be sure we have the right person."

There was silence on the phone line for a long moment. "File for overtime," Ike said. "And be careful. Take your radio."

"I'll go armed," Addie said. "If I see anything important, I'll call you tonight or tomorrow."

"And I suppose if you don't call, don't bother you," Ike said. "Because you'll be busy."

Addie rolled her eyes. "See you Wednesday," she said.

She hung up the phone quietly and looked over at Tracey. He was involved in playing a four-wheel-driving game that she'd started

183

for him on her computer. She walked over and picked up the *AFTERThought* card again. Besides the apparent connection between the group and the adhesives plant, there was, of course, the tentative connection between the group and her own brother. That was a part of the puzzle she wasn't sure she wanted to reveal, even to Tracey, if, indeed, she could even explain it.

"We never did get a chance to look at whatever Gil stored at Bobbie's place," she said.

"No," Tracey said, "I kind of forgot about that last night. You think that has something to do with all of this?"

Addie shrugged. "I don't know. Maybe we can find out more about that later."

"Sure," Tracey said. "We can drop by Bobbie's this evening. Bobbie likes you. She thinks what you do is pretty cool. You and her could get to be friends. And I could get in that bedroom and take a look at Gil's stuff."

Addie went to the bedroom and strung some gear onto a leather belt, choosing the same equipment she'd taken with her during her trip to the bear-hunter's camp. She started up her car, running better now that Tracey had tuned it, and they headed out through Buenavista and through the rice paddies and farmland to the north. Tracey directed Addie out the farm road that branched off the main highway by the Preserve's Visitor Center. They followed it east across the river bridge above the pulp mill, then down a dirt road to their left.

"This must be pretty close to Roslyn's new timber sale," Addie noted.

"Yeah, it's going to be just east of here, I think, out along the East Bank," Tracey said.

The dirt road they were following intersected a pipeline clearance, a wide cleared strip through the forest beneath which a buried gas or oil pipeline ran. Addie parked there. She managed to pull the car far enough off the road that it was hidden in the heavy

184

brush that was taking advantage of the extra sunlight in the clearance. They had planned to walk along the pipeline and then strike off through the woods, but a side road, apparently newly-cleared, led towards the Lejeunes' camp. Instead of crashing through the brush along the pipeline following the Preserve's boundary, they decided to use the road.

"Last time I was here, this was just a four-wheeler track," Tracey said. "But it's been a few years."

As they approached the river they slowed down, keeping an ear out for any vehicles. Tracey suggested they walk back in the woods now, off the roadway. The Preserve boundary, marked with paint on the trees, ran close to the road. Finally, they came to the camp itself.

"Wow," Addie whispered, standing off behind a tree. "I thought you said it was ratty."

"Used to be," Tracey said. "You can't see it from down on the river, so I didn't realize they'd done all this."

The camp now consisted of three buildings, each about twelve by twenty, with plywood sides, real windows, and small solar panels near them on braces on the ground, in a large cleared area. There was even a satellite dish on top of one building. Two new-looking Polaris four-wheelers were parked side-by-side. There was a large campfire ring outside one of the buildings with logs set out around it as seats.

They walked down to the edge of the river and followed the bank. Moored in a small slough to the north, they found an old, lightweight aluminum jon-boat, a new fourteen-footer, and a bigger utility boat.

"Sea Ark," Tracey said, pointing to the newest one. "One of them could be the one I saw George using."

There were no cars or full-sized vehicles parked at the camp. It seemed quiet and deserted.

185

"I don't think there's anybody here," Tracey said. They cautiously walked into the camp itself. Tracey inspected the quads. "There's thousands of dollars' worth of stuff sitting out here."

"Tens of thousands," Addie said. "They're definitely getting a bunch of money somewhere. I wish I could get in one of those buildings."

"I doubt there's locks on them," Tracey said helpfully.

"No, I don't mean that," Addie said. "I may not be on duty, but I'm still acting as a law enforcement officer. I'd need a search warrant to enter any of these. Even if the doors don't lock."

"Oh." Tracey cupped his hands to the sides of his face and looked through one of the windows. "Lots of furniture in there," he said. "Bunk beds, chairs, desk, table." He moved to the next one. "This one too. Like a little house." He walked towards the third one, which sat back away from the river at an angle along the road, and cupped his hands on the window. "Looks like a meeting room. A couple of laptops."

Addie joined him and squinted to see through the glass. There was a large table with folding chairs in half the room, and several lightweight desks and file cabinets. Paperwork, including maps, were scattered around on the tabletops. There was also a set of bunk beds along one wall, as if the cabin was used for sleeping quarters as well as a planning or meeting room. Addie brought her gaze up and found parallel sets of hooks along the wall next to the bunk. Gun racks, she thought.

Back behind the conference-room cabin was a battered shed which had once been painted red. It had glass windows and a tiny front stoop.

"That's the original building that was out here, the one I remember," Tracey said. "Last time I was here, it was the only building."

Addie approached the shed and tried to peer in through the window nearest to the river. "Looks like they're just using it for

186

storage, now. There are a few bags and cans and stuff, but I can't read the labels on them through this filthy window."

"Does it look like a meth lab?" Tracey wondered.

"I don't see anything that would suggest a meth lab. Some of the chemicals in those cans could be used for manufacture, but I don't know that for sure, because I don't know what they are. No glassware or cold tablets or anything else I've been taught to look for at labs."

She shook her head and took a last look around the camp. "Well, I guess that's enough. I don't really see anything illegal. They're not encroaching on Preserve property."

They began walking out down the road, more relaxed now that they knew there was no one at the camp. Addie glanced back over her shoulder, trying to figure out how everything fit together.

"Shit," Tracey said suddenly, with enough feeling that Addie snapped her head back around. A man she had never seen was standing fifty feet ahead of them in the road, a rifle in one hand, the barrel resting in the palm of his other hand.

"George Cole," Tracey said.

Chapter Fifteen

George grinned, but otherwise stood stock-still. Addie cautiously hooked her thumb under the hem of her T-shirt in the back and began to slowly pull it up to where she could draw her pistol if she needed to. Tracey might trust George, but she knew him only as a meth manufacturer who took pot-shots at her boat in the woods, and she wasn't at all sure how he'd feel about her.

"Well, Trace, I been expecting to see you out here, but I didn't expect you to bring your warden girlfriend," George said.

"I heard some rumors that the Lejeunes' were expanding their camp out here," Addie said quickly. "I wanted to make sure they weren't encroaching on the Preserve. Our boundary is right over there. But I don't see any problem here. We were just leaving."

"That right?" George cradled the rifle in the crook of one arm and pulled a cigarette pack from his shirt pocket with the other hand. He shook the pack until a cigarette popped up, pulled it out with his teeth, then put the pack away. Addie felt her adrenalin level rise. It was a Camels' cigarette pack.

"You know this is private property," George stated.

"I know," Addie said, "but it was too hard to walk through the woods, so we walked along the road. Anyway, it's not posted."

"Besides, I got invited out here," Tracey said. "Van told me to stop by any time."

George eyed Tracey from under his brows as he lit the cigarette. Then he switched his gaze back to Addie. "Uh-huh. You armed?"

"Maybe," Addie answered, stepping back with one foot into a balanced stance.

George grinned at her. "Don't worry. I was just curious. Tracey here told me I took a few shots too close to a fed. Said you coulda shot me back. I sure appreciate you not doing that."

"I don't go around shooting into the woods at targets I can't see," Addie said pointedly.

"So I guess you know that's my stand out there, now," George said casually. "I guess Tracey told you that. I wasn't sure where the Preserve boundary is over there. Is that what you came out here for, to bust me for that?"

"No," Addie said, "you're right; the boundary's not well marked over on the East Bank. I'm not even sure myself whether that stand's on our property. I don't think it is. It's probably on private property, maybe Roslyn."

George threw his cigarette down suddenly, ground it out in the mud, then picked up the butt and put it back in his shirt pocket. When he spoke, his tone had changed from off-hand to abrupt.

"So what are you doing out here, then? Because you're not looking at the boundary, walking around peeking in through the windows and grubbing over those four-wheelers and talking about meth labs," he said.

He must have been watching them for some time, Addie realized, and from close enough to overhear their conversation. She wished she'd been more observant, but George was obviously good at sneaking silently through the woods.

"If you're not out here looking to bust me for that stand, then you came by hoping there'd be no one here at all so you could poke around," George continued. "Otherwise you would've come in the evening when you knew people were going to be here, or on the weekend. So don't give me this looking-at-the-boundary shit."

"Hey," Tracey interjected. "She's with me, remember?"

George said nothing.

"We were looking at the boundary, like she said," Tracey continued, "but we were thinking we might run into you, too. We need to talk to you about a couple things, but we wanted to make sure nobody else was around to hear. That's why we were poking around. We were just waiting to see if you'd show up."

189

George raised his eyebrows. "Didn't sound like you were looking for me, the way she told me you were just leaving."

"How would she know who you are? She's never seen you before."

"Okay," George said, looking straight into Addie's eyes. "I'm George Cole. Now you know. So what did you want to talk to me about?"

"Didn't you hear what happened to Francis?" Tracey asked.

"I heard Francis is dead, yeah," George said slowly. "I heard you found his body back up some slough off Thief Creek. Skeeter told me about it yesterday. Gil told him somebody shot him."

"Somebody?" Tracey asked. "Nobody told you the rest of it?"

"Rest of it what?"

"There's a lot more to it. A lot more. It's gonna take some telling, and it involves you and me and guns and drugs and all sorts of shit." Tracey looked around. "You sure there's nobody else out here?"

"Of course," George sneered.

"Well, good. It's too damn hot out here. Let's go sit in the shade somewhere. You got any cold drinks?"

"In that cabin," George nodded towards the cabin closest to the river. "There's a cooler inside with some Coke."

Addie turned reluctantly and followed Tracey to the cabin. He pushed open the door and she followed him in. She did want to see what was inside, but she didn't like the idea of being confined and possibly trapped.

Tracey slid an ice chest out from under a plywood-topped table near a window and fished three sodas out of the mostly-melted ice. He pulled up a chair for Addie and one for himself, popped the top on Addie's soda for her, and put one for George on the table. George sat down next to the door between them and the exit. Addie felt her anxiety level go up another notch. She sat down and sipped her soda nervously.

George leaned back in his chair, balancing on the back legs with his back against the wall. He laid his rifle across his lap, his right hand gently resting on it, forefinger lying along the trigger guard. Addie guessed it had been no mistake he'd admitted shooting at the cans on the boat. He was subtly letting her know what a good shot he was. And she knew better than to try to outdraw a drawn weapon. He was smart enough to have taken control of them without laying a hand upon them.

"Where the heck were you when we came in?" she asked, hoping to put him more at ease.

George grinned. "I set up a tree stand just off the road and I use it as kind of a guard post. People don't look up above eye level most of the time, and if you keep still people can look right at you and not see you. You folks walked right by me. I climbed on down and followed you in to see what you were doing."

"So that's what you do out here? You check out anybody who comes in to the camp?"

"Yeah, there's too much stuff here that could get ripped off if the word got out it was sitting around unguarded. Van pays me to act as a guard when nobody else is here."

"I'm kind of surprised you'd be out here at all," Tracey said. "I'd of figured Francis would stay away from you. Thought he might be real nervous about you being back around."

George shrugged. "Francis doesn't come out here much. He plays landlord, shows up and tells Van what else he wants in order for them to keep using the camp, Van agrees, and he goes away. Then Van gets him some of what he wants, and things are good for a while."

"Looks like Francis is getting a good deal," Addie said. "These guys must have some money."

"Sure they do," George said. "Don't ask me where they're getting it from, though. They don't tell me and I don't ask."

George took a swig from his soda. "Besides, I don't bear Francis any grudge. Not much, anyway. He played his cards better than I did, that's all. And he's the one that told Van about me, that I might be available to help out around here. I've got a good thing going here, and that's due to Francis. I'm sorry he's dead, no matter what some folks might say. Him and me were friends once. We made a stupid mistake and things got screwed up, but that don't change what came before."

George looked down for a moment, as if remembering. Addie felt an odd jolt, as if he was echoing her own thoughts of the night before. And despite the Camels, if he was lying, he was doing a good job of it, she thought. She noticed that he referred to Francis in the present tense, as if he was still alive, which would be less likely if he had actually killed Francis and seen him dead.

Tracey put his soda down and leaned forward. "You said Gil told Skeeter somebody shot Francis?"

"That's right," George said. "Skeeter said they'd all been figuring Francis was staying up in Aynesworth with some friends because him and Brenda had a fight. But I guess now Gil thinks Doug Raney lost his temper and popped Francis, maybe over some deal gone bad or maybe Francis was hitting on Doug's sister."

"Does that theory make any sense?" Addie asked.

"Not much," George admitted. "I don't know if Gil is too busted up to think straight, but the only deal Francis and Raney were in together was that Raney fenced a few pounds of venison down at his family's butcher shop in Buenavista when Francis got a deer. Wouldn't be nothing to kill someone over. And Francis sold his jewelry out of The Jewelry Bug, that's Doug's sister Bug's shop, but I never heard Francis was putting the moves on Bug. Or that Doug would've been pissed off if he had."

192

Addie considered that. Raney had been in possession of meth that matched the drugs on Francis, although there was still the issue of the rifle.

"I've been hearing a couple other names thrown around, myself," Tracey said. "See, I wrecked a car into Thief Lake a couple weeks ago. It was Virg's old '68 Dodge, the one I always wanted to borrow when I was a kid."

"I remember that one," George grinned. "You haven't changed much, have you, Trace? Still can't keep out of trouble to save your life. But what's that got to do with Francis, for Christ's sake?"

"I wrecked it on the night Francis disappeared. I was driving Brenda Doheny home from Duckhaven – don't give me that look, it don't mean nothing," Tracey interrupted himself as George raised an eyebrow, "and I lost it in the rain and went off at that tight turn by the old mill. I was trying to figure out how to get it towed out of there with the least amount of hassle, you know, but it got found before I could deal with it. When the cops towed it out, there was a bunch of crank in it that I didn't know about, in a cigarette pack. And there was a rifle in there, one that wasn't there before I dumped the car in the lake."

"That's right," Addie put in, "and it's got the initials 'GC' carved in the butt. It's pretty distinctive."

George sat up and the front legs of his chair thumped on the plywood floor. "What are you trying to say?"

"Well, it was consistent with the weapon that killed Francis. And there were drugs found with his body that match the drugs found in Tracey's car," Addie said. "The drugs in Tracey's car were in a Camels' cigarette pack, and I just saw you pull a Camels' pack out of your pocket. Whoever put that rifle and the drugs in the car probably killed Francis."

George's mouth hung open for a second. "Well it sure as shit wasn't me! I wouldn't have dumped my own rifle in a car in the lake

193

where it would be sure to be found if I had. I'm not a fucking idiot. And I'm not making crank again!"

"Well, then, somebody's setting you up to look like this is your fault," Addie pointed out, trying to keep her voice calm. "Who would have access to one of your firearms? A rifle, about thirty years old, with 'G.C.' carved in the stock? You said Gil thinks Doug Raney killed Francis. Would Raney really have access to that rifle? Or would someone else?"

"Look," Tracey said. "The most obvious person to have done this is you, and if you didn't, then someone is going to a lot of trouble to make it seem like you did. There aren't that many people who even know you're back around, other than these guys in this militia, or whatever it is."

George hesitated. "But why would anyone kill Francis and set me up for it?"

"I was hoping you would know that," Tracey said, "because there are some folks who think I must have had something to do with it, given all this stuff was found in the car I was driving on the night Francis went missing and in the right area. Virg already worked me over pretty good, but it's nothing compared to what I'm going to get if they try and pin this murder on me."

George did not reply. Addie hoped he was beginning to come to some conclusions of his own.

"Look, George, I already know this group isn't just a militia," she said. "It's probably some kind of a strike team or action group. And we know Francis was hanging around with guys from the adhesives plant and he may have taken them out hunting with him. And we know Doug Raney sold Ray Kenworth some crank, and he told Ray he was getting it from somebody named George."

George began to protest, but she didn't allow him to interrupt. "If you didn't kill Francis for revenge, and Doug Raney didn't do it, then the next most logical thing is that someone from this group killed him. Maybe it has to do with drugs. Maybe Francis

194

threatened to turn them in for manufacturing. And now they're using you as a convenient scapegoat."

"That doesn't make any sense at all," George said. "Nobody's involved in any drugs around here. I wouldn't be hanging around these guys if they were and neither would Francis. Neither would Gil. I don't understand why Raney would say he got crank from me or why there would be any with Francis. He never did the stuff even when we were making it."

"Could Francis have found something out that they didn't want him to know? Something important?" Addie asked.

"I don't know what," George said, and shook his head. "Damn, with all this, the cops are probably already looking for me. Good thing I haven't been home for a couple days." He looked up at Tracey. "I can't risk getting busted. I can't risk the rest of the guys, either. This camp is a good thing for me. Getting in with this group was a good thing. If everything goes all right, I'll have something I can do for years, something I can get into. But not if I get busted because of some trumped-up charge."

Addie was beginning to get edgy again. "There's no reason for you to be busted," she said. "You could go in to the cops yourself, tell them what you know. It sounds like these guys might have set you up. You don't owe them anything."

"I owe them everything," George said. "Nobody else around here would hire me. I'm an ex-con with no skills. I didn't get into any vocational program like Francis did. Van pays me for what I do best and lets me use his boats and four-wheelers. And Van wouldn't set me up the way you say. You don't understand this guy. He has a vision, a thing that he's going for. He's not like anybody else I've ever known. I know he wouldn't do me wrong. Something else is going on, and I don't know what it is, but I'm going to figure it out. And you're not going to be able to go anywhere until I do."

"Don't try and keep us here against our will," Addie warned him.

"If I let you go, you'll send somebody to pick me up for being a felon in possession of a firearm and they'll throw the book at me on suspicion of murder," George pointed out. "I'm not stupid. Once they get me in there, they'll quit looking for whoever really did this to Francis. There's no way I'll get out of this."

"But there is," Addie said. "There are some things that don't fit with you being the murderer. I don't believe you are now, after talking to you. And I'll never mention I saw you with a firearm. Your help is too valuable. That's the deal I'm willing to strike. Let us get out of here now, before any of the rest of these guys show up. Maybe you'll be able to pick up some more information if you stick around, just by listening. You could pass it on to me. If you promise to do that, I won't tell anyone I saw you today. I give you my word."

George seemed to be wavering. He squinted as if in thought. In the silence, Addie heard the whine of a boat motor out on the river drop in key as it slowed. A boat was heading for the camp. The prop guttered as the pilot tilted the motor up at the mouth of the slough.

George jumped up and peered out. "Gil Lejeune," he said, positioning himself behind the door, his rifle up. "I wasn't expecting him down here today. He usually only comes by on weekends. Maybe he's looking for me. Maybe he thinks I killed his brother like everyone else does."

"No, he doesn't," Tracey said quickly. "He said he didn't think you were involved, the other night over at Bobbie's place. And you said Skeeter told you Gil thinks Doug Raney did it. Don't do anything stupid."

George kept his position. "I'm not taking any chances. Why would he come here now, when he knows nobody but me is here? That story about Raney could be a cover-up."

Addie could see Gil walking up the bank from the slough towards the open door of the cabin. He, too, was carrying a rifle in

196

one hand. He stepped in, glanced around, and stopped short. George's rifle was pointed at him, gut-level.

"What the hell's going on?"

"Listen, Gil, I didn't have anything to do with Francis. No matter what it looks like," George said.

"Are you pointing that thing at me?" Gil asked incredulously.

"Hell, him and me were good friends, once," George continued, keeping the rifle in place. "I never held anything against him. There's no way I would ever have done this thing."

"I know that," Gil snapped. "Quit pointing that thing at me and tell me what the hell's going on."

After a long moment, George dropped the rifle barrel so that it pointed at the floor near Gil's feet. Gil waited a few seconds, then carefully leaned his own rifle against the wall, near the door and on the side away from George.

"Well?" he asked, nodding at Tracey and Addie. "What are these two doing here?"

"I saw 'em poking around, looking in the windows and stuff," George said. "When they went to leave, I figured I'd find out what they were doing."

"Good idea," Gil sneered. "So you were having a nice neighborly chat with the warden, and when I show up at my own camp, you decide to point a rifle at my gut."

George shook his head, turning briefly to look at Addie and Tracey. "They told me about Francis and about my rifle and the drugs in the car. I thought maybe you would think I had something to do with it."

"Well, I didn't think so," Gil snapped, "and I don't appreciate coming into my own camp and having a goddamn gun pointed at me."

Gil scanned the cabin briefly, breaking his eye contact with George and ending the confrontation. "When is Van supposed to be down here?"

"He said he'd come down-river this afternoon."

"Anybody else around?"

"No," George said, "not yet. But everybody's supposed to be down here tonight. Van called some kind of a meeting."

"How did these two get here?"

"They walked in along the road."

"Well, they didn't walk all the way here," Gil snapped, turning to Addie. "How did you get here?"

"Ike dropped us off," Addie said quickly. "He's going to pick us up at the farm road. If we're not there, he'll get worried. He should be there soon."

Gil snorted. "I doubt that. Good try, though. I bet they drove in and left their car somewhere. Why don't you go find it and make sure it's not drawing attention? I'll stay here with these two until Van comes down. And keep an eye on the entrance road, just in case someone is looking for them."

George hesitated. "So you're going to make 'em stay here until Van comes down?"

"Look," Gil said. "This is my camp. I'll get screwed if anybody figures out what's going on out here. You know and I know by now that Van and the rest of them are probably fugitives. If she gets away, we'll have the whole goddamn county and all the feds in the area down on us. We can't trust Tracey now, either, because he's messed up with her. I don't know what the heck we're going to do with them, but they can't go anywhere right now. We'll have to let Van make the final decision."

"All right," George said, "I'll go see if I can't find their car. But I need to figure out what the hell is going on. Looks like I've been set up, and I don't like it."

"No, I guess you don't," Gil said.

George narrowed his eyes. "I guess if you wanted somebody to take the fall for Francis, it'd be me you'd pick."

"If I was setting you up, it'd mean that I had something to do with my own brother's death," Gil retorted. "You should at least be bright enough to know I didn't. I have a damn good idea who did. But right now, we need to make sure Ike or somebody else isn't coming in on this camp, because I don't want to get busted, and we need to make sure her car isn't sitting out in some obvious place. So why don't you go find it?"

After a few moments of indecision, George slung his rifle behind his shoulder and walked out the door. Gil took a deep breath and let it out slowly.

"What the hell are you doing, Gil?" Tracey demanded as George faded quietly into the woods. "You better not even think you're going to keep us here if we want to leave."

"Well, that's exactly what I think!" Gil snatched his rifle up from beside the door. "I don't want to hurt you, Tracey, God knows I don't, but I'll do what I have to do to keep you here now. You walked into something you don't even understand, and you walked in at a bad time. I want to take out the fucker that killed my brother, and there's only one way to do it. I'm not going to let you get in my way."

"You could at least tell us what's going on," Tracey said, facing Gil down despite the rifle. "Maybe we could even help you. Did you ever think of that?"

Gil shook his head. "Nobody can help me now. I'm in this too deep. I've got to take care of this my own way, myself."

"Look, we already know a few things," Tracey said more calmly. "We already know it probably wasn't George who killed Francis. And I know you know that too: you must have figured something out the other night at Bobbie's when I told you about the rifle and the drugs, because you said right then you didn't think George had anything to do with Francis being missing."

Gil smiled grimly. "No, I knew as soon as you told us about that stuff in the car that it wasn't George who'd put it there. I knew who it was, too."

"Do you really think it was Doug Raney?" Addie asked.

Gil laughed bitterly. "Hell, no. I went down there anyway and asked Doug about the crank. He said he got it from some guy who said his name was George, but it wasn't George Cole. Sounded like maybe it was Charlie."

Gil set the rifle down again and began pacing the cabin. "That's why I'm here. Charlie might've been in on it, but Van killed him or at least he set it up."

"How do you know it was Van?" Tracey asked.

"Because I was here when George gave Van a couple of old rifles to get rid of for him. Van was supposed to fence them somewhere and give George the money. George got the money, so I guess he assumed Van sold them."

"But instead he kept them, or at least one of them, and when the time came, he had a perfect set-up," Addie said. "And does Van smoke Camels, too?"

Gil shrugged. "He doesn't smoke, far as I know. George smokes whatever he can get on sale. Right now it's Camels. Van probably just grabbed an empty pack. I don't know how he would've got hold of the crank, but it wouldn't have been hard. Heck, Charlie's a chemist. Maybe they even made it themselves. And once Charlie made some up, he gave it to Doug Raney and said his name was George. People would make assumptions."

"That means it was premeditated, planned in advance," Addie said. "Maybe even a long time in advance. But why? What was Francis doing that made them think they needed to get rid of him? Was it because he figured out what they're doing out here? Or he figured out they're wanted somewhere else?"

"No," Gil said, "or they'd have to kill me and George and everybody local they ever deal with wherever they go."

"Then what?" Tracey said. "What made Francis so bad?"

"His own stupidity, and mine for not stopping him sooner," Gil said bitterly. "He pushed Van too far. I told him we had a good deal here and not to mess it up. But Francis always thought he knew what he was doing, that he had it under control."

"What did he do?" Addie asked.

"He got these guys here in the first place, is what," Gil snapped. "That was the start of it."

"You mean he knew these guys before they ever moved down here?"

Gil leaned on the edge of the table and crossed his arms. "No, he didn't know them specifically. He went out to that program in Colorado. They had this big final project to all do together, a commissioned piece for some group of art collectors. While he was out there he got talking to the guy that was kind of the go-between between the collectors and the center. Francis had kind of got it in his head that we needed to go back to the way things were a long time ago, have less impact and less laws and all. You know the way he was."

"Sure," said Addie. "You too, kind of."

Gil glanced at her. "Anyway, he got talking to this guy, and the guy told him he belonged to some sort of group that protested against companies that caused pollution and other environmental damage. So Francis told him about Roslyn and that they were looking to sell their adhesives plant and how it might be a good opportunity to close the place down and stop some pollution. The guy came back later and said yeah, they were interested. Francis got him some information and told him they could use his camp. The plant got bought out eight months ago and Van's group showed up about six months ago and moved right in. It's been a good deal up 'til now."

Addie had a sneaking suspicion she knew who the liaison Francis had been talking to was, but Gil hadn't mentioned any name, and she wasn't about to jog his memory. "But things went wrong along the way somehow," she said. "Did you guys realize exactly what these guys were planning to do here?"

Gil shook his head. "No, and I still don't know for sure. I know at first Francis thought they'd buy out the plant and just close it down to make a statement, but that's not what happened, obviously. I don't know why all these guys need to be here or what they're going to do with this camp in the future. But Francis thought he figured out what they were doing. Only thing is, he told Van what he'd figured out and pissed him off."

Gil pushed himself off the table. "I got George out of here so he wouldn't find out the whole story, because if he does he'll get in Van's face, and I want Van to think everything is fine until I get him alone. Then I'll take care of him once and for all. I was hoping to catch him alone tonight. But if I can't, then sometime tomorrow I ought to be able to catch him when none of his little gang is around. Then I'm gonna blow his brains out. I hope you didn't tell George too much. I don't want him to get in the way. I'll have to keep him out of it, one way or the other."

"But if Van's really a murderer, he may kill us when he shows up," Addie pointed out.

Gil shook his head. "I don't think so. You don't know Van. He doesn't want to attract any more attention than he has to, not that kind, anyway. A dead fed would for sure bring attention, even if some dead local boy ex-drug-dealer didn't."

Tracey glanced at Addie. She was working her T-shirt slowly up over her belt to give her access to her gear. She stood up and stretched as though the chair was bothering her back.

Gil looked up and moved hastily towards the door, positioning himself between them and the exit. Addie leaned casually on the chair back. "Gil, if Van knows you know whatever Francis was doing, you're in just as much danger as Francis was," she pointed out.

Gil smiled grimly. "No, I'm not. Because I'm going to get Van before he has a chance to get me."

"That's a real dangerous chance to take, Gil. What if Van figures out you suspect him? George said you usually don't come down here except on weekends. He's going to wonder what you're doing here tonight."

Gil shrugged. "Van usually comes downriver by himself, and he usually shows up first. George may be here, but I doubt he'll stop me, and I won't let you two stop me. And if he does come with the other guys, I'll lie. I'll tell him I think somebody else did it, and then I'll wait. I'll get him in the end."

"That's a stupid idea, Gil," Addie said. "What about afterward? When he shows up dead, everybody will know you did it. All his buddies will know, and they'll be gunning for you."

Gil shrugged. "After he's dead I won't care. But once he is dead, I'm going straight for the stuff Francis had and I'm gonna turn it in and get everyone busted, Howie and Jesse and Charlie and the whole lot."

"If you're going to turn in what Francis had on this group anyway, then a better idea is for us to go to the police right now, get you to swear out a complaint, and we'll pick Van up based on the evidence."

"Bullshit," Gil said. "I don't want Van arrested. I want him dead. No, now that I know for sure it was him, I'm going to take care of it myself."

"You do what you have to, then, but we won't be any part of it," Addie said. "We're leaving."

"You're not going anywhere. I can't let you mess this up. You're going to have to stay, now, until I deal with Van."

Addie had worked her left hand up under her T-shirt hem and removed her pepper spray canister from her belt. She was holding it down behind her thigh out of sight. She walked quickly towards the open door.

Gil stuck out an arm as if to block her path. Addie raised both arms together and checked Gil across the chest as hard as she could with her right forearm while she discharged a short blast of pepper spray into his face with her left hand. The shock of the cold blast coupled with Addie's strike to his chest put him off balance. He staggered, and Tracey shouldered him in the gut. Gil hit the wall of the cabin hard, and Addie ran out the open door, gagging on the back-spray from the pepper spray. Tracey was right behind her. She saw he'd had the presence of mind to grab Gil's rifle from where it stood beside the door. Unless Gil had access to another firearm and she'd missed his eyes, he wouldn't be shooting at them.

They raced around the side of the building and back down the road. George was down that way, she knew, maybe even at her car. They'd deal with that when they got there. But they were not more than fifty yards along when a large yellow pickup truck came roaring up the road towards the camp. They stopped short, and Addie turned towards the woods.

"We won't be able to get across the slough that way!" Tracey yelled. "The boats! Go back to the boats!"

They turned and ran back towards the shore of the river and the inlet where the boats were moored. Gil stood by the corner of the building they'd been in, leaning over, hands on his knees, spitting and gagging. The big pickup stopped just behind them; she heard Gil yelling hoarsely at whoever was in the truck.

They slid down the bank to the boats and Addie leaped into the little lightweight aluminum one. Tracey yanked loose the bowline and gave the boat a good shove as he stepped in. He stumbled, grabbed for the gunwale, and fell over the bow box into the boat, dropping Gil's rifle into the water near the shore. There was no time to try and retrieve it. Addie scrambled to the stern and grabbed the ripcord on the motor.

Two men appeared on the bank above them and began to slide down. Just as they got to the water line, Addie got the motor started and accelerated out of the slough into the river, barely in control.

As they popped out of the slough entrance they nearly collided with a big, low-riding jon-boat. Startled, Addie pulled in the tiller, and her boat yawed to the right, going crosswise to the current. It tilted with the sharpness of the turn, and the bow popped up. The bigger boat crunched into their right side and slid under them. The little boat rolled violently.

Addie was flung out of the boat to the downstream side. She caught a glimpse of Tracey falling, and she had a quick impression of the gunwale of the boat coming up and over. Then the brown muddy water of the river closed around her.

The river was deep here, where it cut into the bank in the bend. The weight of her clothes and the pistol and other gear on her belt drove Addie straight to the bottom. She floundered for a minute; she was an adequate swimmer, but she could feel the resistance of her own weight and the pull of her wet jeans and shoes. She kicked and clawed for the surface.

As she came nearer the surface, she was swept into a clot of dead down trees lodged against the bank in the bend. Addie came up through the branches, fighting to get her head up. But the branches caught on her gun holster, ripping through her T-shirt. The current pulled her under, entangling her further in the limbs.

Desperately, Addie grabbed at the branches, tried to disentangle her gear, and clutched at the trunk above her head at the same time. The surface of the water was just a foot above, but she could not get there. Her air was running out; at any moment she'd be forced to gasp a lungful of the warm muddy river water. She could feel the pressure at the edge of her eyes, and knew it was only seconds before she lost consciousness.

With the last of her reason, she let go of the tree altogether and fumbled for her belt buckle. As the belt flapped loose, she grabbed the buckle end and pulled, feeling first her badge case, then her extra ammo and handcuffs, and finally the gun holster pop free as the belt pulled them up against her belt loops. The branch that had been wedged between the holster and her hip waved loose. Addie made one last effort. Her head came just above the surface of the water, and she gasped for air and clung to the tree trunk while her legs swept underneath.

Fighting for air was for a moment the only thing she could do. As her mind cleared, she scanned the river for any sign of Tracey. All she could see was the bottom of the aluminum boat, which had flipped completely over and floated half-sunk down the river around the bend. She wanted to yell out for him, but was still too breathless to do anything but gasp.

She heard a motor behind her. She turned her head to see the big utility boat slide up crosswise to the current. She was afraid for a moment that it would crush her against the tree trunk, but the driver kept it in place just above her. A man in the front grabbed her arm, reached down, and got the back of her waistband. With one heave, he dragged her clear of the tree trunk and up over the gunwale of the boat and dropped her on her back on the floor.

Addie looked up from where she lay into the face of the driver. He was a tall blond man, with a short haircut and a military-green shirt. She knew she was looking at Delevan Bates.

Chapter Sixteen

"Well, well, Addie Derange," Van said.

Addie struggled to sit up in the bottom of the boat. She stared at him.

"Yeah, I know who you are," he said. "You're Logan Derange's sister."

Addie pushed herself up to her knees and grasped the gunwale of the boat. She wondered if she could leap out of the boat back into the river and hope to get away.

Van ran the boat up hard onto the bank inside the mouth of the slough. The jolt threw Addie off balance and she fell sideways, knocking her ribs on the side of the boat's middle bench seat. George, returned from his mission to locate her car, grabbed the bow and held the boat against the bank.

"Charlie, go see if you can find Tracey down the river," Van told the man in the bow of the boat. "I'll send Trent and Troy on down to the bridge. He'll likely come out there if you don't get him. George, go fetch that little boat back before it sinks altogether. Then take a walk down through the woods in case he comes out on this side of the river."

Van dragged Addie to her feet by one arm and walked her off the boat as Charlie clambered past them into the stern.

Up on the bank, Van grabbed the hem of her shirt and yanked it up over her waistband.

"Where's your gear?" he asked.

"I dropped it in the river," Addie gasped. "It got caught on the trees."

Van poked her in the back with his fingertips and urged her up the bank towards the cabin. She went. She could see that any attempt to escape would be futile. Besides Van, Charlie, and George, the two men who'd come up in the yellow truck were in camp. Gil sat outside at the fire ring, spitting on the ground and washing his face with water from a plastic jug held by one of them. He squinted up at her with red and running eyes. Addie felt a twinge of compassion. She'd experienced pepper spray herself, in training.

Van escorted Addie inside the cabin. "Sit down," he ordered. Addie sat on one of the chairs and ran her hands from her forehead to the nape of her neck, squeezing the water out of her hair. Van picked a towel off one of the bed frames and tossed it to her. Then he grimaced.

"What the hell did you do to Gil?"

"Pepper-sprayed him," Addie said.

"That's what I thought. Don't go anywhere," Van ordered. "I need to make sure he's not going to have a goddamn asthma attack or something. It still smells like that stuff in here."

Addie slumped in the chair, trying not to breathe too deeply. Fortunately, she'd sprayed Gil near the open door, and because she'd been very close to him, most of it had settled on him. Still, there was a distinct peppery odor in the air. At least Gil would probably be unable to carry out his threat to execute Van with his eyes swollen and his rifle at the bottom of the slough.

Van returned in a few minutes. He grabbed another chair and sat down directly in front of her. He leaned forward, rested his arms on his knees, and clasped his hands. He had intense, sharply focused brown eyes, and he met and maintained Addie's gaze.

She looked away, uncomfortable with his proximity and scrutiny. She had no idea what he was planning to do with, or to, her, but if Gil was correct, this man was a killer. She was obviously his captive now, and her first responsibilities were to protect herself and to try to escape if she could.

"Well, you know what I'm wondering?" Van began in a conversational tone, without the sharpness he had used before. "I'm wondering what you're doing out here today, Miss Logan Derange's sister, macing people and stealing one of my boats."

"And I'm wondering how you know my brother and what you think you're doing," Addie retorted.

Van nodded. "Well, I'll tell you how I know your brother, and I'll tell you exactly what I'm doing, not what I think I'm doing. But you haven't answered me. Don't you think I have a right to know why you were stealing one of my boats?"

"You're keeping me here against my will," Addie said, ignoring his question again. "I want to make that clear."

Van sat back a little. "I'm fully aware of that," he said. "I think that may change. But if not, I'm prepared to continue to keep you here against your will, at least temporarily."

Addie sat still, trying to comprehend everything she'd learned within the last few hours. She was exhausted and half-drowned, alone, and without any of her defensive equipment or her phone, which she'd left in her car. At least her keys were in her pocket; if she did manage to get away, maybe she'd be able to get to her car and escape. But until she had a chance, maybe her best bet would be to cooperate, to make him think she was interested in what he was saying.

"We weren't stealing your boat," she said as calmly as she could. "We were just borrowing it."

Van laughed shortly. "Well, I didn't really think you were stealing it. I think you probably came here to investigate this place and ran into a couple people you weren't expecting and you were trying to get away. Gil told me he tried to stop you from leaving and that's when you sprayed him and took off."

"He's lucky that's all I did."

Van snorted. "Is that a threat? Remember, all your stuff is at the bottom of the Deuce. But I'm not going to hurt you, anyway. I want to talk to you. I've been wanting to talk to you for some time."

"Oh? Why are you so interested in talking to me?"

"Well," Van said slowly, "I believe you have some idea who we are and what we do. And I suspect you're curious about us for more than just professional reasons. I think you've got a personal interest in us."

"You have no idea what my interests are," Addie said.

"Maybe not," said Van, "but I do know your brother, and I know what his interests are. He's told me some things about you and I've found out more on my own. And I know you're hanging around Tracey Cole. Given your situation with your brother and with Tracey, I think you're fairly open-minded. I think you can see through to what's going on underneath. You're not willing to condemn someone for his actions before you understand his motivations."

Addie said nothing. She had somehow expected a brutal man, but Van's voice was gentle and persuasive. He sounded reasonable and articulate. She began to have some hope that she would be unharmed, might even be released, if she seemed cooperative.

"I'll tell you what," Van said. "I'm willing to tell you everything you want to know about this operation on one condition."

"What condition is that?"

"Just that you listen to what I have to say, and that you withhold judgment until you have the whole story."

"Okay," Addie said. "I'm willing to listen. Don't expect me to agree with you at the end, though."

Van nodded. "I'm glad you're being up-front with me. You see, you and me are on the same side here. Of course you know whatever Tracey has been able to tell you about us. I guess you might have talked to George and even Gil about us, and I suspect you've figured out a few things on your own by now. You probably know more than you think you know."

"I guess I haven't put it all together, then," Addie said, "because I still don't know what you're doing out here. Everything looks on the up-and-up. We were only trying to get away from Gil because he was all upset about finding us out here at his camp."

"So why did you come out here today, then? You must have suspected something."

When Addie hesitated again, Van spread his hands. "Look. I said I'd tell you whatever you want to know. I meant it. Is that something I'd say if I planned to hurt you? I wouldn't tell you what I'm doing in that case, and I wouldn't care what you thought. I'd just lock you up somewhere, or bash you over the head and dump you in the river, or whatever. That's not my intention."

Addie shrugged. She was wavering. Van almost sounded believable, but she didn't want to be taken in. On the other hand, she wasn't sure she trusted Gil's conclusions. He didn't seem to have a lot to go on. She was curious, too, especially given Van's apparent association with Logan, and she still thought it would be best to seem cooperative.

"Okay," she said, "I thought there might be a meth lab out here. I came out today looking for it, but I didn't find one."

"No," Van said with a grimace. "Did you think Francis' death was a drug deal gone bad, then?"

"Not really a drug deal," Addie admitted, "I thought maybe Francis found out this militia was making meth and he threatened to tell the authorities in order to get rid of George again. So somebody bumped him off and set it up to look like George did it."

Van squinted at her. "Well, that would be a logical conclusion. Wrong, but logical. But you don't really think we're a militia, do you?"

Addie wiped away a trickle of river water that was rolling down her forehead from her hair, partly to give herself some time to formulate a response. It hadn't escaped her that Van wouldn't have been able to correct her conclusion if he didn't know the real situation.

"I know you must be connected to *AFTERThought*," she said. "Somebody put a business card with the logo on it on my porch."

211

Van smiled slightly. "We knew Logan was going to get in touch with you. We just wanted to let you know we were here and around town."

Addie glanced at him. Of course, she'd ignored Logan's call, so she didn't know what he'd been intending to pass on to her. "But I didn't know what *AFTERThought* was. I had to look it up on the Internet."

Van looked surprised for just an instant. "Oh? So what did you find out?"

"After I began thinking about what was going on with Francis, I started looking for information about the adhesives plant, because I knew all of the militia guys work there," Addie said. "I looked up Adrian Sora's other holdings and found out he owns wind farms and fuel-cell companies. That didn't seem to fit with the adhesives plant. Then I thought maybe the plant was a front for producing anhydrous ammonia for meth. But making meth didn't seem to fit in with Sora, either. I noticed that his holdings were listed on the *AFTERThought* website, so then I thought that maybe this group isn't actually a militia, but some kind of environmental strike team."

Van nodded. "I like that definition."

"So if you're such an environmentalist, what are you doing working in an adhesives plant? That seems pretty contradictory to me," Addie said, trying to turn the tables and force Van to talk. Despite Van's promise to tell her whatever she wanted to know, so far she had been the one doing the talking.

"Maybe, but I'm under no illusion that I can go out and save the world all at once without causing any harm ever again. There's give and take in this business. If I have to associate with less than environmentally-correct people or businesses in order to accomplish what I want to do in the long run, then I have no qualms about that."

"Right. I wouldn't call my brother environmentally correct," said Addie.

Van shrugged. "We hedge our bets by dealing with people like Logan, people who on the outside seem average but who have something to lose by having everybody know their private business. That gives them a reason to keep quiet."

"People like George Cole, too, I guess."

"Sure," Van said, "George has a lot of skills we can use. He's an expert tracker and marksman and he's been teaching some of the guys what he knows. He's available to guard this camp when everybody else is working. But he's not the kind of person we'd let in to our inner circle or tell all the details."

"And Tracey?" Addie asked with a stab of conscience, remembering that he might be hurt or drowned in the Deuce. "Were you trying to recruit him into this group? Or were you using him for something else?"

Van thought for a minute. "Well, I figured he could help out around this camp the way George does. We know he can keep his mouth shut. We didn't manage to get him to say anything controversial and didn't come away from our trip with him knowing anything more about his political leanings than when we started. That's good. I like people who can keep things close. But I also needed some information from him, which I got."

"What information?"

"Locations, who owns what land. Don't worry, it's not like he was revealing state secrets."

Addie heard another truck's engine and then the slam of doors as more people arrived in the camp. Van glanced out the door momentarily, but then brought his eyes back to her. "Is this all beginning to make sense?" he asked.

Addie rubbed her face and ran her fingers through her damp hair, wondering how much information she could extract from Van. "Some of it. I'm not clear on exactly what you're doing here or who controls everything. I gather that this *AFTERThought* organization

213

comes up with the targets they want you to hit and sends you out on the job."

"No, *AFTERThought* doesn't have anything to do with that," Van corrected. "Each environmental strike team, as you've called us, is semi-independent. That's safer for all of us. You looked at the website?"

Addie nodded.

"The foundation's run by Mike's daughter June now. She doesn't have direct contact with us, not even cell phone numbers. We communicate with her through the Internet, mainly. But she has turned us on to potential funding sources from time to time. The Soras are the funding source for this particular set of operations."

Van shifted slightly in his seat. "Adrian Sora and Mike Gerschoff go way back," he said. "They both lost their wives to cancer that may have been caused by industrial pollution near where they lived in New York. They both became environmental crusaders in their own right. They just took slightly different routes to accomplish their goals. Adrian was already a successful business owner, and he figured he could do his best work within the system, using it against itself.

"That's what he's been doing with the adhesives plant. Rosyln's holdings were on our radar, and when we found out about the plant being for sale we saw a great opportunity. Adrian's son and one of his buddies put together a deal to co-manage an ammonia facility with the fertilizer factory next door. It was pretty easy to get folks in where we needed them, with a little help from plant management. The plan was to requisition and siphon off a variety of chemicals, from anhydrous ammonia, urea crystals, and nitric acid to ammonium and potassium nitrate. We'd have the supplies to make all the explosives we needed for years, plus a bunch of other chemicals we could use for all sorts of purposes."

214

Addie raised her eyebrows. "So the anhydrous ammonia is for explosives, not methamphetamines. And you were planning on using some of those to blow up the Roslyn pulp mill?"

Van shook his head. "No. You're right that Roslyn is on *AFTERThought*'s shit list. But that's not how we operate. We're divided into different teams. We're an advance team. We secure the funding, set up base camps, and recruit local people to work with us and maintain the camps until we need to use them. That way there'll be equipment and supplies ready. We choose and map out the targets, get coordinates and do some of the surveillance so the folks who do the actual strike can come in, do what they need to do without attracting attention, and get out. By that time this particular little group of people will be long gone, though."

"So when you've got everything set up the way you want, you just pick up and leave, go on to the next place, the next assignment?" Addie asked.

"More or less," Van answered. "I've been doing this for more than ten years. I've been all over the country, everywhere from New York to southeast Texas. It's a good set-up for me. I'm like you. I want to work outside, I want to use my brain, and I don't want someone hanging over me all the time. I want to travel around. And I want to do something that fits in with my philosophy. Can you understand that?"

"I guess," Addie said, grudgingly.

"I thought you would," Van said. "See, I really believe in what I'm doing. I believe it's the right thing to do, and I believe it's the right way to do it. I realize that I live by the sword and I'll probably die by it someday. But I accept that. This is the only way to bring about what I want to accomplish."

His eyes brightened as he continued and his voice became more animated. "Throughout history change has been accomplished by small radical groups of people who move the general opinion a small step at a time away from what was once the accepted norm.

215

Right now we've got to move away from fossil fuels and decentralize energy, transition to renewable sources. That will insulate us from terror strikes against centralized power producers and protect our environment so we'll be able to provide for ourselves in the future without dependence on other countries. I like to focus on big energy-related businesses that use their political clout to keep us dependent on them. Some of the guys prefer other targets. But we all have a common goal: reducing environmental abuse by bringing attention to the practices of specific companies."

Van scooted his chair around slightly, so he was sitting at an angle to her rather than directly in front of her. Addie could now see out the door of the cabin. She felt slightly less trapped, as if Van had suddenly relaxed his guard.

"And, Addie, I guess you're a lot like me. I guess you'd prefer to work with no one looking over your shoulder. You want to make your own decisions. In an agency like yours you're lined into all these little chores that don't mean anything. Isn't that right?"

Addie shrugged uncomfortably.

"You don't really have much in common with the people you work most closely with. What about Ike? His family is all cops, going way back. He doesn't understand, can't even imagine where you came from. If he found out about your brother, about you, he'd never trust you again. It wouldn't be fair; you're as dedicated to protecting the environment as he is. Probably more so: he does it because he likes being a cop, you do it because you have a philosophy behind it, you believe in it."

Addie shook her head. She didn't know how he knew about Ike, but he was voicing things she had thought herself. She didn't like him cutting that close to the truth.

"Look, Addie," Van continued before she could interject, "you're isolated here. The only people you can trust with your personal background are people like Tracey Cole, and he and his family don't have any real understanding of what it is you're trying

216

to do or how dedicated you are to protecting the Preserve and places like it. You've had enough time to figure out that all you're doing in this job is catching the little fish. You bust someone for dumping a washing machine in the river, but there's a pulp mill dumping dioxins right across from it. You bust someone for riding a quad on the Preserve, but some timber company's clear-cutting up to the boundary. You bust somebody for fishing without a license, but some oil rig is leaking crude into the waterways and salt water's spilling into the creek. You think you're making a difference here?"

Van's voice had become intense, passionate. He seemed to be voicing things she had never wanted to tell herself. She fought to remind herself that he was a criminal, possibly a murderer.

"You didn't answer my question," Van pushed. "Are you doing what you really want to be doing? Are you having the impact on the world that you really want to have?"

"What are you really asking me?" Addie demanded.

"You know what," Van said. "You know how to run boats, drive quad-runners, you know about the system and about how officers think and work. You could be invaluable to us. You get all the toys you want, computers, whatever. No boring, repetitive schedule. You get to travel all over the country with nobody looking over your shoulder. And even more important, you get to hang around with a bunch of people who are committed to the same causes you are. People who actually believe in the same things you do, who can suspend judgment the same way you can in order to get the job done in the end. And you get to play at being whoever you want to be. You re-invent yourself each time we go somewhere. We work as a family. We take care of each other. We know what we're doing with our lives. You could be a part of that."

Addie laughed abruptly. She couldn't believe what he was asking or that he was serious. His ideas almost made sense: he would probably have more impact on the earth than she ever would

217

in her life. And the freedom and the sense of belonging to a group of people who thought the way she did were enticing.

"And if I don't? If I don't want to join you?"

Van sat back slowly. "I won't hurt you. I'll set it up so you can get away or get found after we leave tomorrow. Or I'll just let you walk away. You can go back to doing what you do, to checking fishing licenses and hiding your past from Ike and from yourself. You won't have the information you'll need to be able to track me or the proof to cause any of us any harm. But I think I know you. I think I understand you. I think I know what decision you'll make."

Addie sat silent. This time she did not bother to deny that he knew anything about her. Damn Logan. He'd obviously talked to Van in depth about her, not just surface likes and dislikes, but her deepest motivations. Yet Logan hadn't warned her; his message had been about some map. Was it perhaps a code he expected her to understand? Or a meaningless message, intended to throw off anyone who might be listening to her answering machine?

Addie realized she was staring blankly at the floor, her vision turned inside. She glanced up. Van was watching her, still only a few feet away.

"You want to know how I know Logan?" Van asked. "I first met him about ten years ago, right when you were starting college. At that time he had dozens of those pots around his place, maybe hundreds, plus other artifacts, the kinds of things people will pay thousands for. My operation at the time, my first operation, was being financed by a guy who happened to be a collector of such stuff. Part of the deal was that I obtain certain items for him and launder their patrimony if it was questionable. So I ended up moving artifacts for Logan. He financed your college education by selling those pots."

Addie dropped her gaze uncomfortably. He was right, of course. Although she had never asked, and Logan had never outright told her, she had always known.

218

"You wouldn't want the people you work with here to know you were a pothunter when you were a kid or that your brother is still involved with that sort of thing," Van pointed out. "But it's not just a matter of integrity. It's a criminal matter, and you and Logan could both still be liable, especially Logan, with the stuff he has sitting around.

"And believe me, if we get busted, our trail is going to lead back to Logan and his ranch, and all this is going to come out. Someone is going to figure it out. And eventually it is going to lead right to you as well."

Addie still did not reply. She had nothing to say.

Van got up and returned his chair to its place under the table near the window. "I'll be back in a few minutes," he said. "When I come back, I'll answer any more questions you've come up with. And then I'm going to need an answer from you, because I can't waste time. Time is one thing I don't have right now, and that means time is one thing you don't have either."

Van walked out the cabin door, leaving Addie staring after him, a chill creeping over her as his last words sank in. Those words seemed to be a threat, and she still saw little reason to completely disregard Gil's suspicion that Van was Francis' killer. Van hadn't denied it; in fact, he had skipped over it entirely, focusing instead on his desire to recruit her into the group.

She put her elbows on her knees and her head in her hands, trying to think. A storm of possibilities and responsibilities seemed to swirl in her mind. She found herself puzzling over how all of them, Van, his group, the Soras, *AFTERThought*, her brother, had found each other, had even begun to discuss the things they now appeared to take for granted. It would be a gamble each time Van approached someone new, she realized, and he would have to be fairly certain what the outcome would be or it would be too risky. He must have been sure about what he'd seen in her. Maybe he had been right. Certainly it seemed true that she had more in common

219

with some of the members of Van's group than with some of the people she lived and worked with. And Logan, the one member of her family she'd been closest to, trusted them and had worked with them. Indeed, it appeared she owed her college education, in a roundabout way, to Van.

She looked up as she heard George's voice outside the door. He was talking to a man with close-cropped red hair and a smile that turned up sharply at the corners.

"Hey, Howie," George said.

"Hey," Howie said. "Did you see any sign of Tracey?"

"No, he must still be in the river or he must've gone over to the other shore," George said. "I'll guarantee he didn't come out of the river on our side between here and the bridge."

Addie felt her heart sink, but she tried to convince herself that George was mistaken or even lying.

"Gil said you went looking for where they parked their car earlier. Did you find it?" Howie asked.

"No," George said. "They must have parked it out on the farm road off the shoulder somewhere."

Addie was puzzled. The car was hidden, but not so well that someone looking for it couldn't have found it. It was in a fairly obvious place. She doubted that George had missed it.

"Okay," Howie said. "We'll take a look for it when we go drop off that truck later tonight. If it's that concealed it probably isn't attracting any attention anyway. We can leave it alone for the time being. Remind me when we go."

Addie wondered if George had been trying to find out more about the circumstances surrounding Francis' death. She was sure Gil wouldn't tell George anything more. But George could have been figuring things out for himself. It would have been easy for him to decide Van was involved in setting him up, with the information about the gun and the cigarette pack.

220

Van stepped back into the cabin and motioned to the bottom bunk of one of the beds. He sat down and scooted to the wall so that his back was supported.

"Come sit next to me and let's talk a little more," Van said, smiling. Despite the smile, it was an order rather than a request, and Addie crawled onto the bed next to him.

"So, what do you think? Do you have any interest at all in my offer?"

Addie hesitated. She still thought it was in her best interest to agree with him, no matter what her ultimate decision might be. "I'm still listening to what you're saying, let's put it that way."

"Good," Van said. "I wouldn't want you to jump into this if you aren't sure. I need people who are committed, people I can trust."

"I have some other questions, then," Addie said. "I can't make a decision without knowing exactly what I'm getting into and exactly what kind of people I'd be working with."

"Fair enough," Van said. "I'll tell you what you want to know. I'm willing to take that risk if it means the possibility of recruiting you. Besides, I'm adept enough at hiding by now that no one will be able to find me when I leave here, even with what I'll tell you."

Once again he had dropped his voice so that Addie found herself actually leaning towards him in order to hear what he was saying. She leaned back again, torn between wanting to seem like she trusted him and her own shock at being perversely attracted to him. She realized Van was using a variety of techniques to keep her attention and build her trust, some of which she'd been taught herself in interviewing classes. She glanced at him and noticed that he'd rearranged his legs and arms to mimic her own body posture. Clever, she thought: a rapport-building technique.

"First, I want to know the truth: what happened to Francis and why? Now that I know about the chemicals at the plant, I have a

221

good guess," she said, drawing on what Gil had told her earlier. "He blackmailed you, didn't he? He found out you were siphoning off anhydrous ammonia, and he threatened to expose you."

"All right," Van said with a sigh. "I can see you're following a line of logic that's leading right to me. You're not totally wrong. How much detail did Logan go into with you?"

Addie squirmed. "I didn't actually return his call."

Van blew his breath out audibly. "So this is all new to you?"

"I guess so," Addie replied.

"Well, you're doing better than I thought at figuring out what's going on, then," Van said. "Let me fill you in on a few things. It's true that Francis tried blackmail, if you want to call it that. He told me he'd got some information I really wouldn't want anybody else to know. He didn't make any specific demands."

"What exactly did he figure out?" Addie asked.

"Well, Francis mostly worked at shipping and receiving at the adhesives plant, but he would sometimes fill shifts at the fertilizer plant. Ammonia goes out to the fertilizer plant, and urea and formaldehyde and adhesives go out to buyers, and waste goes out to waste disposal sites. Since he was working at both places, he noticed that the ammonia supplies coming in to the fertilizer plant weren't always matching what was leaving the adhesives plant."

"Observant of him," Addie said. Apparently Francis had been taking his job seriously.

"Yes. He had computer access at the plant because he was responsible for entering receiving records, and when he noticed the discrepancies he got a little paranoid that he'd done something wrong. He didn't want to tell anybody that he might have messed up. So he checked the computerized inventories and financial records, intending to correct anything he'd screwed up."

"A receiving clerk had access to plant financial records?" Addie snorted. "That doesn't sound very secure."

Van shook his head. "He didn't. He used Altara Sora's password. She's the administrative assistant, Andrew's daughter. She kept a list of passwords in her desk, like a lot of people do. They worked different shifts, but he told her he'd bring some of his jewelry and leave it for her to check out, but that he didn't want to leave it in her mailbox since it was valuable. She told him she'd leave her office open and he could drop it on her desk and lock up on the way out. He went through her desk while he was in there and found the list. Then he got into the records and found two sets of books covering the same time period, but different from each other."

"Someone was falsifying inventory," Addie nodded, "and of course that means someone knows about the discrepancies and is covering for them."

"That's what Francis thought. So he began to keep an eye on things, and he figured out that certain chemicals would be labeled as waste, shipped out as if they were going to the waste disposal site, and these same two guys would always be the ones who transported those loads. Francis knew those two guys are part of the militia, Trent and Troy Brock.

"He figured the anhydrous must be for some big methamphetamine operation somewhere. He got paranoid we were making meth on his property, or that we'd get caught making it somewhere else and be tied to him through the camp. He knew with his background, he'd be screwed if that happened. He was okay with us using his property, with the laptop and the ATVs and the boats and all, but the methamphetamine thing freaked him out.

"So he downloaded both sets of inventory and receiving books onto the laptop we gave him, copied them onto disks and made a set of paper copies for good measure. Then he came to me and told me what he'd done. He suggested I might want to think about what he knew and how valuable it might be to me."

"But he was wrong," Addie said. "You said you're not using the chemicals for meth production. So why didn't you just tell him that and ruin his blackmail plan?"

"I did, sort of," Van said. "You have to understand that only our inner circle, these guys I travel with, know all the ins and outs of what we're doing. I have to keep a few secrets. So I told him we didn't have the proper disposal permits for all the waste we were producing and we were shipping it to Louisiana under the table. I pointed out that there wasn't some big influx of meth in the area lately, like there would be if we were manufacturing it."

Addie looked at him. "And?"

"And I pointed out what a good deal he had going with us here. I pointed out that if he turned us in for illegally shipping waste, we'd have to split and the cops would probably confiscate the boats and the laptop and the ATVs and ransack his camp and maybe go through his house. So his plan wasn't in his own best interest."

"What would actually happen if someone got hold of those copies?" Addie asked. "Would Andrew Sora just be able to pass it off as someone on his staff illegally dumping waste without his knowledge?"

Van shifted. "Maybe. Me and my crew here could certainly just split and disappear. It wouldn't be a big danger to us. But Francis didn't know what he had. He didn't just copy the specific files that showed the double books. He went ahead and backed up the whole system onto his own drive. There's a whole lot more information there. For example, there's a breakdown of the expense account I used to purchase these boats and the ATVs and other equipment, which was money that came directly from Adrian Sora. If a trained financial investigator got hold of that stuff, it could start to fall in line. The connections could be made."

"So Adrian could be compromised," Addie said, "and he can't go underground. He's someone who could be found easily and he has a lot to lose." And if the Soras stood to be exposed as financiers of an eco-terrorist operation, that was a good enough reason to kill Francis, she thought. "What did Francis say when you told him it was a disposal scam?"

"Well, he wasn't stupid. He realized that he didn't want to mess up what he had going here. I kind of turned the tables and told him he better give us everything he'd copied, the laptop, the disks, and the paper files, or I'd cut him off. I said I was willing to give him a chance. I figured he'd eventually come around and I wasn't in any hurry at that point. But he kept stalling."

Addie squinted in the shade of the bottom bunk. "What has this got to do with Logan?"

Van looked down for a minute. "You might know that we came here and started using this camp because your brother put us in touch with Francis. He met Francis at this rehabilitation center in Colorado."

"Circle of Life," Addie said. "I know that. I guess maybe Logan figured I'd eventually be able to help you out, too."

"That was the plan, but Logan wanted to ease you into it carefully. Things kind of came to a head faster than anyone anticipated. It would have helped if you'd actually called him back. You'd understand a lot more about what's going on," Van said reproachfully.

Addie crossed her arms. "You obviously don't know much about my relationship with Logan."

"Maybe not. My younger brother travels with me. He's the one called Jesse, the blond out there by the fire ring. To me, he's the one person in the world who understands how I grew up, what my childhood environment was like, what our family's like, what my motivations are. If he called me for any reason, I'd jump. I wouldn't ask questions. He'd do the same for me. He'd do anything for me, without question. Even kill somebody if I told him to, or if he thought he needed to protect me. It's hard for me to imagine a brother-sister relationship that isn't like that, I guess."

Addie studied his face as she digested that. Was he suggesting that he'd asked his younger brother to kill Francis for him? And, almost more important at this point, was he right about Logan? If she'd returned his call, what would she have done for him? Memories of the times she'd lied to protect him flashed across her mind: that time they'd been pulled over with a load of just-pilfered pottery in the trunk, and other times.

She shook her head to bring herself back to the present. "It doesn't matter. The fact is, I still don't know what happened."

"Well, while Francis was at that Circle of Life place the last time, he stole a map. It's important to one of Logan's clients, and they want it back. It took a while to figure out who did it, but they narrowed it down to Francis. Logan's the one who brought it in to the center in the first place and let the students look at it. And then he couldn't figure out how to get it back." Van snorted derisively.

Addie's mind returned to the cryptic phone message from Logan, how he had been worried that it might be "too late". Had Logan guessed that Van might resort to force to retrieve the map?

"So eventually I told Francis I knew he'd taken the map and that I wanted that back, too, and if he didn't return it along with everything else pretty quick, I'd turn him in for it," Van continued.

"That probably pissed him off," Addie said.

"Yeah, it might not have been a very good technique," Van admitted. "He got mad. He told me that if I didn't cooperate, he'd go to the cops himself, not just with the files but with the map. And he told me he knew what it was and that it could be tied to illegal pot-hunting and laundering in Colorado, that it could be tied directly to Logan, and that it could be tied directly to you."

Addie stared at him.

"Now, I might be willing to sacrifice you, and I might be willing to sacrifice Logan, but there's a bigger issue. Logan's gotten way too close to June Gerschoff. June, *AFTERThought,* and a bunch of Logan's clients can be linked directly to illegal activities through

226

that map," Van said. "We needed to get it back. But once again, things didn't go exactly as planned."

"How so?" Addie asked.

"We didn't get the map back before Francis died. I freely admit it was us who went through his house and Gil's house. Me, in fact, and Howie. We ransacked the two places looking for the map. We took the laptop, but we didn't find the paper copies either."

That had happened after Francis' death, Addie thought, although only someone who had killed him would have known that he was dead at that point in time. On the other hand, would Francis have trusted Van enough to go hunting with him after an encounter such as Van had described?

"Seems like to me you had a couple reasons to get rid of Francis, then," she said. "He was trying to blackmail you, and he had this map."

Van squinted at her. "Those might be some pretty good reasons, but I still thought Francis would come around eventually. His being dead is actually an inconvenience, because now he can't tell us where the copies are. So I didn't kill Francis and I didn't order him killed."

"Then who did?"

Van crossed his arms. "Well, I don't know, although with some of the stuff I've been hearing, I have a pretty good idea. But there's not much to be done about it at this point."

Addie wasn't sure she believed him. It still made sense to her that he'd just get rid of the blackmailing ex-con and not have to worry about the threats to himself, his group, and Adrian Sora. It also made sense that he'd stop short of admitting to murder before he had her firmly recruited into the group. But she didn't think she was going to get much more out of him. "So now what?" she asked.

"Now that Francis' body has been found, people are going to start putting two and two together pretty fast, like you did. That means we're in danger. It's too risky for us to stay. But we can't

227

leave without those files and that map. We can't risk having them out there, ready to be used in some sort of blackmail on the one hand or pointing out a pretty damning set of circumstances to the cops on the other.

"I figure the map's with the paper copies of the files. The only reason we haven't left yet is that everybody's waiting on me to figure out where Francis stored those records and get them back. We know they're not at the Dohenys', and they're not at Gil Lejeune's old camp on Widow Slough. That was the information I got from Tracey, about where that camp's located, and we checked it. But it's possible Gil knew what Francis was planning to do. That leaves one other logical place for the records to be. I'm betting Gil has them and he stowed them at Bobbie Cole's place."

"You're planning on going to Bobbie Cole's place to find the copies before you leave," Addie concluded.

"Tomorrow morning. That'll be my last shot at it."

"Does Gil know you're leaving tomorrow?" Addie asked.

Van shook his head. "I don't really want Gil to know, because if he's got those copies and the map, and he knows what he's got, he may try to use them right now. I suspect he thinks one of us killed Francis, no matter what he says about Doug Raney. He'd probably rather take out whoever he thinks did it himself, but if he thinks that won't be possible, I bet he'll go to the police. So you did me a favor. Gil's going home so he can get a shower and wash that crap off and recover. You got Gil out of here for the evening so he can't see that we're packing up or hear us talking about it and he'll think he's got more time to deal with things on his own."

"What about George? He may take the blame for Francis' death after you leave, especially since it looks like somebody set him up."

Van studied her. "How do you know George didn't do it?"

Addie stopped short in her reply.

"Anyway, there's not enough evidence," Van continued. "We'll move George out of the area for the time being, give him enough help to hide out elsewhere for a while, and when things blow over he can come back if he wants to. He'll be fine."

"What about me?" Addie asked hesitantly.

"I'm taking a chance no one will know you're missing until at least tomorrow. I do know your days off are Monday and Tuesday, so I guess it could even be Wednesday before your partner notices you're gone. You'll come with me tomorrow. Then, if you change your mind, I'll let you off and you can say you were kidnapped. And if you decide to stick with us, you'll already be under way."

Van crawled out from under the bunk. "Come on. I've got to get Howie and George going. They're dropping a truck up at Magnolia Slough so we'll have it there for tomorrow. None of us are going back to Aynesworth tonight, or ever, for that matter. It's too risky now. We'll sit around the fire for a while and have a couple beers. Then we're going to get a little sleep. You'll sleep with me."

Van laughed as he looked down at Addie's expression. "Don't look so alarmed. I'm a saboteur, not a rapist. You're just sleeping in the same bed with me so you don't get up and disappear in the middle of the night. And I'm a light sleeper; I'll feel if you move. Come on."

Chapter Seventeen

When the little aluminum boat was thrown to the side, Tracey was flung out and into the river. The gunwale, coming up quickly as the flat-bottomed boat flipped onto its side, smacked him in the back of the head, nearly knocking him cold. Tracey, with his history of a skull fracture, did not deal well with knocks to his head.

He felt the tepid water of the Deuce River around him, but for a few moments he could see nothing. The current was swift along the bank, and he turned so he was floating feet first, not fighting it, but allowing it to carry him along. Tracey had been swimming in the Deuce all his life, and keeping himself afloat was almost automatic.

In a minute his vision cleared a bit, and he took a few strokes and brought himself up through the murky water. As he surfaced, he found himself inside the upside-down boat. There was enough space between the water's surface and the hull for him to bring his head out all the way. He grasped the single oar in the clips on one side for support, and allowed himself to float downstream with the boat.

He didn't know where Addie was, but she wasn't under the boat, that was for sure. And it was probable someone would come after the boat, to try and get it before it sank. It was not made to float upside-down, and was already lolling to one side. The air trapped in the bottom escaped from the higher side in large bubbles, reminding him of the sinking car.

Tracey took a deep breath, ducked back under the water and pushed himself off to the side. He swam underwater, downstream, for as far as he could, trying to put distance between himself and the boat. When he could hold his breath no longer, he came to the surface, shook his hair off his face, and looked around quickly.

He found himself close to the bank. He'd been swept around a small bend, and the boat Van Bates had been piloting was nowhere to be seen. Tracey grabbed a root sticking out of the mud and hauled himself up quickly. As he reached the top of the bank he heard a boat motor, and threw himself down on his belly behind a cypress. Keeping as flat to the ground as he could, he wriggled close to the base of the tree and raised his head just enough to be able to see out from behind it. A boat swung back and forth across the river slowly. He could see a single occupant, with a dark ponytail and heavy build.

As the boat passed, Tracey pulled himself up to a sitting position and leaned against the cypress, gingerly rubbing the back of his head. He felt confusion and nausea rising, and recognized those as signs of a concussion. He had dealt with those symptoms for years, every time he'd banged his head even a little, and he had a pretty good idea about how things were going to go. He didn't know how bad it was going to get, but it had been a hard hit, and he knew he was going to have to make some decisions to protect himself as soon as possible.

The men who were searching for him would look along the shore if they failed to find him in the water. Van would expect Tracey to haul himself out downstream at the bridge where the farm road crossed the river. Probably, he'd send someone down there to keep a lookout for him. That made it a bad way to go, although the nearest civilization was down that way, at the pulp mill. He was sure they wouldn't leave anything to chance. Maybe they'd even send George out to search. That would be bad news, because George understood the river shore and the piney woods almost instinctively. Tracey knew he needed to get out of the area, but he was in no shape to travel. His only real choice was to hide as best he could for the time being and hope that things would get better.

He found a hollow near the bank where the roots of an old fallen tree had ripped out, and crawled into it beneath the decaying root system, looking for snakes. He pulled the spidery limbs of yaupon brush down over the opening as best he could. Then he

231

slumped down again, cradling his head on his arms, lying half on his stomach so that if he passed out and vomited he wouldn't choke. He heard a sound in his ears like the boat motor, coming closer and closer, up over the bank, and his vision clouded over.

Tracey awoke several times during the night, too confused to be able to figure out where he was. He awoke again just as the sun began to rise over the river. He crawled shakily out of the hollow, trying to figure out if he'd gotten so drunk he'd passed out in the woods. He had a wicked headache, and still felt nauseated and confused.

Slowly, the events of the evening before began to come back. Almost immediately, he felt an overwhelming sense of guilt. He didn't know where Addie was or what was happening to her, but whatever had happened, she'd gotten involved in it because of him. He'd suggested they come out to the camp and told her it was safe, and she'd gone along because she was trying to get him out of the trouble he'd gotten himself into by dumping the car in the lake to begin with. If he'd never taken that car, they would never have gotten into this situation.

He began to figure what he could do. Going upstream from the Lejeunes' along the east bank would be useless. It would just put him into the Bottoms, and there was nothing there but a maze of waterways and George's stand at the bear-hunter's camp.

If he swam across, even if he could keep himself from being swept downstream towards the bridge, he'd come out into the Preserve, with no settlements anywhere close. He'd then have to hike out towards Duckhaven or down towards the highway. His memory of the day before seemed incomplete and he was having a hard time keeping things in order in his mind, but he knew that he needed to get help. He couldn't risk getting caught swimming the river, and trying to negotiate the woods to the west would be a waste of time.

He was too sick from the bang on his head to try and hike out to the pulp mill overland, although that was the closest route to civilization and the easiest way for him to avoid detection. There was one other possibility, the only one that seemed to make any sense in his condition, but he knew it was risky.

He got unsteadily to his feet and looked around, trying to gauge where he was in relation to the camp. He knew he was south of it, downstream. The dirt road they'd driven in along ran northwest from the farm road that passed the pulp mill until it intersected the oil-pipeline clearance. That was where Addie had parked her car.

Turning his back on the river, he headed into the woods, listening for any vehicles or voices and watching for the Lejeunes' entrance road. In his distraction and haste, he tripped repeatedly over vines and underbrush. Each jolt traveled painfully through his head, causing bursts of light at the sides of his field of vision.

He reached the cleared swathe under which the oil pipeline ran and stepped out into knee-deep brush and deadfall. Out from beneath the cover of the trees, the early morning sun stabbed his eyes and augmented his nauseating headache. He staggered across the pipeline, ducked into the woods on the opposite side, and kept going through the forest, easier than trying to negotiate the three years' worth of brush along the clearance.

A few minutes later he came to the dirt road. There were multiple fresh tire tracks; obviously a number of vehicles had driven up it recently, or a few had driven up and back a number of times. Instead of walking along the road itself, he kept just off to the side in the trees.

As he approached the intersection he slowed down, listening and looking carefully. If someone had found the car, they'd surely be watching it. But perhaps it hadn't been found. They'd tucked it away in the brush, and it was gray, not an obtrusive color. Then again, perhaps Addie herself had taken it. He had no idea what she was doing or where she was. He had a good idea that she wasn't free and

233

safe, though. She would surely have alerted the county, they'd have come in on the camp by now, and things wouldn't be so quiet.

Tracey could see the brushy area where the car was parked. He saw no one around, but then, they wouldn't be out in the open. He crossed the road and could see the top of the roof. It was still there. He circled the car carefully, back in the woods, looking for any signs of people. No one. He made a complete circle, then stopped. He had to risk it, now.

Tracey took a deep breath and walked over to the car. No one stopped him. He yanked open the door, which was unlocked, and slipped in to the driver's seat. He knew Addie had taken the key, but he thought there might be another key somewhere. Just give him a few minutes to search, and he might be able to find it. If not, he might be able to hot-wire the car and start it that way.

"Just get me out of this situation, let everything be all right, and I swear I'll clean up my act," he muttered under his breath in a kind of prayer. "I won't do stupid shit anymore. I'll get a job, I'll fix up the car, I'll do whatever Virg wants. Or heck, I'll get a good enough job that I'll move out on my own and do what I want."

He leaned over and yanked open the glove compartment and pulled everything out. No key there. He pulled down the visor over the driver's seat, and an object fell out on his lap. Addie's cell phone. He picked it up and took it out of the clip-on holster. He could barely focus on the tiny numbers and letters, and the strain brought his stomach up into his throat. He remembered Addie saying she didn't usually wear it because it rarely got reception out in the Preserve. But the little screen showed a bar in the upper left-hand corner.

He hit the 'contacts' button and the list came up at Ike's name, apparently the last person Addie had called. He punched the number and held the phone up to his ear, but nothing happened. When he looked at it again, the single bar was gone.

"Crap." Tracey stared at it for a long moment, trying to figure out what to do next. Addie had called Ike before leaving the house, he was fairly sure. Ike knew where they were going. It was worth sending a text, hoping it would go through where a phone call wouldn't or that it would send itself if he could get to somewhere with better reception.

The amount of concentration required to hit the correct buttons on the small screen made him dizzy. He managed to enter the words 'Camp need help' and hit 'send' before he felt a wave of nausea overcome him. He tossed the phone on the seat, got out of the car and vomited in the brush a few steps away, feeling the pressure behind his eyes and in his sinuses. After a minute, he felt considerably better. He spit a few times and returned to the car, groping under the front bumper and along the wheel wells for a spare key.

He found it behind the license plate inside the rear bumper. He pulled out the little magnetic box and dumped the key out, then dropped the box in the brush. He jumped back in the car and stuck the key in the ignition, simultaneously reaching for the door to pull it shut.

But the door did not shut. Irritated, Tracey glanced to his left. George Cole was standing there, blocking the door with one hand on the window frame. In his right hand, he held his rifle.

"Thanks for finding the key," George said. "How much of an idiot do you think I am?"

Tracey said nothing. He gazed up at George, feeling a wave of defeat.

"I found this little car last night, when Gil first sent me out to look for it," George continued. "I decided not to tell 'em, though, because I figured I needed to do some thinking, and I didn't want to play all my cards."

"Yeah?" Tracey asked. "So what card are you going to play now?"

235

George contemplated him for a moment. "Well, there's a few things I could do. I could march you right back up to Van."

"If you do, Van'll kill me," Tracey said. "After you were gone, Gil told us he knew Van killed Francis. It made sense when he explained it, but don't ask me to repeat it all right now. Gil said he was going to kill Van for revenge. We got away from him, but then we ran into Van. I guess you know the rest of it, but I don't know if you realize what it is Van's been doing here or who he really is."

"No, I guess I don't. But now I have to agree with Gil, it looks like Van might have knocked off Francis and then set me up for it. Or at least had it done, if he didn't do it himself."

"Van's playing you for a fool," Tracey pushed. "He must have been planning this for a long time. You can't go back there now, with or without me."

"But if I don't go with Van, the cops are going to haul my ass in on suspicion of murder, not to mention a bunch of other stuff I'm not supposed to be doing. And I have no kind of alibi. One thing I do know, Van's been on the run for at least ten years, and he's good at putting distance between himself and whoever's looking for him. He could put that distance between me and whoever's looking for me, too. If I screw this up, it's over for me. I'll end up back in prison."

Suddenly George snapped the rifle upright and moved towards the car. "Move over," he said. "I'd rather make you drive, but I can see you're in no shape, and I don't want to get in a wreck."

"Where are we going?" Tracey asked as he scrambled over into the passenger seat. He palmed the cell phone and casually stuck it down along the side of the seat as he moved.

"I got an errand to do," George said. "Plus, there's someone I need to talk to. Someone who might know a little bit more than we give him credit for. You're coming with me until I figure out who I'm going to trust and how I'm going to save my ass."

236

George cranked the ignition, then put it in reverse and careened backwards onto the dirt road.

"What about Addie?" Tracey asked as George cranked the wheel and maneuvered so the car was straddling the ruts in the mud caused by the recent heavy traffic.

"She's there at the camp," George said. "She's with Van. He's been talking to her. I don't know what's going on, but Van's got something on her, I think. Something to do with her brother. Anyway, you can't help her now. There's nothing either of us can do until they're away from that camp."

Tracey slumped back in the passenger seat. At least Addie was alive and, for the moment, safe. But he didn't like knowing she was with Van. He thought about the text he'd sent to Ike, and suddenly realized the way he felt about Van must be the way Ike felt about him.

It seemed like a long time before they saw the farm road ahead. As they came out of the woods and up over the road shoulder, Tracey glanced down the farm road to the left, towards the pulp mill. A couple hundred feet away, he noticed a big yellow pick-up truck parked on the far shoulder, facing their direction. The passenger side door was open, and a man sat partly inside, with one leg out. George veered to the right, spinning his tires in the loose dirt, and accelerated towards the bridge. Tracey turned in his seat and saw the man pull his leg in and slam the door. Then a couple of elbows and a rifle came out the passenger side window of the truck.

"Shit," George swore. "It's the Brock brothers. They think I'm you or Addie. They don't know it's me."

George gunned it as the car's tires hit the pavement, and the little car, newly tuned, responded by picking up speed. Tracey saw the truck swerve and dirt spray from the tires as the driver accelerated off the shoulder and onto the asphalt. The passenger was still leaning out, bracing himself on the door frame. Tracey ducked his head apprehensively, and a rifle round shattered the rear window.

George downshifted and hit the gas again. They were making time on the truck as they crossed the bridge over the Deuce River, but the road from there on was wide and open, with cleared shoulders and a good, long view. The passenger would have an easy time of it, even from a distance away, if he was a good shot.

"Idiots," George yelled as he yanked the wheel back and forth, weaving across lanes and trying to make them harder to hit. "Van'd kill them if he knew they were shooting at us like this. They were supposed to stop you or Addie, not kill either one of you. They're not bad enough shots to be hitting the windows when they're aiming for the tires or engine. I know, I taught 'em how to shoot."

At least one more shot hit the car in the tail; Tracey wasn't sure if more came in through the shattered back window or not. He leaned forward and gripped the dashboard for balance, trying to keep his head down. The straightaway seemed to last forever, although at that speed he knew they'd reach the highway intersection inside of twenty minutes.

As they came around the bend in the road where it began to run south toward the Preserve's Visitor Center, Tracey saw red-and-blue flashing lights coming their way. They were going more than a hundred miles an hour now, sure to attract attention. George waited until the patrol vehicle was in clear view, then stepped on the brake and laid rubber down the road, finally fishtailing off into the wet grass of the shoulder. Then he yanked the emergency brake handle and the little car stopped abruptly. Tracey threw open the door and rolled out onto the grass. He looked through underneath the car and saw the white patrol car's nose dip as the driver hit the brakes. Then the yellow pickup flashed by in the other direction, and he heard three shots impact the car.

George was splayed across both seats, trying to stay out of the line of fire. "Get in!" he yelled, grabbing the back of Tracey's shirt.   Tracey scrambled to his feet and threw himself back into the car. He could not see the yellow pick-up; it had apparently continued on its track to the west. But the white patrol car had pulled a U-turn on the farm road several hundred yards behind them and was roaring back in their direction.

George accelerated and fled before the patrol car. Tracey peered through the shattered glass of the back window. He was fairly sure it was Buster Brighton. At the next dirt road, George stepped on the brake, then fishtailed off the farm road and gunned it again. The patrol car screamed on by, lights flashing, more interested in the pick-up with the gun out the window than in them.

"You could have stopped and let Buster know we were okay," Tracey said reproachfully. "Or told him what was going on and asked for help, even."

"Yeah, I think he figured out we're okay when we started driving again," George laughed grimly. "I think he figured out it wasn't your girlfriend in this car, either. But he decided to go after the gun out the window rather than after the stolen vehicle, which, by the way, is what this is. And I can't afford to get busted now. Nothing's changed as far as that goes. And I doubt he's all by himself; he's going to have everybody and their brother out looking for this car, and everybody else out at that camp. We got to ditch this car somewhere fast."

"Yeah?" Tracey said cynically, "we're headed the right direction. I know a good lake you could dump it in."

"Hmmm." George glanced over at him. "Not a bad idea, cousin."

Chapter Eighteen

Outside at the fire ring, Addie perched tensely on a log. Besides Van and Howie, the core group consisted of Charlie, with long, dark hair in a ponytail; Derek, a talkative storyteller; Silas, a compact athletic young man; and Jesse, Van's younger brother, who resembled him strongly physically, but was taciturn and intense and spent most of the evening working on a laptop computer connected to a car battery. There were also two others, Troy and Trent Brock, the men who had been in the yellow truck, but Van sent them down to the bridge to wait and see if Tracey came out there. Howie and George were gone for a while shuttling a pickup to Magnolia Slough, and Charlie took Gil home in a boat, towing Gil's boat behind, since his eyes were still too swollen for him to navigate safely.

Derek and Silas were on dinner duty, and Addie was eventually presented with a plate of decent barbecued chicken and a baked potato.

"We would offer you venison, but Jesse didn't come home with anything last time he went hunting," Silas said pointedly. Jesse shot him a poisonous look and the two locked eyes for a moment.

"I think venison is disgusting, anyway," Derek said hurriedly. "Nasty stuff if you ask me. I don't eat beef or pork, or any mammal meat, for that matter. I stick with fish and fowl. Gotta be careful about the fish you catch around here, though. I hear some of them can be loaded with dioxins and other chemicals..."

Howie had returned with a case of beer, and he offered her one with a smile.

Addie hesitated a moment. "Sure, why not?" she decided. Howie popped the top for her. It was ice-cold and Addie shivered after the first swallow: the sun was going down and she was still damp from the river. A minute later Howie reappeared with what was obviously one of his own jackets and draped it over her shoulders. Addie stuffed her arms into it gratefully. It was too big, but it was weather-resistant and warm.

Derek soon launched into a series of stories about his days working as an Emergency Medical Technician, many of which Addie could relate to. She found herself laughing along with Silas and Howie, but she tried to keep an eye on what else was going on around the camp. Jesse didn't join them in their story-telling, and in fact, often when she glanced at him she found him glaring at her. Other than Jesse, everyone seemed friendly and they treated her as though she was already part of the group, although she noticed that Van kept a close eye on her when she went off to the outhouse at the edge of the slough.

Late in the evening, Van pulled Charlie aside, off near the river. She couldn't hear what was going on, but from their body language she guessed it was some sort of disagreement. Charlie shrugged and gestured, apparently denying some accusation or question. When Van returned to the fire ring, he bent and spoke to Jesse, but Jesse brushed him off, refusing to go with him. Van's jaw tensed, but he relented and rejoined the group.

Eventually the beer was gone, and Van, who was sitting next to her on the log, got up. "Come on," he said. "Let's get some sleep." Addie followed him while the rest of the group went off towards the other two buildings. There were only two bunks in the front building, which seemed to be used more as an office, and it appeared that Van had claimed that one as his personal space.

Addie spent the night on the bottom bunk pressed between the wall and Van. She knew she needed to sleep, to prepare herself for whatever the next day would hold, but she couldn't force down the thoughts that kept circulating in her mind. It seemed like she went over the same things again and again: her conversation with Van, his offer, her brother's involvement with the group, their past together, the missing files, and then, finally, with a sleep-defeating

241

jolt of adrenalin, the fact that Tracey was missing and possibly drowned in the Deuce.

She awoke in the middle of the night to the sound of whispered voices. She could feel that Van was no longer in the bed. She was lying on her stomach, and she raised her head a bit, allowing her eyes to adjust to the dark. Van stood near the cabin door, one hand braced against the wall, talking face-to-face with Jesse. Addie strained to hear. The tone of their voices was tense, she thought, but she could only make out some of the words.

"It's dangerous," Jesse said. "Think about who she is, what she does."

"I know you don't like it," Van whispered, "but this is my call. Look, I know how to take care of this group. I can't afford to have you going wildcat on me again. I swear I'll relegate you to the strike team."

Jesse turned impatiently towards the door. Addie laid her head down again quickly. Van returned to the bed and climbed in quietly. Addie could hear his breathing in the dark and knew he lay awake, as she did. Obviously Jesse was not in favor of her admittance to the group, but there seemed to be more to the conversation. Had Jesse made some decision on his own of which Van disapproved? She thought back to Van's confrontation with Charlie and Silas' comment about Jesse's latest hunting venture. Maybe Jesse and Charlie had taken their own initiative without the rest of the group's knowledge or assent, and the group members were just now beginning to figure things out. But she wasn't confident that she'd interpreted things correctly. Addie pulled the blanket over her ears and turned to the wall, willing herself to sleep.

Van was up and stirring before dawn. He lit a lantern on the table near the door and Addie was roused by the smell of kerosene burning and the low hiss of the gas. She stood up and wrapped the wool blanket around herself in the damp of the morning. She could see the faint light of the impending sunrise.

242

Van stepped outside, stretched, and whistled. The rest of the men joined Van and Addie at the cabin.

"Where the hell are the Brock brothers?" Van asked no one in particular when the group was assembled inside.

"Still down at the bridge, I guess," Howie said. "I think they were figuring they would take a last look around for Tracey once it got good and light. They were going to look for her car, too." He nodded at Addie. "We forgot to look for it last night. George was driving like a bat out of hell, like he usually does. I was worried about just keeping up with him but still keeping far enough behind that I wouldn't slam into him if he broke a goddamn axle on that two-track."

Silas and Derek both laughed appreciatively. Apparently George's driving was a matter of common knowledge. George himself was not in the cabin, though.

"Well, if they haven't found Tracey by now, it's too late. We need to get going," Van said. He spread out a number of colorful short-range personal radios on the table and frowned.

"I don't think the Brock brothers took one," Howie said, pointing out two matching blue ones. "They would've had one of these."

"Idiots. And they don't have cell phones. So we have no contact with them," Van grumbled. "Well, I hope they're back soon. Are you guys ready to go?"

"Yeah, we can leave any time, soon as we get this coffee brewed," Charlie said. He was heating a pot of water on a gas-powered burner on the table. "I took down the solar panels and satellite dish last night and packed up most of the files."

Van turned to Silas. "How about you?"

"I'm going now."

"When you drive out of here, see if you can't find the Brocks down by the bridge and send 'em back to me to help break down.

243

Wake 'em up if they fell asleep," Van said. Silas nodded as he left the cabin, heading for one of the trucks. Van turned to Howie.

"Howie, you load up one of the quads in Derek's truck and you two get out of here now. Don't screw around, okay? No last minute sneak attacks on the way out of town. I want you safe. There'll be plenty of opportunities for action in the future."

"Silas gets all the fun this time, huh?" Howie replied.

"This time. We don't need you up there."

Howie looked down for a moment, as if deciding whether or not to argue, but then he nodded. "Okay, Van. You don't want to leave the quads here?"

"We'll take two and leave two for Gil," Van said. "You take one and I'll take one in my truck."

Van grabbed a mug from the table and poured himself a cup of coffee. He poured a second and handed it to Addie.

"Charlie, you might as well go now, too," he said. "Go out to the east along the farm road. Don't go through town in case something's happening with the Brock brothers, or in case anybody else gets picked up."

"Okay," Charlie said. He pulled a pair of glasses from his shirt pocket and settled them on his nose. "Give me one of the radios. I'll keep in touch with Howie. If either of us has any problems, we can ditch one of the vehicles and take the other."

"Good," Van said. He stuck out his hand to Charlie. "See you, then, hopefully in a couple-three days."

Charlie grabbed a briefcase-style bag from the floor, and he, Jesse, Howie, and Derek left the cabin. Addie heard them yelling to each other outside, and the rattling of the ATV engine as they loaded Derek's truck.

"Where are the guys headed off to?" Addie ventured.

Van gave a half smile. "You'll find out soon enough." He ran his hand through his hair. "Well, if the Brock brothers don't show up pretty soon, they'll just have to take care of themselves. I can't wait around for them. You and me will head out in my pickup, that Chevy Howie and George picked up last night."

"Where is George?" Addie asked, glancing around.

"Poking around somewhere out on the river, I guess. He's supposed to meet us up at Magnolia Slough Road. He'll come up in one of the boats. After we meet up, he can take the truck that's stashed up there, and you and me will go in mine. Are you finished with that coffee? Grab some stuff and let's get started."

Addie picked up two camp lanterns and the folding stove and followed Van out. She didn't see Gil, either. It surprised her a little that he hadn't come up with some excuse to return, looking for his chance at Van. His absence gave her a glimmer of hope, though. Perhaps he'd had a change of heart, and he'd let someone know what was going on at the camp.

Charlie pulled a set of aluminum ramps out of the bed of the green truck and ran the ATV up in the back.

"You climb up there and strap it down," Van instructed Addie. She climbed into the truck bed and began attaching the straps to the ATV. She watched as Charlie and Jesse pulled away in a green Subaru wagon, towing a boat trailer with one of the utility boats on it. The car had Illinois plates, barely visible as it turned in the clearing. Addie squinted, trying to memorize them.

Derek and Howie finished loading their truck and walked over to Van. Van shook hands with Derek, then Howie. As Howie began to turn, Van pulled him back suddenly, still gripping his hand.

"Don't do anything I wouldn't do," Van said seriously. It sounded to Addie more like a warning than a trite farewell.

Howie grinned. "Never," he said. "Be careful, man."

Van continued to grip Howie's hand for another few moments. "If for some reason I don't meet you there, take care of things. You know what I mean."

Howie sobered, meeting Van's eyes. Then he jumped into Derek's truck and followed Charlie down the dirt road. The sound of the engine faded away in the early morning. That left just Van and Addie at the camp.

Van looked up at Addie in the truck bed. "Just about ready," he said. "Silas should have started shift by now."

"He's not leaving today?" Addie asked.

"Yes, he's leaving," Van said. "But he's going to set a little accidental fire at the adhesives plant first. That'll get rid of evidence, close the plant, and hopefully get our friends up there out with an insurance payment. It'll also be a good distraction for the local authorities. He's supposed to get things going as soon as he comes on shift. And we need to be away from here in case he gets caught."

"He's doing it while people are there? Isn't that dangerous?" Addie asked in some alarm.

Van shook his head. "He knows what he's doing. Everybody will be out safe."

Van leaned against the side of the truck and gazed at the morning mist rising off the Deuce. A great blue heron launched itself from its nighttime perch in a cypress across the water and winged heavily up the channel. Van studied it, squinting as the sunlight flickered off the surface of the river. Then he turned suddenly and looked up at Addie. Their eyes met, and Addie experienced a strange feeling, a combination of fear and curiosity.

Van turned abruptly and walked a short ways down the access road, his back to her, his head cocked as if listening. Addie hooked one of the ATV straps into a loop installed in the truck bed and yanked it taut, then rocked the ATV to make sure it couldn't shift.

"Hey!"

Addie looked up at the shout. Van was running back towards her at full speed. Addie realized she could hear a vehicle coming in along the access road. She wondered if it was the Brock brothers, but only for a second.

"Get down!" Van yelled. He grabbed Addie by the arm and yanked her over the side of the truck, half-supporting her. She landed awkwardly, and Van gave her a terrific shove towards the slough.

As Addie regained her feet, she saw a flash through the trees. Not the Brock brothers: they'd been driving a yellow truck. A white vehicle, maybe, she realized with a flash of both hope and fear, a police vehicle of some kind.

"Get to the boats! Now!" Van screamed at her. He brought his rifle around to the front, holding it with the butt up against his shoulder and his hand on the trigger guard, ready to raise and fire at a second's notice. Addie wasn't sure if the threat was meant for her or if Van planned to shoot at the vehicles as they came into the clearing.

She hesitated only a moment, then complied: if they escaped in the boat, Van wouldn't shoot at the cars, she quickly decided. And Ike, Buster, or any number of other people she knew could be in those cars.

As she slid down the bank, she saw the first vehicle roar into the camp clearing. It stopped short, a wise move on the part of the driver, who couldn't know what or who he would find. Van jumped into the boat after her, shoved off, and started the motor, his rifle on its sling clanging against the housing. The motor faltered, then caught, and they were out of the slough and onto the river, leaving the camp behind at full speed.

"Those were cop cars," Van shouted over the whine of the motor. "Somebody's onto us."

"Do you think Silas got caught?" Addie asked. "Or Gil turned you in?"

"I don't know what happened, but I'll bet it had something to do with the Brock brothers not coming back. That or Tracey managed to get away and get help. I hope to God Charlie and Jesse

247

and Howie and Derek were clear. Keep an eye out for any other boats on the water."

Addie glanced back at Van, who was studying the river ahead. Jumping into the river didn't seem a viable option for escape, given her last experience. She would have to wait for a better opportunity, if, indeed, that's what she intended to do. She realized she wasn't trying very hard to escape; her mind still rocked back and forth on the edge of decision.

"If the Brock brothers got caught, it's not the end of the world," Van mused. "They're new. I just picked them up in San Antonio six months ago. They don't know much about our organization. They don't know about the support system or the financing. But if Silas got caught, it's bad news." He glanced up, catching Addie's eye. "Do you know how to get to Magnolia Slough?" he shouted over the motor noise.

"Of course," Addie replied, "but we can't get there from the river. It's off Thief Creek."

"I know. I want to get to the end of Magnolia Slough Road, not the slough itself. That's where the truck's stashed."

Of course, Addie remembered, the end of Magnolia Slough Road was also where Bobbie's house and the inventory copies were located.

Van kept the tiller cranked up, the boat skipping around the bends in the river. Dirt from muddy feet on the bow dried in the wind and flew off in clumps, stinging Addie's bare face. Her sunglasses were lost or left somewhere, and she squinted into the glare of the morning sun on the river. She thought she could see a haze developing over the trees. It began to consolidate into a column: it looked like smoke, maybe from the adhesives plant.

She turned around and yelled back to Van. "If you want to get out near Magnolia Slough Road, you'd better pull up along here some place. Otherwise you'll get under the bank, and we won't be able to climb out."

Van slowed the boat and ran it over towards the west bank of the river. There was a shallow flooded backwater behind a little river island. Addie directed them into the backwater and Van put the boat up on the shore. Together, they pulled the boat up the sand and into the woods. Right where they pulled it into the brush, they came upon a second boat. It was a small Sea Ark.

"George must be here already," Van said as they walked by the boat. "Maybe he's waiting at the truck."

Addie frowned and looked back over her shoulder as they passed the boat. She had come around the left side while Van walked up the right side. As she passed the boat, she saw a dent and scrape on the left side bow. Skeeter's boat, she thought. One of the utility boats had gone with Charlie and she and Van had the other one. George should therefore have come up river in the second small jon-boat, the one without a dent.

They walked quickly north and uphill through the pines towards the bluff where Bobbie's house stood. Van carried his rifle on its sling across the front of his body, with one hand resting on the stock to keep it from swinging.

Partway up the hill, they paused. It was already hot. Addie wiped her brow on her sleeves and pulled out the collar of her T-shirt to allow some air to filter down between the cloth and her chest. Van gazed up the slope through the woods towards the top of the rise where Bobbie's house stood. He swung the rifle on its sling so that it lay against his back, rather than across his chest where he had been carrying it.

At that moment, Gil stepped out of the woods. He held a pistol in one hand, and as he approached he pointed it directly at Van's chest.

A surprised expression passed briefly over Van's face, then he brought his hands out to the sides, palms up, as if in a gesture of surrender. "Hey, what's up, Gil?" he asked.

"You killed my brother and now it's your turn," Gil growled. "I just wanted to look you in the face instead of shooting you in the back like the coward you are, like you did to Francis."

Van smiled slightly and shook his head. "I didn't kill Francis," he said. "If you're going to kill me, go ahead, but if you do you'll never know the truth."

Gil's eyes flicked away for half a second. In a single, sweeping motion, Van twisted his body to the side and grabbed the pistol with his right hand. Then he brought his left hand up under the barrel, knocking the muzzle up into the air, and yanked down on the gun, against Gil's twisted wrist. Gil yelled, and a single shot went off. Addie flinched; the shot went over Van's left shoulder. Van yanked again on the gun, now loose in Gil's grip but still hung up on his trigger-finger. Gil yelled in pain again, going down to his knees, and Van shook the gun loose. Then he kicked Gil in the face, knocking him backwards. Gil sprawled on the ground, blood running from his right forefinger and his face. Van quickly flipped the pistol around so it was pointing the right way, at Gil.

Addie leapt forward almost without thinking and grabbed Van's arm. Van wheeled around, but Addie held on. She clutched the pistol and tried to twist it out of his hand. But Van hadn't wasted his time just pretending to run a paramilitary camp: he knew what he was doing, and he was stronger and taller than Addie.

Van stepped forward and punched the pistol towards her, then yanked it back, breaking her grip. Then he shoved her shoulder violently and swept her leg out from underneath her as he stepped past her right side, throwing her onto her back on the ground.

Addie grabbed for the pistol and managed to get a hand on the barrel again as she went down, yanking Van towards her. As Van bent forward, his rifle slid around him so Addie got a frightening view down the barrel for a moment. She turned her head quickly, and the swinging barrel knocked her in the temple, disorienting her.

She managed to keep a grip on the pistol barrel. For a few seconds they were in a tug-of-war. Van, crouched over her, tried to jerk the pistol out of her grip, and Addie, on her back, did her best to hold on. Then Van suddenly let his arm go slack. He jumped to his feet and jerked his body sideways, yanking his arm straight with the force and the speed of his turn. With her arm loose from Van's unexpected release, Addie was unprepared: Van's sudden movement straightened her arm out with a snap.

She felt her shoulder separate from the socket. Her fingers opened, and Van had the pistol. At the last second, as Van jumped away from her, Addie clawed at the rifle sling. The rifle slid over Van's head the rest of the way and fell on the ground beside her.

Addie rolled up onto one knee and snatched the rifle off the ground with her left hand. Her right arm felt numb and unresponsive, but she had shot a rifle with her left hand before. She pulled the butt in against her shoulder and looked up.

Van stood a few feet away, leveling the pistol at her. He was holding it extended, his body turned sideways to her. His finger was on the trigger and the barrel was pointed at her chest. She had the rifle pointed in his direction, but without a second hand to steady it, it wavered from side to side.

As she looked up and met Van's eyes, she knew he had her. He had the advantage; he could shoot her at any moment. But he stood stock still, the pistol steady in his hand, the muscles of his arm taut, and did not pull the trigger. It seemed to Addie that time slowed, and her mind raced through every possible action she could make without settling on any one of them.

The crack of rifle fire sounded in the clearing. Van jumped and a look of alarm crossed his face. He went down on one knee, bringing the pistol across his chest. Then he collapsed forward silently. His eyes, as he fell, continued to lock Addie's. She stared until his body hit the ground and his head turned, breaking his gaze.

251

Gil seemed to come to his senses. He rolled to his hands and knees and then scrambled to his feet, staring into the woods. It was definitely a rifle shot, and definitely not from close by. Addie had not fired. Someone else was shooting at them.

Gil scooped up the pistol, now loose on the ground. Addie forced herself to her feet, clutching the rifle, and stared uncomprehendingly at Van, who lay sprawled.

"Come on! Run!" Gil yelled at her. Addie willed herself to action, and together they stumbled out of the clearing and through the line of trees south of the bluff. Bobbie's house was less than a hundred yards away.

Addie ran for the front door, expecting to hear another shot at any second, with no time to guess at the motive or targets of the shooter. She was gasping for air by the time they reached Bobbie's doorstep. She stumbled into the door and it swung open, unlocked and unlatched. Gil staggered in after her. Once inside, he slammed the door and locked it, his breath coming hard. He sniffed and wiped his bloody nose on his arm. His right forefinger was obviously broken.

And then they were standing face-to-face in the living room. Gil still held the pistol, and the blood crept down onto his upper lip again. Addie held the rifle in her left hand, too close to Gil to bring it up.

There was a long moment of silence. They remained face-to-face, eyes locked.

"I was going to kill him back there," Gil finally said.

"But you didn't," Addie said. "Somebody else did."

"I'm screwed now, aren't I?" Gil asked. "They'll get me for everything, for all of this."

"I don't know what they'll get you for," Addie said, "but at least it won't be murder. I think you can make a case that you didn't know who they were or what they were planning when they asked to

252

use your camp. And after you began to figure it out, you were afraid of them."

"Yeah, but I'll have a harder time explaining why I tried to keep you out at the camp."

Addie nodded. "You will." She glanced at the pistol. "Look, don't do it again. You go where you need to go. I'm not even going to try and stop you. Just leave me here."

Gil hesitated and looked towards the door. Addie knew he could take the boat they'd come in. He might even be able to find the truck Van had been talking about.

"The door was open," he said suddenly. "Bobbie always locks it when she leaves."

"Do you think somebody else is in here?" Addie asked nervously.

Gil turned and crept towards the back of the house quietly, keeping the pistol tucked in by his side, using his left hand. Addie ducked into the kitchen, putting the bar-height counter between her and the rest of the house. She raised the rifle to rest across the counter and pulled the butt in to her left shoulder again.

She watched Gil as he made his way into the hallway. He stood back away from the first door, leaning a little sideways to peer into the room. Then he pushed the door open further. He quickly checked the other rooms the same way before returning to Addie.

"There's nobody here, but they were here," he said. "There were two boxes I stored in the spare bedroom. That's what Francis had on Van; that's what they killed him for. Now they're gone."

He sat down heavily on the arm of a chair in the living room, looking stunned. Without the copies, Addie realized, it would be difficult to prove that anything strange had been going on at the adhesives plant. She left the rifle lying on the counter and went into the living room, cradling her right arm with her left.

"Who else knew about them, knew they were here?" she asked.

"I don't know. Nobody. I figured Van might guess. That's why I came here." He twisted his wrist and looked down at the pistol, studying the side of it, then looked at the end of the barrel.

Addie saw the motion and guessed at the idea behind it. "Gil, don't even think it," she said, lowering her voice to force his attention.

"Why not?" Gil readjusted the pistol in his hand, as if testing its weight. "Why the hell not? Francis is dead. Van's probably dead now, that's all I was waiting for. What do I have to look forward to? Years of my life in prison?"

"No," Addie said. "It's not that bad."

"Yeah," Gil said, getting to his feet, "it is that bad. But not in here; not in Bobbie's house. She doesn't deserve that."

He walked slowly to the door, but then turned abruptly and transferred the pistol awkwardly to his injured right hand. Then he plunged his left hand into his pocket.

"Here," he said, and he took a few steps back towards Addie and held his hand out. Automatically, she put her hand out, and Gil dropped something small and heavy into it. "Francis gave it to me a couple days before he disappeared."

Addie glanced at her palm and saw a silver-colored metal pendant. When she looked up, Gil was already back at the door. He unlocked it and pushed it open.

"Jesus Christ!" he exclaimed, jumping back in alarm. Through the open door, Addie could see a semi-circle of patrol cars blocking Magnolia Slough Road, doors swinging wide. A multitude of firearms were pointed in their direction.

"Put the gun down now!" an amplified voice commanded. Gil, apparently too startled to remember his own intentions, obeyed immediately, placing the pistol on the ground just outside the door. He raised his hands. Addie slipped the pendant into her pocket and stepped out beside him, raising her arms as far as she could with her injured shoulder. She felt relief flood through her. She could see a big white pickup parked behind the row of cars: Ike was there.

It took only a few minutes for the officers to take Gil into custody. Addie found herself being hurried back behind the row of cars towards the pickup by Ike, who wrapped a protective arm around her back to escort her to safety. She looked up at him, registering the expression of alarm and concern on his face.

"I'm okay, Ike, I just have a wrenched shoulder," Addie said, more calmly than she felt. Ike steered her to the passenger seat of his truck and pulled out his first-aid jump-kit. He fashioned a sling quickly from a triangular bandage and bound her arm to her chest with another. Addie grimaced as the binder pressed on her ribs. They were bruised as well, from her fall in Van's boat.

"You have some kind of mark on your temple," Ike said, examining it. "Looks like a circle."

"From the barrel of a rifle," Addie replied. She didn't elaborate. "I'm dying of thirst."

Ike pulled his ice chest out of the back of the truck and popped the top of a soda for her. "Probably from the adrenalin," he said as he handed the can to her. "My mouth always gets dry when I get an adrenalin rush. Think I'll have one myself."

"How did you know we'd be here?" Addie asked.

"I got that text on your cell phone," Ike said. "When I couldn't get hold of you all night or this morning, I went by and saw that your car wasn't at your house. I figured something must've gone wrong out at the Lejeunes' camp."

"What text?" Addie asked.

Ike looked at her for a moment. "I got a text from your cell number. You didn't send it?"

"No, my cell phone was in my car, I think, and I haven't been with my car since yesterday. What did it say?"

"It said 'camp need help'," Ike said. "Whoever took your car must have sent it."

255

"Where is my car?" Addie asked.

"We don't know right now," Ike said. "After I got the text I called Buster and asked him to respond because I was all the way down in Buenavista. He went out towards the camp and met a gray Toyota coming at him at a hundred miles an hour, being chased by a yellow truck with a passenger who was shooting out the window. Buster decided to go after the truck rather than the car, but he got the plate, and when he ran it, it came back as yours. But he said there were two guys in it. He thought one of them might have been Tracey."

"And they were being shot at?" Addie asked in concern.

"Yeah, but Buster said they must've been okay, because the car turned off the highway and kept going. Anyway, several of us went in to the camp, but there was nobody there when we got there."

"No, we were just leaving," Addie said ruefully.

"So when we found the camp empty, and with Buster's info about the car, we started trying to figure where Tracey would go if he was hiding or in trouble. We had units check the Radners', including Dennis Radner's house, and his grandpa's place on Pine Slough, and finally we came up this way, to his sister's. The first unit here heard a gunshot in the woods and saw two people run into the house with firearms. When we got here we came in quiet, and we could see you guys moving around in there. So we were ready when you came out."

Addie nodded. "But you still haven't found Tracey."

"No, or whoever it was he was with, or your car. The county did stop that yellow truck, though, just west of town. Last I heard they were negotiating a surrender with the occupants. But right now I need to get you over to the hospital, or at least an urgent-care," Ike said. "You need to get that shoulder X-rayed. You can tell me everything while I drive."

Ike fastened Addie's seatbelt for her. The dirt road was rough, and the jouncing made Addie's shoulder ache. She tried to

256

distract herself by answering Ike's questions and asking more questions herself.

"What's happening at the adhesives plant?"

"There's a fire going on there," Ike said. "We'll be able to see the smoke from the highway. The fire started in the office complex, and they're trying to contain it to keep it from spreading into the manufacturing area and becoming a giant hazardous-materials scene. No injuries, though, as far as I've heard." Ike glanced at her curiously. "Why did you ask about the adhesives plant? How did you know something would be going on there?"

"It's too complicated to explain right now," Addie said. "Does anybody have any idea where George Cole is?"

"No," Ike said. "Buster sent some units over to the Dohenys' boat ramp to check for your car there. He thought there might be some connection with Skeeter Doheny and that George might be hanging out there. They didn't find anyone, but there were the remains of what appears to be a little one-pot meth lab in one of those old houses along the slough. Skeeter is missing, too."

"Skeeter's boat is down in the woods on the shore," Addie said. She stopped, considering. There were a lot of questions still unanswered in her mind.

At the urgent-care, it took several hours to get an X-ray and a consultation with the doctor. Ike kept her company and took notes as she told him what had happened out at the camp and who had been involved, leaving out the part about her brother and Van's offers to her.

Finally the doctor viewed the X-rays and decided that while her shoulder had been dislocated, it had returned to the socket by itself. There was little that could be done, other than let it heal and keep it in a sling. Ike stopped at a pharmacy and Addie picked up a prescription for pain pills.

"I guess I shouldn't take one of these now," Addie said, reading the side of the bottle. "They'll probably knock me out."

"Go ahead. I think you should go home now and try and get some rest," Ike said. "I'll take this information you gave me and we'll see what we can do with it. When you've had some sleep, of course, somebody will want to do a full-scale interview with you to get everything you know. But it can wait until tomorrow. In fact, it should wait until you've had a chance to get your head together."

Addie swallowed one of the pills and slumped in the seat, beginning to feel the effects of the last two days. But as they turned onto her street, she sat up suddenly.

"Hold it."

Ike hit the brakes. Parked along the curb near her house, Addie saw a beat-up green pickup truck. She wasn't sure, but she thought she'd seen it out at the camp the evening before. It looked like the one Van had sent Howie and George to stash up at Magnolia Slough.

Ike drew his pistol and slowly drove towards Addie's house with his left hand on the wheel, his window open. There was no one in the truck, and Addie saw no one she didn't recognize in the neighborhood.

But as they drew even with her front stoop, Addie did see someone. Outside her door was a buck-toothed, redheaded kid, dressed in jeans and an over-sized military shirt. He was sitting on a copy-shop box. And behind him, in the shadow of her porch, leaning against the wall with his arms crossed and one leg up, was Tracey Cole.

Chapter Nineteen

Ike re-holstered his pistol and Addie jumped out of the truck almost before he could pull to a stop. She stumbled on the curb, nearly going to her knees. The grin on Tracey's face disappeared, and he jumped off the side of the porch and grabbed her arm.

"You doing okay?"

Addie couldn't help but smile at the familiar phrase, despite the pain. "I'll be okay. It's just a sprain," she answered, gesturing at her shoulder. Then her own smile faded. Tracey's clothes smelled like dried river mud and his hair was tousled and tangled, but what concerned her most was what appeared to be dried blood on top of one shoulder.

"What about you? Where have you been? Are you all right?"

Tracey guided her towards the house. "Yeah, getting better. I got my head smacked by the boat and I think I got grazed by a bullet on top of my shoulder. I didn't even notice when it happened, I was too damn scared. But it's not too bad. It'll be okay."

Ike came up on Addie's other side and put a hand protectively on her back. "I'll bet you were in Addie's car when Buster saw it. One of the shots from those guys in the yellow truck grazed you, didn't it? You should've stopped and told Buster what was going on. We could have avoided a lot of this."

Tracey glanced at Ike, but spoke to Addie. "George was driving. I would've stopped if I had a choice. I'm sorry about your car," he added.

"Where is it?" Addie asked.

"In Thief Creek," Tracey shrugged, with an embarrassed grin. Ike gave a hopeless gesture. "It's down the boat ramp in between Gil and Francis Lejeune's places. George put it there so no one would see it and find us before he could get away. It's pretty shot up, but it should be easy enough to tow back up the ramp."

"Come on, Addie," Ike said, urging her up the front steps. "Let's get you inside and sitting down. Then we can talk about what happened. Where's your key?"

With some effort, Addie extracted her house key from her right front pocket with her left hand, to avoid using the injured arm. Ike took it and let them into the house. Then he brought the boxes in one at a time and set them on the living room floor.

Addie let herself gingerly down onto the couch next to Tracey. After a few minutes of fumbling around in the kitchen, Ike managed to locate glasses and ice cubes and poured four sodas. He handed one to Addie, one to Tracey, and held one out to Skeeter, who was skulking behind the armchair just inside the door. Despite his obvious discomfort, Skeeter took the soda.

Ike put his own glass on the coffee table and knelt on the carpet to open the battered cardboard boxes. Addie leaned forward, and Ike pulled the boxes closer to her so she could see. As he pulled up the lid, an odor of damp cardboard and musty paper wafted into the room. Inside were water-stained sheaves of copy paper, as well as several unlabeled thumb drives, CDs, and zip disks.

"It looks like copies of financial records," Ike said. He made a face at the mildew and closed the boxes up again without touching anything inside. "We'll have to get these to someone who knows what to look for in them," he said. "I have no idea what any of this means."

"All that stuff may help explain why Francis was murdered," Addie said. She realized as she spoke that no one else in the room knew the true circumstances leading to Francis' death. "They're financial and inventory records from the adhesives plant. They should show that anhydrous ammonia was being siphoned off. Van told me Francis tried blackmailing the group using these copies," she summarized quickly. "These records may also show a link between Van's group and the financiers of his operations, the owners of the adhesives plant."

260

"I guess we have you to thank for these, Tracey," Ike said grudgingly.

"Nope, Skeeter," Tracey corrected.

Addie and Ike looked at Skeeter, who glanced towards the door. Ike got up and pushed the door shut. "You're not going anywhere, Skeeter. You've been involved with a group of people who committed a lot of crimes. You're going to have to talk to someone about all this. You don't have to talk to us right now, without your Dad or some other relative with you, but I can't let you leave, either."

Skeeter shrugged self-consciously. "Okay, then, I'm not talking. You're after Van, but you don't know anything about him. Van isn't a bad guy like you think. He's the greatest person I ever met. He gave me the best things anybody ever gave me. And he was setting it up so Francis and Gil and George could make money out of that camp."

"But he also killed Francis," Addie pointed out. "Didn't Francis take care of you? I know you spent a lot of time down at the Lejeunes'."

Skeeter looked at her sharply. "Van didn't kill Francis," he said decisively. "He couldn't have and he wouldn't have."

Addie frowned skeptically. "Skeeter, the gun used to kill Francis was one George gave to Van to sell for him."

"That's right, and Van gave it to me," Skeeter continued, despite his earlier refusal to talk. "He said he couldn't get any money for it anyway. But he made me promise not to tell George he hadn't gotten rid of it."

Addie's heart sank. Skeeter was obviously attached to Van, and word of his death would certainly come as an unwelcome shock, especially if Skeeter didn't believe Van had killed Francis.

After a few more moments, what Skeeter had said began to sink in.

261

"So you had the gun, the one that belonged to George, the one used to kill Francis," she said carefully.

Skeeter stared at her, but said nothing.

"And your boat," Addie pointed out. "It has a dent on it with paint scrapings that match Tracey's car."

"And there's a meth lab up at your family's boat ramp," Ike put in.

"No!" Skeeter shook his head. "I know what you're trying to say! I'm not an idiot! But it's not the way it looks!"

"How is it, then?" Ike pressed. "How do you explain all that?"

Skeeter came around from behind the armchair. "I don't know how to explain everything, but that lab up at my place was Charlie's. He only used it one time, just before Francis disappeared. He ran an electric line over from the big house on Marker Slough. But Charlie told me never to let anybody know about that lab. He told me if I kept quiet he'd get me a new rifle. He did, and I gave him that old gun of George's. So he was the one who had that gun."

"But what about the boat?" Addie persisted. "Could Charlie have used your boat?"

"Sure. I took the boat down to the camp the night Francis went missing. Van took me to Buenavista to see my cousin Pet, and they took me to the movies. It was pouring rain out, so we left my boat at the camp and took Van's truck. That's how I know he couldn't have killed Francis."

"So Charlie could have had access to your boat that night," Addie mused. "And he manufactured meth just before Francis went missing. Was he at the camp that night? Was there anybody else out there?"

"Sure, Charlie was there and Jesse was there. Not the Brock brothers, though. And I think Howie and Derek and Silas were home in Aynesworth, but I don't remember for sure."

"Skeeter, what time did you and Van get back to the camp?" Ike asked.

"'Bout ten-thirty or eleven, I guess. Real late. I spent the night there so I wouldn't have to take the boat home in the rain and the dark."

Addie and Ike glanced at each other. So the boat had been at the camp all night, and there had been plenty of time after Van had returned from Buenavista for him to make it to Francis' place.

Skeeter fell silent, and neither Addie nor Ike pressed him further. There would be time to digest all of it, and figure out the how and the why, later. Ike turned to Tracey.

"So how did you come to be in possession of these records?"

Tracey gave Ike an odd look, but then he told them about his journey through the woods, about getting the car and the chase with the yellow truck and Buster, and how George had brought them to the Lejeunes' and rolled Addie's car into Thief Creek.

"Skeeter was hanging out at Gil's," Tracey said to Addie. "Me and George sat down and went over everything we knew. Then Skeeter told us Van went out to Gil's old camp on Widow Slough looking for a couple boxes a while back, maybe from a copy shop, but he hadn't found them there."

"I told Tracey and George I thought those boxes were at Bobbie's house," Skeeter put in.

Addie looked at him. "And you knew that because you heard Gil tell Bobbie he needed to store something that belonged to Francis at her house."

"How'd you know that?" Skeeter asked, with a quick incredulous smile.

"Because I heard the same thing. I was down along the river, the night Bobbie held that party out at her camp. And afterward I thought I heard someone back in the woods. That must've been you."

"Yeah. But I didn't remember until Tracey and George said something about it."

Tracey continued. "George said Van had him and Howie park that green truck up at Magnolia Slough Road, right near Bobbie's house. It seemed like a weird thing to do, unless there was some reason for Van to need to stop there when nobody was likely to be home at Bobbie's. We didn't know what was in the boxes, but we figured it might be something important. We went up there in Skeeter's boat, found the boxes and stowed them in the truck."

"And then what?" Addie asked, studying Tracey's face.

Tracey shrugged and avoided her eyes. "Well, let's just say me and Skeeter split with the boxes and the truck."

"What about George?" Ike asked.

"Don't know," Tracey said. "He didn't come with us."

"And what about the shot from the woods, the one that killed Van?" Addie said, and then bit her tongue. She glanced at Skeeter, who stared wide-eyed at her.

"Don't know about that, either," Tracey raised his eyebrows. "I never heard it. Me and Skeeter must've been gone by then."

"You know, if you're withholding information..." Ike began, but Addie hushed him.

"It doesn't matter," she said. "Whoever shot Van was reacting to what he could see from the woods, and I'm sure it looked like Van was going to shoot me. Whoever it was did what he did to save my life. He probably saved Gil's life, too."

Addie looked down at her lap as an image reappeared in her mind: Van's eyes, locked on hers as he fell to the ground. He almost certainly believed she had shot him. He had gone to his death with both of them believing wrongly about the other: he, that she had betrayed his trust, and she, that he was the killer he might not be.

"I can't think about this anymore right now," she said, looking up at Ike and Tracey. "I need to get some rest. I'm feeling those pain pills and I'm tired and dirty and just about used up."

"I'm sorry, Addie," Ike said immediately, a note of concern in his voice. "Do you want me to stay here with you?"

"I'll stay," Tracey said quickly. "You need to take care of Skeeter. You can take him in to juvenile or wherever he needs to go. And you can take care of these boxes. I can't."

"I guess you're right," Ike said grudgingly. "I'll check back later this evening. You let me know whatever you need."

"Thanks, Ike," Addie smiled. Ike put a hand on Skeeter's shoulder to escort him out of the house. Skeeter had not spoken in several minutes, and the look on his face was now one of defeat, rather than the defiance he'd first exhibited.

"You want me to bring those boxes out so the kid doesn't get away from you?" Tracey asked from the couch. Ike looked back at him and the two locked eyes for a moment. Tracey slid his arm off the couch back and down around Addie's shoulders.

"If you feel like being useful," Ike said icily, turning back towards the door. Tracey pushed himself off the couch and followed Ike out with one of the boxes, then returned for the second. Addie heard the engine of Ike's truck turn over, but it was a long moment before Tracey returned.

"What did Ike say to you out there?" she asked.

"Nothing," Tracey said. "Do you have any beer? I could use one right about now. If you don't, I can walk down to the gas station on the corner. Except I don't have any cash."

"There are some in the refrigerator," Addie told him. "Help yourself."

"You want one?"

"No, what I really want is to wash up. Besides, I shouldn't have one with these pain pills."

Addie gratefully stripped off her filthy clothes in the bathroom and stepped into the shower. Clean and dry, and with her arm readjusted in the sling, she began to feel a little better.

265

"Me next for the shower," Tracey said as she came into the living room. "Can I throw my clothes in your washer?"

"Of course," Addie said. "I'm starving. How about we order a pizza?"

"Good by me," Tracey said, looking out the living room window. "There's a cop here with a tow truck."

"Probably impounding that green pickup," Addie said. "It's evidence, now."

"You don't think any of those guys are still around here, do you? That they might show up here tonight or something like that?" Tracey asked.

"No, I think they're all gone," Addie said, but at the same time she wondered: where had they gone? When the five remaining members of the core group met again at their intended destination, and discovered Van was dead and the Brock brothers arrested, what would they do? It was likely they'd hide out for a while. And, while all of them together might attract attention, she realized her brother's ranch would be a good spot for one or two of them to lay low.

Tracey was looking at her.

"Ike told me the two guys in the yellow truck were pulled over outside Buenavista earlier," she said quickly. "Van's dead, Gil's arrested, and the others have probably blown town by now. The only one I don't know about is George."

"Oh, I wouldn't worry about him," Tracey said. "What do you want on the pizza?"

Addie put her good hand on her hip. "So far this afternoon, you've avoided talking to me about George twice and about Ike once," she noted. "You're pretty good at side-stepping the issue."

"Practice," Tracey grinned. "Comes from years of living with Virg Radner, trying not to tell him what I've been up to."

After Tracey got out of the shower, Addie carefully bandaged the bullet graze on top of his shoulder with gauze and tape. When the pizza arrived they sat on the couch, using the coffee table to spread out the pizza box, plates, and drinks.

"I guess you won't be able to go back to work for a while," Tracey noted, as Addie fumbled to fold a slice down the middle with her left hand.

"I can't go back to work right now, anyway. All my gear is at the bottom of the Deuce River," Addie told him. "Even if we could put a diver down in that area and he could find my stuff, it would be in pretty bad shape."

Tracey grimaced. "No diver would be able to find it. The bottom of the Deuce is about two feet of loose silt. Your pistol probably sank like a stone. But don't you have extras?"

"Pepper spray, yeah, but we don't have a firearm in a caliber I've qualified with. We'll have to request one."

Tracey consumed the rest of his slice. "I guess I need to call Virg and Bobbie and tell them I'm all right. I mean, they might not have missed me. They might just think I'm staying at the camp or somewhere else. But they might have heard some rumors. I think Buster was looking for me everywhere he knows I've got family. And I'll bet everybody knows the glue factory had a fire. Plus, a lot of people have scanners. They could have heard stuff on the radio."

Tracey pulled the cordless phone out of its cradle on the kitchen counter and punched the buttons. "Hey Virg, it's me," he said, glancing at Addie. "Yeah, I'm fine."

There was a pause. "I didn't tell you where I was going to be 'cause I didn't know," Tracey continued. "I figured I'd be home Sunday night, but then some things happened." He glanced at Addie again. Sunday night was the night they had left Bobbie's house.

"Right now?" he asked, and grinned. "I'm at Addie's house. Yeah, Addie Derange. In Buenavista. There's been a lot of stuff going on the last couple days. It has to do with the glue factory fire. No, I'm not involved with it, at least not that way. Can you have Billy pack up some clean clothes and send 'em down with James?

267

The ones I've got right now are pretty bad. Because I fell in the Deuce, plus there's a hole in the shoulder of my shirt where I got shot. And blood. I'll tell you about it later, okay?"

He rolled his eyes and hung up the phone. "Virg wasn't any too happy he hasn't heard from me in three days," he grinned. "I guess it didn't help when he found out I'm down here with you."

"I guess he had to find out at some point," Addie said. "I'm about beat, Tracey. These pills are knocking me out. I'm going to bed. You can go ahead and use the phone all you want."

In her bedroom, Addie checked the pockets of her pants before tossing them in the laundry basket. She felt the hard lump of the forgotten pendant in there and pulled it out. She sat down on her bed to examine it.

It was disk-shaped, silver, about an inch-and-a-half in diameter, and carved in the shape of a curled, sleeping mouse. It was fairly thick and heavy. It was very well done, very detailed and properly proportioned. She was somewhat surprised; she hadn't realized Francis was that good.

There were four tiny holes in the sides, as if small struts could be inserted to secure it somewhere. She flipped it over to see if the back was signed. The back was flatter than the front, still carved, but the small mounds of the mouse's back and haunch were muted so that it looked more like topography than an animal, with hills, river valleys, and tributaries. There was an odd series of small, incised dots, with no discernible pattern, and the silver was etched with shallow lines tracing the contours.

Addie felt her heart begin to beat a little faster. Indeed, the back looked like topography because it was topography.

It was a map.

Chapter Twenty

Addie studied the hills and valleys and the tiny points on the back of the mouse pendant. The map was non-referential: it didn't have city or mountain names or roads. If you didn't know where to start, you wouldn't be able to read the map and figure out where to go. You could spend years trying to compare it to topographic maps, and it might fit generally into any one of many different areas.

The topography was certainly much too extreme for southeast Texas. The elevation in the Deuce River Preserve only varied by about 50 feet. The mouse-map, if it was an accurate representation, showed what could only be described as canyons and mesas. There were seven small marks on the map, each tucked into one of the tiny river valleys.

Addie squinted at the map, her mind fuzzy from the pain medication. It was awfully small-scale, more like a keepsake than a functional map, perhaps meant to remind the owner of places he had gone.

A suspicion snuck into Addie's mind. She had seen similar maps before. Logan wasn't a jeweler, but he kept coded maps of dig locations on paper and he provided keepsake maps to his clients, often drawn by him by hand. This was almost certainly such a map.

Van had obviously known what he was looking for, although he'd scrupulously avoided mentioning the form of the map to her. It explained the snapped chain next to Francis' body: whoever had killed Francis had expected it to be there. But Francis had given it to Gil a few days before, realizing that Van was looking for it and that he might be in danger, or perhaps hoping to improve his hand in the blackmail dance he and Van were performing. When it hadn't been on him, Van and Howie had been forced to ransack the houses looking not only for the paperwork but for the missing pendant. But

269

Gil had already taken the paperwork, first to Widow Slough, then to his own boat, and from there to Bobbie's house.

Of course, that meant that if Jesse had indeed killed Francis, he'd admitted it to Van. Otherwise, Van wouldn't have known that the map hadn't been on Francis. But that still didn't answer, to Addie's satisfaction, why the map was valuable enough to kill for. In this non-referential form, it could hardly be enough to implicate a collector. It would be an important keepsake, but she couldn't see someone ordering the thief murdered to retrieve it. Surely another piece could be done to replace this one.

She turned it once again and looked at the four little holes in the sides. She wondered if it was intended to be part of some larger piece, into which it could be mounted. But there was no way to figure that out at the moment. She couldn't ask Van any more questions, and that left, most probably, only Logan to whom she could go for answers.

Addie put the pendant in the top drawer of her nightstand and lay down carefully on her bed. She awoke the next morning to the smell of coffee. Tracey handed her a mug as she walked out of the bedroom in her bathrobe. He had thrown his clothes in her washer and dryer, so they were clean if not quite spotless.

Around nine o'clock, the phone rang. Addie jumped and pushed herself off the couch, where she had slumped in a pain-pill induced stupor, staring at the T.V. Tracey had borrowed ten dollars and walked down to the mini-mart and gas station a half-mile away to pick up a few items.

"It's Ike. How are you feeling?" Ike said as she answered.

Addie cleared her throat. "Okay. Just a little groggy from the pills."

"I called last night to check on you but Tracey answered and told me you were asleep already."

"Sorry, I crashed pretty early," Addie responded. "I didn't even hear the phone." She was slightly amused to find out Tracey had answered her phone as well as made the morning pot of coffee. He seemed quite at home in her house.

"That's probably for the best, anyway. Listen, there's an FBI agent here from Houston," Ike said. "We contacted the FBI due to the kidnapping and the possible eco-terrorism connection. If you're up to it, I'd like to bring him by to go over a few things with you and do a formal interview."

"Sure," Addie said. "Just give me enough time to get dressed. Tracey will be back in a few minutes. The agent might want to interview him as well."

Ike grunted. "Don't rush. We won't be by until afternoon. There are a few things we need to take care of first. I've been up all night helping secure things at the Lejeunes' camp and showing agents and all sorts of other people how to get from point A to point B around here."

"I'm sorry," Addie said. "Don't overdo it, Ike. Take care of yourself."

"It's all right," Ike replied quickly. "I'm actually kind of enjoying it. It's something different. It feels like I'm doing something important for a change. You never know; maybe I'll get some contacts in the FBI and switch agencies. Though I'd really hate to have to go back through basic academy at this point in my career.

"By the way," he continued, "Nobody ever found Skeeter's boat yesterday. Just that big utility boat and Gil's truck up near Bobbie's place, and another fourteen-foot jon-boat on the bank downstream from the camp. County's still searching the rental houses of all the militia guys in Aynesworth. Anyway, I'll see you at one."

Addie hung up the phone and stood in the kitchen considering for a minute. The boat downstream from the camp must have been the one George had taken Tuesday morning, and he had left it there when he found Tracey and took her car. And then he'd slipped away as easily as the morning mist on the river in the summer sun. She wanted to assume that he'd been the one to pull the trigger of the rifle that killed Van. She didn't want to consider the other possibilities.

Ike and the FBI agent stopped by about one o'clock, arriving not in Ike's truck but in the agent's large, midnight-blue four-door sedan, incongruous in Addie's neighborhood, which was heavily populated by pickup trucks and rusting sub-compacts. Ike arrived at the door carrying two large plastic garbage bags.

"This is stuff from your car the FBI said we could release back to you," Ike explained apologetically. "There are a couple boxes from your trunk in the bags. I have the paperwork from your glove compartment, too. Most of it's pretty soaked, but you might be able to salvage some of it."

Addie had forgotten the boxes in her trunk. "Dump them on the back porch, will you, Ike? I'll go through them later. There are a few tools I may be able to save if they're not too rusty already."

She shut the porch door after Ike deposited the dripping bags on the flagstone. The photos were undoubtedly completely ruined. Another connection to her past had been wiped out, erasing the slate even more cleanly. It would be even easier now for her to make a complete break, to sever all ties with her past and continue to build the new life she'd started two years ago. But she hadn't forgotten the way she had felt about Van's proposition. Nor had she forgotten her rekindled memories of her brother.

She joined Tracey, Ike, and the FBI agent at her coffee table. The agent introduced himself as Lionel Odrup and sat forward on the couch with his elbows on his knees and his hands clasped.

"Basically, Addie, we've divided the investigation into a number of parts. First, there's the murder of Francis Lejeune. Then, there's the murder of this guy you're calling Van Bates. Third, there's attempted murder by the two guys in the yellow truck. Two of those happened on federal property, but one is going to be a state crime. Then there's the arson at the adhesives plant and stockpiling anhydrous ammonia for illegal purposes, possibly with interstate transport of materials, although we don't know where the stuff was being stashed yet. And there's kidnapping and holding you and Tracey against your will. Lastly, there's the association of this militia group with domestic terrorism and possible financing and support networks. Of course, all of them are tied together. My specialty is domestic terrorism, in particular extremist environmental groups."

Addie nodded. The term 'domestic terrorism' suddenly seemed to make everything more sinister. She wondered if Van had thought of himself as a terrorist.

"Anyway, my job today will be to get a good, thorough statement from you and pass on that information to my team. I'll also be responsible for updating you on what's going on and what we've found so far, probably through your partner Ike, here."

Ike adjusted his body armor importantly and leaned forward. "Here's some interesting information." He laid out a neatly organized list, with bullets and notations, on the coffee table. Addie smiled. This was something Ike enjoyed, ordering and labeling things. And because he enjoyed it, he was good at it. A penchant for organization and detail might, she considered, be a good trait for someone who was angling to become an FBI agent.

"These are the personnel records from the adhesives plant," he said. "They were on file with the Chamber of Commerce. Take a look at the names I've highlighted."

Addie read off the list of names. "I recognize some of them, but not all of them."

"Well, I recognize all of them," Ike said. "I told you Silas Casey was a Union Civil War general and so was Delevan Bates. So was Jesse Reno, or Renault, and so are all the rest of them I've got highlighted."

"So they're all pseudonyms," Addie said. "That's not surprising. But it's interesting that they chose a theme."

273

Odrup picked up the list. "But these aren't just fake names: they're complete false identities. Some of them have a couple years' worth of paper trail associated with them. All of them were able to present drivers' licenses, Social Security cards, and other identification for employment purposes."

"Are you going to be able to figure out who any of them really are?" Addie asked.

"We know who two of them are," Odrup confirmed. "The men arrested by the county for shooting out the window of their truck are brothers whose real names are Troy and Trent Brock, from San Antonio. They were employed as truck drivers for the adhesives plant about six months ago and claim to have gotten involved in Van's group because it was a militia. Neither of them will admit to knowing anything further.

"We've got three evidence techs out at the camp lifting prints from the pickup truck and the quads and laptop and other equipment left out there, and hopefully we'll be able to identify some of these guys that way. But if they don't have police records, that's not going to help us a lot."

Odrup put a photo in front of Addie on the coffee table. "Here's one guy we think we've identified, though."

Addie picked the photo up and studied it carefully, but there was no doubt in her mind.

"That's Howie."

"You sure?" Odrup asked. "He'd be six years younger in that photo than he is now."

Addie nodded. "I'm sure."

Tracey looked over her shoulder. "I'm sure, too. I took him and Van out on a fishing trip. I kind of got the impression he was Van's right-hand man."

Odrup nodded. "That's likely. This is J. Howard Cannady. He disappeared six years ago on Lake Erie in a solo sailing accident, presumed drowned, but his body was never recovered. It was big

274

news in the Great Lakes area, because his Dad's a major shipping magnate and Howie was a sailing champion as a kid. Some folks thought he might have 'disappeared himself'. I worked around there back then and I remember the case. We knew he was involved with extremist environmental groups before he disappeared. Anyway, I got in touch with his Dad and asked him to email us a photo."

"What about this guy Van?" Tracey asked. "Who is he, really?"

Odrup sat back and blew out his breath. "Don't know," he admitted. "We got the coroner to roll fingerprints from him, but nothing came back. There's no paper trail on him, nothing. He's like a ghost. I'm not sure how we're going to figure out who he is, either, because no one is going to come forward and admit to being involved with him in any way."

Addie thought about that for a minute. "Maybe there is someone, a person who can say she knew Van without admitting to having been personally involved with him," she said.

"Who would that be?" Odrup asked, squinting at her.

"June Gerschoff, the lady who runs the *AFTERThought* website."

Odrup grinned. "Now, there's a thought. I've dealt with June before. She's always been cooperative. She's pretty smug about their system, and she has a right to be. We've never managed to prove any link between her and any of the groups she publicizes. I think she actually enjoys dealing with us, because she knows there's nothing we can do to her. It's free speech, she's not committing any crimes, and of course she thinks she's doing the right thing."

"Do you think she'll tell you who Van Bates really was if she knows?" Addie asked.

"Can't hurt to try," Odrup grinned. "I'll give her a buzz tonight. She's not hard to get hold of. She has a legitimate business and phone number."

Addie and Tracey spent the rest of the afternoon giving Odrup their statements about events at the camp. Addie sat out on her back porch while Tracey gave his account, so as not to overhear what he said. Odrup didn't want each of them contaminating the other's statement. It was strange to be treated as a victim and a witness, rather than as the law enforcement officer she was used to being. She distracted herself by going slowly through the wet box with the tools and car parts in it, drying them and laying them out on the flagstone. Finally she peeled away the soaked cardboard on the second box and removed handfuls of stuck-together photos. She didn't try to separate them.

When it was her turn, Addie worded her statement carefully. She didn't leave anything out she felt might be instrumental to finding or identifying members of the group, but she didn't tell Odrup anything about Van's proposition to her, or about her brother's involvement, or about the pendant. No one else had been there to hear what Van said to her, except possibly George Cole. She knew George could have told Tracey some of what he'd heard about her and Logan. But it would be partial information at best, and it wasn't likely Tracey had repeated any of it to Odrup.

"Have you interviewed Gil Lejeune yet?" she asked Odrup when she was done describing the camp and the circumstances leading to her being in the woods near Bobbie's house.

"No, why?" Odrup asked.

"I'd like to talk to him."

"What for?"

"Well, the way I see it, he tried to rescue me back there in the woods. He put himself in danger to do that. I'd like to thank him."

"I doubt he was trying to rescue you," Ike snorted. "More like he was trying to kill Van. Anyway, you won't be able to talk to him until he's out of 72-hour psychiatric hold. I'll let you know, if you want."

"Please do," Addie said. She found herself feeling sorry for Gil, and less inclined to blame him for what had happened. His actions had been motivated not by greed, or by malice towards her, or even idealism, but by his understandable desire to avenge the death of his brother.

In the middle of Addie's interview, they took a break and ordered take-out Chinese food. After their meal, Ike finally succumbed to his exhaustion and fell asleep in a corner of the couch. Tracey moved into the bedroom, taking the TV with him, stretching the satellite dish cable down the hallway. Addie was left alone with the FBI agent as she struggled to put the events of the last days in chronological order.

By the time Ike and Odrup finally left, Addie was too tired to do anything but sit propped up in bed and watch a few minutes of TV while Tracey picked up the remains of their meal and stowed the little cardboard containers in slots in her refrigerator. Irritated at her inability to stay awake, she decided she'd quit taking the pain pills the next day. She wanted clarity of mind, and the medication was clouding her judgment.

She awoke the next morning finally feeling a little more normal. Tracey was up before her once again, and once again had made a pot of coffee. They had lunch with James, who dropped by to give Tracey some clean clothes and drove them downtown squeezed together in the front seat of his air-conditioning service truck.

After they ate, James drove them to his shop and loaned Tracey their old service truck, and Tracey and Addie went car-shopping. Addie was growing impatient with her lack of mobility, her shoulder was feeling better, and the insurance company had assured her that her car would be considered totaled. She finally picked out a two-year-old green Jeep Rubicon.

Tracey left from the dealership to go back to Mill Lake. Addie drove home carefully. The Jeep was an automatic and not difficult to drive without straining her shoulder, at least on city streets. She parked it where she had parked her Toyota, to the side of her front walkway, up off the street. As she got out and closed the door, Ike's Preserve patrol truck turned onto her street.

"Hey, is this yours?" Ike asked as he swung out of the truck.

"Yep, just picked it up."

"Nice." Ike walked around it and surveyed the exterior. "Pop the hood, let's check it out," he said enthusiastically.

Addie popped the hood, and Ike took a look inside. "I'm not big on Jeep products, but it's clean. It's bigger than the car you had, and four-wheel-drive's always nice to have."

"That's what I thought," Addie said. "You want to come in?"

"Where's Tracey?" he asked, glancing around.

"Went home."

"Ah," Ike said in apparent satisfaction. He held the screen door for her. "I just stopped by to pass on some news and let you know how things are going with the investigation."

Inside, Addie set the keys to her new Jeep on the counter and poured Ike a glass of iced tea. Ike sprawled on the couch in typical position, with his long legs stretched out and one ankle crossed over the other. He looked as though he'd finally gotten some sleep.

"How are things going with the FBI, Agent Ike?" Addie teased.

"Pretty good. Odrup's going to interview Gil later this afternoon. He's out of psychiatric hold and in a regular lock-up. Odrup said he'd recommend dropping or reducing some of the charges against him if he'll cooperate and testify against the Brock brothers and anybody else we eventually arrest. If he does cooperate, he may be able to bail out, provided someone can come up with the money."

"Thanks for letting me know," Addie said.

"A couple of agents have been going through the files in those boxes," Ike continued. "The paper copies are inventory records

278

and records of movement of chemicals between the adhesives and fertilizer plant and waste disposal. Like you suspected, they've been modified. But they're just copies of the latest records as of the time Francis printed them out. They don't tell us who changed what, when, or who knew about it. Apparently the administrative assistant is claiming Francis stole her password and changed the records to either cover up his own mistakes or blackmail the company."

Addie considered that for a minute. The cover story wasn't far off from what had actually happened, and it would probably be pretty hard to prove different. "Are the paper copies all just those inventory records then? Nothing else?"

"That's it," Ike confirmed.

"And the computer disks and thumb drives?"

Ike shrugged. "More of the same. Just company records, with normal mistakes. So far they haven't found anything particularly suspicious. Odrup's got the mileages from the company trucks that were used to transport waste loads, and they're using those to establish a perimeter to look for where stuff may have been dumped or stored, but it's going to be difficult to prove the Soras knew anything. Their insurance company is going to go ahead and pay for damage to the offices."

Addie looked out the window. So even with the files in hand, they weren't going to be able to implicate Adrian and Andrew Sora. The connections between Van's group and the financers, and between the financers and Gerschoff, were well covered, perhaps better than Van had realized.

"Ike, I have to come back to work soon. I'm going stir-crazy," Addie said.

"Fine," Ike replied, grinning. "You can probably come back on light duty any time you want. And since your arm isn't healed yet, and we're still waiting on a replacement weapon for you, I guess you'll just have to spend your time going to meetings and taking care of the administrative side of things."

279

Addie grimaced. "Yeah, I guess I will. But I'll do it, Ike, and do it without complaint, partly because I'm bored and I want to come back, and partly because I owe you for taking up my slack this past week."

"Don't worry about it. You don't owe me. It was a great chance for me to get to work with the FBI," Ike said. "If you do the administrative stuff for a while, it'll more than make up for it, because I'll get to continue working the case. Besides, you'd do it for me, wouldn't you?"

"Take up your slack?" Addie asked. "Ike, you wouldn't know how to slack off if your life depended on it."

Ike grinned. "Why don't you change your days off to weekends, and come back in on Monday morning? That way you can be around all week when the administrative folks are in."

"Yeah, great idea," Addie said sarcastically. "You know, this shoulder's getting better real fast. I think I'll be off light duty by next week."

"Good to hear it," Ike said. "I'll let you know if we hear anything else." He hesitated. "There is one more thing. You know we've had a crew searching the area near where Van died and we've searched the green truck and interviewed Skeeter."

"So?"

"So, Skeeter says he was with Tracey the whole time and he didn't see him with a rifle, and if Tracey did have one and hid it after shooting Van, he did a damn good job. So I guess he's off the hook for murder. His cousin's another story, though."

"No, George is on the hook for being a felon with a firearm. But Van was pointing that gun right at my face, and he'd just finished beating the heck out of Gil. Whoever shot him did it to defend me and saved my life. I'll testify to that in court if I have to."

Ike looked down and nodded. "I just thought you'd want to know."

"Thank you, Ike. It does take a load off my mind," Addie said.

After Ike left, Addie grabbed her credentials and a pocket recorder, jumped in her Jeep, and headed downtown. Gil was being held in the city lock-up, which was also a federally-approved facility. She wanted to get there before Odrup.

At the jail, she showed her ID and asked for Gil.

"Would you like a private interview room, ma'am?" the jailer at the desk asked.

"That would be great."

"Would you like us to turn on the cameras? All the interview rooms are video-ready."

"No need. I brought a recorder. I don't need video."

The jailer nodded and led Addie to a small interview room. She sat behind the table and waited, wishing she'd brought something to look at besides the walls.

In a few minutes, the door opened and Gil walked in. The jailer held the door open for a moment. "We monitor all the rooms while interviews are in progress on that camera over there..." he pointed, "...no sound, but we'll be watching in case anything goes wrong."

"Thanks." Addie smiled and the jailer shut the door.

Gil sat down across the table from her silently. There was a dark bruise spreading from the side of his nose across his left cheek and his eyelid was swollen from Van's kick. His right forefinger was splinted and bandaged. His dark eyes met hers steadily.

"How are you doing?" Addie started.

"I'm fine. I'm not going to kill myself," Gil said.

"You were thinking about it," Addie replied. She hadn't turned on the recorder; she wasn't interested in a record of what they were saying.

"I changed my mind."

"Okay. That's good. An FBI agent named Lionel Odrup is going to interview you this afternoon. Did they tell you that?"

Gil shook his head. "No."

"I told him you risked your life trying to rescue me in the woods," Addie said. "I sure appreciate that."

Gil raised his eyebrows but said nothing. The corner of his mouth twitched slightly.

There was a slight pause. "So, do you want the pendant back?" Addie asked quietly.

"No. I don't know what it means. I figure maybe you do," Gil said. He kept his fingers interlaced on the table before him, but glanced up at the cameras.

"No one's recording this," Addie said. "What else do you know about that pendant? Did Francis make it?"

"I think he stole it. He came back with it after his last session at that Circle place they shipped him off to. He didn't make it, I'm pretty sure about that."

"Why are you so sure?"

"Because," Gil said, "he isn't, wasn't, that good. He makes his stuff with a kind of clay that you bake, and it gets hard, then you make a mold out of it. He used pewter for the final pieces, it's softer and melts at a lower temperature than silver. He didn't have access to the equipment to do silver. But that pendant's silver, for sure, and it's good. If you look at it, it's really detailed."

Addie nodded. "Did you ever look at the back?"

Gil shrugged. "Yeah, there are a bunch of little holes in it. I figured they might have had little jewels in them or something at one time."

"Did Francis tell you anything else about it?"

"No. He gave it to me just a few days before he disappeared. I don't know why."

Gil leaned forward across the table and studied Addie's face. "You think someone killed him for that pendant, don't you?"

282

"I'm not sure," Addie said. "You knew he was blackmailing Van with records from the adhesives plant, right?"

Gil sat back and nodded. "Yeah, he told me. I thought he was an idiot. And when he told Van, Van pointed out how good we had it and how Francis wouldn't want to mess that up. Francis didn't like to admit he was wrong, but he was thinking about giving those papers back. But he never did before he got killed. After he got killed, I figured Van did it to get those papers because Francis was stalling. But now I'm not so sure."

"Me neither," Addie admitted. "It seems unlikely Francis would trust Van enough to go hunting with him after all that."

"That's true. But if Van didn't do it, who did? Who wanted that pendant back that bad?"

"Oh, I suspect it was someone from Van's group at the very least," Addie said.

"Well, Francis usually hunted with Jesse or Silas," Gil said. "He kept doing it even after he had his little to-do with Van. You think one of them might have done it?"

"That's my guess. Maybe they did it to get the papers back, maybe they did it to get the pendant back, or maybe Jesse did it for both those reasons but also because he was pissed at Francis for threatening his brother. You think that could be a possibility? You knew them better than I did."

Gil nodded thoughtfully. "Well, if anyone threatened my brother, I guess I might get mad too. In fact, I might get madder than if they threatened me. But they didn't end up with the pendant." He raised his eyebrows. "They might still want it back."

"I bet, especially now that they've killed someone for it. They've got a lot invested in that thing, now. I'd appreciate it if you didn't mention it to Odrup."

"Okay." Gil looked down at his hands. "I don't know why you don't want him to know, but I won't say anything about it. I just want to know who really killed Francis, and why."

283

"Me, too," Addie said. "I promise I'll let you know what I find out. Let me just say this: you were ready to kill the man who killed your brother. Jesse might have killed Francis to protect his. There are things I'm willing to do for mine, too."

Gil stared at her for a long moment. Then he nodded. "Guess I'll see you around, then."

"Guess so." Addie picked up her recorder and stood up.

"Too bad the cops took those nice new Polaris four-runners," Gil said as she went to the door. "Guess I'll have to ride my old one on the Preserve now."

Addie turned sharply to look at him. There was almost the hint of humor in his tone, but she wasn't quite sure. She rapped on the door, and the jailer opened it and let her out.

Chapter Twenty-One

Back at home, Addie sat down at her computer. She hadn't been on-line in several days, and she needed to clear her inbox. She scrolled down the list, deleting those with questionable subject lines and unknown senders. Partway down the list, she stopped abruptly. One of the subject lines read 'About Van'. She checked the sender's name, an abbreviation she didn't recognize, then opened the email.

"This is June Gerschoff," the email began. "At 4:00 your time today, click on the link below. Sign on using your email as a user name and your last name as a password. I have temporarily enabled your log-on. We will be able to chat for fifteen minutes before your log-on is disabled. All records of our conversation will be deleted."

Addie glanced at the clock. It was three-thirty.

She hurried to her bedroom and yanked open the drawer of her nightstand. Then she grabbed her cell phone and took two photos of the pendant, one front and one back. She downloaded them onto her computer and trimmed them closely before she returned to Gerschoff's message and clicked on the link. She didn't question how June had obtained her email address. But she could feel her heart pounding: why had Gerschoff chosen her to contact, and what was it she wanted to say?

"Are you there?" she typed after signing onto the website.

"Yes. I understand someone may be looking over your shoulder," came the reply. "I'm not worried about it, but you might want to consider how worried you are about it."

"No one is looking over my shoulder," Addie typed back. "I told no one about your email."

"Okay," came the response. "I received a call from an FBI agent last night asking me to try and figure out the real name of an environmental crusader whose pseudonym was Delevan Bates. Let's say I've done a little research. The man's name was Willem Van Gelderin, age thirty-nine, and he originally came from Oregon. You won't find any police records on him. However, he was a surveyor at one point in his life and I suppose he might have been fingerprinted by his employer."

Addie reached for a pen and scrap paper she kept by her computer and scribbled the name.

"Thank you," she typed back. "This will not only help the investigation, it's also the right thing to do."

"I doubt it will help the investigation much. I will also pay for any costs associated with cremation and transportation of the remains back to Oregon or here to Colorado once the body is released."

Addie raised her eyebrows. That was unexpected. "I'll pass that on," she typed. She took a deep breath. She could feel her heart beating as she embedded the two pictures in the chat box.

"Are you missing something?" she typed, and hit the enter key.

There was a significant pause before the next message returned. "Very interesting. I assume you have the pendant in your possession? Odrup didn't say anything about it to me."

"It's in a safe place."

"Of course. Do you know what it is?"

"I know it's a map, and I know Francis stole it from Circle of Life while he was there."

"Well, here are a couple of pictures for you," June said. In a minute, two pictures appeared in the chat box. Addie clicked on the screen to enlarge them.

The first one was of the metal sculpture she'd seen on the Circle of Life website. In this photo, though, most of the holes were filled with small round objects similar to the mouse pendant, each depicting an animal curled to fit within the contours of its circle. Addie could see what appeared to be a bear, an eagle, and a dog or coyote, and there were a number of others. There was a hole in the middle right side, at three o'clock, where, she suspected, the mouse pendant was missing.

The second picture was a close-up of part of the piece, with two of the pendants flipped over to show their backs. Addie could see that the contours of their backs fitted together with the lines and contours on the rest of the piece, forming a much larger and more detailed map.

"This art project was commissioned by a group of southwestern Indian art collectors, through Logan," June continued. "What they wanted to do was incorporate a set of historic silver pendants, with the backs modified, into a metal wall sculpture. The idea was for the Circle of Life group to create the main structure of the piece.

"When viewed from the front, it's an intricate American Indian motif, with the pendants incorporated. But if the pieces are flipped around so their back sides show, a detailed map emerges, showing sites from where the clients' pieces were taken. Each piece is secured with four pins, so it can't rotate easily. In order for them to be flipped, two of the pins have to be retracted using a magnet.

"The metalwork is intended to cover a secret custom-built, climate controlled cabinet with some of the collectors' pieces stored in it. The items stored in there couldn't be exhibited: body parts, teeth, skulls, things like that. The mouse pendant is the only one that can be completely removed, and it can then be inserted into a slot in the cabinet and slid forward to release a latch. None of the other pendants fit, as they are all slightly different sizes, with the mouse being the smallest.

"Logan brought in the historic pendants in order to provide the students with an example of something they could make and allow them to study them. Apparently that's when Francis took the mouse pendant. He identified with it as it's often seen as a symbol of the artist. The piece wasn't completely assembled before the Circle

287

of Life group left. During assembly, it was discovered that one of the pieces was missing.

"Of course it can be re-created to serve the purpose it was intended to serve, but the piece you have is part of a historical collection, besides being incriminating in the wrong hands."

"Is it yours?" Addie asked when June was done.

"No. But it's very valuable to someone, and that someone wants it back."

"Bad enough to kill for it, or to order someone killed?"

"I deny any knowledge of that act," June replied. "I certainly didn't order or suggest it. The decision was made by the person who committed the act."

"What more can you tell me about Van or any other members of his group?"

"A few things. Van went by "Van" before he became Delevan Bates, probably why he picked that alias. His brother Joseph would be going by the name Jesse Reno. He's ten years younger. Their folks were survivalist types, anti-establishment. They grew up in a semi-isolated enclave. The kids were encouraged to learn self-defense, firearms, survival skills, etc. After Joe got in some trouble, Van took him on the road with him, and shortly thereafter they disappeared off the radar."

"You seem to have done some pretty thorough research," Addie typed.

"You could put it that way. I was involved with Van for a while."

"I see," Addie replied. "Then I'm sorry for your loss, and for the circumstances."

"Yes. It's been a few years, but we remained in touch, as you're undoubtedly aware."

People seemed to think she was aware of more than she actually was lately, Addie thought.

June continued, "You should know that I've been in an intimate relationship with Logan for about the last year."

"I see," Addie typed, not particularly surprised. Van had intimated as much. "I'm not sure what you know about the circumstances, but Francis, the man who's dead, was blackmailing Van, and Van had turned the tables on Francis regarding the theft of the map. I know you've disavowed any knowledge of this murder, but would you guess that Francis' refusal to hand over the map would be enough for Van to kill him?"

"You have to understand Van's influence over everybody who worked with him," June typed. "People automatically did for him what they thought he wanted, whether or not he actually asked them to do those things. Specifically, Joe is still heavily dependent on Van emotionally. Van represents the only way of life Joe has known as an adult, the only stability in a world where he has been on the run for ten years."

"That sounds like you think Jesse, or Joe, might be willing to take out someone who he thought was threatening his brother or the group, whether or not Van asked him to do it directly. Is this something Jesse might have done?"

"I can't tell you one way or the other. I will tell you that Joe has killed before, when he was a teenager. It was during a fight with another kid. That's when Van took him and they disappeared. Van's death will be a huge blow to Joe. Anybody he can associate with it may be in danger. That means you. That is one reason I wanted to contact you. I do not espouse violence against people in order to accomplish environmental protection and I do not publish reports of incidents where people were purposefully or needlessly injured. But you need to understand I have no direct control over any of these people."

"Thank you for the warning and for the information," Addie typed when the words ceased coming. "I assure you I was not directly involved in his death, and repeat my condolences."

Once again, there was a pause before the message began to return. "Thank you for your sympathy, but I intend to hold Van up as a martyr. I think his death may galvanize certain groups and bring focus to the immediacy of our mission. You should realize that this isn't over yet."

"What do you mean by that?" Addie typed.

"I mean that these groups and individuals will continue with these actions as long as they feel it's the only way for them to motivate change in this nation. And this: it isn't over for you personally.

"I want to say this to you: sometimes our relatives do things we don't agree with. But that doesn't alter our past. You can never erase the time you've shared with someone you've known for many years. You may take different paths in life, but eventually those paths tend to run close to one another, because the thought patterns constructing them are the same. You can't negate the influence of your upbringing."

Addie did not reply. Her fingers hovered over the keys, but she wasn't sure what to say.

"Of course, it's up to you what you do with the pendant and how you deal with it. I won't tell you one way or the other. That's your decision. It's your life."

There was a space beneath the words, then a final line:

"I talked to Logan last night. Be very careful if you choose to visit. Keep in touch."

The screen flashed and was replaced by a white background with the words, 'Your session has timed out' printed across it. Addie sat back in her chair. Was June warning her that the remaining members of the group were at Logan's place? And what would Jesse do if he thought she was responsible for Van's death? He hadn't wanted her in the group in the first place. Surely June wasn't warning her about Logan himself.

Addie clicked on her "Favorites" drop-down menu and brought up the *AFTERThought* website. After June's words, she was not surprised to see that a memorial for Van occupied the main page. Addie stared at the close-up photo, taken somewhere with a large expanse of water behind him. He was looking off camera, somewhere over her right shoulder. His hair had been longer then, and he was smiling as the wind whipped it around his face. A sudden wave of emotion washed over her. She told herself it was because of the shock of having witnessed Van's death. But she also had to admit that she was disturbed she had never really come to a final decision: if Van had not been shot, if they had gotten the copies and gotten away from Gil, what would she eventually have done? Where would she be at this moment? He could have killed her, there in the clearing by Bobbie's house, and he hadn't done it. He had wanted her to accept him, to believe in what he was doing. He had given her one last chance to make her choice, and it had cost him his life.

Addie turned the computer off. She saw Van's eyes in the last few seconds of his life, riveted on her own. Now that she had the story behind the pendant-map, she wasn't sure what to do with it. She could, of course, turn everything over to Lionel Odrup and tell him how *AFTERThought* was connected to her brother and to Francis, and how they were both connected to Van's strike team. Possibly the information would lead eventually to the discovery and arrest of the rest of Van's group. It was more likely, though, that it would lead to problems for Circle of Life, and certainly for Logan and all his clients.

She thought about what June had said. Should she abandon Logan because of what he had done in the past? On the other hand, if she reestablished some kind of contact with him, could she continue to live the double life she had been living? If the truth came to be known, what would happen to her career, to her relationship with her co-workers, particularly Ike? Despite their different backgrounds, she was fond of Ike and wanted his respect and approval as a senior member in her field.

Addie rubbed her face with her hands. She was going to have to make some sort of decision. Sitting there agonizing over it was driving her crazy. No one could fault her for talking to her own brother; no one would even have to know. She got up and went to the phone, and, before she could change her mind, dialed Logan's number, which she knew by heart. But after a few rings, a recorded message kicked in.

"We're sorry, but the number you have dialed is no longer in service. If you feel..." Addie hung up. Perhaps she'd mis-dialed. It had been a long time since she'd called that number. She pulled out her address book and checked, then dialed the number again. The same voice replied. The number was no longer in service.

She tried information, but no number was listed for Logan Derange. Stunned, she gave up and sat down again. He had told her he was at the same number in the message he'd left on her answering machine, so the number had been changed in the last two weeks. She could call Blake, but if Logan had changed his number it was likely he hadn't given it to Blake, either. She was sure he had an email address, but she didn't know it. She could write a letter, but that seemed somehow too formal and too restrictive for what she needed to say. Abruptly, she also realized that the FBI might in actuality know more about her brother's activities than she gave them credit for. It was possible Logan's phone had been tapped, or his email and other mail monitored. That left only one option open: if she wanted to talk to him, she'd have to do it in person. But did the fact he'd changed his number now, at this point in time, mean he no longer wanted her to contact him?

The sound of a car on her quiet street caught her attention. She looked out to see a gray station wagon pull up to her mailbox. It was the rural delivery contractor. The driver rolled down the window and inserted a handful of mail, then set a box down below. Addie walked out to retrieve it.

As she deciphered the scrawled return-address, she felt a sudden adrenalin surge. She stood holding it in her hands for a moment, examining its size and shape, the weight of it.

Inside she sat on the couch with a pair of scissors and carefully cut the brown tape. The box was packed with pale yellow straw-like padding. Addie worked her hands down underneath it and pulled the object out, balancing it on her palm: round and white, the pale clay of the pottery slip accented with red Colorado dust in the hairline cracks. She thought of the photograph Tracey had examined not long ago, when she'd held that piece of pottery once before. Now it had been repaired: the large chip missing from one side had been artfully cemented back in place. It was whole, entire, and complete.

Addie sat for a long time in the middle of the couch with the pot on her lap, her hands cradling it gently. She looked deep down into the hole on top, into the dark within. Logan had extended his hand again, holding out the container of their shared past. Did he know she had no way to contact him, now that she wanted to?

She looked up as she heard the telltale rattle of the muffler on the old air-conditioning truck. She quickly set the pot back into its box. The vehicle choked to a shutdown outside her door. Tracey was back.

"Hey," he grinned as he came into the house. "Grandpa Joe's throwing a barbecue at his place this evening. You want to go? There'll be a whole bunch of folks there. He invited some people he works with at the Preserve, too."

"Sure, sounds fun," Addie replied. She brought the box back into her bedroom. Impulsively, she took the mouse pendant out. She weighed it for a moment in her hand, then carefully slipped it through the opening in the top of the pot, into the dark interior. Then she placed the box on the top shelf of her closet.

She grabbed a windbreaker and went back out to the living room, where Tracey was waiting on the couch. "Ready to go?"

"Sure."

"What did you do this morning?" she asked as they headed out to the truck. "Work on the car?"

Tracey grinned. "Good guess. Talked to Bobbie and James, too."

"Oh? What about?"

"About moving in with them. I been thinking about it for a while. That's a three-bedroom house up there. The only thing that third bedroom's being used for is to store junk, mostly Gil's."

"What did they think about that?"

"They're good with it. We just got to get Gil to move all that stuff out and back to his place. Shouldn't be any reason he can't do that now. I'll have to pay Bobbie some rent. I'm living free at Virg's place, but James said they might be able to use me part time at the air-conditioning place, and I can use this truck."

"What does Virg think about that plan?" Addie asked.

Tracey shrugged. "He seemed to take it okay."

Addie studied him for a minute. His tone was the same as those times when he'd avoided talking to her about Ike or the incident at Magnolia Slough.

There were at least a hundred people already at the get-together by the time they arrived. Three barbecues smoked in the big back yard, and small groups gathered in the shade on lawn chairs, overturned tubs, picnic tables, and blankets. There was a small enclave of Preserve employees off to one side, including Ike.

Tracey went off to find drinks and let his grandfather know he'd arrived. As Addie wandered towards the garden, she noticed Gil standing with Bobbie a short distance away. He looked up and made eye contact with Addie. They held each other's gaze for a few seconds.

Addie turned as amplified sound came from the direction of the back porch, which was covered by a red-and-white striped awning and shaded from the afternoon sun by the house. A local band, all in jeans, white button-down shirts and red suspenders, was warming up. Other people were clearing tables and chairs from the flagstone, creating a dance floor. The chairs were set around the outside so those not interested in dancing could sit and listen.

Addie walked over towards the porch, meeting Tracey halfway there.

He nodded towards the back of the yard. "They're going to play a little pick-up softball over there. You want to play?"

"No, you go ahead," Addie said. "I'll sit here and listen to the music."

Tracey trotted over to join the softball game, and Addie moved a plastic chair into the shade from the house, setting it at an angle where she could view either the game or the dance floor easily. She alternated between watching Tracey and watching Virg Radner, who was a good dancer and much in demand.

Eventually, the late afternoon heat and humidity brought Virg to a halt, and he sat down next to Addie in the shade, breathing heavily and wiping his brow. The band began a slower tune, and Virg scooted his chair closer to her and leaned forward. Addie turned towards him.

"Listen, I don't know how involved you're planning to get with Tracey," he began.

"I don't know either," Addie said truthfully. "Right now I'm just taking things one day at a time."

"Fair enough," Virg replied. "I just want you to know what you're getting into."

Addie crossed her arms defensively. Virg raised a hand.

"I'm not going to try and talk you out of anything. I realize there's a big age difference between you and me, but it was worth a try. I just want to make sure you understand Tracey is pretty dependent on his family to make sure he stays out of trouble and gets things done. I think it was partly because of his childhood, maybe because of that crack on the head, and maybe he takes after his Dad a little more than anyone would like to admit. Junior was never real highly motivated to succeed, either. I'm not sure if Tracey will ever really get out on his own."

"He's moving out of your place and in with James and Bobbie," Addie pointed out, hoping Tracey had actually told Virg that.

"What good will that do?" Virg asked. "Bobbie and James have over-protected him for years. At least I make him take responsibility for what he does."

"Maybe it'll be good for him just to make a change," Addie said. "Anyway, right now I'm happy to let things be the way they are. I don't expect Tracey to suddenly get into a business suit and go make a white-collar career."

Virg nodded. "Okay. Let's hope you're right, and this is a good thing for him. Because one thing is, I really do care about what happens to Tracey. I raised him the same as I raised my own sons, and I want to see him make his way in the world. I don't want him to go from being dependent on one person to being dependent on another."

"You mean you think he might become dependent on me," Addie said.

Virg shrugged. "I guess relationships are kind of a matter of dependency anyway." He looked up. Tracey was returning from the softball game.

"I think I'm about due for a drink," he said. "I'm sure I'll be seeing you around."

"Is the game over?" Addie asked as Tracey threw himself into the chair Virg had been occupying, almost upsetting it.

"No, Dennis told me to quit," Tracey replied. "I was pitching and I accidentally hit Ike with a softball."

Addie fixed him with a reproachful stare.

"It was an accident. You know what all these guys in Van's group made me think about?" he asked suddenly.

"What?" Addie replied.

"I was thinking how they all move around all over the country. They get jobs wherever they go, they meet people, get to do all sorts of things. They've probably seen what this whole country is like. They know something folks who stay their whole life in one place don't know. Me, I've never been out of southeast Texas, except to Louisiana, and that don't really count."

"Were you thinking you want to go somewhere else?" Addie asked in surprise.

"Not permanently. Just to check it out. You know where I was thinking of going?" Tracey said. "Austin."

"Austin?" Addie repeated. "Why there?"

"Because my brother Jackie lives there. You know I haven't seen him in fourteen years."

Addie stared at him. "Fourteen years?"

"Yeah, after Jackie's thirteenth birthday party, where I got my head smacked, Jackie went to Austin to stay with my mom's cousin and her husband. They thought it would be good to get him out of this area, get him into a bigger city where maybe he could fit in better. And I haven't seen him since. Barely even talked to him."

Tracey looked off towards the softball game, where someone had made a good hit and was running the bases, accompanied by cheers of encouragement. "You know, he was one of my best friends when we were little kids. We got in a lot of trouble together." He grinned, then sobered. "I don't even know if he wants to see me. But I would kind of like to see him, I think. I don't really care what he's like, you know? What he's doing with his life, I mean. He's still my brother. I think about him pretty often, but all I can do is hope he's had a good life."

297

Fourteen years, Addie thought. Compared to that, the two years in which she hadn't seen Logan seemed brief.

"Tell you what," she said. "Let's you and I go on a road trip. We'll take my new Jeep. We'll go up to Austin to see your brother, and then we'll go on over to Colorado to see mine."

Tracey looked at her seriously. "I would like to do that. But I don't even know how to get in touch with Jackie. I guess maybe Virg does, or my mom."

"I don't know how to get in touch with Logan, either," Addie said. "He changed his phone number and he either didn't get a new one or it's unlisted. We might just have to go and hope he's there when we get there."

"I'm okay with that."

"You realize it might be dangerous," Addie warned him. "There's some stuff you don't know about Logan. He's involved with Van's group. It's complicated. I'll tell you more about it later if you want. But the thing is, the remaining members of the group could be at his ranch, or at least in the area. And besides them, there's another team somewhere, the actual strike team. You know they're all going to be upset that Van is dead, especially Jesse. And I'm pretty sure it was Jesse that killed Francis, not Van."

"Well, I don't really want to visit those guys," Tracey admitted with a grimace. "But we might be able to kind of sneak up and see if they're there first."

Addie laughed. "It's not good sneaking-up territory. But we could visit Blake, my other brother, out at my family's farm first, and he might be able to help."

"That's the fat blond kid, right?" Tracey asked.

"Not fat and not a kid anymore, but yeah, that was him in the pictures. He's a farmer now, manages my family's farm and takes care of my dad, who's got early senility. He works hard. He and I don't have much of a relationship, but I'm willing to bite my tongue and be nice in order to see Logan. There are a few things I really need to ask him."

"So," Tracey asked, "when do you want to go?"

"Soon," Addie answered. "While I'm still on light duty and can't do anything constructive at work anyway." She thought briefly about what that would mean for Ike, but she suspected that the main part of the investigation would wrap up soon anyway, and the FBI would return to Houston.

"I've always wanted to go to that place where you can stand in four states at once," Tracey mused.

"Four Corners," Addie said. "We can go there, too. We can go over to Arizona and New Mexico and visit Acoma and Hopi and some of the other places where they still make pottery like the ones you've seen in my photos."

Tracey nodded. "Can I see those photos again sometime? The ones of you and your brothers when you were a little kid?"

"No," Addie told him. "They were all ruined when my car went in the water."

"I guess that's my fault, at least partly," Tracey said apologetically.

"It doesn't matter," Addie said. "Maybe I can get some copies from Logan while we're out there."

Tracey laughed. "You're sure you're not afraid of being in the same car with me? Seems like a lot of 'em end up in the drink."

"There won't be a lot of places we can end up in the water in the southwest, unless we manage to run into Curecanti Reservoir or Lake Powell," Addie said. "Besides, if you hadn't dumped that Dodge in Thief Lake, we'd probably never have gotten together."

She leaned back in the plastic chair, slowly relaxing now that the decision was made and the plans were finally laid. She thought about the little pot at home, and how Logan had repaired the chip in the side to make it whole. She would bring the pot with them when they went to Colorado. Like her, it needed to go back from whence it came, to complete the circle she'd begun ten years before when she removed it from its place of rest.

About the Author

K.A. Krisko is the author of a number of fantasy fiction novels and literary short stories. She grew up living in national parks, where her father worked as a ranger. Her mother, a William and Mary graduate in English Literature, encouraged her to write, read, and recite poetry competitively. Her father took her on star walks and taught her about lightning. Later she became a ranger herself, and worked in parks from Texas to California. She now lives in northern Colorado with her two Australian Cattle Dogs, Page and Carter. She enjoys walking and hiking with her dogs, skiing and snowshoeing, and reading and writing.

http://www.kakrisko.com
http://www.stolenworld.com

Other works by K.A. Krisko:

Novels:
Stolen (Book One of the Stolen Trilogy)
Crypt of Souls (Book Two of the Stolen Trilogy)
Hyphanden's Box (Book Three of the Stolen Trilogy)
Cornerstone: Raising Rook (Book One)

Short Stories:
The Snow Deer and Other Stories (short story anthology)
One Wet Dog (stand-alone short story, also in Happy Endings II)
Almost A Dog (Happy Endings I)
The Possessed RV (American Blue: Real Stories by Real Cops)
Mother Bear (Wisdom of Our Mothers)

Of Words and Water:
The Natural Seize in the 2013 volume
The Name of the Dog in the 2014 volume

Sneak Peek at Book Two!
'On Second Thought'

Van's group is scattered and disoriented. Addie's been roped into trying to rescue one of them. At the same time, she's trying to reconcile with her own family. Meanwhile, someone is murdering cows on her brother's farm...

She was DRT, Dead-Right-There.

Howie rolled sleepily out of bed in the tiny, one-room cabin at six a.m. and, since there was no plumbing, staggered to the front door to let himself out. The rough-hewn door opened outward, but when he pushed on it, it didn't move. He pushed a little harder and rattled the knob, assuming it was stuck, but to no avail. He shoved on it with his shoulder, bracing his feet against the turned-up edges of the warped floorboards, and managed to get it open about an inch. That was when he saw the red-brown cow fur.

She had apparently settled herself in for a nap right on the front porch, lying with her bulk up against the door. Howie prodded her a few times with his fingers through the slot between the door and the frame, then fetched a poker from near the little wood-burning stove and poked her with that. There was no response, not so much as a twitch of hide.

He retreated and went to the single window in the south wall, small, four-paned, and cloudy with grime. After banging and shaking it several times, he managed to break the thick layers of paint around the casement and shoved it up about fourteen inches. He grabbed a wooden chair, stepped on it, and began threading himself through the slot head-first, supporting himself by bracing his hands against the outside wall as he wriggled further and further out.

Finally he yanked his feet through and rolled awkwardly onto the dirt next to the cabin. He sprang up quickly, backed off a few steps, and cautiously peered around the front corner of the cabin, side-stepping to give himself a better view.

There was no doubt about it. She was dead. Not of natural causes, either: she'd been shot in the head. Howie could see the small round hole between her ears. Eight hundred pounds of murdered cow lay smack on the porch, right up against the door.

How in the hell he could have slept through a cow being shot on his front porch was beyond him, but Howie didn't feel he had the luxury of puzzling over it just yet. The cabin sat in a small group of cottonwoods on the edge of a deep wash that eventually became a ravine. A hundred yards away was Logan Derange's ranch house, and near that the big Quonset hut that served as a storage room and garage, the stables, and the corrals. There were no trees between Howie and the ranch house, but there were a number of large red cows scattered here and there.

Feeling a bit like a paranoid fool, Howie darted barefoot from the edge of the cabin to the first large, live cow in the field. In a way, it was a useless endeavor: if someone was lying in wait for him, Howie had no way of telling where that person would be or from which direction a shot might come, and thus he might inadvertently end up on the wrong side of any particular cow. But taking a measure of cover comforted him to some degree.

He worked his way quickly to Logan's back door, opened it carefully, and slipped inside. His senses were heightened: there was the possibility that something had happened to Logan or that someone dangerous might be in the house. But nothing seemed amiss, and as Howie crept through the big back kitchen he could see Logan sprawled on the couch in the living room, watching T.V. He was not dead. He stretched and yawned as Howie watched him.

Howie let down his guard and stepped into the living room. Logan turned his head quickly.

304

"Didn't hear you come in," Logan said, returning his attention to the T.V. "Coffee's on, but it's not ready yet."

"There's a dead cow on the cabin porch," Howie replied. Logan turned to him once more, fixing him with the expressionless gaze that was his typical response when faced with anything unusual or unexpected.

"Yeah, they die some times," he said after a moment. "I'll call Mr. Gotter and have him send 'round a front-end loader to pick it up."

Howie shook his head. "Didn't die of natural causes. Somebody shot it."

Logan frowned. "You sure?"

"Yeah, well, I didn't do a full autopsy or anything, but there's a bullet hole in its head."

Logan got up and shuffled through the hall into the kitchen. He was shorter and thinner than Howie, with tousled dark hair, and he was wearing a white T-shirt, flannel pajama bottoms, and no shoes. He stopped in the kitchen and poured himself half a cup of coffee from the old, yellow, electric coffee-maker, tested it, and then poured the rest of the mug full. Cup in hand, he walked to the back door, held open the screen, and stared out at the cabin and the dead cow.

"Yeah," he said, "there it is."

Logan let the screen door slam and set his coffee mug on a bureau. He pushed his feet into a pair of cross-trainers that were sitting near the door, leaving them untied. He shuffled out, Howie following, and made his way through the cows to the cabin, circumnavigating cow pies along the way.

Logan leaned over and looked at the hole in the cow's forehead. "Pretty small hole," he said. "Pretty stupid to shoot a cow in the forehead with that small a caliber if you want her to die. There's a bunch of solid bone right up there."

305

He walked slowly past the cow, looking at the ground. "Blood trail," he noted, pointing it out. The two of them followed it for two hundred yards across the field to another group of cottonwoods, where Logan stopped.

"Well, it looks like she got shot around here," he said, pointing to where the blood trail began. "She didn't die right away, but eventually the head trauma got her."

"At least that explains why I didn't hear anybody shooting in the middle of the night," Howie said, feeling a measure of relief.

"Still pretty close," Logan pointed out. "You must sleep pretty good."

"What about you? Did you hear it?" Howie demanded.

Logan smiled. "Nope. But I'm not worried anybody's out gunning for me, either."

Howie frowned at him in dismay. "So tell me this, why would someone be out here shooting Mr. Gotter's cows in the middle of the night?"

Logan thought for a minute. "Got no idea. Could be it was a sick cow they wanted to put down, though that seems like a poor way to do it. But I expect it's a coincidence that it managed to die right on your doorstep. Unless someone shot it and then, like, led it over there and waited for it to die."

"How likely is that?" Howie asked.

"Well, there are footprints going along that blood trail," Logan said casually. "Boot prints, like cowboy boots. So I guess there's some possibility."

Howie studied the ground. It was hard-packed dirt mixed with ground-up cow crap. But now that Logan had pointed it out, he could see at least part of a boot print here and there. He followed the blood trail back to the cabin. There were several partial prints right around the front porch. Someone had definitely been standing there with the dead, or dying, cow, in the middle of the night. Right outside his door.

Logan turned and headed back to the house. "I'll call Mr. Gotter and have him send someone over to get it off your doorstep. It's his responsibility. I got that written into the grazing lease."

Howie followed him, wondering if he could set up some sort of warning system or maybe get a dog. At the house, Logan kicked off his shoes again and made his way back to the living room, leaving Howie to pour himself a cup of coffee. In some ways Logan's extreme calm in all circumstances was irritating, but Howie recognized it as a coping mechanism probably developed over centuries by hard-working farmers, ranchers, and others who worked the land and had little control over major events in their lives, such as weather and natural disasters. It didn't do any good to get worked up over things you couldn't do anything about anyway. You just took a look and then figured out where to go next.

Howie had been at the ranch for nearly a month now. It had been their planned meeting spot following their retreat from southeast Texas. Howie, Derek, Charlie, and Jesse had all arrived as planned. Silas had shown up a little later. He came bearing the news that Troy and Trent Brock had been arrested, which wasn't a disaster, but wasn't great, either. Van, however, had not arrived.

After a couple of days, everyone started getting worried. Then Logan got the phone call from June Gerschoff, the manager of the Alliance For Tactical Environmental Response, or *AFTERThought.* Van had been shot dead by an unknown assailant, supposedly while kidnapping a federal law enforcement officer and having beaten up a local man whose brother he, Van, had purportedly killed.

Logan broke the news to Howie, Derek, Silas and Charlie; Jesse was out at the time. After the initial shock, Derek and Silas quickly decided it was time to cut their losses and take some time away from the group, at least until the heat was off. They'd only been with the group for three years, and it would be easier for them to reestablish a work history and identity than for Howie or Charlie.

307

Charlie decided to make himself scarce for a while as well, heading to the Santa Fe area where his sister had property. Howie wasn't particularly sad to see him go. He suspected Charlie had been involved in the murder of Francis Lejeune, at least peripherally. He knew Van had suspected that, as well.

It fell to Howie and Logan, then, to break the news to Van's younger brother Jesse. Jesse had been on the run with Van for more than ten years, since he was a teenager. He knew no other life and had no work history, only an arrest warrant for manslaughter waiting for him back in Oregon. He took it hard, as Howie had been afraid he would. After his initial disbelief, he collapsed onto his knees in Logan's living room, howling with rage and grief, pounding the wooden floorboards with his fist. Howie's half-hearted attempt at comfort had been met with a violent withdrawal. Howie and Logan elected to leave him alone. Although he sympathized with Jesse, whom he'd known for six years, Howie also saw some measure of justice: he was pretty sure Jesse had murdered Francis, and this must have been how Gil Lejeune had felt upon hearing of his brother's death. Gil had thought himself responsible for his brother's demise, and Jesse probably felt the same, since it was ultimately his actions that had led Addie Derange to the camp and had led to the group's hasty exit from the area.

The following morning Jesse was gone. Howie and Logan were concerned about him, but they couldn't exactly report him missing to the police. They spent a few days trying to track him into the canyons nearby and driving around the nearest towns, but with no luck, and eventually they quit looking. Jesse was going to have to find his own way out of the morass that was his life, and they could only hope that he wouldn't eventually lead authorities back to Logan's ranch, or return there himself bent on some twisted idea of revenge.

Howie really had no place to go, after six years on the road with Van. He'd stayed at Logan's, but the old cabin was inconvenient and it wouldn't be a place he could live for the winter. He was reluctant to ask Logan if he could move into the main ranch house. Logan needed some privacy, and he hadn't specifically invited Howie to stay there, after all. It was a big house, but it was Logan's, and Howie felt like a guest who was overstaying his welcome.

He told Logan he just needed some time to clear his head. In reality, nothing at all was clearing in his head. Without Van's guidance, he had no idea what to do with himself. He had been Van's right-hand-man, it was true, but Van had the charisma, the vision, and the organization to make the contacts and get things rolling. He had the personal ties with June at *AFTERThought*. Plus, Van had worked closely with Jesse. Jesse was the one who handled the computer systems, the encryption and coding, and the financial systems that allowed them to launder money from contributors. Without him, the core group couldn't function; the two brothers had been vital. Howie and Charlie had really been secondary, and Silas and Derek, though important, had been even less necessary.

Whether Logan, who had known Van for longer than Howie, was grieving or not was difficult for Howie to tell. Logan was quiet and reserved and rarely revealed what he was thinking. But Howie was almost as devastated by Van's loss as Jesse had been.

"You want more coffee?" Logan asked. Howie had wandered into the living room and had been staring blankly at the TV news. Logan had meanwhile gone back into the kitchen and retrieved the coffee pot. He tilted it side to side, demonstrating that there was coffee left.

Howie shook his head. "No, I'm going for a ride, if you don't mind. I need to get my head together after starting the day like that."

"That's fine. Horses need exercise, anyway." Logan fixed him for a minute with his calm gray eyes, then turned back to the TV. "It's your way of paying rent."

Howie stared at him for a minute. Sure, maybe he could work for, or with, Logan, at least for the winter. It would be an option, if Logan would let him stay. It was quiet and peaceful here, at least when cows weren't dying on his doorstep. He could exercise the horses, maybe do some work around the place. He pushed open the screen door and headed for the cabin.

Damn it, he had to get back inside. He couldn't go riding barefoot. He grabbed an old wooden stool off Logan's porch and took it across to the window on the side of the cabin. It was beginning to heat up and flies were gathering. He hoped Mr. Gotter or one of his boys would be there soon.

Howie threaded himself back in through the window, dressed, and, after a moment's thought, slipped his pistol in its clip-on holster over his belt, more for ease of mind than anything else. He pulled his shirt down over it and slid back out. He was getting better at it, but the rough old windowsill was hard on his stomach if he went through head-first or his legs if he went through feet-first. He tried to pull the window down once he was outside to keep the flies from getting into the cabin, but it was sticky and warped.

Howie ducked between the wooden rails of the horse corral and walked slowly towards the bay Morgan, his favorite. The Morgan kicked and trotted away, tossing his head and herding the subordinate geldings. Howie draped the halter over one hand and deliberately followed the horse from one quadrant to the other, and eventually the Morgan, perhaps eager for some exercise, stood still. Howie held up the fading green halter, and the horse dropped its head through the loops.

Brushing the dust out of the Morgan's coat and listening to him chomp a little grain was calming, almost meditative, and Howie worked slowly, first with the rubber stripper, then with a soft brush. He kept his mind on what he was doing and tried not to let it stray. He'd learned not to allow himself to think about Van's death, at least not the specifics of it. It was too disturbing. Even worse were the

310

little nagging thoughts that tried to nudge their way into his mind: who'd shot Van, anyway? Had it been Logan's sister? He didn't know the details, and he wasn't sure when, or if, he'd ever want to. But on top of those thoughts, invariably, came the unwelcome realization that he was living with the brother of a law enforcement officer who'd been held involuntarily at the camp, and that she was apt to be looking for the rest of the group, including him, either to arrest them on suspicion of murder, suspicion of criminal damage to property, or for her own personal revenge.

Done with the brushing, Howie saddled the Morgan and worked the snaffle carefully into its mouth. Howie had grown up on the Great Lakes, and although horses had been available, they had never interested him. He'd preferred sailing. But now he wanted the silence of mounted travel, not the grind and cough of a quad-runner's engine. And after all, riding a horse was a little like sailing: they were both non-motorized and required skill rather than raw power.

The Morgan trotted eagerly down the dirt road from Logan's place to the farm road, a two-lane strip of pavement mostly connecting one farm to another. Howie rode the shoulder, which was broad and brushy, and only a few cars zipped by before he turned off, heading overland towards one of the canyons cut into the big flat-topped butte that bordered the basin. In the distance, he saw a bucket-loader trundling along the road towards the ranch: Mr. Gotter's hired hand or one of his sons, come to remove the dead cow, he guessed. The Gotters leased Logan's land, so all the cattle belonged to them.

It was cool in the shady spots in the canyon and hot in the sun, and the horse settled down into a mileage-covering walk. Howie relaxed, letting the Morgan have its head. There was little for it to eat in the canyon bottom and nowhere for it to go but forward. When they came upon small streams, he allowed it to drink and splash for a few minutes before they traveled on.

311

It was an hour before Howie dismounted at a place where a box canyon cut into the main drainage and a trickling stream intersected the creek-bed. In the intersection stood a huge, block-shaped boulder with an overhanging lip. Under the lip was built a tiny cabin, walls of stacked and interlaced driftwood. It had remained undisturbed since its owner had abandoned it: his cast-iron cookware still sat stacked in a back corner. Chipped into the makeshift sill above the open doorway were the words "1906 – SINK".

Logan had shown it to him. It was a place where they'd collected arrowheads when Logan was a child. On days when he wanted to ride, Howie often went there. It was silent and peaceful and he could keep his mind quiet, holding back the tide of remorse, and also the fear, not only of those who might be searching for him, but also of the unknown future. There had been few in life Howie had been willing to follow. For the past six years he had followed Van, but now Van was gone, and Howie felt himself twisting, with no clear direction.

Involuntarily, his thoughts turned to the last few words Van had said to him at the camp. Van had told him not to 'do anything I wouldn't do', but he'd also told Howie to 'take care of things' if he didn't show up at Logan's house. Now Howie struggled to figure out what things, exactly, he should be taking care of. Had Van referred to Jesse and Charlie and their involvement in Francis' murder? Or had he meant that Howie should try to keep the group together, try to continue what Van had started?

He wished he could talk to June. He didn't have direct contact with her, though. Only Jesse, Van, and Logan had a number where they could reach her if needed. He'd met June when Van had been going out with her. She was dark and driven, and he'd thought she and Van were a good match. Van was tall, blond, good-looking, athletic, outgoing, and charismatic, and they were about the same age. Logan was just the opposite: slender, dark-haired, quiet, laid-back, unmotivated, and younger than June. Howie had wondered if June's relationship with Logan after her break-up with Van had been just a ruse to stay in touch with the group. He thought she was still in love with Van, and she must be hurting now. If he could talk to her, she might be willing to give him some insight, some direction, even though she was supposed to stay out of the field operations. She might know more about what Van had planned and what his thoughts had been regarding his brother and the group. He wondered if he could find her number on Logan's phone, or maybe contact her through the website and ask her to call him.

He shook his head, clearing his thoughts, and looked for his horse. He caught the Morgan and swung up into the saddle, feeling some ease in his mind from the peaceful ride. After all, no one official had shown up at Logan's house in the month since they'd left east Texas, and none of the other group members had been arrested as far as he knew. Maybe things were going to be okay. Maybe he could get in touch with June, get some ideas and a direction from her. Maybe he could function without Van.

As he came out of the mouth of the canyon, where he could see down and across the broad valley in which Logan's ranch was situated, he pulled the horse to a halt. He scanned the valley carefully, squinting in the midday sun. He felt on edge, as if someone was watching him.

He guided the horse carefully and slowly back to the farm road and Logan's drive, keeping a watchful eye on the ranch and the area around it for anything unusual. But he saw nothing out of place. Maybe it was just hyper-vigilance, brought on by the events of the last month and the morning.

As he brought the horse around to the corral, he saw Logan, fully dressed now, step out of the house, keys in hand. Logan looked up at Howie and reached out to take the horse's bridle to stop it. Howie swung down. That was an unusual thing for Logan to do; usually he'd just let Howie take the horse back to the corral himself.

"Going somewhere?" Howie asked.

Logan nodded briefly. "Something's come up. I don't know how long I'll be gone. The back door's unlocked. But Howie, listen." He paused, as if searching for the words. "You can stay here as long as you want. But things may get a little unsafe. You understand? You'd do best to keep your head down, keep it quiet. Don't go into town for the time being. Just tell me what you need and I'll get it. And for God's sake move your truck into the Quonset hut."

Logan turned and walked quickly to his truck, jumped in, and started it up. Howie stared after him. That was out of character, he thought. What the hell had happened? Things didn't just 'come up' in Logan's life, as far as he could tell. Logan led one of the most laid-back, unhurried lives he could imagine, with very few scheduled demands upon his time.

He brushed down the Morgan quickly and turned it back out into the corral, where it immediately rolled in the dirt. The cow was gone from the porch, only some drag marks and blood and the tracks of the bucket-loader in the yard. Howie gratefully let himself in the door of the cabin, rather than going through the window. He grabbed his keys and started the black pick-up he'd registered in Texas under his pseudonym, Thomas H. Ruger. The front part of the Quonset hut was a garage and workshop of sorts; the back half was a storage area for some of Logan's artifacts. Howie pulled the truck in beside a couple of ATVs and a small tractor and closed the hut back up.

He wished Logan had been a little more specific. He was already enough on edge without vague threats and warnings. He looked up at the rise to the east of the ranch, where the two-lane road came over. He didn't really like that rise: someone could sit up there and look down, spying, watching. He didn't care for the ravine behind the property either. It was too good a way to sneak up on the place. He felt his stomach turn over: so much for breakfast. But he wasn't sure what else he could do. Logan hadn't told him to flat-out

314

leave, only to hide the truck and lay low. So there couldn't be that big a problem, could there?

Coming Soon! Check www.kakrisko.com for updates!

www.ingramcontent.com/pod-product-compliance
Lightning Source LLC
Chambersburg PA
CBHW062109170626
46813CB00002B/381